Una-Mary Parker
Drawing extensive
social editor of *Ta* ~~~ prominent member of the
social scene, Una-Mary Parker has written a dramatic
and compulsive novel of sensual suspense. Her previous international bestsellers, *Riches*, *Scandals*,
Temptations, *Enticements*, *The Palace Affair* and *For-
bidden Feelings* are all available from Headline and
have been extensively praised:

'A compulsive romantic thriller' *Sunday Express*

'Deliciously entertaining' *Sunday Telegraph*

'Scandal . . . saucy sex and suspense' *Daily Express*

'This novel has everything – intrigue, romance,
ambition, lust' *Daily Mail*

'Blue-blood glitz at its best' *Prima*

'Will keep you glued to the page' *Daily Express*

'The characters ring true and the tension mounts
nicely' *Sunday Express*

Only The Best

Una-Mary Parker

HEADLINE

First published in 1993
by HEADLINE BOOK PUBLISHING

First published in paperback in 1994
by HEADLINE BOOK PUBLISHING

10 9 8 7 6 5 4 3 2

ISBN 0 7472 4169 4

Printed and bound in Great Britain by
HarperCollins Manufacturing, Glasgow

HEADLINE BOOK PUBLISHING
A division of Hodder Headline PLC
338 Euston Road
London NW1 3BH

**This is for Edward Duke,
with my love, always**

PART ONE

New York
1990

Chapter One

Beverley had never been to such a glamorous party in her life and for a moment she wished she was one of the guests. The very air about her seemed to be shimmering with opulence, carrying wafts of designer perfume, scented flowers and tantalising aromas from the lavishly laden buffet in the adjoining room.

As she stood behind the reception desk, with the four other young women from Highlight Promotions, checking invitations and requesting the guests to sign the visitors' book, she watched spellbound, forgetting her back ached, and that her new shoes, bought in a hurry at Saks that morning, pinched her feet. Her eyes were dazzled by the jewels worn by the beautiful women and her ears seduced by the rustle of silk and taffeta; this was the party of the year, if not the decade, held in the New York Public Library on Fifth Avenue, and even if she was only here to work her butt off, at least she was *here*! Able to watch each arrival as guests braved a storm of flashlight bulbs; able to observe Elaine Ross, tonight's hostess and the Queen of High Fashion, welcome everyone with her own brand of professional charm.

Beverley had realised from the beginning it was a

3

party that would set Manhattan buzzing. Held to celebrate the fiftieth anniversary of *Chichi*, the glossy magazine that was even more popular than its rival, *Vogue*, Elaine, the editor-in-chief, was making damned certain it was going to be a success. If it wasn't, heads would roll. Especially the heads of those who worked for Highlight Promotions, the public relations company Beverley had worked for during the past ten months. Responsible for all the arrangements, including getting the press here tonight, there was one thing they hadn't been able to organise and Elaine Ross had not expected it of them: she intended taking full credit for it herself. Through her contacts in England, she had been able to secure the presence of Princess Diana who was in New York to attend the official opening of an exhibition of royal paintings and artifacts, lent by the Queen, held at the Metropolitan Museum.

This was the pinnacle of Elaine's career after eight years as editor, and as she awaited the arrival of the royal guest, Beverley watched her closely, curious to see if she showed any sign of nervous tension. There was none. As she stood beside Cass Sternberg, *Chichi*'s publisher, there was only a look of supreme triumph on Elaine's face. This was her moment. Dressed as always in her signature creamy white, with pearls round her neck, each as big as a quail's egg, and large pearl earrings, she looked cool and confident, her position as New York's top fashion magazine editor unassailable.

Suddenly, the entrance lobby was bathed in the brilliant illumination of television lights, and there was a palpable ripple of excitement. Then Elaine stepped forward, and amid an explosion of flashbulbs, Princess Diana appeared, tall and blonde, in a sensational dark blue beaded evening dress, with sapphires and diamonds blazing at her throat and in her ears. The two women, one so fair and the other so dramatically dark, shook hands, and Elaine expressed her welcome. Princess Diana, looking even more beautiful than Beverley had expected, smiled and laughed and seemed regally at ease.

Earlier, Elaine had handpicked those whom she considered suitable for presentation, and now she led the Princess to these exclusive groups, while all around the hubbub of muted voices carried on a running commentary in tones of suppressed excitement.

'Isn't Princess Di just beautiful!'

'Did you ever see such a wonderful dress?'

'And yet they say she only buys from British designers.'

'Get a look at those sapphires! They're unreal!'

'They were a wedding present from the Emir of Kuwait, you know.'

Then the Princess moved on down the room to meet more people and the buzz of conversation shifted to talk of Elaine Ross.

'How did the bitch pull it off?'

'You've got to hand it to her, haven't you?'

'Did Oscar de la Renta *give* her that white dress for tonight?'

'Of course she *has* increased *Chichi*'s circulation figure to one point four million!'

On and on it went, the back-stabbing and sniping, as Elaine stayed close to Princess Diana's side, while the new 'in' band, Tito Puente, provided the background music, which mingled with the popping of champagne corks and the clink of glasses.

Everyone who was anyone was here tonight and the gathering resembled a convention of international jet-setters rather than a publishing party. Designers like Paloma Picasso, accompanied by her husband Rafael Lopez-Sanchez, rubbed shoulders with socialites like Nan Kempner and Betsy Bloomingdale. English Dukes and Duchesses, over for the royal exhibition, exchanged banalities with Bill Blass and Karl Lagerfeld, who kept his face half hidden behind a pale yellow fan.

Tonight, for one very special magical occasion, Elaine Ross had gathered under one roof the crème de la crème of New York, Paris, London and Rome. It was a party that would be remembered for years to come, a display of wealth beyond comprehension, a unique gathering of artistic talent, worldly wit and international fame, graced by royalty, aristocracy, and the elite of New York, and in the centre of it all one slim elegant woman, her black hair cut fashionably short, her make-up immaculate, her position supreme. Elaine Ross had scored tonight and her rivals and enemies would never be allowed to forget it. Princess Diana's picture would appear on the next cover of *Chichi*, and there would be a twenty-eight-page supplement featuring the Princess at tonight's party. Eat your heart out, *Harper's Bazaar* and *Vogue*, thought Elaine with satisfaction.

Beverley watched, fascinated and intrigued by Elaine. She thought her an exquisite bird of paradise; exotic, poised and brilliantly clever. All the things Beverley would love to be one day. Beauty *and* business acumen seemed almost too much to find in one woman, but Elaine had both. Yet there was something about her that disturbed Beverley, a flaw in the otherwise perfect façade. No matter how dazzlingly Elaine smiled, revealing perfect white teeth framed by lusciously painted scarlet lips, her eyes remained cold. Aloof. And very distant. It was as if, beneath the soft allure of clinging cream silk and the pearls with their subtle sheen which made her skin glow warmly, there lay hidden a heart of ice. Had the price she'd had to pay for her success been too heavy? Or had she been forced to make sacrifices to satisfy her ambitions? It seemed she never smiled from the heart, only with her mouth, and Beverley longed to know the reason.

'Don't imagine *Chichi*'s party is going to be any fun for us,' Beverley's immediate boss, Mary Stapelton, told them when Highlight were first given the job of organising the event. 'Elaine Ross is a bitch! I've worked for her before, and I'm telling you, she'll be phoning us at eight-thirty every morning for weeks ahead for no better reason than to keep us on our toes. She's demanding, tyrannical, and she treats everyone who works for her like dirt.' Mary's clear grey eyes were candid, her tone warning.

'Oh, great!' exclaimed Faye Mallory, a tall thin girl who had been with the company for several years, and who would be working with Beverley on this function, together with Lisette Attwood and Nina Klett.

Highlight Promotions was divided into four main sections, each run by an account executive with the help of four assistants. Mary Stapelton was in charge of publicising restaurants, clubs, art galleries and high-profile functions. The five women, all under thirty, made a lively team and they all got on well together. They were also thankful to have got into the most fun section of the company, whose other public relation interests covered industry, commerce and home products.

'At least we'll get to see Princess Diana,' Beverley had remarked, when they'd been informed by Elaine to expect the future Queen of England.

'Don't count on it,' Mary warned. 'You'll be lucky to get a glimpse of the top of her head in the crowd. We'll be on the reception desk that night, checking everyone's invitation, so don't expect a ringside seat!'

They all laughed, knowing she was probably right, but they were nevertheless excited to be working on such a glamorous project.

Beverley Franklin had only been living in Manhattan for the past year, although she was no stranger to New York, and considered herself fortunate in having a job at all when the recession was affecting so many people. Born and brought up in Stockbridge, Massachusetts, she was the second child of Rachael and Daniel Franklin, both of whom were teachers. Money had never been plentiful, but she and her sister Jenny, and her two brothers, Josh and Tom, had received a thoroughgoing education from their parents, so that she developed an appreciation of literature and art. Rachael and Daniel Franklin were dedicated teachers and had always encouraged their four children to study.

'There is nothing more precious than a good education,' Daniel was fond of repeating at frequent intervals, and his two eldest children had heeded his words, even if the two younger ones so far showed no signs of following their example.

At twenty-seven, Josh Franklin was a lawyer, practising in Washington. It was his ambition, in time, to enter politics. Beverley, who was twenty-three, had won a scholarship to Wellesley College, where she majored in Literature and French. She also took several art courses

8

and finally graduated with a BA and high honours. It was her parents' proudest hour, for she had fulfilled all their dreams. Now, a year later, working for one of the top public relations companies, she was able to pursue her love of the arts and of music, and while the other girls at Highlight rushed off to discotheques and bars in the evening, Beverley was more likely to be found engrossed in a concert at Carnegie Hall or Lincoln Center.

Jenny and Tom seemed uninterested in carving out good careers for themselves; Jenny, at fifteen, had announced she wanted to quit high school in favour of working in a big department store, whilst twelve-year-old Tom was obsessed with baseball and could talk of nothing else.

Shortly after Beverley had arrived in New York, she'd found herself a small but sunny apartment on West 57th Street from which she walked to the Madison Avenue offices of Highlight every morning. She also earned enough money to buy herself some new clothes, a requisite of the job, because she was in daily contact with clients and the general public.

Tonight, for instance, she was expected to look good. Everyone knew that they had organised *Chichi*'s party, and the managing director of Highlight, Charles Floyd, wanted 'his girls', as he referred to Mary Stapelton and her team, to do him credit. Along with the black high-heeled pumps that were now killing her, Beverley was wearing a simple black sheath dress, and her hair, an outstanding feature because of its dark chestnut tints, was confined into a business-like trendy twist. Normally it cascaded around her shoulders, rich and lustrous, but tonight she knew she had to appear svelte. Unlike a lot of people with auburn hair, her skin was unblemished with not a freckle in sight. Instead it was a pale clear cream, and her eyes were hazel with tiny golden flecks. If Beverley did not consider herself to be beautiful, her friends did, and her loveliness was natural, too. Apart from a little mascara and a peach-coloured lipstick, she wore no makeup.

Mary Stapelton broke into her thoughts at that moment as she eased one aching foot out of her shoe. 'We'd better get the press packs assembled.'

'Yeah, okay,' Beverley replied, bending down to open the boxes of folders that had arrived from the printers earlier in the day.

Elaine Ross had stipulated that each guest be given a copy of the latest edition of *Chichi* in a folder containing a photograph of herself, the history of the magazine, together with facts and figures about advertising and circulation, plus a resumé of forthcoming special features and articles. She'd also persuaded a French perfume company to give phials of Excite to all the women guests and a bottle of Arousal after-shave to the men. Beverley, Lisette, Faye and Nina were to hand them out to the guests when they left, from behind the long reception table in the lobby.

It was now ten-thirty and Beverley was tempted to slip off her other shoe as well, figuring that if she remained behind the table no one would see her feet. Just as she was beginning to feel a delicious sense of freedom in her almost numb toes, there was a sudden bustle of activity across the room and she realised Princess Diana was about to go.

Struggling to push her feet back into her shoes, she caught sight of the ethereal-looking princess, her blonde

head towering over Elaine's dark one. Then, with a
jolt of mixed horror and excitement, she realised the
princess was breaking ranks, moving away from Elaine
and the planned route across the red carpet to the exit,
and making straight for them. There was confusion
among her accompanying entourage as everyone,
including her lady-in-waiting, wondered what was happening. Elaine, hovering by her side, was trying to tell
the princess she was going the wrong way.

'Ma'am . . .' she whispered urgently. The cameras
were all lined up by the exit, waiting to get a final shot.
The crowds in the street were expecting to see Diana
emerge any second now. 'Ma'am . . .' said Elaine desperately.

But Princess Diana paid no attention. Walking
towards the five young women from Highlight, she
reached Mary first, her hand outstretched.

'Have you had to work very hard tonight?' she asked
sympathetically.

Beverley saw Mary's eyes bulge as she gave a silent
gulp.

'They've all worked hard tonight, Ma'am,' Elaine
butted in, meaning to sound helpful, but her tone was
dismissive, as if that was what they'd been paid to do so
it was no big deal.

Princess Diana had shaken Mary's hand now and was
moving down the line of amazed young women. Faye
wondered if she was supposed to curtsey, like she'd seen
English people do in photographs. Nina wondered if she
ought to say 'Your Majesty' and Lisette looked as if
she was going to faint.

Suddenly the princess was face to face with Beverley,
and she was smiling and asking her if she'd worked for

the promotion company for very long?

'Nearly a year, Ma'am,' Beverley replied, feeling suddenly breathless. The princess had exquisite skin and her blue eyes were beautifully and subtly made up. Beverley gazed at her, spellbound.

'Is it fun? Do you get to organise a lot of amusing parties?' Princess Diana was asking, with a warm smile.

'Sometimes,' Beverley replied, catching Elaine's cold expression as her eyes swept over her black dress critically. 'This one has been really special though, even if it has been a lot of work,' she added truthfully.

Princess Diana nodded understandingly, and then, with a final smile, moved towards the exit. There was another explosion of flashlight bulbs, and the crowds surged forward to see the future Queen of England, and then she was gone, whipped away in a large black car, accompanied by outriders and followed by other cars carrying her entourage.

Mary, Beverley, Lisette, Faye and Nina stood there, staring at each other in shock, bereft of words, their eyes popping with delighted astonishment.

'My God!' breathed Beverley. 'Was that a dream I just had?'

'I could have *died* when she came over to us like that!' Faye gasped.

'But why did she come and talk to us?' Nina asked. 'Did you expect it? I didn't!' She was red in the face with excitement. 'Wow! Wait 'til I tell my boyfriend! He'll freak! He's always had the hots for Princess Di!'

'Let's face it, none of us expected it,' Mary pointed out, her hands shaking. 'And the person who expected it least of all was Elaine Ross! Did you see her face?'

'But I don't understand,' Lisette exclaimed. 'Why us?'

'I read somewhere she likes to talk to the people who really do the work, not just the socialites,' Mary explained. 'Someone must have told her we organised tonight – and let's face it, we did! The caterers, the florists, the printing and mailing of the invitations, dealing with all the acceptances and refusals . . . dealing with Elaine Ross every day! God, I think we deserve medals! *Chichi* may have paid for the party and Elaine may have been the hostess, but, girls, who did all the work?'

They all nodded, thrilled now to realise the honour they'd been paid; knowing that their boss, Charles Floyd, who was among the guests tonight with his wife, would be pleased with the recognition they'd been given.

'I'm still in shock,' Mary commented, her hands trembling.

'*You're* in shock,' Beverley quipped. 'Wait till I tell my mother! She'll be so thrilled the whole of Stockbridge will be told.'

'Wait until I tell *my* mother,' Nina thrilled. 'Coming from the Bronx, she'll be amazed to know I was even here tonight. When I tell her who I shook hands with . . .! My, she'll go crazy.'

'Princess Diana is the world's heroine, isn't she!' Faye observed. 'A sort of cross between Madonna and Mother Teresa. I have a feeling I'm going to wake up in a minute and find the whole thing was a dream.'

Guests were leaving now, floating out on to Fifth Avenue in a mood of euphoria, knowing tonight had been a very special occasion, maybe even a once in a lifetime experience for some. Outside the cars were lining up and the photographers had left with the departure of the princess. The caterers had started to clear away and the cleaners were moving in to sweep away the debris left by a thousand revellers.

Beverley and the others took a final look at the room that had accommodated the gathering of the decade. A melancholy scene of drooping flowers and burnt-out candles met their gaze.

'Well, I suppose that's that,' Beverley observed sadly. There was a definite feeling of anti-climax in the atmosphere now. 'The party's well and truly over. We'd better be getting home.'

'Not a moment too soon,' Mary remarked briskly. 'Sorry, girls, I expect you're dead on your feet but I'll still expect to see you on time tomorrow morning. We've got that art gallery launch to work on. It's only two weeks away and there's still a lot to be done.'

They all nodded. It was good to have another project to look forward to, another event to organise and promote.

'See you in the morning,' Mary called out as she hurried away, anxious to leave. Very much a loner, she lived by herself and few people were taken into her confidence.

Nina turned to Beverley. 'Want to share a cab? I pass right by your apartment.'

'Yeah, that would be great. Thanks.' They waved goodnight to Faye and Lisette. An empty yellow cab cruised down Fifth Avenue at that moment, and hailing it, they jumped in.

'That was some night, wasn't it?' Beverley remarked, leaning back and closing her eyes.

'It sure was, and the whole thing went off without a hitch, too. Even Elaine Ross must have been pleased.'

Beverley started taking the pins out of her upswept

14

hair, letting it fall to her shoulders in abundant waves. Then she shook her head, so that her hair rippled freely.

'Ah, that's better,' she said with relief. 'I don't know what was hurting me the most – my feet or having my hair screwed up.'

Nina yawned. 'Who cares? We got to meet Princess Diana tonight and that's something we can dine out on for the rest of our lives.'

A few minutes later the cab stopped outside her apartment block and the two girls said goodnight. The long day, that had started at six o'clock in the morning for Beverley, was now nearly over. In five minutes she could be in bed, and in ten fast asleep. She could hardly wait.

Beverley's two-room apartment was on the fifteenth floor. Getting out of the elevator, she crossed the landing quietly so as not to disturb her neighbours. Stepping into her own small hallway, she switched on the light while she re-locked her front door and put on the safety chain.

At that moment she heard a thud coming from the direction of her living room and for a moment she froze with fear. There had been several burglaries in the apartment building recently, and the superintendent had warned everyone to be sure to lock their doors.

Another thud followed the first. Paralysed, she held her breath, too frightened to move. Her heart roared, pounding in her ears, and then a voice spoke.

'Bevs? Is that you?'

Beverley gasped and leaned against the wall. 'Christ! You scared me out of my wits!' Fumbling for the living-room light switch, she remembered she'd said her kid sister could stay a couple of nights. She'd even left a spare set of keys with the super so Jenny could let herself in.

'I'd clean forgotten you were here,' Beverley said, flopping into the one armchair. The sofa, which pulled out into a bed, was already occupied by Jenny, who was curled up under a blanket. 'It's been such a helluva day, I completely forgot you were staying.'

'Gee, thanks. I'm glad I'm such an important part of your life.' Jenny grinned at her, blinking under the bright central light. 'Why are you dressed to kill?'

'You know why. I told you. We had this party tonight, for *Chichi*'s fiftieth anniversary. I got to shake hands with Princess Diana, too,' she added triumphantly.

'Oh, yeah? And Prince Charles asked you to marry him, I suppose,' Jenny scoffed good-humouredly, propping herself against one of the soft cushions.

'It's true. Princess Di came over and shook hands with all of us,' Beverley assured her. She eased her painful feet out of her shoes and groaned with relief.

Jenny was sitting bolt upright now, wide awake. 'You're kidding!'

'It's true, but I'm too tired to tell you all about it now. Have you any idea how long I've been on my feet?' She looked at her wrist watch. 'Nearly nineteen hours and I'm dead. If I don't go to bed now I'll be in no shape to go to work in the morning.'

Disgruntled, Jenny lay down again. 'Then I won't see much of you tomorrow?' she complained.

Beverley dragged herself to her feet. 'You knew the score when you invited yourself to stay here, honey chile,' she pointed out reasonably. 'I'll be back by six-thirty tomorrow evening, so we can do a movie or eat out somewhere.'

Jenny, who was eight years younger than Beverley, was so different they might not have been related. She was into loud pop music, trendy threads, New Age symbolism and, of course, boys. Cuter-looking than Beverley, with golden brown hair which showed russet tints in certain lights, she had none of her sister's openness. With Beverley people knew where they stood. She was direct, honest and sincere, with a very warm, vivacious personality. Within weeks of arriving in New York, she'd made a clutch of good friends, both men and women, and was equally popular with both. But it went deeper than that. She was also liked and respected. People didn't take advantage of Beverley, and they didn't bad-mouth her. They knew they could trust her, with work, with confidences, with their reputations, and they did.

With Jenny it was different. There was a mischievous slyness about her greyish-blue eyes and a wanton slackness about her full mouth. Slim, with a tiny waist, long legs and breasts slightly too big for the rest of her body, she oozed sex appeal. Whereas men instantly liked Beverley, and in time grew deeply fond of her, it was Jenny, even at fifteen, whom they desired on sight. Jenny whom they longed to go to bed with. The trouble was she knew it, and had always known it. Flirting was second nature to her, and she'd quickly mastered the art of manipulating her father and Josh. She'd always been able to wheedle her way into getting whatever she wanted and people, especially men, fell for it every time. Since the age of twelve she'd been dating several high school boys, but whether she'd got into more than heavy petting Beverley didn't know and didn't want to know. Their mother had assured Beverley she had nothing to worry about, and that Jenny knew all about safe sex, and that she mustn't feel responsible for Jenny's behaviour. Nevertheless, she couldn't help worrying at times.

Beverley had dated a lot of law and business students at Harvard while she'd been at Wellesley, but apart from one romance when she'd been twenty, which hadn't worked out, she hadn't met anyone she cared deeply enough about to want to make a serious commitment. Not that it worried her in the least. One day she was sure she'd meet the right man and have the perfect relationship, but in the meantime she was enjoying her life, with its freedom and independence, and wasn't in a hurry to change anything.

'What am I supposed to do with myself tomorrow, then?' Jenny demanded with a touch of petulance.

'But you know I work,' Beverley replied patiently.

'Take the day off then.'

'No way. We're frantically busy in the office and there'll be lots of loose ends to tidy up after tonight's party.' Beverley went into her bedroom, which led off the living room, and started to undress.

'Call up and say you're sick,' Jenny shouted from the sofa.

'I can't do that.'

'Oh, come on, Bevs. Why are you so dumb? Take the day off and we'll have some fun. God, Bevs, I only get to come to New York once in a while. The least you can do is take some time off.' Her voice was querulous and shrill now. Beverley recognised the beginning of one of Jenny's tantrums. She came slowly back into the living room, wearing a knee-length tee-shirt patterned with tiny red hearts on a white background. With her hair tumbling round her shoulders she looked younger than Jenny, but there was a determined glint in her gold-flecked eyes.

18

'Cut it out, Jen. I'll meet you for lunch, but I warned you you'd have to look after yourself if you came to say, so stop being such a pain.' Firmly, she switched off the living-room light. 'I'll see you in the morning, but right now I *have* to get some sleep. Good-night.'

'Goodnight,' Jenny replied grudgingly, knowing she was beaten. It wasn't often she could pull one over Beverley, but it was always worth a try.

Beverley climbed into bed and sank luxuriously into the softness of the mattress. It was wonderful to lie down at last. Turning on her side, she curled up under the duvet.

'Beverley,' called a small voice from the next room.

'What is it?' she rolled on to her back again and hoped Jenny wasn't going to try and talk all night long.

'I need some new clothes. I've got nothing to wear and there's a high school dance next week and I'm going with the dishiest boy you've ever seen called Eddie . . .'

That's what she says about them all, Beverley thought. Hank . . . Jimmy . . . Matt . . . Steve. The list was endless.

'So?' she asked aloud.

'Where shall I go to get something?'

'What? Oh, for God's sakes, Jenny. It's one o'clock in the morning and I'm . . .'

'But can you lend me some money? Mom only gave me a hundred dollars. How am I going to manage on a hundred dollars while I'm here, and buy something new to wear?' She sounded pathetic now, all poor-little-me, and it was designed to make Beverley feel sympathetic towards her. It had the opposite effect.

'Please! Do me a favour! It was good of Mom to give

you anything. And why should I stump up so that you can go shopping? Now, go to sleep.'

The alarm clock shrilled piercingly at six-thirty the next morning, awakening Beverley from a deep slumber. Groping, with eyes still shut, she reached out and switched it off, unable to believe it was morning already.

'Oh, no,' she groaned, curling herself up into a foetal position. Then she remembered that she had to wash her hair and iron her navy blue linen skirt before she went to the office. Rolling out of bed she went to the window and drew back her green and blue stripy curtains. It was a glorious morning, the sky washed clean by an earlier shower, the air fresh and cool.

Creeping on tip-toe so as not to disturb Jenny, she slipped into the bathroom, tiredness forgotten. The exciting thing about working for Highlight was that there was always something new to look forward to. A new challenge, another mountain to climb. Already her mind was working on the next project, the opening of the new art gallery. There was to be an exhibition of modern paintings for the first month, and an opening night party to which two hundred people were being invited. Today, it was Beverley's job to send off the artwork for the catalogue to the printers. Stepping into the shower, she hummed cheerfully to herself. Right now, she reckoned, life couldn't be better.

'So what's wrong with wanting to be like Madonna?' Jenny demanded, her face filled with indignation.

It was an hour later and Beverley was trying to get

breakfast, tidy the apartment, dress herself and listen to Jenny, all at the same time.

'Grow up!' Beverley laughed. 'You can't sing, for one thing. You can't act, either.'

'So?' Jenny stood in the middle of the living room, her legs encased in black leggings, over which she was wearing a multi-coloured tee-shirt. Holding her hair-brush up to her mouth, pretending it was a microphone, she launched herself into what Beverley presumed was a recent Madonna hit.

'Ple-ase!' She clapped her hands over her ears. 'Give me a break, Jen. It isn't even eight o'clock yet!'

She shrugged. 'Okay. So where are we going for lunch today?'

Beverley puffed up the soft cushions and gave the room a final inspection. 'I'll call you from the office when I know what time I can get away.'

'But that means I'll have to wait in all morning. I wanted to go and look at the stores,' Jenny grumbled.

'Oh, God . . . then come to the office. Twelve-thirty.' Beverley gulped down her coffee. 'You know where it is, don't you?'

'On Madison Avenue?'

'Yes. Number 386, between 68th and 69th. We're on the third floor. Go to reception and ask for me.'

'How do I get there?' There was a whining note in Jenny's voice.

Beverley clasped her forehead in mock despair. 'How do you *think* you get there, Dumbo? You do what every-one else does in New York. You walk. You know? You use those things on the end of your legs! Now I must go or I'll be late.' Grabbing her handbag, she glanced around the apartment for the last time. 'Try and keep

21

the place tidy, Jen,' she begged. 'You know how I hate coming back home at night to a mess.'

'Elaine Ross wants someone to take round the contact prints of the photographs of last night's party,' Mary announced at eleven o'clock. 'Can you drop them round, Beverley? She's at her apartment on Park. Here's the address.'

'Sure.' Beverley took the slip of paper on which Mary had written the details. So far, she'd dealt with the new gallery's catalogue and finished the mailing for the launch party. A breath of fresh air would do her good.

Half an hour later, Beverley was being shown by a black maid into one of the most elegant drawing rooms she had ever seen. It exuded pure luxury with its lavish decor, fabulous European antiques and an exotic profusion of flowers and paintings, fabrics and silk rugs. Through the large windows that formed two walls, Manhattan could be seen, spread like a richly textured tapestry.

'Will you wait in here, please, miss,' the maid told her. 'Miss Ross will be with you in a minute.'

Beverley sat down gingerly on a Louis XVI chair, upholstered in pale blue watered silk, and prayed she wouldn't knock anything over. There were carved jade figures, ivory carvings, silver-framed photographs and enamel trinket boxes arranged on several occasional tables dotted around the room, and on a pedestal in the corner a huge orchid plant trembled with delicate white blooms. Silk Chinese rugs, pale blue wild silk curtains and silk-covered sofas added to the sensuous delicacy which epitomised Elaine herself.

Beverley had heard that Elaine lived alone; an ivory

22

figure in an ivory tower, she reflected, looking around.
Yet persistent rumours linked her name with *Chichi*'s
publisher, Cass Sternberg. It was Cass who had groomed
her over the past ten years, building her up so that she
was now the most influential magazine editor in the
United States. Some said they'd been lovers for the past
fifteen years, and that the only reason they'd never married was because Cass had a wife and three teenage
children whom he refused to leave. Others insisted their
relationship was purely platonic, built on mutual respect
and comradeship. Beverley looked around, searching
for evidence of a male presence, but there was none.
Even the silver-framed photographs showed the egotism
of the owner of the apartment. There was Elaine meeting the President, Elaine shaking hands with Frank
Sinatra, Elaine with Joan Rivers and Ivana Trump at a
benefit concert, and Elaine in a bathing suit, sitting on
a beach, with a group that included Prince Rainier. No
doubt, Beverley reflected, there would soon be another
addition to the collection: Elaine and Princess Diana
smiling and laughing together, as if they were lifelong
friends.

At that moment, Elaine marched into the room, her
winter-white flannel slacks accentuating her slim hips.
With them she wore a creamy shirt and white cashmere
blazer, dazzling with gilt buttons. Large gilt earrings
glinted beneath the trim cut of her black hair, and as
usual her make-up was immaculate.

'Ah, the photographs,' she said crisply. 'Are they any
good?'

'They're great,' Beverley assured her, handing over a
large brown envelope.

'Ummm . . . but would you know?' Her tone was

crushing. She drew the sheets of contacts out of the envelope, and Beverley noticed her long nails were painted with natural-coloured varnish except for the tips, which were white. On her left hand a large square-cut emerald glinted in the light, reminding Beverley of a recent article she'd read in *Chichi* in which Elaine had urged readers to trade in their engagement rings for larger and better stones to reflect their husband's growing prosperity. It was just the sort of thing she would think of, Beverley thought.

Elaine had taken the photographs to the window, and was examining them through a silver-framed magnifying glass. From time to time she drew in her breath with sharp gasps of exasperation. 'Jesus, that's terrible,' she muttered, and then grudgingly: 'That's not so bad.' At last she turned back into the room.

'Give me a chinagraph pencil,' she commanded, without even looking up.

Beverley offered up a silent prayer of thankfulness that she'd remembered to bring one of the special type of pencils for marking up glossy photographs with her. Elaine grabbed it without a word of thanks.

'I'll mark the ones that you may use, to submit to the press in general,' she said, scoring around the ones she liked best. 'The rest are to be destroyed, including the negatives. I won't have bad pictures of myself lying around.'

Beverley looked at her levelly, the gold flecks in her eyes cool for once. 'Very well. We have no control over the pictures taken for *Woman's Wear Daily*, though. It's entirely up to them to choose what they want to reproduce.'

Elaine turned slowly to look at her, her almost black

24

eyes sweeping from the top of Beverley's chestnut hair, held back from her face by two combs, to the slim legs in navy blue tights and matching shoes. Her expression was one of pure hostility.

'Who do you think you're talking to?' Then she shrugged her narrow shoulders as if she were secretly amused by something. 'I suppose to a girl like you, up from the country, last night must have been very exciting. Just don't let it go to your head, dear.'

Beverley flushed, her creamy skin suffused with red. 'I don't think there's any chance of that,' she replied gravely. 'My parents brought me up to be completely underwhelmed.' She took the envelope from Elaine and, with a polite smile, turned to leave the room.

'Wait!' Elaine commanded. 'In future, I want to deal with Charles Floyd direct. Highlight charged me a fortune for last night. I think I deserve to deal with the boss, and no one else.'

Beverley inclined her head coolly, to indicate she understood. Then Elaine spoke again.

'What's your name?'

Beverley turned, delighted to be given the opportunity of having the last word. 'Miss Franklin,' she replied with quiet dignity.

Jenny was waiting for her in the office reception when she got back, looking unusually chic in a red and white checked dress with a red belt and red sandals. She'd looped her hair up with red ribbon, so that it hung in soft blonde tendrils around her face, and with the addition of bright red lipstick, she looked about twenty-five.

Beverley stopped short in her tracks when she saw her, before giving a cry of deep irritation. 'Really, Jen, do you *have* to borrow my entire wardrobe without even asking me? That's my best dress, and it's new.' Then she caught sight of her sister's feet. 'My new shoes, too! You'll stretch them! Your feet are bigger than mine.'

Jenny looked sullen. 'You have the money to buy nice things and I don't,' she replied. 'You wouldn't even lend me a few dollars to go shopping. What am I supposed to do?'

Beverley caught her by the arm and pushed her in the direction of the elevators. 'What we don't do is talk about it in the lobby, in front of the entire workforce of Highlight on their way out to lunch!' she hissed.

'Well, I can't help it,' Jenny wailed, stumbling into the elevator. 'Mom's so mean to me . . .'

'Will you shut up?' Beverley mouthed. The elevator was crowded but Jenny was quite prepared to discuss family matters in a loud voice, no matter who was listening. When they reached street level, she started again.

'If Mom would only give me some money . . .'

Beverley led the way long the sidewalk until they came to a small Italian restaurant. When they were settled at a table for two in the window, the waiter presented them with the menu. Lunch out was an extravagance Beverley didn't usually indulge in, instead taking a corned beef on rye or a bagel with cream cheese back to her desk, washing it down with a Diet Coke. However, she figured she should give Jenny a treat.

'What are you going to have?' she asked, skimming the menu.

Jenny decided she was starving. 'I'll start with the seafood salad, and then I'd like the pasta with the mushrooms in cream. Get a look at that trolley, too. Have you ever seen such gorgeous desserts. Wow! I'm enjoying myself now.' She gave a sigh of contentment.

Beverley burst out laughing. 'I'm glad to hear it!' She gave the waiter the order, choosing gnocci in tomato sauce for herself.

'Let's have some wine,' Jenny suggested, as she preened herself for the benefit of the waiter.

'I've got to work this afternoon, Jen,' Beverley protested. 'If I have wine I'll fall fast asleep at my desk.'

'Do they sell wine by the glass?' Jenny urged. 'Then I can drink wine and you can have water.'

'Thanks a bunch! Anyway, you're under-age.' Beverley turned to the waiter. 'We'll have a bottle of mineral water,' she said firmly.

Over lunch, Jenny started grumbling once again. 'I want to come and live in New York, and work in Saks,' she announced.

Beverley had heard it all before. Her parents were trying to get Jenny to continue her studies and there had been many family arguments on that score. As to living in New York, they were dead against it, and Beverley was inclined to agree. Some girls of fifteen were very mature, others were a danger to themselves. Jenny belonged to the latter category.

'If I lived with you, we'd have a great time,' she was saying in a loud voice, and Beverley noticed the two men at the next table staring at her sister. Their hungry eyes were devouring every inch of her long legs, crossed, with the skirt pulled high above her knees, and her breasts, which swelled temptingly above what had been a demure neckline when Beverley had worn the dress. Aware of the effect she was having, Jenny was playing with the tendrils of hair that trailed from the sides of her face, and then Beverley saw one of the men lick his lips and close his eyes. A moment later Jenny was glancing across at him with a knowing look, enjoying the sport of long-range seduction.

'Will you stop it, Jenny,' Beverley whispered, frowning.

'Why should I?' Jenny's mouth curved with amusement. 'It's fun. I bet he's got an erection.' Her eyes swept over the man's body, lingering on his crotch. 'He's rather sweet.'

Shocked, Beverley glared at her. 'You're behaving like a hooker!' she hissed.

'I'm having more fun than you,' Jenny retorted.

'I don't plan to get myself raped one of these days,' Beverley said angrily. 'You're a fool, Jen. It's crazy to go flaunting yourself in front of strangers.'

'My, my! Miss Goody-Two-Shoes is a prude, isn't she?' Jenny mocked. 'Listen, what are we going to do tonight?'

'Tonight? We could see a movie, I suppose.'

Jenny grimaced. 'Boring. How about going to a disco?'

'We don't have anyone to go with.'

'That's no problem! Let's go to a singles bar, find a couple of guys, and get them to take us to a disco.'

'Are you out of your mind?' Beverley exclaimed. 'Mom would kill me. We'll go and see a movie and then I'll splurge and take you somewhere nice for dinner. We might go to the TriBeCa Grill. It's owned by Robert De Niro, Sean Penn and Mikhail Baryshnikov, and is always full of show-biz people. That should appeal to your desire to hit the high spots.'

'Just the two of us?' Jenny looked crestfallen. 'Don't you have any boyfriends you can call up? It'll be no fun on our own. I might as well have stayed at home, if I'm only going to be going out with you.'

Beverley, hurt at Jenny's attitude when she was trying to give her sister a good time, suddenly decided to do some straight talking. 'Listen, Jenny, you're behaving like a spoilt brat. I didn't invite you to New York, you asked yourself, so stop being so ungrateful. I'm not here, you know, to provide you with clothes, shoes, money and boyfriends, as well as giving you a good time.'

Jenny turned scarlet and for a moment Beverley thought she was going to burst into tears. Instead she jumped to her feet, grabbed the red purse she'd also borrowed from Beverley's closet and stormed out of the restaurant.

'I can have a good time without you!' She flung the words over her shoulder as she nearly collided with an elderly couple who were entering the restaurant. Aghast, Beverley heard Jenny swear and then push her way out into the street without a word of apology.

The two men at the next table were grinning now, obviously amused. Beverley finished her lunch and tried to look composed, but inside she felt a mixture of annoyance and fear. New York was no place for a fifteen year old, with a hundred dollars in her purse and the wilful nature of a two year old, to go running around on her own. Jenny was becoming more uncontrollable every year; something would have to be done soon or she'd go completely off the rails. Beverley decided it was time she talked to her parents about Jenny's future, before it was too late.

Beverley got back to her apartment at half-past six, but there was no sign of Jenny and it didn't look as if she'd been back since lunch either, judging by the state of the bathroom, living room and bedroom, where half the clothes had been pulled out of the closet. Grimly, Beverley started to clean the place for the second time that day.

Her apartment was her pride and joy, and she'd managed to transform the simple square rooms into an inviting and attractive home which reflected her personality. White walls and a highly polished wooden floor had been embellished with blue and green kilims, framed Erté posters, an antique crewel shawl, which she draped over the sofa-bed, and an easy chair piled high with ethnic cushions. Along one wall, an arrangement of various-sized baskets held her collection of cassettes and videos, magazines and newspapers, dried grasses, plants and shells. Along the opposite wall stood the white bookshelf she'd brought from home, and this was packed tightly with her beloved collection of books.

Next-door, her bedroom echoed the stylish theme of cane and basket-weave, ethnic fabrics and scatter rugs, and as she continued to tidy away the mess Jenny had left, Beverley felt a glow of satisfaction at the little home she had created for herself. It hadn't cost a fortune either; just an eye for putting together arrangements of objects that blended and harmonised, against a simple backdrop.

It was eight o'clock and there was still no sign of Jenny. Where the hell could she be? The possible answers sent a chill of apprehension through Beverley. The sooner her sister went back to Stockbridge the better. She made herself an omelette and turned on the television to watch the news channel.

By ten o'clock, she was seriously worried. Jenny could be lying mugged in some gutter, raped in a back alley, or even drugged senseless. She knew her imagination was getting the better of her, but couldn't quell the rising panic that kept blotting out all coherent thought. For a moment, she thought of phoning home to see if Jenny had gone straight back to Stockbridge, but then she decided not to alarm her parents. It was unlikely Jenny would have returned. She was most probably drifting around the singles bars of New York, looking for someone who would take her dancing, and could be anywhere from the Bronx to Battery Park.

At midnight, lying on the living-room sofa, she fell asleep. Earlier she'd planned to phone her mother if Jenny hadn't come home by twelve o'clock, but now, oblivious to everything, she slept on and still Jenny hadn't returned.

Chapter Two

A chilly grey dawn slowly brought New York back to life as the rising sun touched the skyscrapers with a pink glow, reflecting in a million windows so they sparked with sudden fire, warming the atmosphere, freshening the air, wakening the people. Soon, all was hustle and bustle down on the streets and sidewalks, while up on the fifteenth floor of an apartment building on West Fifty-Seventh Street, Beverley was awakened by the pain in her neck. Slowly, her eyes opened and she looked around her living room with a puzzled expression. Then, with a yell, she jumped to her feet, swaying dizzily for a moment, remembering.

Jenny. That was it. Where the hell was Jenny? Instinctively, she rushed into her bedroom and there, sleeping as peacefully as a baby in her bed, lay Jenny. She was wearing one of Beverley's nightdresses, too.

'Jenny!' Beverley bawled angrily. 'Where have you been? Don't you know you had me worried sick? What time did you get in? Why didn't you wake me?'

Jenny opened her eyes and smiled sleepily. Then she rolled leisurely, stretching like a cat, on to her back.

'I didn't want to disturb you,' she replied reasonably.

'Disturb me? Didn't you realise I was going out of my

mind? I nearly called the police. Anything could have happened to you.' Now that Beverley knew Jenny was all right, relief made her madder than ever. 'This is the last time you stay here,' she admonished. 'I want you to pack your bags and leave this morning. I'm not going to endure another twenty-four hours of hellish worry just because you want to go on the town. It's selfish, thoughtless and utterly irresponsible of you.'

Slowly and carefully, as if her head hurt, Jenny sat up and leaned against the cane bedhead.

'Cool it, sis,' she said with maddening calm. 'I had a great time. You should have come along, too. I went to a fantastic club on the East side, called Jeric-O, and I met up with a really nice girl called Maxine. She introduced me to these great-looking guys, and the next thing we were dancing the night away! I've never had such a good time. I didn't get back until nearly five o'clock this morning,' she added proudly.

Beverley sank on to the end of the bed. 'And that was it?'

'Yeah. Why?'

'How old did you tell them you were?'

'I didn't. Anyway, nobody asked. Oh, come on, Bevs. I had a few Coke and rums, that was all. They weren't into drugs or anything.'

'Well, haven't you been the lucky one?' Beverley commented drily. 'It doesn't alter anything, though. You've got to go home. Being responsible for you has aged me ten years overnight.'

A pillow hit the back of her head as she left the room.

'I think you're mean!' Jenny shrieked. 'It's no fun being around you. I wanted us to have a good time together but you're a real wet blanket.' She was crying now but Beverley didn't react. For Jenny's own good, she must go back to the country where she could come to no harm. Going into the kitchen, Beverley made some coffee, and a few minutes later Jenny appeared, looking woebegone and wiping her eyes with the backs of her hands.

'I only wanted to party,' she said brokenly. 'Don't make me go back home, Bevs. I hate Stockbridge. There's nothing to do. I'm so bored at home, I could kill myself.' She sounded so genuinely upset that Beverley went over to her and put her arms around her.

'I'm sorry, honey,' she said sympathetically, 'but it is for your own good. You've no idea what a dangerous city this is. There are people out there who are crazed, on drugs, psychotic and diseased. Some would kill for a few dollars. They have guns, knives, and they're not afraid to use them. Coupled to which, the city can no longer afford to provide enough police to patrol the streets like they used to. I know you think I'm being stuffy, but I'm not. This is not a safe place to be, especially for a young girl who has lived all her life in a quiet country backwater.'

'How was I to know that?' Jenny whined.

'Jen, you know it perfectly well, because we had this conversation the last time you were here. Six months ago, in fact. You've got to go home today. Let's have some coffee and then I've got to get to work or I'll be late.'

Jenny took her mug of coffee back to bed with her, and watched Beverley as she slipped into a dark emerald wool suit that set off her hair to perfection. With it she wore black high-heeled shoes and large gilt earrings.

'You're so lucky, Beverley,' she grumbled.

Her sister looked at her candidly. 'Not lucky, Jen, hard-working. I've worked my butt off, all my life, to have what I've got today. I nearly killed myself studying to get that scholarship to Wellesley, and then again to get my BA, and I've never stopped working.'

'But you've had opportunities,' Jenny insisted, unconvinced.

'Don't think you can send me on a guilt trip, because it won't work,' Beverley pointed out. 'Don't give me all that crap about my being "lucky". You could have everything I've got one day, if you'd only study harder at school.'

'But school is such a drag! I don't want to waste time studying. Just you wait, Beverley. One day I'm going to be richer than you. One day I'll be really rich, with a big apartment in the Trump Tower and lots of designer clothes, and I'll go out every night and drink champagne and have a wonderful time.'

Beverley grinned in spite of herself. 'I'm sure you will, Jenny. Meanwhile, get yourself packed and I'll phone Mom and tell her you'll be home this afternoon.'

When Beverley returned from work that evening, Jenny had left and the apartment was reasonably clean and tidy. It wasn't until she was getting ready for bed, and wanting to decide what to wear to the office the next day, that she realised Jenny had taken two of her best suits, a silk blouse and a pair of black high-heeled sandals with a matching purse.

'This guest list sure looks good,' Mary Stapelton remarked, ticking off the list of acceptances for the opening of the Herman Art Gallery.

Beverley, writing the press release on her word processor, looked up. 'It'll be hard to equal *Chichi*'s party when it comes to VIPs!' she remarked.

Mary laughed, looking quite pretty. In repose, her face had a pale plainness that made it closed and secret-looking. 'Nothing will ever match up to that,' she admitted. 'Nevertheless, this one isn't bad, considering.'

Beverley hadn't seen the guest list herself because Mary, with Faye's help, was looking after it while her job was to write a few enticing paragraphs that would hopefully inspire journalists to come along and make their own assessment of the exhibition.

'How many shall I tell the caterers to expect?' Lisette asked as she sat at her desk surrounded by menus and wine lists. The five women shared one large open-plan office, with Lisette and Beverley sharing two adjoining desks, so they faced each other, while Faye and Nina had the same arrangement on the opposite side of the room. Only Mary, as head of the department, sat alone at a large fumed oak desk which she always managed to keep scrupulously tidy. She looked up now to answer Lisette's question.

'Let's say one hundred and fifty,' she replied. 'As usual, of those invited two-thirds accept, and of those who accept, two-thirds actually turn up.'

'How do you know that?' Beverley asked, intrigued.

'It's a statistic catering managers always go by, and it rarely fails.'

'Right. Then I'll order champagne for that number,' said Lisette, making notes. 'Have you any preference for canapés?'

Mary nodded. 'Tell them not to produce anything messy or too big. We want to serve little pop-in-the-mouth morsels that won't drop greasy crumbs on the beautiful new gallery carpet, and that won't make the guests' fingers sticky. There isn't a kitchen there either so it's no good them bringing canapés that need heating. Make sure the caterers provide an average of half a bottle of champagne per head ...'

'As much as that?' Beverley cut in. She'd been listening intently because she'd been put in charge of organising the catering for the next function they were scheduled to do, and was trying to pick up all the tips she could.

'Some people will tell you a third of a bottle per head is enough,' Mary explained, 'but if you really want a party to go with a swing, you should allow for half.' She did some quick calculations. 'Tell the caterers we'll need seventy-five bottles ... make that eighty to be on the safe side, and allowing for emergencies, tell them ninety. Extra people sometimes turn up at the last moment, and it's the kiss of death if the champagne runs out. But make sure, Lisette,' she added, 'that you get it sale-or-return.'

'Okay.' Lisette nodded in understanding. 'Glasses, ice, fresh orange juice, mineral water, flowers, food ... anything else?'

Mary thought for a moment, considering, her long straight brown hair falling to her shoulders like silk. 'We'll need a visitors' book, so that the guests can sign in.'

'Okay.'

'Faye, I want you to help Nina on the night,' she continued. 'I'm going to have my hands full showing the press around the new gallery, and talking to the art critics. We mustn't forget we're also there to promote the artist as well as the gallery. I want you to check the guests and get them to sign in.'

'What will you want me to do on the night, Mary?' Beverley asked.

'I want you and Lisette to mingle and give out any information that might be required. Who knows, some people might actually want to buy the works of Anatole Kanchelski.'

The girls laughed and Beverley held up one of the leaflets depicting a painting of scarlet swirls on a purple background. 'What the hell is it?' she demanded.

'Search me,' Nina replied, giggling.

'It's called "Ukrainian Soliloquy",' said Beverley. 'Oh, for God's sake, it's a joke!'

'It's not much of a joke at twenty thousand dollars,' Faye remarked.

'Is the Herman Gallery going to specialise in this junk?' Nina asked.

'There are people who take this type of art very seriously,' Mary pointed out. 'For goodness' sake, don't be heard to scoff at it, or we'll lose the account.'

'Be honest, Mary. It's total crap,' Beverley protested.

'But the gallery don't think so and they're our clients. I think there's something you're not realising,' she continued seriously. 'It's important we believe in what we're promoting otherwise we won't be doing a good job.'

'We can pretend to like something, can't we?' Nina asked.

'Up to a certain extent only. Obviously we can't like everything, but we should at least try to understand it and appreciate that, while it may not be to our taste, others could like it. Do you understand what I'm saying?'

Beverley nodded, but Lisette, Nina and Faye still looked doubtful.

'Do you like every single thing we publicise in this

39

department?' Faye asked directly.

'On the whole, yes.' Mary sounded positive. 'It may not be to my personal taste, but I can always see the merit in it. Charles Floyd told me when I joined Highlight six years ago that I must never handle an account I really hated because I wouldn't do a good job. It's up to us to spread enthusiasm for a product, or a client, and that's something you can't fake. It has to be real. There's nothing more infectious than enthusiasm, and then success breeds success.'

They all nodded, getting the point. If you wanted to inspire others, you had to be inspired yourself.

'Have you turned down many accounts?' Beverley asked, intrigued.

Mary shrugged. 'Half a dozen over the years.'

'And you've never regretted your decision?'

'Never.' She shook her head. 'Usually the product failed because not enough people liked it either, or the client went down the tubes. You have to have integrity. Falseness stands out like a sore thumb. If you hate Anatole Kanchelski's paintings, don't look upon them as works of art but as colourful decorative canvasses to hang on a wall in a modern setting. And if you really can't say anything nice about them at the opening party, don't say anything at all.'

'Well, the gallery's nice anyway,' Beverley said thoughtfully.

They all laughed. 'That's right, Beverley. You plug the gallery and we'll say nice things about the artist,' Nina giggled.

'Okay, girls,' Mary commanded, 'let's get this job wrapped up. There's tons of other work we've got to get on with, like the press breakfast for Marcus Klein to

launch his new brasserie, and all the arrangements for
the opening of the new SoHo boutique.'

In good humour and working well together the girls
got on with their various jobs, while Mary perused the
guest list for the Herman Gallery once more, and
thought about the 'session' she'd had with her best
friend Pamela the previous evening.

'Come early,' Pamela had said, when she'd invited Mary
to dinner. 'John doesn't usually get back until after
seven so come straight over from your office and we'll
have a session before he gets home.'

Pamela and John Hanworth lived on Fifth Avenue, in
a magnificent duplex furnished with a unique collection
of English antiques bequeathed to Pamela by her grandmother who had been British. Much of it was Chippendale, the wood glowing from countless years of loving
polishing, but there was also a William and Mary chest
in the hall, an Elizabethan oak refectory dining table,
and a very fine George III desk. When Mary had first
visited the Hanworths, whom she'd met through a
mutual friend who was an interior designer, she realised
they were in a class of their own. Cultured, highly educated and also very rich, they lived in a world which was
seemingly unrelated to the nineties.

John was a lawyer in an old established firm that had
been started by his late grandfather and was now run by
his father, and Pamela dabbled in buying and selling
small objets d'art, but as Mary had observed, more
buying than selling went on because Pamela couldn't
bear to part with anything that was beautiful.

When Mary arrived, Pamela welcomed her raptur-
ously, holding on to her arm as she led her across the

cool black and white marble squares of the hall floor and into the elegant living room beyond. The atmosphere was instantly seductive, heavily laden with the sweet fragrance of large vases of white lilies and lit softly by oyster silk-shaded lamps.

'Everything's ready,' Pamela exclaimed, as excited as a child giving a party. She was wearing a brightly coloured Japanese kimono over black slacks and heavy gold chains hung from her neck. Mary looked around, her eyes lingering on taupe velvet sofas piled up with petit point cushions in soft shades of pink and blue, on delicate landscapes on the walls framed in carved gilt, on polished mahogany and rosewood, walnut and satinwood. Pamela was standing in the window now, framed by the gold and rose silk brocade curtains that had once graced a noble house in England. Before her was a small square table covered with a dark blue velvet cloth.

'Come and sit down,' Pamela indicated one of the chairs that stood in readiness. With mounting excitement, Mary seated herself. Going to Pamela for 'sessions' had become like a drug; she couldn't keep away, she had to know, she had to find out . . . Deep and dangerous in her silken parlour, Pamela had Mary under her spell, and Mary couldn't resist.

From a drawer in the table, Pamela withdrew a pack of strange-looking cards, covered with delicately coloured images. More oblong in shape than normal playing cards, they looked like miniature works of art, and each bore a printed title.

Pamela leaned forward, her voice low and intense, her frizzy blonde halo of hair a wild tumbling profusion of snarled locks. She was the Medusa look-alike of Fifth Avenue, the wildly eccentric lover of beautiful things who didn't care if people thought she was odd. 'Shuffle them and then cut them twice,' she breathed.

With hands that trembled, Mary picked up the cards, suddenly sick with nerves. What were they going to say today? What were they going to tell her, this time? She'd been going to Pamela for 'sessions' for several months now, secretly of course. John would have freaked out if he'd known his wife's hobby was telling fortunes. Not that she did it for anyone outside her circle of close women friends, but nevertheless he disapproved of anything like that, declaring that no one was supposed to know what the future held.

Mary had finished shuffling the long narrow cards. She cut the pack twice and then sat back and looked at her friend apprehensively.

'That's great,' said Pamela. Then she laid out the cards in a circle, with one in the centre, on top of which she laid another card, crossways. Mary found herself looking down on the cards she herself had shuffled for this first 'spread'. There was the Page of Cups, the Horseman with Six Wands, the Queen of Wands, the Queen of Cups, the King of Swords, the Knight of Swords, the Queen of Pentacles, the Lovers, the Hangman, and the Wheel of Fortune. On the many occasions she'd come to Pamela's to have her fortune told, Mary had learned what most of the individual cards were called, but it took years of study to learn the significance of the cards in relationship to each other when placed in a circle.

'Well?' she asked, digging her nails into the palms of her hands. Pamela had been astonishingly accurate in telling Mary things about her past, and once or twice her predictions had come true, too, even if they had only dealt with her job or her colleagues. Nevertheless, when she'd asked Pamela about 'the most perfect man', Pamela had instantly spotted him as the Page of Wands, depicted in Medieval costume and holding a long stave.

'Here he is,' Pamela had announced triumphantly, stabbing the card with a heavily ringed finger. 'He is a faithful lover, young and fair, an envoy of glad tidings.' Then she paused and laughed gleefully. 'I just *knew* he was right for you when I invited him to dinner to meet you. Now the cards can tell us what's going to happen.'

Through Pamela, Mary had been asking the cards for signs, for the past six weeks, and according to Pamela, the forecast was encouraging. True to what the tarot cards had prophesied, the 'most perfect man' had invited her out twice, though the relationship had not blossomed further than a goodnight kiss on the cheek. Nevertheless . . .

'Look at this!' Pamela exclaimed excitedly. She was pointing to the other cards that surrounded the Page of Wands. 'He will soon be in close proximity. I can see lightning strike . . . as if he's just discovered something. You're on his mind, that's for certain.'

'What else?' Mary urged, leaning forward. She was worrying that John might come home at any moment and they'd have to stop.

Pamela studied the cards intently, one hand pressed to her temple. 'There's love here . . . an overwhelming passion, he's a very passionate man . . . but there's also a storm, like an explosion . . . Do you know anyone who loves going to concerts? They're going to be part of the pattern . . .'

Pamela kept talking for another ten minutes, but Mary had almost ceased listening. She was hung up on the words 'An overwhelming passion . . . He's a very passionate man' . . . and that was all she wanted to hear. For six weeks, ever since they'd met at a dinner party given by Pamela and John, Mary had been crazily in love with the 'perfect man', and all she could think about was how wonderful it would be to be lying in his arms while he made love to her.

Beverley and the others changed in the office washroom for the opening party of the Herman Gallery because there was no time to go home first. She'd brought her best dark blue dress to the office that morning, and now as she slipped into it she added gilt earrings and a simple gilt necklace to complete the smart but business-like look. Thankfully, she reflected, Jenny hadn't gone off with her best pair of dark blue shoes and tights. Jostling with Mary, Lisette and Faye for the only mirror in the washroom, she pinned up her hair, added a touch more mascara, freshened her pale copper-coloured lipstick and dabbed a touch of Lancôme's Trésor behind each ear. Charles Floyd had given them all Trésor for Christmas, so no doubt they'd all smell exactly the same tonight.

As they got ready to leave the office the usual panic started.

'Has anyone seen the visitors' book for tonight?' This from Nina.

'You have got all the press releases?' Mary was demanding of Faye.

'Yeah, they're all here,' she replied, stuffing them into a box.

'Yes, but have you got the ones about Anatole Kanchelski as well as the ones about the Herman Gallery?'

'Yeah, of course!' Faye sounded offended that anyone would think she'd forgotten something so important.

'I can't find the visitors' book,' Nina was bleating, frantically.

'It's here,' Beverley assured her.

Nina fell on it as if it were valuable. 'Oh, thank God!'

Suddenly Lisette spoke in a stricken voice. 'Where are the catalogues? I haven't even seen them, today.'

'Cool it, guys!' Mary remonstrated. 'The printer was delivering them direct to the gallery, remember?'

'Yeah, and I checked an hour ago, and they've arrived,' Beverley assured her.

'Is there anything else we need to take?' Lisette fretted. Out of all of them, she was the one who always got in the greatest panic at the last moment. 'Anyone got a pen?' she asked suddenly. 'The guests will need a pen to sign in.'

'It's all under control,' Mary said calmly. 'Come on, you guys. Stop fussing around and let's go. There are two cabs waiting to take us.'

When they arrived at the Herman Gallery on East 96th Street it was five o'clock and the caterers were putting the last touches to the arrangements. A long table covered with a white damask cloth had been placed down one side of the long room, and from here the champagne would be served. Silver platters of canapés, protected until the last moment by clingfilm, were laid out on small tables around the gallery, and in each corner arrangements of magnificent flowers exuded a heady perfume.

'Wow!' Beverley exclaimed, impressed. 'Even Anatole Kanchelski's paintings look half-way decent!'

Under the carefully directed spotlights, they did bring a certain decorative quality to an otherwise sterile-looking gallery.

'Who's coming tonight?' Nina asked.

'The usual "in" crowd, I suppose,' Faye replied vaguely.

'Any special celebrities?' Beverley asked. 'Any royalty?'

Nina laughed. 'I don't think Anatole Kanchelski has quite the pulling power of Elaine Ross.'

Beverley sighed. 'Wasn't that a night to remember? Imagine actually meeting Princess Diana. When I told my mom, she didn't believe me at first.'

'I don't think any of our moms believed us,' Lisette chuckled. 'Mine accused me of being drunk!'

By six-thirty the gallery was crowded. Rich well-dressed socialites mixed with artists in scruffy clothing while the photographers snapped away, and the girls from Highlight made sure everyone signed the visitors' book, received a catalogue, and was given any information they wanted.

Beverley, standing to one side surveying the scene for a moment, realised that, as at many functions, people had come to see and be seen. The paintings on the walls only served as something to remark upon when the banal flow of conversation dried up.

'Aren't you drinking?'

She spun round and found herself looking at a tall well-dressed man of about thirty. He was wearing a dark blue suit with a fine white pinstripe, a white shirt and a silk tie in deep burgundy with a tiny white spot. Candid blue eyes twinkled as they looked into hers from a

47

tanned face lightly scored by laughter lines, and his grin was slightly roguish.

'Hello. My name's Anthony Amesbury. Can I get you a drink or are you on the wagon?' His English accent was pleasantly modulated and not as fearfully cut-glass as some of the British accents she'd heard. And his manner was easy and charming.

'Hi,' Beverley replied, liking him instantly. 'I'm Beverley Franklin, and I never drink while I'm working. Is there anything I can tell you about the gallery or the artist?'

Anthony Amesbury raised quizzical fair eyebrows, and under the gallery spotlights she saw his hair was fair too.

'Is the artist a friend of yours, then?' He asked the question so carefully, so tentatively, she burst out laughing.

'I've never met him in my life, but I'm helping to publicise his work. Don't you think his paintings are . . . vibrant?' She paused for a beat. 'And vivid?'

'That's one way of putting it,' he chuckled, glancing at the swirling bright colours which looked, in some cases, as if they'd been thrown at the canvas. Then he looked back at her. 'There are other things I'd rather look at, though.'

Beverley felt a glow in her cheeks. 'Of course, not everyone is into modern art,' she said lamely. 'But Anatole Kanchelski is highly thought of by some of the critics.'

'I'm sure.' He looked askance at the paintings once more. She caught the whimsical expression in his eyes and laughed.

'Is there anyone you'd like to meet?' she asked, mindful that Mary had said she was to help look after the guests and no one must be allowed to stand around on their own.

Anthony looked back at her. 'Not really,' he said with sincerity. 'Do I have to meet other people? I'd much rather talk to you . . . unless I'm keeping you from your work?'

'No, not at all.' She looked around the gallery. 'Everyone seems to be having a good time.'

'Well, speaking for myself, that's true.'

Their eyes met and she realised he was impossibly handsome. Everyone's idea, in fact, of a good-looking, polished Englishman. She'd always gone for tall blond types, ever since she'd first started dating, but Anthony Amesbury was better looking than anyone she'd ever seen before. There was an added plus, too. Unlike so many handsome men, he seemed quite unaware of his looks.

'How long have you been doing promotional work?' he asked, breaking into her thoughts.

Beverley told him briefly about her job.

'So you obviously live in New York?' he asked.

'Yes. My home is in Massachusetts, but I have a tiny apartment on West 57th Street,' she replied. 'Where do you live?'

'On the upper East side, 88th Street, between Madison and Park.'

'I know the area, it's very nice.' She wanted to go on talking to him but Mary was looking at her across the crowded gallery and she knew she ought to be mingling. As if he sensed what she was thinking, Anthony took hold of her elbow and moved nearer one of the particularly large paintings which consisted of splodges of orange and indigo, streaked across with black, and entitled: 'Moonshine in Tibet?'

'Why don't you try and explain these pictures to me?' he suggested. 'I can see I'm sorely in need of education.' The suppressed laughter in his voice was plain.

'Sure,' she replied confidently, and then started laughing. 'Where shall I begin?' Suddenly she felt as if she'd known Anthony all her life. The atmosphere between them was so relaxed, they might have been old friends.

They went slowly round the gallery, looking at the pictures but talking about other things, although afterwards she couldn't recall a word that was said. Then she heard him asking her out to dinner.

'I know a lovely Italian restaurant, just two blocks away from here. Their calamari is out of this world, and if you like osso buco, this is the place to go.'

Beverley looked round the gallery. To her surprise, almost everyone had left while they'd been talking. Mary and Faye were standing by the entrance, saying goodbye to a prominent art critic from the *New York Times*, and Nina and Lisette were gathering up the left-over catalogues.

'My God, I'd no idea it was so late!' she gasped, looking at her wristwatch. 'It's nearly nine o'clock! What's happened to the evening?' She turned to Anthony in astonishment. 'Have we really been talking all this time?'

He nodded. 'I'm afraid I've monopolised you all evening, but you can slip away now, can't you?'

Beverley looked up at him, and knew she wanted to go out with him more than anything. She'd never met anyone quite like him before; incredibly good-looking, charming, intelligent, funny, and very much his own man. It took her three seconds flat to make up her mind.

'I'd love to, but first I must check with my boss that she doesn't need me to stay any longer.' Beverley hurried over to Mary, letting Anthony follow her more slowly.

'Is it all right if I go now?' she asked. Mary looked up from studying the visitors' book and her eyes were icy. 'I think we've done everything, haven't we?' Beverley added, faltering slightly. She'd never seen Mary look so angry, and wondered what had happened to upset her.

'I think *we've* done everything,' she said, indicating Nina, Lisette and Faye.

Abashed, Beverley flushed. 'I'm sorry . . . I was talking to the guests and didn't realise how quickly the time was passing . . .'

'Well, the party's over so you might as well go,' Mary snapped. Then she turned and stalked off, brushing past Anthony. He looked after her, frowning in a puzzled way.

'God, that was a bit heavy,' Beverley remarked when they got into the street. 'I wonder what got into Mary? I've never known her to behave so strangely before.'

'I was going to thank her for inviting me tonight but she rushed off,' Anthony said. 'Never gave me a chance. Something must have upset her.'

Beverley looked surprised. 'Is she a friend of yours?'

'We've met a few times at the home of some mutual friends, and then we've gone to the cinema together or to a restaurant – she's more of an acquaintance than a friend, really. She's a nice girl but she certainly behaved oddly tonight. Actually, I don't know why she invited me. Perhaps she just needed people to help fill up the gallery. I do get asked to quite a lot of things when they need to swell the numbers.'

'How come?'

'Oh, you know how it is.' He spoke lightly. 'Here we are. La Tavernetta. I hope you like it after the build-up I've given it.'

Beverley smiled, determined not to let Mary's behaviour get to her. 'It certainly looks great.'

After they'd studied the menu and Beverley had made her choice, Anthony ordered dinner with the quiet expertise of someone who regularly frequents restaurants, and then he asked her what she'd like to drink.

'You're off duty now, remember?' he teased. 'How about a dry white wine?

'Sounds great.'

'We'll have a bottle of Frascati,' he told the waiter.

Beverley settled down to enjoy herself. Throughout the evening Anthony had been asking her about herself, but now she longed to know more about him.

'You're living permanently in New York?' she began, praying he'd say yes. It would be quite a blow, she realised, if he were to announce he was only here for a few weeks before returning to England. They'd only just met, but already she had the strangest feeling that fate had brought them together tonight. Never in her life had she felt so instantly bowled over by anyone, and she found herself feeling apprehensive as she waited for him to answer.

'Yes, I'm here on a permanent basis,' he replied, smiling, as if he too was thankful to be staying. 'I'm a securities analyst. I've got my own company, and I spend my time analysing US stocks in hi-tech areas.'

'Who for?' she asked, intrigued.

'US investors buy my research for their own use. Mind you, with this dip in the market caused by the recession, I don't have as many buyers as I'd like.'

'And where is your office?'

'I share a small office on Madison and 60th Street with another analyst who specialises in stock in the engineering area. We share a secretary which helps to keep down the overheads and works very well. Of course, it involves a lot of business luncheons with company executives, but I love the buzz you get in New York. Nowhere in the world is quite like Manhattan. I was so pleased to get my Green Card, I celebrated for about a week,' he added, laughing.

'But your real home's in England?' Beverley asked.

Anthony nodded. 'Yes. Bucklands. Just outside Oxford. My brother, who's fourteen years older than I am, lives in the family home. He loves England, but I always had the feeling that the grass was greener over here.'

'And is it?' She looked smilingly into his blue eyes. They were such an amazing forget-me-not shade, unlike any other eyes she'd ever seen.

Anthony was shaking his head. 'Not financially it isn't. Normally it would be a lot better, but this damned recession is screwing up everything.' He sighed. 'Never mind. As long as one can make a living it's okay, and things are bound to get better sooner or later.'

At last the evening came to an end, much sooner than Beverley would have wished, but it was after midnight and she had an early start the next morning.

'Thank you for such a wonderful evening,' she said, as he saw her to the door of her apartment building. She wanted him to kiss her and yet she was glad when he didn't. Tonight had been too special to be reduced to the level of a casual date. He'd already said he'd call her to arrange for them to see each other again, very soon, and that made her realise tonight had been special for him too.

'I'll call,' he promised softly. Then he was gone and she was inside the lobby where the doorman sat sullenly reading the baseball results in the newspaper.

'Good evening,' she called out gaily as she strode to the elevator. He didn't reply, but she didn't care. Tonight had been magical from the moment Anthony Amesbury had started talking to her at the party, and already, in some crazy way, she was missing his presence by her side.

As soon as Beverley walked into the office the next morning she knew something was wrong. Mary was sitting at her desk, talking to someone on the phone, her head bent over the instrument as if she was making a private call. Nina, Faye and Lisette looked uneasily at Beverley as she sat down at her desk.

'Hi!' she said, with her accustomed breeziness.

The girls nodded back, but continued working busily at their desks as if they all had too much to do to talk to her. When Mary finally came off the phone, the atmosphere dropped to below freezing.

'Hi!' Beverley said again, smiling at her boss.

The daggers were out again in Mary's grey eyes, flashing like steel. She made no answer.

'Is anything wrong?' Beverley asked tentatively now. Everyone seemed to be behaving strangely; what on earth could have happened? 'Are you all right?' she asked, concern in her voice. Mary looked dreadful, with dark circles under her eyes and her face tight and strained.

'I'm fine. Why shouldn't I be?' she snapped back.

Beverley blinked. 'No reason,' she said slowly, 'but what's the matter?'

'I don't like unprofessional behaviour.'

'Who's been acting unprofessionally?'

'If you call the way you carried on last night, behaving in a professional manner, then I've got news for you.' Mary was glaring at her now, with open hostility. 'Your bad manners were noticed by everyone. It was unforgivable of you to throw yourself at one of the guests . . . and then to monopolise him all evening until he was embarrassed into having to ask you out to dinner.'

'Hey! Wait a minute,' Beverley cut in indignantly. 'If you mean Anthony Amesbury, he came up to *me* and started talking. Then I showed him all the pictures . . . and before I knew what had happened, the party was over and he was inviting me out to dinner. I didn't hang on to him on purpose. It just sort of happened.'

'You could have introduced him to other people and then got on with the job you were supposed to be doing,' Mary pointed out angrily. She looked almost ugly now, with her long lank hair framing her pinched face.

Beverley looked in confusion at the others. 'I kept looking around to see if anything needed doing,' she said. 'Why didn't one of you ask me, if you needed help?'

Faye and Nina shot her a sympathetic look, but Lisette was watching Mary closely. The silence in the office was broken only by the nervous tapping of Mary's pencil against her coffee cup. No one spoke.

'I'm really sorry if I've upset anyone,' Beverley said in bewilderment. 'I honestly wasn't aware I was doing anything wrong. There were enough of us there, including the owners of the gallery, to talk to all the guests.

And if I'd seen anything that needed doing, then of course I'd have done it.'

Mary lifted her chin scornfully and for the first time Beverley realised how unattractive she was. 'The next thing you'll tell us is that you had no idea who he was.'

Beverley's eyebrows arched in surprise. 'Of course I know who he is. His name is Anthony Amesbury, he's English, and he's a self-employed securities analyst with a shared office on Madison and Sixtieth.'

'Are you pretending you've no idea who he really is?' Mary persisted.

Beverley looked at her and it was obvious she had no idea what Mary was talking about. 'What do you mean?'

'He's Lord Amesbury. The Viscount Amesbury. Younger brother of the Earl of Cumberland,' said Mary solemnly.

'Oh?' Beverley wanted to laugh. Mary's manner was so serious and ponderous, it was as if she'd said he was the Pope or something. Nevertheless, what did impress Beverley was that Anthony hadn't flaunted his title the previous night. Not by a word or a hint had he indicated he was a member of the aristocracy.

'Is that all you can say? "Oh"?' Mary stormed.

'Well . . .' Beverley started to giggle. 'What am I supposed to do about it? Call him up and apologise for not curtsying to him?'

'Now you're being absurd, but he was one of our VIPs and . . . and . . .' Mary started floundering for words, and went scarlet in the face as if she were fighting back tears.

'I'm sorry,' Beverley said, appalled. What on earth had brought this on? Mary seemed to be beside herself with misery and anger. Suddenly, she jumped to her feet and rushed out of the room, her hand covering her mouth as she endeavoured to hold back the sobs.

'What the hell was that all about?' Beverley asked, stunned.

Lisette spoke softly. 'Mary met Anthony a couple of months ago, at a friend's house. I think the friend was trying to do a spot of match-making because she's asked them on several occasions. Recently, I believe, she's been encouraging Mary to believe that Anthony is interested in her. That's why Mary invited him last night. I suppose she hoped he'd take *her* out to dinner after the party. She's absolutely crazy about him, has been for weeks.'

Beverley covered her face with her hands. 'Oh, my God,' she said slowly. It all made sense now. Anthony had admitted he'd met Mary at a friend's house, but he'd said . . .

'How close are they?' she asked the others.

Faye, who knew Mary best, answered in positive tones, 'They've only been out together twice. I know for a fact he's never even kissed her, except a goodnight peck on the cheek. Only the other day she was beginning to wonder if he was gay, because he's shown no interest in her at all.'

Beverley leaned back in her office chair reflectively. Gay he most definitely was not. Uninterested in Mary, maybe. From the way he'd spoken about her, he regarded her as a friend, nothing more.

'When you left with him to go out to dinner last night, I thought Mary was going to die,' Nina said breaking into her thoughts. There was no reproach in her voice, just wonderment.

'You really had no idea he was a Viscount?' Faye asked.

Beverley shook her head. 'No idea at all. Oh, God, I hope this isn't going to change things.' All her early morning fantasies of having a straightforward relationship with a great guy were becoming hideously complicated.

'I never got to see the guest list,' she explained. 'If I'd realised he was really a lord, I'd have presumed he was a VIP and wouldn't have carried on like he was Joe Shmoe.'

'Do you think you'll be seeing him again?' Lisette asked.

'Yeah . . . I'm certain of it,' she said slowly. Last night, she was sure, had been the beginning of something special.

'Then for Christ's sakes, don't let on to Mary,' Lisette warned. 'That is, if you want to keep your job.'

Beverley looked suddenly worried. 'As bad as that, d'you think?'

'And the rest! You should have seen her face when you left the gallery last night. She stormed off, refusing to talk to anyone, and she was in a terrible state.'

'I'm sure Anthony doesn't realise she's gone on him,' Beverley pointed out. 'I don't think he's a two-timing type. It struck me last night that he barely noticed her.'

'That's what Mary said when she saw him chatting you up. "He doesn't even realise I'm in the room." '

'Oh, this so embarrassing.' Beverley looked distressed. 'I wouldn't hurt her for the world. I honestly had no idea . . .'

'Hush!' Nina said suddenly. 'I think she's coming back.'

They heard footfalls coming along the corridor, and when Mary came into the office again they were all busily shuffling papers while Beverley was dialling her own home telephone number, just to look busy.

Mary marched back to her desk, ignoring them all, and after a minute she too started using the phone. Soon real work overtook pretending to be busy, and it was lunchtime before they realised it.

'Okay, you guys. I'll see you later,' Mary said with forced brightness as she left the office. It was one o'clock, the time they all took a lunch break.

'Whew!' Beverley said softly when she'd gone. 'That was a sticky morning! Do you think I've been forgiven?'

'As long as you never mention the wretched man's name again, I think you'll weather the storm,' Faye joked. 'But I wouldn't like to be in your shoes,' she added.

'Not even to become a peeress?' Nina echoed. 'Getting the best table in the restaurant, having people bow and scrape to you, wearing a diamond tiara ... Oh, well ... yeah, maybe!'

Giggling helplessly, they left the office to cram a quick snack and some shopping into their lunch hour.

There was a message on Beverley's answering machine when she got home that evening.

'Hello. Anthony here.' The English voice was deep-timbred and rich. 'I was wondering if you were free for dinner tonight? I thought if I collected you at eight, we could go to Le Cirque? This is my number if you'd like to call me when you get in. I hope you can make it. Goodbye.'

Beverley grinned, loving the way he spoke. Some time ago, she'd seen Prince Charles on television making a speech at the White House dinner, and Anthony's voice reminded her of the Prince's. Then she decided to have some fun. Dialling his number, his answer machine picked up the call. As soon as she heard the go-ahead bleep, she started talking.

'Miss Franklin wishes to thank Lord Amesbury for his very kind invitation to dinner, which she has much pleasure in accepting, and she will look forward to seeing him at eight o'clock.' Then she dissolved into giggles. Talk of a touch of the Emily Posts! Her mother was going to be riveted when she told her she was going out with a British peer of the realm, a real live lord. Then she smiled, glad that she hadn't realised who he was when they'd met. Whatever happened now, as far as she was concerned he'd always be just Anthony, the man with the exciting blue eyes and lopsided smile. And much, much more.

He phoned back when she was in the shower, and she dashed into the bedroom, dripping water everywhere, to take the call.

'Eight o'clock really is all right?' he asked.

'Fine,' she assured him, wondering what to wear.

With a growing sense of excitement, Beverley brushed her hair until it shone like rich polished chestnuts, then she went to the closet, still unable to make up her mind whether to wear a simple white suit she'd bought recently, to replace one of those Jenny had taken, or a deep lilac silk dress, which was gathered up at the side, forming a large floppy bow on the left hip. Le Cirque was a dressy place she knew, though she'd never been there before. She held first one outfit in front of her as she looked in the mirror, and then the other. After a few minutes she decided on the lilac silk. It went brilliantly with her hair, and she even had some earrings made of fake amethysts that would look perfect.

When Anthony arrived, she was ready and knew she looked good.

'Hello,' he said, looking as if he could hardly believe his eyes. The light from the living-room windows behind her shone with late-evening sunshine, so that her hair glowed like a fiery halo, and she was smiling up at him, the gold flecks in her eyes glinting.

'Hi,' she replied softly. Leaning forward he kissed her on the cheek, a social gesture only but one he managed to imbue with tenderness.

'You look marvellous,' he said softly.

'Thank you.' Beverley stood aside to let him in and he walked straight into her living room, looking around appreciatively. 'How beautifully you've done this room,' he remarked. 'I love all your baskets.'

'You have no idea how useful they are,' she replied candidly.

'And ornamental, too.' Anthony was gazing at her, thinking he'd never seen anyone lovelier. Her hair was pure burnished bronze in the reddish glow of the sinking sun, and her eyes danced with merriment. At thirty, he'd had a lot of girlfriends, but none of them had been like Beverley. There was a vibrancy about her that made him want to do crazy things like grab her hand and run barefoot through Central Park, or take a trip in a helicopter and drop leaflets all over Manhattan proclaiming his love for her. For that, he realised with an inner jolt, was what had happened. He'd fallen head-over-heels in love and he didn't care who knew it. To hell with the English girls who had been thrust on him by a succession of ambitious mothers since he'd been twenty; to hell with caution! The girls he'd left behind were bland beside this fiery-headed goddess; creamy milk beside this sizzling champagne lady.

'Are you ready to go?' he asked Beverley, his voice not quite steady. She nodded, her face glowing.

They were shown to the best table when they arrived at Le Cirque, and if Beverley hadn't already known Anthony was titled, she'd have been left in no doubt, as all the waiters greeted him as 'M'Lord', and hovered round their table to make sure everything was perfect.

'Do you like champagne?' Anthony asked quietly. If all about him was ostentation, he himself played it very low key.

'I love it.'

'Good.' He ordered a bottle of Dom Perignon while they decided what to eat, and lulled by his expertise, Beverley realised that it was very nice to be looked after. Especially by one who knew the ropes.

Tonight Anthony felt extravagant. Not that his work was showing much of a profit, and contrary to what most people thought, he did not have a private income either, just because he was titled. The small legacy his father had left him was invested against a rainy day, otherwise he had to survive on his earnings. Being the younger brother of an earl meant that everything had gone to Henry; Bucklands Castle in Oxfordshire, the estate which included a farm, and then there were the priceless family heirlooms. The paintings by Van Dyck, Rubens, Rembrandt and Canaletto, the fine furniture, some of it examples of Chippendale's work, the tapestries from Aubusson, the Grinling Gibbons carvings; Bucklands Castle was a treasure trove of magnificent artifacts, and although Anthony knew they'd never belong to him personally, he was perfectly content to have Henry look

62

after them for future generations.

The Amesburys were of ancient lineage, able to trace their family tree back to Thomas Amesbury who had an estate near Oxford during the reign of King Richard II in 1377. One of his descendants was made a Viscount in 1732, ennobled by the then King for his good works in the community, and by 1764 the family had also been granted an Earldom and given high office at Court. Anthony's elder brother, Henry, now held the title of Earl of Cumberland, whilst Anthony as the second son became Viscount Amesbury when Henry succeeded to the title on the death of their father. So far, Henry only had a ten-year-old daughter, Lady Juliet, and Anthony knew that if no son was born, he himself would succeed to the Earldom.

One day he'd explain to Beverley all the ramifications of British titles, with all their quaintness, but right now, he just wanted to get to know her. He had a feeling she wouldn't put too much significance on a title anyway. Of all the girls he'd met, she seemed to have the most sensible priorities and he could tell from just talking to her that she was completely unspoilt.

'Isn't this fun?' she said suddenly, looking around the restaurant with eyes that sparkled with enthusiasm. 'I've never been here before.' There was something so fresh and unaffected about her manner that Anthony smiled, longing to take her hand . . . put his arms around her . . . then he sighed inwardly. He'd be lucky if she allowed him to kiss her on this their first real date. Beverley was not the sort of young lady you could buy with an expensive dinner. He dragged his mind and eyes from her shapely figure back to the menu.

'How about lobster?' he suggested.

'Actually, I have a weakness for crab,' she admitted. 'I'd love the Crab Mornay, with a green salad.'

'And asparagus to start with?'

'That's pure temptation,' she said, grinning. 'Yes, please.'

After he'd given their order, he longed to ask her a hundred things about herself, but he wasn't sure where to begin. Paramount in his mind was the worry that there might already be someone special in her life. But then he had the feeling she'd probably have refused to go out with him if she already had a boyfriend.

The champagne was brought to their table and poured into two fluted glasses. It glowed, golden and bubbly, and he raised his glass to Beverley.

'To your very good health,' he said softly.

'And yours,' she replied, amused by his Englishness. No American would have said that, but she liked it because it was sweet and old fashioned. 'Thank you for asking me out to dinner,' she added.

'Let's hope it's the first of many evenings.' Then he added impulsively, 'I'm so glad we met.'

Beverley chuckled. 'So am I,' she said fervently. She hadn't felt so happy in ages, and she asked herself what could be nicer than spending the evening with this delightful man, drinking champagne.

'I noticed, when you left a message on my machine . . .' he began, but she interrupted him, guessing exactly what he was going to say.

'The girls in the office told me who you were.' Her eyes danced with merriment. 'Was it supposed to be a secret?'

He laughed, and she noticed how even and white his teeth were. 'Of course not, but it sort of never came up, did it? I don't think it's very important, myself.'

Beverley decided to take him into her confidence. 'Mary was very angry with me,' she said. 'She ticked me off for monopolising one of her VIP guests and said that I . . .' She broke off, suddenly embarrassed.

Anthony looked surprised. 'Why should she be angry?'

'I think . . . Oh, well, never mind.' Loyally, she decided not to let on that Mary was actually crazy about him. If he was to see her again, it would be embarrassing for both of them.

'We were introduced by mutual friends, Pamela and John Hanworth,' he explained. 'Mary is a nice girl, though not really my type. Anyway, we went out a couple of times, and she offered to show me Manhattan, but I rather like to find my own way around.'

Beverley nodded, not knowing what to say.

'You don't know the Hanworths?' he asked.

'No.'

'They're an interesting couple. Pamela's a bit strange, but John's okay.'

'Strange in what way?'

Anthony shrugged. 'Weird clothes and her hair is like a lion's mane. She buys antiques and is always into something new.'

'Sounds interesting,' Beverley observed. 'Are she and Mary great friends?' It sounded unlikely, she reflected, for Mary was conventional if nothing else.

'I don't know.' Suddenly he chuckled. 'I have an idea Pamela was trying to match-make between us, though God knows why. People are always wanting to marry me off to their best friends or their daughters, and it's embarrassing for everyone! Anyway, I don't think Mary was any more interested than I was.'

'Is that because you've got a title ... that people try to match-make?' she asked curiously.

He laughed. 'It has to be, because I've got no real money and my only prospects are if I can make my business work. My worldly possessions,' he continued, 'are a rented apartment, a few sticks of furniture from home, and a car which I only use at weekends because it's more trouble than it's worth during the week.'

'Yeah, cars can be a real drag in New York, unless you've got a driver.'

'Which I'll certainly never be able to afford,' he said, grinning.

'Don't you miss your family? And England?'

'Sometimes,' he admitted. 'Especially my brother, Henry. He's a lot older than me, but we're very close.'

'And he lives in England?'

Anthony nodded. 'I need the get-up-and-go atmosphere of city life, but Henry prefers to stay at Bucklands.'

'Is that the name of his house?'

He thought of the fourteenth-century castle with its battlements and ramparts, and the ancient drawbridge that spanned the moat, and the Baronial Hall, the walls of which were hung with armoured breastplates, swords and spears.

'It's not exactly a house,' he explained, his face breaking into a grin, 'but it is the old family home.'

'I expect it's quite grand,' Beverley suggested, 'and that's something you can't say about my home. It's a white clapboard house on the outskirts of Stockbridge, near the forest. Both my parents are teachers and very wrapped up in the arts, so it's a perfect place for us to live. The Berkshires are full of museums, and of course the famous painter Norman Rockwell lived in Stockbridge at one time. There's even a Rockwell museum.'

Soon she was telling him all about her family, how Josh was now a lawyer and how young Tom was crazy about baseball, and then of course there was Jenny ... describing her kid sister was a lot more amusing than having her around, she decided. Anthony was soon roaring with laughter as Beverley told him about her high spirits.

'The next time she comes to New York I'm going to lock my closet,' Beverley said, laughing. 'It's too darned expensive having to replace half my clothes every time she hits town.'

'How do you like to spend your spare time?' Anthony asked after a while.

'Going to concerts, art galleries, museums, that sort of thing. When I was at Wellesley, I was constantly taking trips to Boston or New York for concerts or exhibitions.' Talking about her two favourite topics, art and music, her face became alive with enthusiasm and Anthony felt quite embarrassed having to admit how low brow he was.

'And you're an English lord?' she asked in amazement.

He laughed. 'Bang goes another myth! Alongside the fact that most English lords are penniless, nearly *all* English lords prefer a good James Bond movie to an art gallery, any day.'

Beverley looked at him, stunned. 'You're not serious!'

Anthony nodded, vastly amused by her shocked expression. 'I have to confess that in the eighteen months I've been living here, I've never even been to the Metropolitan Museum or Carnegie Hall. I think I've only been to the Victoria and Albert Museum in London once, when I was at Eton, and that was because I was made to!'

'I can't believe it. I thought all you English upper classes were incredibly cultured?'

'The professional middle classes are the ones you'll find at the opera and the ballet, and dragging their children round museums on a Sunday afternoon. The lower classes go to the cinema and bingo, read Mills and Boon and watch Coronation Street on television. The upper classes hunt, shoot and fish, go to first nights at the theatre because they'll meet their friends, and live for racing. The British, you know, are horse mad.'

Beverley started to giggle. 'You seem to have studied the class system pretty thoroughly.'

'It's rammed down our throats, one way or another, from birth,' he explained. 'The British aren't happy unless they're pigeon-holing people into classes. We're probably the most class conscious country in the world.'

'Are your family like that?'

Anthony screwed up his eyes, thinking. 'Probably, but we don't really discuss it, as a family. Henry's kept very busy, running the estate and farm, and he's also Master of the local Hunt, and he sits on various local committees.'

'What about your sister?'

'Jean?' His eyes widened comically. 'She's a magnificent shot. She loves stalking deer in Scotland, she's good at archery, and she can fly fish for salmon with the best of them.'

Beverley imagined an Amazonian type of woman, athletic, strong and rather butch. 'Is she married?' she asked timidly.

68

Anthony burst out laughing. 'Her husband is an army colonel, retired now, and she's got two grown-up children who are absolute weeds!'

The evening flew past, and Beverley suddenly realised it was after eleven. The dinner had been delicious and the conversation had flowed as easily as the wine. Now he was asking for the check, and she was wondering when she'd see him again.

As if he knew what she was thinking, he said: 'Are you doing anything tomorrow evening? Would you like to go to a movie or something?'

'Why don't you let me cook you dinner at my place? I make a mean chicken casserole.'

'I'd like that, on one condition.'

Beverley looked at him askance. 'What's that?'

'You let me bring the wine.'

'Okay.' She grinned. 'You've got a deal.'

Outside a cab was waiting for them. She climbed in and Anthony followed, sitting as close to her as he could. A moment later she felt the warm firm grip of his hand holding hers, and it was as if she'd received a mild electric shock. A tremor ran through her, and when she looked at him, she found his fiercely blue eyes searching hers and her heart did a slow loop-the-loop before juddering to a momentary halt. Then he leaned forward and kissed her. Lips that were hungry for hers pressed down hard, enveloping her mouth. His tongue, strong and firm, probed deeply and she felt as if she was being lifted off the ground and was floating away. He pulled her closer as she responded, and for a moment she grew weak, unable to resist. There was something magnetic about Anthony that drew her to him, and yet to find herself in his arms like this seemed the most natural thing in the world.

69

For a moment he pulled back and looked at her, and when he spoke, his voice was honey smooth.

'There's something very special about you,' he whispered. 'I feel like I've known you all my life. Have you ever had that feeling?'

She nodded, unable to speak. He was still kissing her when they drew up outside her apartment house. Then he walked her to the door and although she was longing for him to suggest he come up to her apartment, she was glad when he didn't. It was too soon. She wanted to savour every inch of this journey to paradise. She wanted to count every golden moment, remember every second, relish every instant. To have rushed things now would have been to spoil this infinitely precious time when they were just getting to know each other.

'I'll see you tomorrow,' he murmured, under the watchful eye of the doorman.

'Yes.'

A moment later he was gone. But there would come a night, she thought, as she rode up in the elevator, when he wouldn't slip away to be lost in the darkness of New York. He'd stay, and they'd be together in a way she knew she'd never been with anyone before.

Chapter Three

'Jenny, you are *not* going to New York again!' Rachael Franklin looked up from where she was preparing vegetables at the kitchen sink and eyed her younger daughter with a steely look that had quelled many an unruly pupil at the High School where she taught. It did not have much effect on Jenny, however.

'I'll do as I like,' she replied pertly. 'I can stay with Beverley.'

'That's not fair on Beverley,' Rachael remonstrated. 'She's got her own life. She's worked very hard to get where she is today, and I won't have you taking advantage of her.'

'She doesn't mind.'

'What about your schooling? You can't just walk out of school when you feel like it, you know.' Rachael's kindly face was anxious, accentuating the tired lines around her eyes.

'I'm sick of school!' Then she had a sudden thought, making her brighten. 'Maybe I'll get a job in a restaurant in New York!'

Rachael gave an exasperated groan. 'You're doing no such thing, Jenny. I'm not having you running around in New York.'

'Why not?' Jenny wailed. 'It's not fair! Beverley's been allowed to go places, for years now; New York, Boston, Washington! Why shouldn't I go to New York?'

'Beverley is a different kettle of fish, and you know it,' her mother reminded her sternly. 'She's smart and she's responsible.'

'And she's your favourite!' Jenny shot back. 'It's always been Beverley this and Beverley that . . . when are you going to give me an even break, for God's sake?' Angry tears filled her eyes, and for a moment Rachael almost relented, but then she remembered how Jenny was always able to turn on the water-works in order to get sympathy, and she hardened her heart.

If anyone had told her thirty years ago that girls were more difficult to bring up than sons, she'd never have believed them, yet it was true. Josh and Tom had been straightforward kids from the beginning, without hang-ups or foibles, but the girls had been a different matter. Beverley was easy now, but during her childhood and teens she'd been too smart for her own good. Frustration had eaten into her deep intelligence; she always wanted to be ahead of herself, to be the best at everything. And only the best would do. Jenny, on the other hand, wasn't smart enough. Her life and interests revolved around boys, clothes and having a good time, and she seemed unable to settle in to her studies. Now she wanted to drop out of school altogether and go and live in New York, and no doubt get into mischief.

'Beverley is not my favourite. I don't have favourites as you know full well,' Rachael retorted. 'Your father and I have always treated you all the same, and you've all had the same opportunities. Josh and Beverley have made the most of theirs, and I hope Tom will too, but you've never even *tried* to do anything with your life, and that's one helluva waste, kiddo.'

Jenny rose from her seat at the kitchen table with an impatient gesture. 'I'll show you all one of these days! I'm going to be rich and famous! You'll see!'

'I'd rather you were just grown up,' Rachael observed quietly.

'What was that?' Jenny stopped and turned round in the doorway and Rachael realised she was wearing a dress she'd never seen before.

'I said I wished you'd grow up, and where did you get that dress?'

'Bevs gave it to me,' Jenny replied blithely. 'I'm going to call her now, and tell her to expect me this evening.'

Faye, Nina and Lisette crowded round Beverley in the office washroom, eager to hear how her date with Anthony had gone the previous evening.

'What's Le Cirque like?' Faye whispered. Mary had gone out to lunch but nevertheless they felt nervous about talking too loudly in case she came back unexpectedly.

'What did you have to eat?' Lisette asked.

'The whole evening was fantastic,' Beverley replied, after she'd answered their questions. 'And guess what? He's coming to dinner at my place, tonight.' Soon, though, she knew she'd want to keep her dates with Anthony private. Seeing him would no longer be washroom gossip she would want to indulge in, but just for today it was fun to describe Le Cirque, and what it had been like, and the delicious dinner they'd had.

'Did you go to his place or yours afterwards?' Nina asked curiously.

'Neither,' Beverley answered shortly. 'It was nearly midnight when we left the restaurant, and then he dropped me off at my apartment.'

The girls could see she wasn't going to say any more and so they changed the subject, but Beverley could think of nothing else. She'd lain awake most of the night thinking about Anthony, remembering everything he'd told her about himself and recalling every detail of their evening together. It was with a light step and a sense of euphoria that she rushed out in her lunch hour to buy the food for tonight's dinner. Chicken, mushrooms, baby potatoes and fresh spinach soon filled her shopping bag, to which she added garlic, herbs, poppy-seed rolls and several large apples, which she decided to bake with honey and cinnamon.

As she staggered back to her office on Madison Avenue, she bumped into Mary in the lobby.

'Hi,' Mary greeted her easily. She seemed to have gotten over being upset about Beverley going out to dinner with Anthony after the gallery opening because she eyed her shopping and remarked gaily: 'Looks like you're feeding the five thousand!'

Beverley hitched the brown paper bags of shopping higher in her arms and tried to look nonchalant.

'Yeah . . . well, I thought it would make a change from a take-out.' It did not sound convincing but she didn't know what else to say. She had a feeling that if she'd said she was expecting Anthony for dinner, it would cast a blight over the entire office.

In awkward silence they rode up in the elevator together and she noticed Mary's face suddenly looked

74

pale and pinched. Uneasily, Beverley realised she must have guessed who was coming to dinner.

'Oh, no! I don't believe it! Dammit, how could she do this to me!' Beverley stood listening to the messages on her answerphone and gasped with irritation as she heard the familiar voice of her sister, cosily informing her that she'd be arriving later on in the evening: 'to stay with you for a few nights.'

It was already six o'clock. Too late to ring home and tell Jenny not to come. Too late to do any damn thing except get on with cooking the dinner, knowing her quiet evening with Anthony was about to be wrecked.

Cursing, she prepared the chicken and put it in the oven. Then she plumped up the cushions in the living-room, put the flowers she'd bought in a vase on the low coffee table, and went to phone her mother. It would help to know whether Jen would be arriving in time for dinner or turning up afterwards.

'I'm sorry, honey, but I have no idea,' Rachael sounded upset and angry. 'I *told* her not to go to New York! That girl's driving me nuts. When she arrives, will you tell her to come right back home?'

'I'll try, but you know Jen. She never listens to anyone. Has she got any money on her?'

'I don't know, but if she needs money to buy her ticket home, will you give it to her and I'll refund you?'

'Yeah, Mom. Okay.'

'You sound very down, Beverley. Are you all right?'

Beverley sighed. 'I'm okay, Mom. But I've got some-one coming to dinner this evening, someone special, and the last thing I need is Jen bursting in! She's so noisy. Not to mention tactless. I'd give anything to head her off, but I suppose it's not possible. You've no idea when she'll be arriving here?'

'I haven't, love. I'm so sorry about this but I don't know what more I could have done, except lock her in her room!' Rachael sounded despairing.

'Don't worry, it's not your fault, Mom. If she arrives late she'll have to spend the night, but she'll go back first thing in the morning.'

There was a pause and then Rachael spoke again. 'Do you think I'm wrong, trying to keep her at home? She's nearly sixteen, but not nearly as responsible as you were at that age, and I wonder if I'm handling her the right way? Would she be less rebellious if I let her go?'

'No, Mom. She *is* too young to be let loose here, without qualifications or any means of supporting herself. She must stay at school. Frankly, I don't want to be made to feel responsible for her just because I live here.'

'I can understand that,' Rachael replied, understandingly. 'Forget I even mentioned it, honey. Tell her she's got to come home.'

Which is going to be easier said than done, Beverley thought as she said goodbye and hung up.

It was now nearly seven o'clock. Time to have a shower and change. Then she'd set the small table in the corner of her living room for dinner, and pray that Jenny didn't turn up until after they'd eaten. One thing was for sure: with her sister around, there'd be no chance of a romantic time with Anthony tonight.

He arrived punctually at eight o'clock, carrying a bottle of wine and a bunch of exquisite pale pink roses. Beverley ushered him in to the living room, and he sniffed the air appreciatively.

'Smells good, whatever it is,' he observed. 'Home

cooking is something I haven't enjoyed since I moved to New York, and I really miss it.'

'Everyone eats out when they entertain in New York,' Beverley agreed. 'Do you cook for yourself, or live on take-outs?'

He roared with laughter. 'What do you think? I'm not sure I even know how to boil an egg! I even go to my local deli for breakfast in the morning.'

'I'm not as bad as that,' Beverley chuckled. 'But I'm afraid I mostly live on salads and cheese and eggs!' As she spoke, he opened the wine, which was already beautifully chilled, while she lit the one large red candle in the centre of the table.

Anthony poured the wine into two of her best glasses, and then handed one to her.

'Here's to home cooking!' he joked. 'May your oven never grow cool, and your saucepan always keep boiling!'

Beverley burst out laughing. They clinked their glasses. 'And may you forever remain hungry!' she quipped.

The fiery blue of his eyes gazing penetratingly into hers took her breath away for a moment, and she blushed crimson at the unintended double entendre.

'Oh, I hope not,' he said quietly, the corners of his mouth twitching.

'I'll just see how the chicken's getting on,' she said in confusion, hurrying out of the room.

When she came back he was examining her collection of books. When she'd moved to New York, the hardest part had been deciding which ones to bring with her and which to leave in Stockbridge.

'You obviously enjoy reading,' he observed. 'Charles

Dickens, Charlotte Brontë, Byron . . . as well as contemporary writers.'

'I love books,' she said simply. 'Reading is a passion with me.' She glanced at the rows of volumes that filled the shelves.

'When do you get time?'

Beverley shrugged. 'Evenings, weekends, whenever I can. On the subway, in my lunch hour . . . I can't bear to be without a book.'

'I can never settle down to read,' Anthony admitted. 'I'm afraid I only skim the financial pages in newspapers and journals.'

'Don't you read in bed at night?' She couldn't imagine how anyone could go to sleep without reading first.

He shook his head. 'I'm asleep as soon as my head hits the pillow. You'd love the library at Bucklands. There must be four or five thousand books, most of them old leatherbound and gilt-tooled volumes. There are quite a few first editions, too.'

Beverley's eyes widened. 'That's what I call a serious library. Don't tell me none of your family reads either!'

He chuckled and refilled their glasses. 'Henry hasn't read a book since he left Eton, to my knowledge, and my mother's sight isn't good enough. Henry's wife, Leonora, pretends to read, but I don't think she does, much.'

'How do you mean . . . pretends to read?'

'Just that! She buys all the new books that come out and stacks them on the coffee table, but she never even opens them. Leonora likes people to think she's highly cultured and well read, but she doesn't know Shakespeare from Sidney Sheldon!'

Beverley laughed. 'What a waste! If I were rich I'd

spend hundreds of dollars a week on books.'

To her relief, they managed to have dinner without being interrupted by Jenny, and by the time she'd made the coffee, and they were sitting talking quietly, she'd almost begun to hope her sister wasn't turning up after all.

Anthony, she realised, was the easiest person she'd ever talked to. And the most interesting. Topics of conversation flowed from one mutual interest to another, and he was telling her all about his trips to Paris and Rome and Venice. She had always longed to travel, and listening to his descriptions of faraway places fascinated her.

'So you've never been to Europe?' he asked at last. Beverley shook her head.

'You'd love Paris, it's the prettiest, most feminine city in the world. Rome is the grandest. And London is fascinating. You must take a trip one day and see it all for yourself.'

'I'll have to start saving some pennies,' she laughed. 'I've only travelled locally. I haven't even been to California! What I'd really like to visit are the art galleries in Europe; the Louvre, and the Uffizi, and the National Gallery in London.' There was longing in her voice.

'I'm sure you will one day,' he said. Looking into his face, Beverley felt her feelings for him well up inside her, and she knew in that moment she wanted to be part of his life. As if he sensed what she was thinking, he leaned towards her and kissed her very gently on the lips. She shut her eyes, and slipping her arms around his neck, returned his kiss. Then he grew more ardent, crushing her mouth under his, holding her so close she could hardly breathe. She wasn't sure how long they stayed like that, it might have been seconds, or a million wonderful years, but suddenly they jumped apart, startled, as the intercom by her front door buzzed loudly.

'What the ... ?' Anthony opened his eyes and looked as if he'd awakened from a long sleep.

'Dammit!' Beverley muttered, pulling away from him. 'That will be the doorman.'

'Who is it? Are you expecting someone?'

She nodded, grimacing. 'It's my kid sister. She threatened to come and stay with me tonight.' Rising, she caught hold of his hand and squeezed it. 'I'm sorry ...' Then she went to answer the internal telephone.

Anthony adjusted his tie and sat upright on the sofa, and listened while Beverley told the doorman to send her sister right up. A kid sister was something he could do without, but he smiled politely as they waited for her.

When they heard the elevator stop, Beverley opened the door, and Jenny came bursting into the hallway and flung down her suitcase.

'Hi ya,' she said. 'You might look more pleased to see me!' Then she strode into the living room and saw Anthony. 'Hi ya,' she said again.

'This is Anthony Amesbury, my sister Jenny,' said Beverley, introducing them. To her mortification, Jenny gave him an appraising look from top to toe, as if she were deciding whether he was sexy or not.

'Well ... hi ya!' Jenny said it more slowly, this time extending her slim tanned hand, the nails painted almost black-red, the fingers covered in cheap silver Indian rings.

'Hello,' Anthony replied evenly, his expression giving nothing away.

'Anyone like some more coffee?' Beverley asked, desperately. Jen would have to turn up tonight of all nights, she reflected. And it was such a tiny apartment there'd be no getting away from her.

'What d'you mean ... more coffee? I haven't eaten yet,' Jenny complained. She looked over to the table in the corner and saw the remains of their dinner.

'I didn't know what time you were arriving, so we went ahead with supper,' Beverley explained.

'Are you kidding? Jesus, I'm starving!' Jenny looked as if she'd been deprived and ill treated. She headed off towards the tiny kitchen. 'Haven't you anything I can eat?'

Anthony stepped forward. 'Shall I slip out and get you a take-away ... I mean take-out as you call it over here?'

'Oh, yeah!' Jenny's pale blue eyes sparkled and she looked instantly good humoured again. 'You're a honey!'

'Oh, Jen, why should Anthony go out to buy you food?' Beverley protested. 'There's some bread in the kitchen, and you'll find cheese in the fridge, and some fruit.'

'It's all right, really,' Anthony said politely. 'I don't mind at all.'

'That's not the point,' Beverley interjected.

'If he's kind enough to offer, why shouldn't he go?' Jenny demanded sulkily. 'You got my message that I was coming to New York, didn't you? You might at least have saved some dinner for me!'

Beverley flushed angrily. She could see this turning into a regular family brawl. Anthony was shifting uneasily from one foot to the other. Then he spoke.

'Look, it's not a problem. I saw a take-out place half a

block away. I'll be back in five minutes.' He nodded in a determined fashion to Beverley. 'I won't be long,' he added with an intimate smile.

When he'd gone, Jenny grabbed her sister's arm. 'Is he for real?' she breathed. 'That has to be the sexiest man I've ever seen! Boy! Where did you find him?'

'That's unimportant,' Beverley replied shortly. 'What *is* important is the fact you're here. Mom wants you back home in the morning.'

'The hell she does. I'm here to stay, Bevs. I'm bored out of my mind in Stockbridge. There's nothing to do at home. It drives me nuts! You've gotta agree it's the back of nowhere!'

'You're too young to be in New York on your own, and I'm not taking the responsibility of looking after you. Mom says you're to go back first thing . . .'

Tears welled up in Jenny's eyes and rolled down her cheeks. 'Oh, Bevs, I'm so miserable. No one wants me. I'm a nuisance to you, and Mom says I get under her feet at home . . .'

She looked so genuinely unhappy that Beverley put an arm around her shoulder.

'You know what you should do, Jen? You should finish high school, then go on to college, get yourself a qualification, and then you could get a decent job, like I did. Once you've done that, you can come to New York and get yourself a place to live. Mom and Dad are not going to let you run wild, doing odd jobs and scraping around for a living, when you could be studying.'

Jenny sniffed loudly. 'You make it sound so easy.'

'No, it's not easy, it's hard work, but in the end it's wonderful to be able to do what you want to do with your own life. Can't you see that? It's so good not to be dependent on anyone else. I just love it.'

'It's all very well for you, you're smart! I've never done well in an exam in my life . . .'

'You never studied for any,' Beverley pointed out.

'But I'm not smart in that way, and I don't really want to be. Oh, Bevs, all I want is something easy to do that brings in enough money for me to have a good time. I want to be able to buy clothes and go to clubs and nice restaurants.'

'Don't you think there's more to life than that?'

'Like what?' Jenny looked blank.

'Oh, come on, Jen. There's something called job satisfaction for a start! And financial independence. And a sense of achievement. Shall I go on?'

'Don't bother.' Jenny picked up the bottle of wine Anthony had brought, and saw it was empty. She plonked it down again with a deep sigh of dissatisfaction. 'I don't want to go home tomorrow.'

'I'm afraid you're going to have to. I promised Mom you'd go back in the morning.'

When Anthony returned with a pizza and a strawberry milkshake, he found the sisters sitting in uncomfortable silence.

'There you are,' he said breezily, handing the food to Jenny. Then he turned and smiled at Beverley. 'I'd better be going, but I'll phone you tomorrow, okay?'

She rose, smiling, loving him for his kindness to Jenny even though her sister was a pain. 'I'll talk to you tomorrow,' she agreed. As he said goodnight to her on the landing outside her apartment, he kissed her lightly and softly.

'Thank you for a wonderful evening,' he whispered. 'The dinner was absolutely delicious.'

'I'm sorry you had to go out and . . .'

He raised his hand, and laid his index finger gently across her lips. 'Don't worry about it. And tomorrow . . .' he kissed her again '. . . tomorrow I'll call you, and we'll arrange something for the evening.'

She nodded, smiling happily. 'See you then.' The elevator arrived with a swishing intake of air and the automatic doors slid silently open. A final kiss and he was gone, but she'd never been so happy in her life. In spite of Jenny's inopportune arrival just as things were heating up, she'd had a wonderful evening and, what was more important, knew she'd be seeing him again tomorrow.

Next morning, things were frantic in the office. Elaine Ross was querying the cost of the caterers they'd used for *Chichi*'s party, which meant Charles Floyd blew his top, and asked Mary what the hell she was thinking of for not getting Elaine to approve every expense beforehand. Then the printers delivered two hundred invitations for a new Mexican restaurant they were promoting, with the wrong telephone number. Nina got the blame for not checking the proofs more carefully, and the whole lot had to be sent back to be reprinted. Finally, a set of valuable coloured transparencies belonging to a client went astray. Faye swore she'd last seen them on her desk. Everyone denied all knowledge. Lisette asked her if she was sure a messenger hadn't picked them up by mistake? Helmeted bike riders were always dashing in and out of the office, collecting or delivering documents, and it wouldn't be the first time they'd picked up the wrong package by mistake.

'Of course not,' Faye snapped irritably. 'They were here an hour ago, and I haven't left my desk.'

Everyone was over-tired and consequently rattled. They were all nearing the end of a trying and hectic week, and things were beginning to get on top of them. Mary looked the worst, with dark shadows under her eyes as if she hadn't slept, and she bit off anyone's head if they so much as asked her a question. Lisette was suffering from a heavy head cold, and it was only Beverley who seemed to be sailing through the week as if she hadn't a care in the world. No press release was too difficult to write, no mail-shot too boring to send out. No journalist was too formidable to talk to and coax to the new Mexican restaurant, and no photographic session too tedious to supervise. The world was her oyster and Mary was once again being friendly towards her.

Then the phone on Mary's desk rang.

'Hello?' she said pleasantly. A moment later her face was a sickly shade of grey as she looked over at Beverley.

'It's for you,' she said. 'The switchboard must have put it through to me by mistake.' Her voice was a dull monotone and her eyes were veiled in misery.

Beverley grabbed her phone, guessing what had happened.

'Was that Mary I spoke to just now?' Anthony asked after he'd greeted her.

'Yes.'

'Oh, God, I'm sorry . . . is it difficult to talk?'

'No, not really.' She tried to keep her voice low, but Mary had got up and left the room, and the others were busy at their desks, pretending not to listen.

'Can you come out to dinner tonight? And maybe go to a movie?'

'That would be great.' In spite of herself, Beverley

couldn't suppress the delight in her voice.

'I'll collect you at seven, shall I?'

'Yes. I'll be ready.'

'Bye now.'

'Bye.' She replaced the receiver, and three pairs of eyes looked questioningly at her. Faye, Nina and Lisette were all grinning, too.

'Everything okay?' Lisette mouthed silently.

Beverley nodded her head, smiling. At that moment Mary came back into the office, and they made themselves look busy again.

When she got home Beverley showered and dressed with care, choosing a slim red skirt worn with a white silk shirt, and a navy blue blazer with brass buttons. Clipping gilt earrings in place, she swept her hair back into a ponytail, and then added red lipstick. Looking at her reflection in the mirror, she was pleased with the result. In fact, she didn't think she'd ever looked so good.

Promptly at seven o'clock, Anthony was ringing her bell, standing in the lobby outside her front door with a wickedly attractive smile on his face.

'Hi! Come in,' she said, holding the door wide. He stepped across the threshold, kissed her lightly on the cheek, and looked around inquiringly.

'Where's your sister?'

Beverley's expression was wry. 'Back home in Stockbridge, screaming and kicking all the way, but she's gone. Would you like a drink?'

'I'd love a club soda.'

'How very American!' she laughed. 'A club soda it is, then.'

'So why did your sister go back? I got the impression she wanted to remain in New York.'

'I know, but she's not even sixteen yet, Anthony, and Mom didn't want her to come here in the first place.' Out of family loyalty Beverley didn't enlarge on the family's desire for Jenny to remain at home where her parents could keep an eye on her.

'I can understand that. This is no place for a young girl to be on her own. I'm not sure I feel all that safe myself at times.' He grinned engagingly again. 'The great thing is to be careful where you go, isn't it? And not to hang around, looking like a tourist.'

'You got it,' she smiled, as she handed him his drink.

They went to see a movie, although afterwards Beverley could hardly remember a thing about it, and then he took her to a small French restaurant on Lexington and 50th Street where the lighting was dim, the decor sophisticated, and the food exquisite. It was a wholly different atmosphere from Le Cirque, much more intimate, and she loved it. Sitting beside Anthony on the grey velvet banquette, cosily set apart from the other diners in a recessed corner, she sipped her wine and felt like pinching herself to make sure she wasn't dreaming. It seemed incredible that in such a short space of time she'd been going out every night with this wonderful man who was everything she'd ever dreamed of; kind, warm, amusing, and incredibly good-looking. The girls at the office kept saying he was 'so eligible', and she supposed it was true, but to her it wasn't what mattered. If he'd been a road sweeper she'd have felt the same about him.

Coffee arrived, and he was holding her hand, and they'd been talking and laughing all evening, although, as with the film, she had scant recollection of what they'd talked about. His very presence was dazzling and she felt distracted.

When he'd paid the bill, he turned to look at her again and the expression in his eyes nearly made her heart stop dead. There was something so direct, so penetrating, that for a moment she had to look away. When she could bring herself to look back, he was smiling at her tenderly, as if he understood.

'Shall we go back to my place?' he asked softly.

Beverley nodded in silent agreement.

Anthony's apartment was larger and far grander than hers, with a living room, three bedrooms, one of which he used as a study, and a very modern kitchen where everything seemed to be made of stainless steel. Simply furnished and decorated in strong masculine colours it had a very comfortable atmosphere, and she immediately felt at home. Table lamps lit all the rooms with a soft glowing light, revealing richly patterned rugs on the floor and well-worn dark green leather sofas and chairs. On the mantelpiece behind some china figurines she saw a row of formally printed invitations addressed to 'Lord Amesbury'. When he saw her looking at them, he put an arm around her shoulder and squeezed her close to his side.

'I'm afraid I somehow got on the mailing list of several New York matrons,' he explained, almost apologetically. 'It's the title they really want at their parties, not me!'

'I'm sure that's not entirely true,' she laughed.

'Well, I have better things to do with my time than go to a lot of boring cocktail parties,' he murmured, and then he turned and kissed her on the neck, just below her ear.

A moment later she was in his arms and he was kissing her strongly and deeply while she clung to him, responding, returning his kisses, pressing herself against him and thrilling at the feel of his thighs against hers.

'I love you . . .' he kept saying as he covered her face and neck with kisses. 'Oh God, I love you.'

'I love you, too,' she whispered back, hardly able to believe that this was happening to her. Suddenly he pulled away and stood looking down at her, his hands either side of her waist. 'I want to make love to you more than anything else in the world,' he said huskily. It was as if he were asking permission and she was deeply touched. Too often, in the past, men had taken her out to dinner a couple of times and then expected to have sex with her, as if she owed it to them. She could remember some very unpleasant moments when she'd refused, and they'd been furious.

She looked up at Anthony now, trusting him implicitly, and her eyes were soft and dreamy. 'I want you, too,' she whispered, going into his arms again, her face pressed to his shoulder.

'Oh, my darling love . . .' This time his kiss was passionate, as if he could never bear to let her go. Then he guided her into his blue bedroom, which had a large double bed covered with a thick blue and white cotton bedspread, and they were lying on it, their arms and legs entwined as he rolled her underneath him. Lying under the pressure of his weight, Beverley suddenly knew what it felt like to want someone with a passionate need.

Since she'd come to New York, there'd been no one special in her life, and the short summer interlude she'd had at college now paled into insignificance. It was almost as if she were still a virgin, and this her first experience. Carefully Anthony removed her clothes, kissing her as her strong slim body became revealed to him. At last she lay naked, her skin creamy-coloured in the lamplight, her hair spread out on the pillow, golden-red like autumn leaves, soft to the touch as silk. For a long moment he stood by the bed looking down at her and then he undressed himself, quickly, as if he could no longer wait.

Slowly and gently he stroked her all over with his finger tips, seeking out her most erogenous zones, letting her take all the time in the world to reach the point of arousal when he knew she would be ready to receive him. Feeling his hands trace the outlines of her breasts and stomach and thighs, she gave little gasps of pleasure, delicately raking her nails across his bare back and chest and up and down his arms. With fingers that left a fiery trail and kisses that scorched, he brought her slowly but relentlessly to a state of readiness, where she was writhing beneath him, crying out for him. Then she cradled his manhood in her hands, feeling the rigid tumescence, guiding him inside her, for without him she felt she would die.

'I want you . . .' she moaned, helpless in her desperate need. He did not answer but instead thrust himself hard up inside her so that she rocked her head from side to side until he found her mouth and, slipping his tongue into its soft wetness, held her down, pinioned to the bed, filled by him, loved by him, taken by him to the deepest fulfilment.

Crying out his name again and again, Beverley held him tightly to her, almost losing her mind as an orgasm shuddered through her, followed a second later by the deep tremor of Anthony's own release exploding inside her. Then they lay spent, gasping for air, shaken by the depth of their feelings. It was a little while later, while they were still lying in each other's arms, that Anthony spoke.

'I've never known it to be like that,' he said fervently. His eyes held a baffled look, as if he were almost unable to understand the intensity of what had just happened between them.

She smiled, gazing into his face. It had been beyond her wildest dreams and fantasies.

For a while they lay together, looking into each other's eyes, and talking softly. Then Anthony got up to fetch glasses of water. When he lay down again, he couldn't resist reaching for her once more, stroking her firm rounded breasts and the golden-red triangle between her legs. Smiling, Beverley reached for him too, loving the flatness of his stomach and the broad line of his shoulders. Before long they were kissing again, and although they had not planned to make love a second time, would have thought they were unable to make love so soon again, bolts of desire shot through them once more, even deeper than the previous time, and with the sweet familiarity of knowing, Anthony took her again, pouring his life into her, riding high together on waves of intensity that left them once again spent.

Four times they made love that night, and it wasn't until a hot summer's dawn crept over Manhattan that they finally fell asleep, still with their arms around each other.

For the next four weeks they saw each other every evening, and most nights were spent together, too, in either Beverley's apartment or his. Nina, Faye and

Lisette saw a great difference in Beverley as the weeks passed; she seemed to glow with beauty and happiness. Mary observed her with cold sad eyes, unforgiving and accusatory. Beverley was careful never to mention Anthony in front of her but couldn't hide her obvious radiance, and it was an awkward situation for both of them. Then came the day when Anthony expressed a desire to meet her family.

Beverley's eyes widened. They were taking a lunch-time stroll through Central Park on a Saturday, and she'd been thinking only a few minutes before that it had been ages since she'd gone home for the weekend.

'We could go next Saturday and stay the weekend, if you like,' she replied.

'Sounds great. How do we get there?' He looked eager at the prospect.

'A flight from La Guardia. That's the easiest and quickest. I'll have to book you into a hotel, I'm afraid, because there isn't room in our house, and Mom and Dad would have a fit if you shared my room. You don't mind, do you?' She looked up at him, handsome in an open-necked shirt and light trousers. He squeezed her hand.

'I think I can probably just survive for one night on my own,' he teased.

'Then I'll ring home tonight, and tell them to expect us,' she said happily. She'd told her mother all about Anthony on the phone, and of course Jenny had given them a full blown description of the 'English lord', but Beverley was longing for them to meet him in person. 'And I'll get Mom to book you into the Red Lion Inn.'

Anthony looked startled. 'That sounds amazingly English!'

'It's a fabulous place, made famous by Norman Rockwell, the artist. You'll love it because it's filled with antiques, and there's a long veranda in the front where you can sit and have drinks looking on to the main street. It's gorgeous on summer evenings. I believe the atmosphere *is* rather English.'

Pamela shook her head, staring at the spread of tarot cards. 'I don't understand what's going on,' she said thoughtfully. She ran her hands with their long nails through her tangle of hair. 'The cards are still saying you and Anthony are going to end up together.'

Mary let out a long low sigh of relief. 'That's all right, then. I don't have to worry?'

'No. There's a lot going on around you, I'll admit that. Turbulent influences are disturbing the atmosphere ... but they won't last.' She tapped the Page of Wands with one long nail. 'There he is, Anthony. A lover, an envoy, bearing favourable testimony about his intentions. He's standing in the centre ... letting it all whirl around him ... but in the end he'll have no choice. The decision will not be his. It is ordained, according to the cards, that you will end up together.' Pamela's voice was low and serious. The silence of her drawing room was oppressive.

Mary stared at the cards too, concentrating on the Page of Wands. Delicately engraved, the antique cards were hand-painted in watercolour. The page in particular appealed to her romantic nature in his richly hued doublet and hose and high leather boots. His cape was flung over his shoulder with a nonchalant air, and he held a long staff which sprouted leaves as if he were about to sink it into the ground. Wavy fair hair showed beneath his plumed hat. In the distance smoky blue mountains and a lake suggested tranquil countryside.

'How long is it going to be before . . .' Mary wanted the favourable outcome so badly, she didn't dare put it into words for fear of incurring the wrath of the gods.

Pamela shrugged. 'You could shuffle the cards again and we could do another spread if you like, but I don't see much point. We know what's going to happen. You and Anthony are going to be together eventually, but they can never give a time scale. It might be months . . . or even a year or so.'

'*A year or so!*' Mary looked appalled. 'Oh, God, surely not?' Her mouth drooped at the corners with disappointment and she looked paler than ever.

Pammy smiled reassuringly. 'Look, you can afford to be patient when you know it's going to work out, can't you? Just get on with your life, and don't talk to other people about him, but be nice and friendly if you happen to meet him . . .'

'It's not so easy being friendly to Beverley,' Mary cut in sullenly. 'I hate her. I'd like to get rid of her, but at the same time I want to keep tabs on the situation between her and Anthony, and working with her is the only way.'

'But you don't discuss him with her, do you?'

Mary shook her head violently. 'Of course not. Faye tells me the odd thing, but I don't even need anyone to tell me, I can sense when she's been seeing him.' Her mouth tightened bitterly. 'I can always tell when they've been to bed together because the next morning she's . . . she's sort of glowing. Christ!' she added passionately. 'I wish I'd never let them meet. I wish she'd never come to Highlight. I wish she was dead!'

* * *

When Beverley and Anthony landed at Stockbridge's small airfield the following Saturday afternoon, Daniel Franklin was there to meet them with the family car. As soon as Anthony set eyes on him, he liked him. He had the same colouring as Beverley and she'd also inherited his direct open expression. Greying now and deeply lined, it was still possible to see that he must have resembled his daughter when he'd been young. The men shook hands, and smiled slightly shyly at each other, and then they all piled into the car. Half an hour later, they turned off the main highway and up a narrow road bordering the edge of a forest. There, set by the roadside and surrounded by a garden, was a white clapboard house, symmetrically built like a doll's house, with four front windows and a front door also painted white. Geraniums overflowed from tubs on either side of the door and Anthony thought he had never seen anything so neat and perfect in his life.

Rachael Franklin came out to greet them, a tiny dark-haired bird-like creature with large dark eyes and a ready smile.

'We're very pleased to meet you,' she said warmly, as she shook Anthony's hand, and then she hugged Beverley, obviously delighted to have her home again.

'Hi, Mom,' Beverley said, laughingly hugging her mother back. A moment later Jenny came bursting out of the house followed by Tom, a serious looking boy who exactly resembled his mother.

'I'm afraid Josh couldn't get home for the weekend,' Rachael explained regretfully. Then she turned to Anthony. 'I expect Beverley's told you he's a lawyer in Boston and has a load of work on right now.'

Anthony nodded. 'Maybe we could go to Boston

sometime and visit him there,' he said, putting his arm around Beverley.

At that moment she caught her mother's eye and they exchanged a look that spoke volumes. He's serious about you, Rachael's eyes seemed to say. I know, isn't it wonderful? Beverley's expression responded. Then Rachael smiled lovingly, and Beverley knew she was glad for her.

'How about a cup of tea?' Rachael suggested, leading the way into the kitchen which was the largest room in the house and Beverley's favourite. They sat in the kitchen around the old scrubbed table much more often than in the living room next door. 'Being English I expect you like tea best, don't you?' Rachael enquired, smiling up at Anthony.

He grinned the boyish grin that always melted Beverley's heart. 'I'd rather have coffee . . . if that's possible, please?'

Tom frowned at Anthony's polite way of talking and his English accent, but Jenny found it entrancing. She sat, open-mouthed and silent for once, hanging on to every word he said.

The conversation flowed easily. To Anthony's relief no one seemed impressed by his title, with perhaps the exception of Jenny, and he liked the Franklin family enormously, thinking that though he might have had a rich and privileged upbringing himself, these people were far more interesting than anyone in his family.

Meanwhile, Beverley watched with relief and happiness as Anthony chatted to her parents. They obviously liked him and that meant a lot to her. Belonging to such a close-knit family, it was important to her that they accept the man she loved. After they'd had tea, she suggested they take a walk in the forest.

'That's a good idea,' Anthony replied, smiling at her, showing her by his expression just how much he enjoyed being with her and her family.

'Why don't we all dine at the Red Lion Inn, tonight – as my guests, of course,' he added, looking at Rachael and Daniel. 'Unless you've already made other plans?'

Tom scowled again, but before Rachael could reply Jenny had already jumped to her feet, her face alight.

'Wow! That would be great! The food is terrific there! Yeah, we'd like that, wouldn't we, Mom?' She looked beseechingly at Rachael.

Her mother's face broke into a smile. 'That's very kind of you, Anthony, but are you sure? We can easily have dinner here.'

'No, Mom. It would be much more fun at the Red Lion . . .' Jenny's voice trailed off. She was about to say they could never afford to go out, but thought better of it. If Beverley was about to get serious with this English lord, then she was all for sharing any of the fringe benefits. At that moment, she made up her mind to be real nice to Beverley in future. She wouldn't take any more of her clothes, or descend on her at inconvenient moments in New York; she'd be as sweet at pie, and if she played her cards right, she might be able to tag along in the aristocratic wash of her sister's boyfriend. It might even get her a trip to Europe! It might also get her a real life lord for herself! Switching on her sweetest smile, she turned to Anthony.

'I think it's a really kind suggestion,' she crooned.

Anthony grinned, pleased. 'Then that's fixed!'

They borrowed the family car to drive into the centre

of the town so Anthony could register at the inn and book a table for the evening in the popular garden restaurant. Then Beverley drove them to the edge of the forest, set on a hill that lay behind Stockbridge to the east.

Parking the car, they started walking up a steep track between the tall trees. Up and up they went, under a canopy of green leaves that was so dense it blotted out the sky. It was so still, so utterly motionless in the forest, that when they stopped to rest in a small clearing, there wasn't a sound to be heard. Beverley leaned back against a tree, slightly breathless from her climb. Anthony stood near her, looking down at the valley below.

'I love it here,' he said suddenly. 'It's so incredibly beautiful and peaceful.'

'I love it here, too. This will always be home to me,' she said softly. 'No matter where I go, a part of me will always be here. In the valley, or this forest, or on the mountain slopes. As far as I'm concerned, this is home.'

Anthony nodded, looking at her tenderly. 'I like your family, too.'

Her eyes met his, and her expression was tranquil. 'I'm glad you do. I can see they like you a lot, too.'

'I'm planning to stay in America, you know,' he said, choosing his words with care, because there was something very special he wanted to say to her.

'You are?' She sounded pleased.

'Yes. I like this country. I like its attitude to people and its basic lack of snobbery. I've decided to stay here, permanently.'

Beverley remained silent, guessing what was coming next, watching him, eyes full of love and trust.

'Will you marry me, sweetheart?' He said it slowly and rather shyly.

A moment later, she flung her arms around him, touched by his sweetly old-fashioned proposal, thrilled and amazed that he had really asked her to be his wife.

'Oh, yes!' she said unhesitatingly.

He held her close, his heart beating wildly, wondering if she'd have said 'yes' if he'd suggested taking her back to England and away from her family. He'd never know now, but it didn't matter. They were going to get married and that was all he cared about.

Chapter Four

Mary looked at her with haunted eyes. 'I'm sorry, Beverley, but you'll have to leave.'

Aghast, Beverley stared back as if she couldn't believe her ears. After her weekend in Stockbridge she'd decided she had to tell Mary that she and Anthony were getting married. It was going to get out sooner or later, and in any case, she'd have to ask for leave. Now Mary had dropped this bombshell.

'Why do I have to leave?' she stammered in disbelief. Surely Mary couldn't be asking her to quit her job because she was still jealous?

Mary rose from her desk and went over to shut the door of their office. Nina, Faye and Lisette were out having their lunch break, and they were alone. She faced Beverley, her face full of misery.

'It wouldn't work . . . I didn't fully realise that . . .' Her voice broke and tears sprang to her eyes. She perched on the edge of her desk with her arms folded protectively across her chest. She drew in a deep shuddering breath. 'I can't go on working with you, knowing that you and Anthony . . . are together . . . married. It's more than I can bear.'

'Oh, Mary.' Beverley felt stricken. Her boss was really

breaking her heart, here in the middle of the office, and all along Beverley only thought that she'd been piqued at her going out with Anthony. She'd never realised just how deeply Mary felt, and the knowledge shocked her now. 'I'm so terribly sorry,' she said involuntarily. 'I'd no idea . . .'

'I fell in love with him the moment I saw him.' Mary was sobbing now. 'I really thought I had a chance . . . he took me out twice, you know . . . and I hoped he would grow to feel the same. The tarot cards told me everything would work out all right in the end. They said . . .'

Beverley looked at her, stunned. 'What tarot cards?'

Mary hung her head, colouring. 'I have a friend who does the tarot cards. She's brilliant. She's never wrong. Anyway, the cards don't lie. They've told me, again and again, that it was really me he'd turn to eventually . . . as long as I was patient and waited,' she added mutinously.

Beverley's jaw dropped and she looked at her boss incredulously. 'You don't believe in all that crap, do you?'

Mary raised her chin defiantly, although the tears were still gathering in her eyes. 'People who are a lot smarter than me believe in fortune telling. What about Nancy Reagan?'

Beverley stood in helpless silence, not knowing what to say. Someone had been deluding Mary, or she had chosen to let herself be deluded, believing what she wanted to believe, despite the facts.

'I'm sure Anthony has no idea you feel like this,' she said awkwardly. 'He regards you as a friend . . . I mean, he was aware that Pamela Hanworth was trying to match-make between you. Perhaps that's why . . .' She paused, feeling stricken. This was the most embarrassing situation she'd ever been in and she couldn't help feeling very sorry for Mary. If Pamela had been encouraging her to believe that Anthony would show interest in her one day, then it was a cruel and heartless thing to do. Mary had stopped crying now and was blowing her nose. When she spoke her manner was abrupt.

'I'm sorry, but hearing you were getting married was a shock. Anyway, I can't go on working alongside you now. It would be too painful. If you want, you can see if there are any jobs going in the other departments of Highlight, but I'd really rather you weren't here at all.' Then she shook her head disconsolately. 'I'm never going to get over this if I have to see you around every day, and I've got to *try* or it'll kill me.' Then she started to cry again, great sobs that seemed to wrench her apart and make her shake all over. 'It seems so unfair. You're only twenty-three and I'm nearly thirty. My chances of finding someone are getting less every year and I really fell for Anthony. He's everything I've ever wanted.'

'Okay, I'll leave,' Beverley said in desperation. She could see Mary was genuinely distraught. They'd never be able to work together again now. No doubt she could get another job but it was all deeply disappointing. She loved being at Highlight and she loved her work. For a moment she felt quite angry with Mary for letting a sick obsession get the better of her. It was costing Beverley her job and she wasn't sure where she'd find another she liked as much. And what was she supposed to do now? Tell her boss to go home and make herself a strong cup of tea? Take the rest of the day off?

'I'm going for a walk,' Mary announced as if she knew what Beverley was thinking. 'I don't want the girls to see me like this.' She did look a wreck – her face blotchy, her eyes swollen and her hair dishevelled. She rummaged in her handbag for a tissue with hands that trembled.

'I'll hand in my resignation to Charles Floyd this afternoon,' Beverley promised.

Mary glanced up at her with eyes shot with pain. 'You won't say why?' she began pleadingly.

'I'll say I'm leaving to get married. That's a good enough reason, isn't it?' said Beverley briskly.

Mary turned to go and then paused in the doorway and looked back, a thin hunched figure with a pale and pinched face. 'I may hate your guts,' she said, 'but . . . all the best.'

Beverley smiled gently, guessing it had cost Mary a lot to say that at the end. 'Thanks,' she replied briefly.

Charles Floyd accepted her resignation with perplexity and regret and didn't seem to believe it when she told him she wanted to give up work in order to get married.

'Is this your fiancé's idea?' She'd told him who Anthony was, and he'd looked suitably impressed. 'Is it because you'll be titled now? You'll be Lady Amesbury, won't you?' he asked.

Beverley laughed. 'No, of course not! I'm sure we're going to need my salary. Anthony's not rich. I just feel . . . well . . .' She paused, hesitating, trying to think of a valid excuse. 'I think I'll need the time off between now and the wedding to see to all the preparations, and then we plan to go to Barbados for our honeymoon. I'll probably start looking for a new job when we return to New York.'

'Do you want to stay in public relations?' he asked.

'I'm not sure,' she replied honestly. 'Some of the time I enjoy the work, but maybe I haven't done it for long enough to know if it's for me.'

'If there's anything I can do, you'll let me know, won't you?'

Beverley thanked him, and they talked for a few more minutes before she left his office. In the space of two hours, she'd announced her intention of getting married and had to give up her job. Everything was happening so fast she felt bewildered. And the damnable thing was that in spite of the fact she'd told Charles Floyd she wouldn't be looking for work until after she and Anthony returned from their honeymoon, she was going to have to get a job, even a temporary one, as quickly as possible. Her savings were meagre, and she couldn't expect her parents to pay for the wedding without some help from her. There was also the rent on her apartment. She'd be moving in with Anthony in due course but in the meantime, the rent was payable monthly in advance and she only had just enough to cover it. When she told Anthony that evening what had happened, he looked stunned.

'How can she be in love with me?' he demanded incredulously. 'And she wants you to give up your job because of it? For God's sake, that's a bit much, isn't it? She *can't* be in love with me, Beverley. I hardly know the girl. I haven't even seen her for months.'

'You've no idea what a state she was in. I've never seen anyone so upset – it was kind of scary. She's obsessed with you, Anthony. She's so obsessed she can't even bear to have me around because I remind her of what's happened. Isn't that dreadful? As she's been with Highlight for six years, it's obvious that I'd be the one to leave if anyone did.'

'But it's totally unreasonable! Why should you be made to suffer because she's got some bee in her bonnet about me? There was never anything between us. We were just friends. You do believe that, don't you, sweetheart?' He looked at her anxiously.

Beverley reached out for him, taking his hand. 'Of course I believe you.'

'Then how did she get like this?' His blue eyes looked puzzled and alarmed.

'I think your mutual friend Pamela Hanworth is to blame,' she said slowly. 'According to Mary, Pamela has been telling her fortune using tarot cards. Pamela, or rather the cards, have prophesied that you will end up loving Mary . . . and she's believed them. This has been going on for weeks if not months, and Mary has been totally convinced that what the cards say will come true.'

His jaw opened and he looked appalled. 'You're not serious?'

Beverley nodded. 'I am. She's been going to the Hanworths' apartment as if Pamela were a professional clairvoyant. Lisette filled me in with more details this afternoon when I told her what had happened. Mary believes in the cards and nothing will persuade her that it's all a load of rubbish.'

'Oh, Jesus! That's awful! What the hell made Pamela do a damned fool thing like that? John will go crazy if he finds out.'

'It probably wouldn't have happened if Mary hadn't been so impressionable and desperate to get married,' Beverley pointed out. 'It's not your fault, darling. You did nothing to encourage her and I think even she would agree with that. I had no idea something like tarot cards could have such a powerful effect on someone.'

'They were banned for a long time in England. Gypsies used them secretly, but it's only in the past thirty years that they've been freely available. I hate anything like that,' he added vehemently.

'I think it's all a load of crap myself.'

'Even so, I'm going to give Pamela a ring and tell her to put things right with Mary, before she destroys the bloody things. Otherwise I'll threaten to tell John, and that will soon make her stop this nonsense,' he said angrily. He went over to the phone in the living room which adjoined his kitchen and dialled the Hanworths' number. A moment later, he was talking to Pamela and his face had turned grey.

'Oh . . . my . . . God!' Beverley heard him say slowly.

She was by his side in a second. 'What is it?' she whispered.

Anthony mouthed the words while still listening to Pamela. 'Mary's taken an overdose.'

Beverley started, and her hands flew to her face. 'Oh, no! Is she . . .?' She broke off, the words sticking in her throat. How could Mary have done such a thing? Over a man she'd been out with twice? It was mad. Sick. For a moment, she felt a wave of anger that anyone could behave in such a way, leaving others to bear unwitting guilt.

'What's happening?' she whispered fiercely, as Anthony continued to listen to what Pamela had to say.

'She's going to be all right,' he whispered back. When he hung up, he dropped on to the sofa as if he was exhausted.

'Did you ever hear anything like that?' he demanded. 'I'm furious with Pamela. She actually admitted she'd been encouraging Mary, doing a "session" with the tarot cards almost daily!' He thumped his fist on the arm of the sofa. 'You know something? I feel terrible about this, and yet I've done nothing to encourage her in any way.'

'I know, love. What did Pamela say had actually happened?' Beverley sat down beside him, slipping her arm through his and holding it close to her side.

'Mary went round to see Pamela this afternoon and told her we were getting married. She insisted on consulting the tarot cards and when Pamela refused, she stormed off in a terrible state, saying she'd find another clairvoyant. Suddenly Pammy got nervous in case Mary did something stupid, so she went round to her apartment . . . and she heard a funny snoring sound through the door.

'She got the superintendent to let her in and they found Mary, lying on her bed.' He paused and then added heavily: 'They only just got to her in time. She's in hospital now, recovering from being pumped out.'

Beverley looked shocked. 'That's terrible.'

'Pamela said she wouldn't be going back to work again this week, so there's no chance of your running into her, which under the circumstances is probably just as well.'

'You're right,' Beverley said, relieved. 'I wondered how I was going to face her again . . . and yet why should I feel guilty?'

'Quite.'

For the rest of the evening, they both felt subdued. Even though none of this was their fault, it had cast a deep shadow over them, and when Beverley turned up at Highlight the next morning, things weren't much better. Somehow the news of Mary's attempted suicide had got out, and Lisette, Nina and Faye were bursting with the news.

'She's going to hate the sight of you,' Nina informed Beverley drily.

'I'm leaving on Friday so she won't have the chance. These are my last few days,' Beverley announced. She'd planned to tell them at the end of the week she'd given in her resignation but now there seemed no point in keeping quiet about it any longer.

They looked at her, astounded. Lisette spoke first. 'You're not leaving to spare Mary's feelings, are you?'

Beverley hesitated for a fraction of a second before she answered. Mary would be resuming work among these girls in the near future, and she was going to need all the dignity and understanding she could get. 'No, of course I'm not leaving because of Mary,' she said stoutly. After all, she'd promised she wouldn't even tell Charles Floyd the real reason for going. 'I'm going to be so busy getting ready for the wedding that Anthony thinks I should do something less demanding for the moment.' She wasn't sure whether they believed her or not but at that moment all the phones started ringing and they were too busy to question her further.

'I will have to find some work, though,' she told Anthony that night. 'My rent is due in a few days.'

'Why don't you move in with me, right away?' he asked eagerly. They were dining at their favourite French restaurant again, as they discussed plans for their wedding. 'Maybe you can find someone to take over your apartment . . . and you know what they say? Two can live as cheaply as one.' He gazed into her eyes with longing.

Beverley laughed. 'And it's been proven that that's completely untrue!' she chuckled. 'It's a lovely thought, though.' She looked back at him, feeling her heart pound at the realisation that soon she could be going to sleep by his side every night and waking up next to him every morning. Suddenly she gave a little cry. 'I've had the most marvellous idea.'

'What is it?'

'Faye is looking for somewhere to live, because she's finding it a drag coming in from Queens every morning. She wants to share with her sister, Hayley. Shall I suggest my place to her?'

'Why not? It's big enough, providing they get on, and she can afford it, can't she?'

Beverley nodded. 'It's a great idea. I'll put it to her first thing in the morning. Oh, Anthony, things are really working out for us, aren't they?' She felt so happy it was as if her heart would burst. For a moment an image of the heartbroken Mary flitted across her mind and she felt so thankful that Anthony belonged to her. He was handing her a glass of champagne across the table now and his smile was wicked.

'Here's an upper cylindrical lubricant for you,' he murmured.

'A what?' She burst out laughing. 'Is that what you call having a drink in England?'

'Only in my family. Henry always calls it that.' His eyes danced with merriment. 'Here's to us, sweetheart. And here's to you moving into my apartment. May we live happily ever after.'

'I'll drink to that,' she replied.

Mary held him close. Hungrily her hands explored his nakedness. Then she drew into her lungs the musky sweet smell of his sweat, and her head swam dizzily with desire. He was entering her now, forcefully and with a single-mindedness that rendered him mute. Lying beneath him, letting him fill her with the hotness

110

of his being, she kept her eyes tightly shut, concentrating.

Anthony. In her bed. Making love to her as she'd always dreamed.

'I love you, I love you,' she breathed, pulling him closer so that his face was buried in her neck. 'Love me, Anthony! Love me, sweetheart . . . love me as much as I love you. Please . . . Oh, please.' She was moaning now and breathing faster, digging her nails into his back, moving her hips so that he could reach deeper. The excitement, mounting every second, was killing her with its sweetness, a sweetness that was sharp like a pain.

'I want you,' Mary cried out with sudden urgency. 'Anthony . . . Anthony . . . I want you!' Convulsing violently as Anthony's dazzling blue eyes, the curve of his full lower lip and the line of his jaw, filled the screen of her mind, she clung to him, wildly. He was hers. Gloriously hers now. They belonged together. They would always belong together. Just as the tarot cards had prophesied.

Mary lay silent and breathless as drops of sweat slid off his body onto hers. Gradually she became aware of the world beyond her apartment. The traffic humming and hooting nine floors below; a police siren wailing piercingly through the streets. Overhead, the engine of a passing plane droned like a sleepy mosquito. Mary kept her eyes shut, savouring this wonderful moment for as long as possible.

He rolled off her at last, and her skin was clammy cold where he had lain as the air chilled their shared sweat. For a moment he sat on the edge of the bed with his back to her. Then he spoke.

'You're a strange girl, aren't you?' he remarked. 'Why

did you keep calling me Anthony? My name's Mark.'

The next morning, at Beverley's suggestion, Faye agreed to move into her apartment.

'It would be perfect!' Faye crowed. 'I've always loved your place and I'm sure Hayley wouldn't mind sharing a bedroom. Oh, it's a great idea, Beverley.' They were still excitedly discussing their plans when the phone on Beverley's desk rang.

'Highlight Promotions.'

'Is that Miss Franklin?' The woman's voice was somehow familiar but Beverley couldn't quite place it.

'Yes,' she replied cautiously.

'This is Elaine Ross speaking.'

'Oh . . . er . . . good morning,' Beverley stammered in confusion. What on earth could the formidable Elaine Ross, top New York editor, acquaintance of jet-setting millionaires and friend of royalty, want with her? For a split second she thought of all the things she might have done wrong that could have roused this awe-inspiring woman's fury. Had she sent off the right photographs of the *Chichi* anniversary party? Had some magazine got some of the captions wrong? Was she . . . oh, God, was she going to take the blame for the caterers' charges being higher than had been anticipated?

'I'd like you to come and see me,' Elaine Ross was saying, cutting across Beverley's panicked thoughts. 'This afternoon if that's possible.'

'All right.' Her mind was really whirling now. What could she have done to warrant this summons? 'Shall I bring anything with me?'

She was thinking of the guest list file, or the press file or the . . .

'You don't have to bring anything,' Elaine said in her cool clear voice. 'Be here at three o'clock.'

I know what it is! Beverley's mind clamoured to remember their last meeting. *I was rude to her. I said I was 'Miss Franklin' and that's why . . . Oh, Jesus!*

'Very well. Three o'clock,' she said aloud, sounding remarkably confident to her own ears. When she put the phone down, she turned to the others and told them what had happened.

'Perhaps she wants Highlight to do the public relations for something else,' Nina suggested.

'No,' said Faye, shaking her head. 'She'd have asked for Mary if it was another promotional job.'

'You're right,' Beverley agreed. 'I think she just wants to give me a hard time, because I didn't bow and scrape to her on the last occasion.'

'She's too busy for that,' said Lisette, 'and I doubt if she harbours grudges and wastes time settling scores.'

Beverley looked down at the crisp blue piqué skirt and long jacket she'd put on that morning, with which she was wearing a silk blouse patterned in splashes of vivid emerald green and dark blue. It was her best outfit and she'd worn it because she and Anthony were going to a concert and then dinner. It was also perfect for a meeting with the most elegant woman in New York.

At three o'clock precisely Beverley was shown into Elaine's large office where windows and mirrors seemed to reflect endlessly, and an ocean of thick white carpeting lay spread before her like a blanket of snow. Lucite furniture, transparent as glass, lamps of cut crystal shimmering like diamonds, and bowls of white flowers completed the dazzling effect. Then a figure, also in white,

113

rose from behind the desk. Outstanding against all the whiteness and in striking contrast to the room were Elaine Ross's black hair and eyes and vivid red lipstick.

'Come and sit down,' she said pleasantly, indicating a chair facing hers.

Beverley felt like tip-toeing forward in case she marked the carpet or knocked something over. Going to see Elaine in her own apartment had been terrifying enough. This was like visiting a queen in her throne room.

'May I offer you my congratulations?' Elaine said charmingly, and she was smiling as if she really meant it.

Beverley stared at her blankly for a moment. She and Anthony hadn't publicly announced they were getting married, so Elaine Ross couldn't be referring to that.

'Charles Floyd tells me you're getting married to Lord Amesbury,' she continued smoothly.

'Er . . . Oh, yes!' Beverley replied, feeling foolish. She'd forgotten they were friends. Charles must have told Elaine.

'Well, that's lovely, isn't it! And are you going to be living in England or staying over here?'

'We'll be staying in New York.' What the hell were all these pleasantries leading up to? Beverley thought, perplexed.

'Good.' Elaine leaned forward, her slim white hands adorned only by the square-cut emerald she always wore. 'I also hear you will be looking for a job, after your marriage.'

Suddenly the penny dropped! Charles must have recommended her, and maybe Mary's attempted suicide had made him realise her real reason for resigning and this was his way of making it up to her.

'Yes, I'd like a job as soon as possible, actually, providing I can have a couple of weeks to go on honeymoon.'

'Your future husband is, I gather, a member of a very aristocratic English family, with a brother who's an Earl. They have held posts at Buckingham Palace as courtiers and equerries to the royal family, I believe?'

Beverley felt like saying, 'Are you asking me or telling me?' She knew Anthony's brother was an Earl, but she'd never heard about the royal connections.

'I'm not really sure,' she said bluntly.

Elaine looked shocked. 'My dear, you must know! You're making a brilliant marriage; you'll be a peeress, and belong to one of the oldest and most noble English families there are! I gather they can trace their family tree back for six hundred years! They own Bucklands Castle, a stately home if ever there was one!'

Beverley burst out laughing at Elaine's scandalised tones at her ignorance. 'The family home is called Bucklands, but I don't know about it being a castle!' she joked. This woman seemed to know more about Anthony's family than she did, but what was the point? Where was it leading?

'My dear unspoilt child!' Elaine chided her gently, but she was smiling. 'You don't seem to know anything about the magnificent heritage of the family you are marrying into.'

'It hasn't seemed very important,' she replied lamely. 'Anthony and I just fell in love at first sight, and it doesn't matter to me about his background,' she added with total honesty.

Elaine leaned back in her chair, her hands up to the large pearls around her neck. She looked slightly shaken. 'You really don't care about it, do you?' she asked in amazement.

Beverley shook her head. 'It all seems so far away. It

doesn't apply to us. Anthony doesn't have a fortune or anything. We're both going to have to continue working, and although we won't exactly be poor, we're not going to be rich either.'

'Well, I've had an idea, and I'd like you to consider it very carefully. One should always maximise one's assets, you know.' Elaine's eyes narrowed slightly as if she wanted to make sure Beverley understood what she was saying.

'Like how? I'm quite good at figures, I'm word processor trained . . .' Beverley began earnestly. 'I enjoy promotional work . . .'

Elaine threw back her head and burst out laughing. It was so unexpected coming from her, who was always so cool and restrained, that Beverley stopped and looked at her, astonished.

'Don't waste your time on all that stuff,' Elaine said, when she'd recovered herself. 'There are hundreds of girls out there who can do all that. I'm talking about you being a Viscountess when you're married. A title like that should be made to work for you, something I'm sure your future husband understands. Now this is my idea. And please hear me out, because it's a multi-layered plan. First, I would like *Chichi* to have exclusive coverage of your wedding. We'd want to take pictures from beginning to end . . . feature your dress and your flowergirls, the reception, the choice of flowers, the guests . . .'

Beverley sat with her mouth open, totting up in her head the impossible cost of the sort of wedding Elaine was describing. Her parents would never be able to run to anything like that. She'd planned a pretty but small wedding in Stockbridge, with a party in the garden of their house afterwards. Elaine was obviously thinking in big bucks.

'But . . . !' she protested.

Elaine raised her hand. 'Hang on a minute. I said this was a multi-layered idea. *Chichi* would sponsor everything, and in return for giving us an exclusive of the most aristocratic wedding of the year, we will give you your dress, the reception with champagne, the flowers . . . everything. It won't cost you or your family a penny.'

Beverley looked at her, stunned. It was the most wonderful idea she'd ever heard of and completely solved the problem of paying for the wedding.

'Added to that,' Elaine continued, 'I'd like you to work on *Chichi*, having your own column, and reporting on what everyone is wearing to New York's top social events. We will call it "Lady Amesbury's Fashion Folder", and every month there'd be photographs of well-known socialites at a variety of functions, and you'd describe what they were wearing, and who the designer was. D'you see what I mean?'

'But I don't know any socialites,' Beverley confessed.

Elaine gave a brilliant smile, showing her even white teeth.

'You will soon, my dear. You will soon.' Then, as Beverley sat bemused, Elaine continued talking, outlining her salary and exactly what would be expected of her.

'Discuss it with your fiancé,' Elaine said at last, 'but you must make up your mind quickly. If we're going to feature your wedding we've got to get on with the arrangements right away. If you agree, we'll also expect you to start work here, as of Monday, to get a "feel" for *Chichi*, to understand our editorial style and layout

117

methods. You won't be starting the "Lady Amesbury" column until after you return from your honeymoon, of course, but by that time you'll have the hang of it.'

Beverley felt breathless, and as she left Elaine's office, her feet hardly seemed to touch the ground. All her problems had been solved. All along she'd been worried about the cost of the wedding, knowing her parents wouldn't accept help from Anthony, and she'd also been worried about finding another job when everything in the country was so tight. Now she was going to be 'Lady Amesbury', with her own column and her name on the masthead. In a daze she walked from the offices of *Chichi* on Fifth Avenue to Madison Avenue and back to Highlight where the girls in the office waited, agog to find out what Elaine had wanted.

'You'll never guess,' Beverley said, still looking stunned, as she sat down at her desk again. It was still only four o'clock, but in one brief hour her whole life had changed. Her prospects were now dazzling. For one thing *Chichi* would be paying her more than Highlight, and she wouldn't be working nearly so hard either.

As briefly as she could, trying to keep her voice steady, she told them what had happened.

'Wow!' was all Lisette could say. Nina and Faye just sat and looked at her with round eyes. Then Faye spoke.

'If that's what marrying into the British Peerage does for you, I'm going to find myself a Lord tomorrow!'

'Me too,' echoed Nina. 'D'you realise you're set for life?' There was no envy in her voice, just admiration.

Beverley laughed. 'I can hardly believe it myself. I can't wait to tell Anthony!'

'He won't disapprove, will he?' Nina queried.

'Why should he disapprove? Who ever heard of

118

anyone disapproving of having someone else pay for your wedding? And throwing in a good job as well? He'll be thrilled.'

'Are you sure?' Lisette looked serious. 'Remember he's an English aristocrat. Aren't they very stuffy? Are you sure he won't think it's all a bit vulgar? You have to admit Elaine is only doing this because of Anthony's title.'

'I know that,' Beverly agreed. 'I'm under no illusions. She wouldn't be giving me a wedding and a marvellous job if I was marrying a cab driver!'

'But won't Anthony dislike having his title exploited? You have to admit it's a very commercial deal, for both you and *Chichi*.'

'I'm sure he'll agree,' Beverley said confidently. 'I'll kill him if he doesn't!' she added, laughing.

Anthony did agree, though. 'If that's what you want, sweetheart, I can't see the harm.' He smiled at her indulgently, unable to refuse her anything. She looked so thrilled when she told him, like a little girl who'd received a prize. He put his arms around her and held her close. 'They're lucky to get you to work for them,' he told her.

Beverley gazed up into his face, her expression quizzical. 'I know I've only had the offer because I'm going to be your wife,' she said earnestly. 'Elaine Ross had no use for me when I was just plain Beverley Franklin, but I don't care. Mom and Dad will be so pleased and proud when I tell them and if you're happy about it, that's all that matters.'

Anthony kissed her gently on the lips, loving her so much he couldn't imagine life without her now. 'And you're all that matters to me.'

119

'I want you to be proud of me, too,' she admitted, resting her head on his shoulder.

He drew back to look into her face and his eyes were tender. 'I'll always be proud of you, love. Tremendously proud. What brought this on?'

Beverly gave a little sigh. 'Elaine made me feel a little dumb today, because she said you lived in a castle and your family had something to do with Buckingham Palace and I didn't know anything about it. Is it true? She said I was making a "brilliant marriage" and that made me feel uncomfortable, like I was a gold digger or something, and had calculated everything. You don't really live in a castle, do you?'

Anthony burst out laughing. 'Are you going to kick me out if I say yes?' he joked.

Her eyes widened, the golden flecks bright. 'You do?' She sounded shocked.

He nodded, amused at her expression. 'I'm afraid so. The family have lived at Bucklands for generations. Henry and his wife and daughter, and my mother, are the only people occupying it now, apart from some old retainers. Believe it or not, I was born in a room in the west turret! How's that for being romantic!'

'Is it a very old castle? What's it like?' Beverley asked, intrigued. 'Do you have any snapshots of it?'

'I don't think so. It's fourteenth century, square-built with a large turret at each corner, and the usual ramparts and battlements, you know.'

'How many rooms does it have?'

He wrinkled his nose, thinking. Then he shrugged. 'I've no idea. I've never counted. Sixty ... eighty perhaps.'

'Sixty or eighty!' She gaped at him, astonished.

'And a moat!' His eyes were twinkling.

'Are you kidding?' They were both laughing now.

'I'm serious. The only way you can enter the castle is across the drawbridge. That's probably why we've never been burgled.'

'So Elaine was right! What about the royal connection? I suppose you're going to tell me that you're a cousin of the Queen of England and she comes to dinner once a week.'

'Not quite! My grandfather was a Gentleman-of-the-Bedchamber to the late King George . . . and my father was an equerry for a while to the present Queen.' There was quiet pride in the way he spoke.

'What about your brother?' She was fascinated by this other world he was telling her about, of courtiers and castles and a heritage that was several hundred years old. It seemed so far removed from their lifestyle in New York and yet it was very much a part of Anthony's life.

'Henry was an equerry for a while. But he likes life in the country far more than at Court, and so he farms now,' Anthony replied.

He grinned at her expression. She looked totally amazed.

'I can understand why Elaine offered me a job and wants an exclusive on the wedding,' she said, slowly and wonderingly. Suddenly she gasped, struck by a thought that appalled her. 'My God, this doesn't mean there'll be royalty at *our* wedding, does it?' Alarm was etched on every line of her face.

Anthony swept her up in his arms again, hugging her with exuberance. No one could ever accuse Beverley of marrying him because of his family connection. They seemed to strike fear and horror in her rather than

121

glee. Then he thought of his sister-in-law, Leonora. How different she was from Beverley! Leonora with her airs and graces had known exactly what she was doing when she married Henry. She'd had him picked out since she'd been eighteen and 'doing' the Season with a pushy mother who was as socially ambitious as she was. Together the two of them had caught Henry in a pincer movement, and now her great quest was to produce a son and heir. Their daughter Juliet, who was now ten years old, wasn't good enough. It had to be a boy who would inherit Bucklands Castle and the title or Leonora would consider she'd failed in life.

'What are you thinking about?' Beverley asked, breaking into his thoughts. 'You're looking quite grim.'

He laughed, kissing her lightly on the tip of her nose. 'I was thinking how lucky I am to have you.'

'And that's why you were looking grim?' Her expression was comical.

Anthony explained. 'I went on to think about my sister-in-law and how different you are. And what a lucky man I am compared to Henry.'

'Will they be coming to the wedding?' She suddenly looked slightly nervous at the prospect. 'What are they going to think of me?' she added. 'Won't they expect you to marry someone very grand?'

'I *am* marrying someone very grand,' he replied gravely. 'The grandest, greatest girl in the world.' He nuzzled her playfully.

'Well, I know what *I'm* marrying,' she parried, tickling him around the ribs.

He let out a yell. He couldn't bear to be tickled. 'What do you mean?' he gasped between shouts.

She continued to tickle him mercilessly. 'I'm marrying

a born flatterer . . . a charmer . . .' They were both giggling now until, struggling to get away from her, he managed to grab her by the wrists. Then he held her close, hands crossed behind her back, so that she was unable to move.

'Now you're my prisoner,' he said, smiling into her eyes.

'How long have I got?'

'A life sentence, my love.'

Her eyes challenged him in the game they were playing.

'No remission for good behaviour?' she asked teasingly.

'Not a chance.'

'That's not fair!'

'Yes it is! Haven't you heard? When she was good, she was very very good . . . and when she was bad she was wonderful!'

Then he kissed her, and after a few moments she was leaning against him, and as he released her hands, she slid her arms around him, holding him so close he could feel her breasts crushed against him. Then one of her slim thighs slid gently between his legs. He groaned, filled with deep longing for her. No other woman had ever aroused him as quickly as Beverley. He wanted to make love to her all the time. Just to see her walking across the bedroom in skimpy bra and pants was enough, but when she came close and pressed herself against him, he ached to make himself a part of her body, to enter her and arouse her as he was aroused himself.

'Oh, Jesus, I love you so much,' he said, burying his face in her neck.

'And I love you.' Her hands opened the front of his trousers and slid inside, holding him with a velvet touch, cradling him gently.

'Beverley... Beverley...' There was almost a despairing note in his voice, as if, no matter how often he made love to her, it would never be enough. Always he wanted more. Always he was satisfied but never sated. He pulled her down onto the floor so they were kneeling, facing each other, and while he opened her shirt and stroked her breasts, she massaged him with her strong but gentle hands.

'Stop,' he moaned after a moment. 'Please stop or I won't be able to wait... and I want to wait until you're ready.'

Then with strong arms he laid her down on the carpet and pressed himself against her, his hands caressing her all the time.

He was the most unselfish lover she could imagine, for even in her limited experience the man had always been more concerned with his own orgasm than with hers. Yet Anthony would somehow manage to hold himself back, waiting until she was on the very edge, crying out for him, and he would enter her swiftly and surely, until she was sobbing with the most exquisite pleasure she had ever known. It was happening now, that wild uncontrollable surge that she wanted to prolong, and yet couldn't wait to have fulfilled.

'Now... Oh, now... yes, yes...' she gasped, as he took her and carried her forward with him, so they were both crying out, never able to have enough of each other, never able to be satisfied for long.

They lay for a long time on the floor afterwards, although her back had begun to ache. Beverley stroked his hair, while he lay with his eyes shut, temporarily exhausted. She had never been so happy in her life. And they were going to have the most marvellous future together.

Two weeks later, Mary decided to try out another singles bar, because she didn't want to run into Mark again. Once was enough as far as she was concerned and he'd served his purpose. Tonight she thought she'd go to The Penguin, on Seventh Avenue and Forty-Fourth Street, arriving in time for what was euphemistically called the Happy Hour. All she wanted to do was to find someone of the right height and build, and with fair hair.

The bar was crowded with groups of young men and women whose awareness of dangerous transmittable diseases did nothing to deter them from looking for sexual adventure. They seemed mostly heterosexual. She glanced around quickly and ordered herself a spritzer. She hated singles bars, they were so obvious, but it was the safest way she could think of to find what she was looking for. A pick-up in the street or in the subway would have been too dangerous. And getting to know someone properly would defeat the object.

Suddenly, out of the corner of her eye, she saw what she was looking for. He was sitting at a table with a group of men, drinking beer, and when he smiled his even white teeth gleamed attractively. Not that it interested her. She'd be able to provide him with a face as soon as they were alone in her bed. It was the size of his hands and the width of his shoulders that mattered. She moved nearer and eyed him more closely. The way the hair curled at the back of his neck was right too, and so was the colour. Just in case her eyes flicked open for a moment, it was a help if that was right. She decided he would do.

With the slow watchfulness of a cat stalking its prey, she moved forward through the crush, her grey eyes gleaming warily. Not for a second did she doubt her ability to capture him and take him back to her lair where she would drain him of all he had to give until she was full and sated. If she had one talent, it was persuasiveness.

Chapter Five

Plans for the wedding were well advanced, and to every-one's delight Elaine had gone along with Beverley's wishes on almost every point, including holding it in Stockbridge.

'Much more stylish than New York,' she agreed. 'We'll stage a really romantic country wedding, with a marquee for the reception, and the church decorated with beautiful garlands of wild flowers and ribbons.'

Beverley's dress had been chosen too, an exquisite gown in cream wild silk with a full flowing skirt, a tight bodice, and sleeves caught up with satin ribbons. Creamy roses were to be tucked into the back of her hair, and Elaine managed to get hold of an antique lace veil which fell into a train.

Beverley and Anthony were going to Stockbridge most weekends now, seeing to all the local arrangements and poring over the guest list with her mother. She was anxious to have child attendants and as she had no nieces or nephews had invited three little girls and a little boy, whose parents were neighbours of the Frank-lins, to be flowergirls and a page, while Jenny, who was almost dying of excitement at the prospect of appearing in *Chichi*, was going to be the chief flowergirl in a long pale blue silk dress, with cream and blue flowers in her hair.

'Isn't it all like a dream?' Beverley kept saying, to anyone who would listen. 'I can't believe it's really happening.'

The whole of the Franklins' garden was going to be covered with a blue and white marquee for the reception, and rooms had been booked at the Red Lion Inn for guests who were coming from a long distance. The menu for the wedding breakfast had, of course, been chosen by Elaine from a top Manhattan catering firm, which she insisted on using, and the food was to be exotic and chic.

'Sometimes I feel I'm still working for Highlight,' Beverley said jokingly to Anthony as they lay in bed one night. There was only another month to go, but already every decision had been made and every detail confirmed. 'Elaine seems to have turned our wedding into a high-powered event! You'd think we were planning a top-rank military manoeuvre. The precision planning is amazing. I don't know about me, but *she'll* have a nervous breakdown if anything goes wrong on the day.'

Anthony laughed. 'But what about you, sweetheart? Are you happy with the arrangements? After all, it is your day, not Elaine's.'

'Yes, I'm happy about everything,' she replied honestly. 'Apart from the feeling of unreality, it's great. And I don't mind feeling I'm organising a professional event, it stops me getting nervous.'

'Why should you be nervous?'

'Every bride gets nervous ... in a nice way. Mostly with excitement, I guess.' She lay back, amazed at how lucky she was to be given a dream wedding. Elaine had

128

also stressed there should be a large congregation, and that the marquee should be filled to capacity, so she'd been able to invite all her old college friends from Wellesley, and her parents were able to ask everyone in the family, including distant cousins Beverley hardly knew. With all their friends and neighbours, it was going to be an unforgettable occasion.

Then Anthony got a letter from his brother. He looked pale and grim as he read it at breakfast.

'What's wrong?' Beverley asked. Since she'd moved in with him she made the coffee and squeezed the orange juice every morning, while he sat on a stool by the counter reading his mail.

'They're not coming to the wedding,' he said. He sounded deeply disappointed.

'What? Your family?' She looked horrified. How could they not be coming? Anthony had told them all about the wedding weeks before, and he'd only been talking to his mother on the phone a few days ago. She went over to where he was perched, and looked over his shoulder at the sheet of pale blue writing paper which bore an earl's coronet printed at the top. It was covered with neat small handwriting.

'Henry says Leonora isn't well and he doesn't want to leave her, and of course my mother is too old and frail to come by herself.'

'Oh, Anthony.' He looked so depressed it broke her heart.

'What about your sister Jean? She's coming, isn't she?'

He shook his head. 'Henry goes on to say that Jean, who is a Justice of the Peace, and does a lot of local charity work, is "too tied-up" to get away.' Anthony flung

129

down the letter. 'Typical! Bloody typical!' he stormed, rising. He started to pace around the kitchen, picking up things and then slamming them down again.

'I'm so sorry,' Beverley sympathised, feeling stricken for him. How was it possible that neither Anthony's brother nor sister was going to come to something as important as his wedding? She could understand about his mother not being able to make it, but the others . . . ?

'I think that's terrible,' she said. As it was, not many of Anthony's friends from England were able to come either. Too far away and too expensive was the general reason given, and he'd understood and not minded. But his own family! 'Why don't you phone them and say they must come,' she urged.

Anthony shook his head. 'It wouldn't do any good, love. If Leonora's ill, I can understand Henry not wanting to leave her, and Mama certainly isn't strong enough to come on her own.' He paused, a wry expression in his eyes.

'I still think you should call them,' Beverley insisted. She'd been longing to meet his family, and it would be deeply disappointing if none of them came to the wedding.

He looked at his wristwatch. Suddenly he came to a decision. Striding over to the phone which was fixed to the kitchen wall, he dialled the number of Bucklands.

'They'll be having lunch in England right now,' he told Beverley. 'There's a good chance Henry will be home.' A moment later, he heard his sister-in-law's voice on the line.

'Hello, Leonora. Anthony here.'

Her rather high-pitched voice, sharp as a steel blade, floated into his ear so clearly she might have been in the next room.

'Ah, Anthony. How are you?'

'I've received Henry's letter,' he said without pre-amble, and watching, Beverley could tell by his manner he didn't like his brother's wife.

'Oh, yes. It really won't be possible for us to get to your wedding, I'm afraid.' Her voice was so loud even Beverley could hear it although she was several yards from the phone.

'Surely you and Henry could make the effort? It is my wedding, you know.' He sounded more hurt than angry.

'I think Henry feels it's going to be a bit of a jam-boree.' Her voice pierced the ether.

'What on earth do you mean?'

'Well ... you know ... I gather the whole thing is being put on by some fashion magazine ... it's all rather infra dig, isn't it?'

'Not in the least,' he said hotly, 'unless you're going to be impossibly snobbish, Leonora. Beverley works on the magazine and is going to have her own column when we're married.'

'Yes, well ...' Her tone was sneering. 'I'm sure that's fine for an American, but really, Anthony, the family's never done anything like that. Frankly, Henry doesn't approve at all.'

'Which means *you* don't like the idea, but you haven't the guts to say so,' he exploded furiously, 'so stop hiding behind Henry. You're a stupid narrow-minded woman, Leonora, and your absence on the day will be no loss at all!' Then he hung up, his face red with anger, and spun round. 'Did you hear her?' he asked incredulously. 'Christ, what a bitch! Did you hear what she said?'

Beverley nodded, looking pale. 'It sounds like they disapprove of me. Is that why they're not coming? Because they think I'm not good enough for you?'

He grabbed her and held her close. 'Don't even think like that, sweetheart. It's got nothing to do with you. Leonora is objecting to *Chichi*'s involvement in the wedding and I think she's making a fuss about nothing.'

Beverley frowned. 'Do you think it's vulgar? Have we done the wrong thing?'

Anthony shrugged. 'It's being done in good taste, so I don't see that it matters. Anyway, it's our decision, not Leonora's.'

'Has she influenced your brother against coming?' She was deeply worried that their getting married was now going to cause a rift in Anthony's family.

'She may have done,' he said casually. 'There are times when she can be really bitchy and she always takes it out on Henry.'

'Sounds like she's not your favourite person.'

'That's an understatement. What is it they say? "God gave you your relatives ... but thank God you can choose your friends"?' She could see he was making an attempt to be light-hearted, but she knew him well enough to know that he was hurt by his family's behaviour. At a time when he would have liked them by his side, they had decided not to give him their love and support. Whatever happens, Beverley thought, I shall never forgive them for letting him down like this. He is getting married over three thousand miles away from home, in a country he hardly knows, and they aren't even going to be there! She looked up into his face, longing to take away his hurt and disappointment. Putting her arms around his neck she reached up and kissed his chin and then the tip of his nose, and finally his lips.

'Well, I'll be there!' she teased softly.

He pulled her close. 'So will I, and we're the only

people who matter, aren't we?'

Beverley snuggled close to him, her cheek pressed to his. She was going to make it up to him for the absence of his family, and she knew her parents would help. Rachael and Daniel Franklin had liked Anthony from the first moment they'd set eyes on him, and they had made him feel warmly welcome. Now, she knew she could rely on them to be there for him, and to love him as parents-in-law, though nothing would ever make her understand the indifference of his own family.

Elaine, on the other hand, did not share her accept-ance of the situation. She was absolutely horrified that the Earl and Countess of Cumberland, the Dowager Countess and Lady Jean Ffitch were not, after all, attending.

'They *must* come,' she retorted. Today she wore cream cashmere and a gold necklace instead of her usual pearls. Her slim hand flew to her throat in a gesture of panic. 'We'll have no titles apart from Anthony if they don't attend.' For a terrible moment Beverley thought she was going to scrap the whole idea, leaving her and her family with bills of thousands of dollars to pay.

'Anthony's best man is coming, and he's a Marquess,' Beverley pointed out.

'He is?' Elaine brightened visibly.

'Yes, he's the Marquess of Goring. He was at Eton with Anthony, and he's his oldest friend.'

'Well, I suppose that's something.' She sounded slightly mollified. 'But won't everyone think it very odd if the bridegroom's family don't attend? What can we tell people?' Her dark eyes flashed with displeasure and Beverley wished she'd never got involved with *Chichi* in the first place. What had started out as a wonderful

133

opportunity to have a magnificent wedding that wouldn't cost her family a cent was slowly assuming the proportions of a nightmare.

'Who else is coming from England?' Elaine was saying. 'Anthony had better invite some more people, and make sure they're titled. I'll ask some people from my VIP list, too. This is serious.'

Beverley's mouth tightened. Perhaps Leonora was right. The wedding showed every sign of being turned into a jamboree, with rent-a-guest . . . as long as they were titled. She longed to turn on Elaine and tell her to forget the whole thing, but how could she? It would bankrupt Rachael and Daniel even to take over the expenses incurred so far and she would probably lose her wonderful new job as well. There was only one thing for it: to try and pacify Elaine.

'I'll talk to Anthony again,' she said, forcing a smile.

'Please do,' Elaine replied coldly. 'Tell him his family really must come. It isn't much to ask, surely. The Earl is Anthony's brother, after all,' she added.

Beverley left Elaine's dazzling white and crystal office, feeling as chilled as if she'd been sitting in a deep freeze. She also had a sick feeling in the pit of her stomach. It had been a mistake accepting Elaine's original offer, and now she was bitterly regretting it. Their wedding day, which should have been an intimate and private occasion, now belonged to Elaine and *Chichi*. A social occasion in the fashion world, where it was more important to be a Someone wearing a designer label than a real person. Hot tears smarted in Beverley's eyes as she realised to what she had committed herself and Anthony. How could she have been so naive as to think she could preserve the sanctity of the occasion when

Chichi was paying for it and Elaine was calling the shots?

Going to the ladies' powder room, she locked herself in one of the cubicles, feeling as if she'd let Anthony down. He'd gone along with Elaine's suggestion to please her and because she'd been excited at the prospect of a dream wedding, not to mention the follow-up job. But it had cost him the presence of his family on the day and for that she'd never forgive herself.

Tears poured down her cheeks as she perched on the lid of the loo. Part of her felt like going back to see Elaine to tell her to forget the whole thing, but once again the realisation of the costs made that impossible. Caterers and florists would want a cancellation fee, and there was her wedding dress which had already been bought, not to mention the flowergirls' and page's clothes. Elaine had also insisted Rachael should wear a dress designed by Oscar de la Renta, with which she was thrilled, never having been able to afford anything better than department store clothes in the past . . . and Jenny was excited . . . the invitations had already gone out and dozens of people had accepted . . . on and on the list went, arrangements that had been made which could not be changed . . . orders that had been given and were too late to cancel. Whether she liked it or not, she was stuck with having 'the Wedding of the Year'. Now it felt as if the whole occasion were being staged just to provide *Chichi* with suitable material to fill its pages. The day was supposed to be a sacred ceremony at which she and Anthony were to make a life-long commitment to each other, not some publicity stunt!

Leaving the ladies' powder room, Beverley came to a decision. She might not be able to cancel the whole thing, but at least she might be able to do something that would make Anthony happy.

Beverley got back to their apartment late in the afternoon. Anthony wouldn't be home for another hour or so, and she was praying that by then she'd have some good news for him. She was in the kitchen preparing a salad for their dinner when the phone rang. With one bound she was across the room, grabbing the receiver from its cradle on the wall.

'Hello?' she said, her heart suddenly hammering so she could hardly breathe.

'Is that Beverley Franklin?' The voice was charming, low and mellow and not unlike Anthony's.

'Yes . . . hello.'

'I'm sorry I was out when you phoned earlier. How's everything going?' It was Henry Cumberland, returning her call.

'That's the problem,' Beverley said nervously. 'Anthony . . . and I are so upset you're not coming to the wedding. He understands about your mother, of course, being too frail, but can't you possibly come? He's really hurt at your refusal . . .' Her voice trailed off. She purposely didn't mention that Leonora had told Anthony they thought the occasion was 'vulgar'.

'Oh dear, oh dear.' He sounded like a kindly Father Christmas figure, and Beverley could just imagine him, rotund and gently jovial, an older, comfortable version of Anthony, in baggy tweeds and heavy country shoes.

'It means so much to him to have you there,' she continued with a note of pleading in her voice.

'Oh dear, oh dear,' he said again, and it sounded as if he were deep in thought. 'The trouble is that Leonora isn't too well, and she certainly mustn't travel.' He sighed gustily and there was silence on the line.

'Couldn't you come on your own? Just for a couple of days? Please?' If she could only persuade him to fly over, she knew she'd feel less guilty at having accepted Elaine's offer. She also knew it would make the occasion complete for Anthony.

There was another heartfelt sigh on the line. Then he spoke.

'No promises, Beverley, but I'll see what I can do. We don't want to disappoint the old boy too much, do we?' He suddenly chuckled cheerily. 'Anyway, I'd like to meet you, so that's a good enough reason to come, isn't it? From all he's told me about you, he's a lucky fella!'

'I think I'm the lucky one,' she replied. 'And I'd like to meet you too.' Already, from just hearing his voice, she knew she'd like Henry. There was something about him that sounded comfortably reassuring. He was the sort of man she felt one could turn to if one needed help and she was profoundly glad she'd phoned him earlier in the day, and left a message for him to call her back.

'Well, don't say anything to Anthony yet, until I see what can be done.'

'But you will try?'

'Yes, my dear, I'll try,' Henry promised.

'I have to take my wife to the Amesbury wedding,' Cass Sternberg protested. 'This is not some publishing convention which we can slip away to. This is going to be a high-profile event. Maxine will hear all about it. How can I possibly go without her?'

Elaine, sitting at the desk in her crystal and white office, glared up at the publisher of *Chichi*, her dark eyes flashing.

'I really had hoped we could be on our own,' she said angrily, 'but I suppose it's too much to ask. When it comes to the crunch, you *always* drag Maxine along.'

Cass, a big man with an urbane expression, balding head and plump cheeks, looked at Elaine in astonishment, his small grey eyes wide with astonishment.

'For God's sake, Elaine, how did you imagine we'd be "on our own", with half the staff of *Chichi* there? And a dozen photographers? And a couple of hundred guests?' There were times when women baffled Cass, and Elaine, for all her savvy, could be incredibly stupid occasionally.

'You know perfectly well what I mean, Cass,' she snapped.

'Well, I'm sorry, sweetheart, but there it is. It wouldn't be worth my life to leave Maxine behind. She came to the Princess Di party, didn't she? You didn't mind then.' With a snort, he turned and lumbered out of her office.

Elaine remained at her desk for several more minutes before rising and going over to the mirror-fronted cabinet in the corner. Opening it, she took out a bottle of vodka, and poured a large measure into a crystal tumbler. Then she added a shot of orange juice, to make it look innocuous if anyone came into her office. It was only four-thirty in the afternoon, but what the hell! She knew how to juggle the balance between alcohol and the anti-depressants she'd been on ever since . . . Elaine went back to her desk and thought about her longstanding affair. Cass Sternberg, financier, publisher, charmer. *Rat*!

Eleven years ago she'd met him when she'd been working on a third-rate woman's magazine. That was before he'd bought *Chichi* and appointed her editor-in-chief. Eleven years of stolen hours when he could get away from his wife, eleven years of subterfuge and lying, eleven years of pretending they were business colleagues when other people were around . . . and the last six years of pure hell.

Elaine sipped her vodka and orange, and felt the glow of well-being it always brought her surge through her veins. Smoothing the white crêpe de Chine of her Calvin Klein dress, she spent some minutes trying to convince herself it had all been worth it. Some days, she was sure that it was, that the sacrifice she'd made to keep both Cass and her job on *Chichi* had been worth all the pain she'd suffered. Those were the up-beat days when she realised the position she'd achieved, when someone referred to her as the numero uno fashion editor, and she rode high on her own success. The rest of the time it was not so good, and she had to depend heavily on her 'props', the pills and the liquor. Even though Cass had bought her a magnificent duplex on Park Avenue, and had lavished money and jewels on her, he could never replace what she'd lost, and her loss would be with her until the day she died.

Working with Beverley, as they went through plans for the wedding, had opened her eyes to her own cynicism. Beverley was so goddamn' romantic about the whole thing, so full of illusions, and Love Everlasting, and Happily Ever After, and all that crap. Look at Maxine Sternberg! Cass told Elaine he'd been faithful to Maxine for exactly eight months after they married, and from then on he'd been cheating on her. Cass couldn't even be faithful to his mistress. Elaine was sure he was playing around with his secretary right now!

She'd finished her drink and decided that another

small one would give her enough of a lift to get her through the rest of the afternoon. Going back to her desk with her refilled glass, she caught sight of herself in the long mirrors that covered one of the walls of her office. The effect was strange. The all-white outfit merged and became lost against the all-white decor, so that her short black hair and scarlet lips stood out, almost detached, as if they were free floating. Then she smiled, remembering that most people thought white was her 'signature', her fashion statement, her desire to be instantly recognisable in a crowded room, her wish to be different. Few knew that in some countries white was worn as a sign of mourning. And am I still mourning? she asked herself. And the answer in a thousand clamouring voices filled her head. Yes-yes-yes-yes!

Elaine slumped at her desk and put her head in her hands for a moment before finishing her drink. She'd made the sacrifice to please Cass and, she had to be honest, to keep her high-powered job on *Chichi*, but the question was, had it been worth it?

There was a knock at her office door, and slipping her glass into the drawer of her desk, she sat upright and switched on her usual smile. No one seeing her would ever guess the pain she suffered inside.

Beverley and Anthony flew to Stockbridge three days before their wedding to see to all the last minute arrangements. During the past week more presents had arrived and they spent the first evening unwrapping them, helped by an over-enthusiastic Jenny.

'Just look at this!' she gasped as each new gift emerged from its cocoon of crisp white tissue paper. Beverley had to agree their friends and relatives had been more than generous.

'We can give a cocktail party for a hundred and fifty guests without having to buy a single glass,' she observed, laughing. They'd also been given a dinner service, cutlery, decanters and table linen, as well as a wide variety of flower vases, three picnic baskets, cashmere blankets and feather pillows, silver salt cellars from Anthony's godmother in England, and a silver tray from the best man, the Marquess of Goring, who was always known as Bertie to his friends. He'd arrived that morning, having flown from England, and with much back-slapping, he and Anthony greeted each other at Stockbridge airport.

Beverley stood watching them, happy that Anthony's best friend had made it even if it didn't look as if his brother would. She'd heard no more from Henry and hadn't liked to contact him again, in case he thought she was being pushy.

'This is Beverley,' Anthony introduced her proudly. 'Darling, my old friend Bertie.'

They shook hands, and Beverley's smile was warm and welcoming. 'I'm so glad you're here,' she said. Her father had booked adjacent rooms at the Red Lion Inn for Anthony and Bertie, and as they piled into the car, she added: 'I hope you're not exhausted by your flight, because from now on it's going to be all go.'

Bertie Goring, who was as tall as Anthony but with dark brown hair and eyes and an attractive thin-featured face, beamed back at her.

'That sounds like a lot of fun,' he commented, his fist gently thumping Anthony on the shoulder as he looked at his friend affectionately. 'Trust Ant to have an exotic wedding on the other side of the world, eh?'

Anthony had told her all about Bertie before he arrived.

'We survived Eton together, in spite of the occasional flogging,' Anthony recalled. 'We were the ringleaders in all sorts of pranks. God knows why we weren't sent down. One year, he and I climbed on to the roof of the chapel and left a po draped in a Union Jack as a mark of our midnight escapade! Then we staggered through university together, playing hard until it was time for our finals when we swotted like hell.' Bertie, he told her, had gone into merchant banking in the City of London, whilst he'd trained to be a stock analyst before leaving England for America. It was nearly two years since they'd seen each other, but the foundations of true friendship had been laid in their youth and so they were able to pick up where they'd left off.

'So what's happening today?' Bertie asked, clambering into the back of the car while Anthony took the wheel with Beverley beside him. His legs were so long his knees almost reached his chin as he tried to fold himself into the confined space.

'Beverley's boss, Elaine Ross . . . the one who's the editor of *Chichi*, you know, very famous lady . . . has organised a dinner party for tonight in the garden of the Red Lion Inn,' Anthony told him. 'There are going to be about twenty of us and you'll meet Beverley's family, so it should be fun.'

Bertie nodded affably. Beverley could see he was an easy going young man, prepared to fall in with any arrangements that had been made.

'All this reminds me of Henry and Leonora's wedding,' he remarked. 'Remember, Ant?'

Anthony groaned. 'How could I forget?' He turned to Beverley. 'Bertie and I were ushers and we had to seat nearly eight hundred guests in St Margaret's, Westminster! The trouble was there'd been a terrific stag party the previous night and we both had raging hangovers!'

Bertie slapped his thigh with mirth. 'And I insulted Leonora's mother by accidentally mistaking her for her grandmother! Oh, God, what a day that was.' Both men laughed at the recollection.

'Was Leonora nervous? I've got butterflies at the very thought of walking up the aisle in front of so many people,' Beverley observed.

Anthony squeezed her hand. 'She was terrified, sweetheart. She lost fourteen pounds during the run up to the wedding . . . but then we did have half the royal family there, not to mention television news.'

Beverley closed her eyes at the thought. 'I can't think of anything worse. Thank God I've only got Elaine to contend with, and that's bad enough.' She looked at Anthony's profile as he drove. 'You'll be there, anyway, to hold my hand.'

He flashed her a teasing grin. 'No, Bertie and I are planning on going to New York for the day.'

'Beast!' She turned to include Bertie in their conversation. 'I can't help thinking how nice it will be when it's all over, though. I've hardly been alone with Anthony for weeks, now.'

'By the end of the honeymoon, you may be so bored with my company that you'll be longing for a crowd,' he remarked.

'Don't you believe it!' Beverley retorted. 'If I had my way, we'd elope! Run away tonight and let everyone have a party in two days' time without us!'

He threw back his head, chortling. 'Can't you imagine Elaine's face if we did! If I didn't turn up, she'd be furious because that would be one title less, to feature in *Chichi*.' But he spoke good-humouredly, amused by Elaine's predilection for society people with titles.

'So what time does tonight's shindig start?' Bertie Goring asked as they drew up outside the Red Lion Inn.

'Eight o'clock,' Beverley replied, glad that Anthony had a close friend with whom to share the coming couple of days. If he couldn't have his family, at least Bertie would be supportive.

'I'm off home so you two can spend the afternoon catching up,' she added, smiling.

Bertie looked at her with warm approval. 'I'm looking forward to meeting the rest of your family. I think Ant's a very lucky fellow to have found you.'

'I think I'm the lucky one,' she replied. As she drove off, Bertie turned to Anthony with a look of frank admiration.

'You've picked yourself a winner there, old chap,' he said, trying to keep the envy out of his voice.

Beverley had chosen a pale yellow dress for the dinner party that night, and it was a perfect foil to her chestnut hair. When Anthony, who'd been having a drink with Bertie before the guests arrived, saw her coming up to the veranda steps of the hotel surrounded by her family, he thought he'd never seen anyone lovelier.

'Has Elaine arrived yet?' she whispered, after she'd greeted Anthony and Bertie. Elaine and her entourage, plus Mr and Mrs Cass Sternberg, had told her they'd be checking into the inn that afternoon, in readiness for the evening's party.

'Right behind you now,' Anthony mouthed back, glancing over her shoulder. Beverley turned, and there was Elaine, in a white faille suit with an enormous stand-up collar, her dark neatly cropped head standing out like a fullstop in the mellow evening light, her dark eyes taking in everything. Already the photographer from *Chichi* was poised to cover every minute of the event, and as she appeared he started snapping away.

'My dear, you look charming,' she said to Beverley, her scarlet lips curved into a smile although her eyes remained cold. She'd worked very hard to turn what could have been a small provincial occasion into a high society event, and she was determined nothing should go wrong. Then she shook hands with Bertie, saying gravely: 'Good evening, Lord Goring.'

Bertie bowed with old-world courtesy. 'Good evening, Miss Ross,' he replied, with equal gravity.

'Oh, jeepers,' said young Tom in disgust. All the pomp and ceremony were getting to him, and he wished his sister was marrying an ordinary guy; or if she had to marry someone special, at least a baseball player.

'Now, behave,' Daniel Franklin admonished his youngest child quietly.

More guests arrived, and Elaine was watching the proceedings with a hawk-like scrutiny. It was important the 'best' people were photographed together. A smart collection from the cream of London and New York society would made a good spread in the magazine, preceding the pages devoted to the wedding itself.

So far everything was going well. Elaine thought Rachael Franklin's dress too dreadful for words but they needn't photograph her tonight, and at least her outfit for the actual wedding looked good because Elaine had chosen it herself. She also wished Beverley's sister Jenny wasn't quite so buxom; her cleavage was more *Playboy* than *Chichi*, but it couldn't be helped. Everyone had arrived now, and the guests were filling the veranda overlooking the street, drinking champagne and causing the local residents of Stockbridge to stop and wonder what was going on in their quiet town centre. Flashlights kept popping, as did the champagne corks, and it was into the midst of this gathering that a taxi drew up at the bottom of the steps. A large comfortable man clambered out, in a creased and slightly shabby grey suit, carrying a mackintosh. While he fumbled with his wallet, the driver unloaded several suitcases and then stood, waiting to be paid.

'My dear fellow, I'm most dreadfully sorry . . .' the man muttered, dropping credit cards and cheque book. 'I'm quite sure I had . . .' He paused as he started searching through his other pockets. The driver was now watching him with undisguised suspicion while the man's agitation grew. Pink in the face and sweating, he exclaimed: 'I know I put them somewhere . . .'

One by one the guests stopped talking as they watched the man frantically search through his pockets again.

Elaine, about to give the order to serve dinner, frowned disapprovingly. Who was this big shambling man in the crumpled suit? His fair hair stood on end, and all the while he was puffing and blowing and muttering something about not being able to find his money.

'Oh, ple-ase!' she muttered aloud, and turning to Cass Sternberg indicated the antics of the man who was getting more desperate by the minute. 'That sort of behaviour, especially here, really is gross, isn't it!'

At that moment Anthony let out a gasp, pushed his way through the guests and bounded down the steps to the road.

146

'Henry? My dear fellow, what the hell are you doing here?'

Henry, Seventh Earl of Cumberland, looked startled for a second, and then flung his arms around his younger brother.

'I can't find my dollars . . . I'm sure I had some. Otherwise I've only got travellers' cheques.' In spite of his agitation, his face was wreathed in delight and relief. 'Damned money,' he muttered, starting to go through his pockets again.

Anthony burst out laughing. 'Here. Let me.' Swiftly he handed the bemused driver the fare. 'So what are you doing here?' he demanded unnecessarily. 'You old rogue! You said you weren't coming.'

'I wasn't, but then . . . oh, what the hell! Here I am. How are you doing, my dear fellow?'

With much back slapping and geniality, the two brothers walked up the steps watched by Beverley who suddenly felt overwhelmed with emotion. It was so wonderful that Henry had turned up after all and she was so glad for Anthony's sake. Her eyes brimmed for a moment, and then Anthony was introducing her, and Henry was pumping her hand up and down, and Elaine was watching the whole proceedings with an expression of disbelief.

'Is this your brother, Anthony? Lord Cumberland?' she demanded in a breathless voice.

Within a few minutes, Henry had been introduced to everyone, Elaine had ordered dinner to be delayed in order to give him a chance to freshen up, and Beverley was watching him with growing affection. No one could help but like Henry. Older, much rounder and more mature than Anthony, he exuded amiability. His quick smile and firm handshake were irresistibly charming, and his merry blue eyes were direct and very honest-looking. In many ways, Beverley could see how Anthony would look in another ten years, a big warm teddy-bear type of man, and she felt so happy Henry had been able to fly over for their wedding. Now she'd met him, she knew the day would have been incomplete without him.

'Can I leave you for a moment, sweetheart?' Anthony whispered in her ear. 'I'm just going up with Henry to his room. We won't be long.'

'Of course,' she replied, understanding how he must want to have a few minutes alone with his brother.

At last they all sat down to dinner at one long table in the garden at the back of the inn. Candles in glass lamps, rising out of garlands of fresh flowers, cast a soft and flattering glow on the guests' faces, and occasional bursts of laughter filled the starry night air.

Elaine sat opposite Cass Sternberg, looking like an exotic night-bird, and from time to time her white satin-shod foot sought his, and then with pointed toe she slid her foot up his calf to his knee. Once or twice, under the cover of the tablecloth, he caught her by the ankle and stroked her instep, whilst all the time they conversed with other people as if nothing was happening. His wife, blissfully unaware anything was going on, chatted to Henry Cumberland and tucked into a dish of wild duck and cherries.

Suddenly, Henry turned to Beverley who was sitting on his other side and started fumbling in his pockets once more.

'Lost your money again?' she asked teasingly. She felt as if she'd known him almost as long as she'd known Anthony.

'Dear me, what have I done with it? No, it's not my money...' His voice drifted off as he searched more pockets.

'What is it?' she asked curiously. Elaine had begun to notice his agitated searching again, and wondered if he was perpetually disorganised.

'Anything I can do, old boy?' Anthony enquired, leaning over Beverley, from her other side.

'Ah...' Henry gave a long sigh of relief, and produced from an inner pocket a small flat box. He handed it carefully to Beverley. 'This is for you, m'dear.'

'What is it?' Intrigued, she felt the soft velvet of the box and realised it was a jewellery box. There was a snap fastening on one side, and when she pressed it the lid flew open. Lying inside was a little note covered with spidery writing.

'It's from my mother,' Henry explained. 'She can't see very well, and her writing's gone to pot!'

Beverley glanced quickly at Anthony, to make sure he was watching. 'It's from your mother,' she said with awe.

Anthony smiled gently. 'So I gather. What has she sent you?'

Picking up the note, she gasped as she saw, lying on a bed of antique white satin, a pair of beautiful diamond drop earrings. 'Oh, how fantastic!' she breathed. 'I can't believe it.'

'They're Georgian, m'dear. Part of the family jewels. Mama thought you ought to have them to wear on your wedding day. She wore them when she married my father, and my grandmother wore them before her. Hope you like them.' Henry spoke in short sentences which took away nothing from the warmth of his voice.

'They're amazing!' Beverley said, deeply touched.

'It's so kind of her.' She picked up the note, and in the

149

candlelight read the faint scrawl.

Dear Beverley,
May you know the happiness that I shared with
Anthony's father, and may you enjoy wearing
these earrings as much as I did. I hope you will
come to visit me one day in England.
Yours affectionately,
Rosemary Cumberland

'Oh, Anthony . . .' She held out his mother's note to
him, too moved to say more. He read it quickly and
when he looked back at her, his own eyes were over-
bright.

'I'm so glad you like them,' he whispered, slipping his
arm around her waist. 'They've always been Mama's
favourite piece of jewellery. They'll suit you, beautifully.'

Elaine was leaning over Henry, long pale arms and
hands outstretched, dying to have a closer look.

'Honey!' she crowed enthusiastically. 'They'll photograph gorgeously! Can we put on the caption that
they're Cumberland heirlooms?'

'You sure can, honey,' Henry shot back in a Texan
drawl.

Then they were all laughing, and Rachael and Daniel
were smiling at their daughter's good fortune, and Jenny
was almost hysterical with excitement.

'You haven't any more brothers, have you, Ant?' she
asked boldly. Laughingly, Henry and Anthony promised
Jenny they'd try and find her a Lord, all for herself, and
she giggled back, and demanded to know how long she'd
have to wait.

At last it was time for everyone to go home, and the

party started breaking up around midnight. The next day, Beverley was going to be busy with all the final arrangements, and Anthony was going to take the opportunity of spending time with Henry and Bertie because it might be a long time before they saw each other again.

'Happy?' he whispered to Beverley as they said goodnight on the veranda steps of the inn.

'I couldn't be happier,' she replied sincerely. She was clutching the black velvet jewel case, and her eyes were almost as bright as the diamonds that lay inside.

'That makes two of us then,' Anthony replied. They kissed goodnight briefly and gently, wishing they could stay together all night, but knowing that, surrounded by their friends and family, it was impossible. But the promise in Anthony's eyes as he looked down at her was plain to see. It was a promise of hot nights of love and long days of companionship and sharing, of talking and laughing and a life they would always share. In two days' time they would be married, and then for the rest of their lives they would be together. For better or worse. For richer or poorer. In sickness and in health. Beverley pressed her cheek against his once again, never loving him more than at this moment, knowing now that they had the blessing of his family as well. Henry was standing watching them with a great beaming smile, and in her hand she still held the jewel case with his mother's note.

It was with a light heart that Beverley returned home with her family that night, knowing the future held golden days for her and Anthony.

Chapter Six

Beverley awoke on the morning of her wedding day to find Jenny standing over her, holding a cup of coffee.

'Mom said to bring this to you,' she said, plonking it down on the bedside table. 'How are you feeling?'

Beverley sat up slowly and looked through the open curtains to the brilliantly sunny day beyond. 'Fine, I think,' she said slowly. Then she frowned. She'd had a nasty dream in which she and Anthony had become separated while walking in the woods. No matter how fast she ran up and down the winding paths, she couldn't find him, and then she found herself lost too, in a part of the forest she didn't know. Panic had seized her, and she called out his name, but then found that she'd been struck dumb. Fear that she would never find him again made her run faster, but then her legs became paralysed and she couldn't move. Beverley shook her head to rid herself of the nightmare and reached for her coffee.

'You don't look too good,' Jenny observed gravely.

'Thanks a bunch! What time is it?'

'Half-past nine.'

'As late as that?' Beverley was surprised. She'd gone to bed early the previous night, because she had expected to be awake by dawn. How could one sleep late on one's wedding morning?

'I want to talk to Anthony,' she said suddenly, climbing out of bed.

'But you talked to him on the phone for hours last night. What more have you got to say?' Jenny couldn't understand all this talking they did. Having a man in your life surely meant lots of kissing and sex. Why waste time talking?

Beverley put on her old blue terry towelling dressing gown over her white cotton nightdress, and ran a brush through her hair. Her eyes still looked troubled and she wished Anthony was there so she could hold him close and have him assure her everything was all right.

'I'll phone him and say "hi", and I'll be back in a moment,' she told Jenny. 'Be an angel and run a bath for me, will you?'

Jenny dropped into an elaborate curtsey. 'Yes, My Lady. Certainly, My Lady,' she mocked. 'Anything you say, My Lady!'

Beverley grabbed a pillow and chucked it at her head. 'Oh, shut up!' she giggled suddenly. 'Nobody's ever going to call me that!'

'Waiters in restaurants will. And girls in shops. And hairdressers. You'll only have to flash your plastic around with "The Viscountess Amesbury" on it, and people will curtsey so deeply they'll drop through a hole in the ground!' Jenny teased with a wicked grin.

'Are you kidding? No way!' Beverley scurried out of the room, and she was laughing too, although there was still an anxious look in her eyes.

When she got through to the Red Lion Inn she asked to be put through to Anthony. After a few bleeps and pings, the operator came back on the line to say he wasn't in his room. Beverley had a sudden thought.

'Could you try Lord Cumberland's room, please? He may be with his brother.'

A moment later she heard Henry's laid-back English voice, and it sounded as if he was chewing something.

'Henry? This is Beverley.'

'Um ... Hello, um, m'dear ... Sorry, I'm eating an egg!' There was a pause, and then he spoke again. 'Anthony and Bertie Goring and I decided to have breakfast in my room this morning, and a jolly good breakfast it is, too.' It sounded as if he'd taken another bite of something. Amused, Beverley asked to speak to Anthony.

'I'll hand you over, m'dear. Nice sunny day, isn't it?'

Anthony came on the line immediately. 'Hello, love? How are you this morning?' His voice was warm.

'Missing you dreadfully,' she said sadly. 'I had a horrid dream in which I lost you and I woke up feeling miserable.'

'Oh, sweetheart! Only a few hours to go and then we'll be together all the time,' he assured her. 'And you've had an invitation!'

'What sort of invitation?' she asked cautiously.

'Henry has invited us to stay with him in the New Year. Won't that be fun? I'm longing to show you Buck-lands, and all the haunts of my childhood. You'll meet my mother, too. She's keen to get to know you. And Bertie says we must stay with him in London.'

As he spoke, Beverley felt a glow of happiness spread through her.

'How wonderful!' she exclaimed excitedly.

They talked for a few more minutes, and the warm

reality of Anthony's voice dispelled the last of her uneasiness.

'I'll see you at the church,' he promised. 'Don't be late.'

'I'm so excited I might even be early,' she quipped back.

Downstairs, the preparations for the reception were well under way as the caterers arranged the buffet tables in the marquee behind the house which had been erected two days before. In amazement, the Franklin family watched as florists transformed everything into a fantasy of flowers and greenery, creating a rose-covered archway at the entrance to the tent. Red carpeting had been rolled out over the grass lawn, and then the three-tiered iced wedding cake was lifted out of the three wooden cases it had arrived in, and placed on a silver stand.

Jenny was agog. As champagne glasses were unpacked, and trays of sandwiches and cakes produced, her excitement increased to fever pitch. Tom, as usual, thought the whole thing a waste of time. He was having to miss a great game on television that afternoon, and was furious about it.

'Why couldn't you have got married on another day, Beverley?' he complained loudly. 'Watching a video is never the same, and someone's bound to tell me who won before I've even seen it.'

Josh, on the other hand, was being very cooperative, helping his father and mother get the house organised, although the guests were to be directed to go straight into the marquee.

At eleven o'clock Elaine drove up with Cass Sternberg in his large limousine to make their inspection of the preparations. He'd managed to persuade Maxine to have her hair done, for the second day running, 'So you'll look great in the photographs, honey', so that he and Elaine could slip away on their own for a couple of hours.

By noon, the hairdresser and make-up artist arrived to get Beverley ready, something she'd tried to resist, but Elaine had been adamant.

'You can't do your own face and hair on an occasion like this,' she'd said in a shocked voice.

Once again Beverley had the sensation that none of this was for real. She felt like a model getting ready for a photo session, or an actress about to play a big scene in a movie.

Rachael, looking very elegant in a sapphire blue silk dress worn with a matching lace coat, came in to Beverley's room in time to help her put on her wedding dress.

'You look lovely, Mom,' she told her mother admiringly. Rachael's hair and make-up had also been done professionally.

'Thank you, sweetheart.' Mother and daughter smiled at each other with deep understanding. The best Rachael could wish Beverley was that she'd be as happy with Anthony as she'd been with Daniel, and her good wishes for her daughter showed in her eyes.

Carefully Beverley stepped into the wild silk wedding dress, feeling as if she was submerging herself in a confection of whipped cream, and then Rachael was doing up the little buttons at the back, and the make-up artist was helping with the row of buttons at each wrist. Then she put on the shoes, dainty high-heeled sandals covered in white silk, while her mother helped to fix the roses and lace veil, spreading it out in a train that flowed to the ground. When Beverley saw herself in the full-length mirror, she gave an involuntary gasp of amazement.

'Is that really me?' she said wonderingly. The girl who looked back at her was beautiful and radiant, and glowing with health and happiness.

Then she reached for the black velvet jewel case and took out the diamond drop earrings Rosemary Cumberland had sent her. A moment later they were shimmering in her ears, adding a dramatic sparkle against the soft sheen of silk and lace.

'Wow!' exclaimed Jenny, coming into the room at that moment. She looked lovely, too, with her blonde hair held back with pale blue ribbons to match her dress.

The sisters laughed happily as they surveyed each other.

'I can't wait for it to be my turn to get married,' Jenny remarked. 'Do you suppose Bertie Goring fancies me?'

'Jenny!' Beverley pretended to scold. 'You're far too young to think of marriage! Anyway, Bertie only set eyes on you two days ago.'

'So? You and Anthony fell in love right away, didn't you? I quite like the idea of being a marchioness. It's a rank higher than being a viscountess, isn't it?'

'Two ranks higher,' Beverley corrected her. 'I've been trying to learn how titles work in England. A duchess is the top rank, then a marchioness, then a countess, and way down the line a viscountess. Of course barons' wives are baronesses, but knights' wives are merely "Lady",' she added knowledgeably.

'How come you're going to be known as "Lady Amesbury" then?' Jenny queried.

'Only a duchess is *called* "Duchess" to her face. Everyone else is called "Lady".'

'Wow! You've learned all about it, haven't you?' Jenny remarked, impressed.

Beverley smiled. 'I don't want to let Anthony down by my ignorance. Anyway, Elaine made me learn the whole system of titles for *Chichi*. I can't get it wrong if I'm to write about all these people.'

At that moment, Josh came to her bedroom door with her bouquet which the florist had just produced.

'Oh, it's exquisite,' Beverley, exclaimed, examining the spray of gardenias, roses, stephanotis and gypsophila.

'Time we got going,' Daniel announced, joining Josh in the doorway. 'The cars have arrived.'

They all looked at each other. It was a momentous moment in the history of the Franklin family. Their second child was getting married in a few minutes, and nothing would ever be quite the same again. For the first time, their close-knit unit of six was being broken up, and Rachael's eyes brimmed with sudden tears. Beverley was the first bird to fly the nest and she couldn't help feeling a pang of sadness.

Beverley, quick to spot her mother's expression, hugged her quickly.

'At least you're going to be living in New York,' Jenny chipped in comfortingly. 'Imagine how awful it would be if you were going to live in England?'

At the local Episcopalian Church a crowd had been gathering for the past hour to watch the arrival of the wedding guests. Eight-foot pyramids of white flowers flanked the entrance and a red carpet had been laid across the sidewalk. Four photographers, hired by *Chichi*, were poised to take as many photographs as they could, while a film team and a television crew stood by to film events as they happened. Amid a buzz of excitement, smartly dressed guests alighted from limousines and then the most chic of all, Elaine Ross, arrived in her limousine. Wearing a white grosgrain suit and a tiny matching hat, she drew gasps of admiration from the crowds. Now there was elegance! they murmured. There was high fashion in all its glory! Escorted by the publisher and owner of *Chichi*, Cass Sternberg, and his wife, Elaine posed like a professional model for the photographers before sweeping into the church. This was as much her day as Beverley's, she reckoned, thinking how wild *Vogue* and *Vanity Fair* and *Harper's Bazaar* were going to be when they saw the spread on 'the wedding of the decade' in *Chichi*. Elaine was also convinced that in time, through Beverley and Anthony, she was going to be able to grab a few more society scoops. It was one of the reasons she'd hired Beverley to write a column.

The church was filled to capacity by two-thirty, and Anthony and Bertie Goring were waiting in position at the top of the aisle for the arrival of Beverley. They were both wearing black tail coats and grey and black pinstriped trousers with pale grey waistcoats. In Anthony's button-hole he wore a white gardenia, and Bertie, nervously patting his pocket to make sure he hadn't mislaid the wedding ring, sported a white carnation.

While the church organ played a Bach fugue, Anthony glanced around at the assembled congregation. Henry was in the pew directly behind him, smiling benignly, and across the aisle, Rachael and her sons, Josh and Tom, occupied the front pew. Behind her sat Elaine, exquisite and fragile, her expression vulnerable for once. I wonder why she never married? Anthony reflected. Suddenly he became aware of a commotion in the street outside as flash bulbs popped and a cheer went up from the waiting crowds. Beverley and her father had arrived. Jenny and the little flowergirls and the page were clustered in the church doorway to greet her as she posed with Daniel for the photographers, and then Anthony felt a frisson of excitement. In a short while they'd be man and wife.

The music changed with stirring chords and the organist was playing the hymn Anthony had especially chosen because it was his favourite: 'Lead us heavenly father, lead us', and there was his beloved Beverley, coming up the aisle with her father. Their eyes met, and as she drew level with him, she gave a tremulous smile. Anthony smiled back, feeling himself glowing with love and admiration, and then he reached for her hand, mouthing the words: 'I love you.' Almost imperceptibly, she mouthed the words back to him.

And so the wedding service began, in the pretty flower-filled church she'd known all her life.

At the end of the hymn the clergyman stepped forward, Beverley handed her bouquet to Jenny, and the familiar litany: 'We are gathered here today . . .' was spoken with loud solemnity.

As in a dream Beverley listened, knowing that the most important words she would ever utter in her life would be in a few minutes when she said 'I will'. Conscious of Anthony beside her, feeling the warm grip of his hand holding hers, she gazed up at the clergyman, intently following everything he said.

The congregation were hushed as the ancient words of the wedding service echoed round the church. On one side, Beverley's family watched with quiet pride, while on the other side of the aisle Henry Cumberland beamed at his brother. And all around them, flowered and feathered hats quivered as guests strained to watch the proceedings in an atmosphere of anticipation.

'. . . If there is any impediment or just cause why Anthony Richard Charles and Beverley Faith Kathleen may not be joined together in Holy Matrimony, let him now speak or forever hold his peace . . .'

The stillness was broken by a sudden shrill cry from the back of the church. 'They mustn't marry! They *can't* marry!'

Everyone spun round, shocked.

'It must be stopped! Stop the marriage!'

The shriek changed to a high-pitched wail and Beverley froze, her face ashen. There was no mistaking the voice. It was Mary.

'He mustn't marry her!' The screams had reached a crescendo. Electrified, everyone in the church craned round to see what was going on. Two of the ushers had got hold of Mary by the arms, and were trying to lead her away. They managed to half lift, half drag her as far as the church door, while she sobbed and screamed hysterically, but then she broke free and, turning, looked directly up the length of the aisle at Beverley. Insanity twisted her features, flamed in her eyes and scalded her tongue with bile.

'That bitch!' she shrieked. 'Stop her marrying him.'

Appalled and shocked, Beverley and Anthony watched as more people rushed forward and Mary was finally dragged away. Minutes later her cries were still echoing in the street outside.

At the reception after the service there was talk of little else. Who was the girl who had interrupted the proceedings in such a hysterical way? And why had she done it?

162

Shaken and still looking pale, Beverley stood just inside the marquee under an archway of white flowers and received the guests with Anthony, Henry and her parents, while Elaine strutted around giving orders to everyone and looking livid.

The television cameras had been allowed into the church to cover the ceremony, and now the story would hit the media in a big way. She wouldn't be able to prevent it although she'd told the photographers from *Chichi* that if they sold a single picture of the disturbance to any other publication they'd never work for her again. Unfortunately she couldn't impose the same rigorous warnings on the TV crew. The story would get into all the newspapers now, taking the edge off her exclusive, and there wasn't a damned thing she could do about it.

'Who was that woman?' Elaine hissed to anyone who might have the answer. In her opinion it was irresponsible of both Beverley and Anthony to have invited someone who was likely to cause trouble.

Embarrassed, Beverley told her it was Mary Stapelton.

'From Highlight? The one who helped organise the party for *Chichi*'s anniversary?' Elaine looked staggered. 'I must get on to Charles Floyd right away. He shouldn't employ unstable people like that in his company. What was it all about anyway?'

Briefly, Beverley explained. It had been a very distressing incident and she felt deeply shocked. Mary had been behaving strangely for weeks, according to Faye, but none of them had expected her to attend the wedding. It was obvious to them all now that she was sick, very sick, and not responsible for her actions.

'I'm so sorry,' Anthony had whispered in the car that took them from the church back to the reception. He shook his head. 'She must be mentally deranged.'

'I know.' Beverley felt deeply sorry for him, too. Through no fault of his, Mary had become completely obsessed, and the scene she had created had upset everyone, with the exception of Jenny who thought the whole think fascinating.

'It's *Fatal Attraction* and *Jane Eyre* rolled into one,' she kept saying.

As in a dream, Beverley floated through the reception, shaking hands, kissing, accepting compliments, and all the while she stayed close to Anthony. Mary's outburst had cast a shadow over her like a black cloud blocking out the sun, like the nightmare she'd wakened from that morning, and she longed to obliterate it from her mind. If Mary was capable of behaving like that, she was capable of anything. Beverley gave a little shiver, and Anthony saw at once that she was still upset. He slipped his arm around her waist and held her close while *Chichi*'s photographers snapped away.

'I'm so afraid it's a bad omen . . . her coming here like that today,' Beverley whispered.

'She's crazy, sweetheart. Anyone can see that. It's actually got nothing to do with either of us,' Anthony whispered. 'She's probably got as big a fixation on you as she has on me!'

'That's what I mean.'

They had no way of knowing how long Mary would be kept in hospital. What happened when she got out? Would she come after them again? And would Beverley be her target, not Anthony? In Mary's eyes, Beverley was the enemy, the woman who had taken Anthony away from her.

'I'll look after you,' he said, smiling down at her as if he knew what she was thinking.

'It's time to cut the wedding cake,' Elaine announced, coming up to them at that moment.

'So soon?' Beverley asked. The time seemed to be flying past, and she wanted this day to last forever.

'I want both Lord Goring and Lord Cumberland to make speeches,' Elaine continued, ignoring Beverley. 'Where are the photographers?'

'Do we have to have *every* moment photographed?' Rachael intervened in a rather pained voice. She was getting annoyed at the way Elaine had taken over every detail of her daughter's wedding.

'Of course,' Elaine snapped back. '*Chichi* has spent a fortune on today, and we want our money's worth.' It was decided that Bertie Goring should propose the health of the flowergirls and page, while Henry proposed a toast to the bride and groom. When it came to his turn, Henry leaned over to Beverley and Anthony and whispered: 'That woman reminds me of a White Witch! I'm sure she's casting all sorts of spells around the place! She terrifies me!'

Beverley and Anthony started laughing. It was the best description of Elaine they'd ever heard.

When it came to Henry's turn to speak, he made it short and to the point. 'Ladies and gentlemen, please raise your glasses to the bride and bridegroom. In the tradition of all fairy tales, may the Good Fairy watch over them, may the Wicked Witch be banished from the Kingdom, and may they live happily ever after!' Then he gave Beverley and his brother a huge wink as he raised his glass.

The Paradise Cove, set on the edge of a stretch of golden

beach, was the most luxurious hotel in Barbados. Anthony had booked the best suite for them and when they were shown into it, Beverley's eyes opened wide with amazement. She had never seen such luxury. The rooms were spacious and elegant, with sofas covered in heavy white linen on which were stacked wild silk cushions in a profusion of pinks and corals and reds. Gleaming white marble floors, scattered with locally made rugs, glistened under the concealed spotlights that shone down from the ceiling, and in the centre, a large glass table held a pyramid of exotic fruit piled up in a basket. French windows led on to a veranda, furnished with cane tables and chairs, and beyond lay the beach and the aquamarine ocean.

'Anthony!' she exclaimed, looking at him with shining eyes. 'It's a dream place. Did you know it was going to be this glamorous?'

'I had a fair idea.' He was grinning at her. 'Let's have a look at the bedroom.'

He led the way through an archway and small lobby where their luggage had been placed beside a walk-in closet, to the bedroom beyond. A king-size carved bed festooned with white muslin hangings dominated the room, which also led on to the veranda. Here orchids planted in great terracotta urns grew in profusion. In the adjoining bathroom gold swan-shaped taps were reflected in the mirrored walls that surrounded an onyx jacuzzi. By the twin handbasins, a small refrigerator was set into the wall.

'Is that for ice?' Beverley asked. 'It's too small for drinks. You'd only get a couple of cans of Coke in there!'

'According to the brochure, the fridge is for keeping your perfume at the right temperature,' Anthony informed her, trying to keep a straight face.

She looked stunned. 'You have to be kidding!'

'No, it's true. Now we'd better buy you some perfume to put in it.' He was laughing now, delighted by her excitement.

Beverley went back to the bedroom and flung herself on to the soft downy bed with a little whoop of joy. 'This place is fantastic!' she said, kicking off her shoes. 'I think I'll stay here for ever and ever.' She thought of Jenny, and how crazy she'd be about a place like this. And wait until she told her about the fridge for the perfume!

Anthony was eyeing an ice bucket on a table in the corner. It contained a bottle of Pol Roger champagne, beautifully chilled, with a small card bearing 'the manager's compliments'.

'Shall we start as we mean to go on?' he asked with a wicked smile.

'We could be alcoholics by the end of two weeks.'

'I'm prepared to risk if it you are,' he replied. 'D'you realise that we can do exactly as we like? No jobs to go to. No Elaine breathing down our necks . . .'

'I'm surprised she didn't want to come on honeymoon with us, bringing along her own photographer, too,' Beverley joked.

Anthony eased the cork out of the bottle and it flew off with a gentle pop. Then he poured the champagne into the two crystal glasses that had been left on a silver tray.

'Here you are, love,' he said, handing her a glass. 'And here's to us.'

'Here's to us,' she repeated softly.

'Happily ever after,' he quoted Henry's toast.

'Happily ever after,' she said, gazing into his eyes, her

heart squeezing with sudden excitement so she could hardly breathe. A moment later she was in his arms, and he was holding her tightly.

'I began to wonder if we'd ever be alone together again,' he groaned, burying his face in her neck. 'We seem to have been surrounded by people ever since we got engaged.'

'Oh, I know,' she replied. 'I've felt the same. Sometimes, when Elaine was going on and on about all the arrangements, I almost forgot it had anything to do with us,' she admitted.

He kissed her then, deeply and tenderly. 'It's got everything to do with us, hasn't it?'

'Oh, yes.' She remembered the day before, when she'd walked up the aisle and seen him standing there, waiting for her, mouthing the words: 'I love you.' She'd mouthed back, 'I love you, too,' and she said it now, again and again, as he began kissing her all over, removing her clothes with loving hands, stroking her smooth warm skin, arousing her to a passion that was as intense as when they'd first made love. Then he took off his own clothes and together they lay on the muslin-draped bed. With gentle hands she was exciting him too, kissing and licking and sucking him until he thought he would go out of his mind if he didn't take her soon. He wanted her so much it was almost unbearable, but she too had become skilled at prolonging their love making, and just when he thought he couldn't wait a second longer, she guided him inside her, holding him tightly, rocking in unison with him, until he cried out and held her as if he could never bear to let her go.

Darkness descended with swift finality over the Caribbean that evening, following a sunset that filled the sky with dramatic swirls of orange and crimson over a now dark sapphire sea. Wandering on to the veranda, in loose cotton bathrobes, Beverley and Anthony finished the champagne, and then walked along the beach, digging their bare toes into the still warm sand. Hand in hand, they strolled until it was too dark to see anything. Then they made their way back to their suite, where Anthony had earlier ordered dinner to be served. He'd had enough of people surrounding them, and he'd made up his mind that on their honeymoon they wouldn't see a soul unless they wanted to.

Already, while they'd been wandering along the beach, a table set with flowers and candles and sparkling silver had been set in the window of their private living room by discreet hotel staff. And he had taken care to choose a typical Barbadian menu of locally caught flying fish with cou-cou, pumpkin fritters, chicken stuffed with herbs, and cocunut cream pie.

'I hope you'll like it,' he said, eyeing the exotic dishes.

'If I don't, we'll order hamburgers tomorrow!' she teased.

'At least the wine's French, so if you don't like the food we can get drunk.'

'I think I'm drunk already.' She nuzzled him like a playful puppy. 'Drunk on champagne, love, sunshine, and being thoroughly spoiled.'

'You deserve it, sweetheart.'

That night they dined leisurely, and when they went swimming at midnight, before going to bed, the warm silky waters of the Caribbean ocean caressed their skins as they floated languorously on their backs, counting the stars in the velvety sky above.

'I wish we could stay here forever,' Beverley said

wistfully as they breakfasted on the veranda the next morning.

'You'd soon get bored with only my company,' Anthony replied smiling, as if he didn't believe a word he was saying.

She kicked him playfully with a bare foot under the table.

'Never in a million years,' she replied stoutly.

He leaned forward. 'Are you sure?'

'Quite sure.' The gold flecks in her eyes glittered, and her smile was roguish. 'Shall I prove it to you?'

'How?'

Beverley flung up her hands in mock dismay. 'He asks me how?' She cast her eyes to heaven. 'Do I really have to spell it out?'

He laughed happily. 'Not really.'

She rose to her feet, catching his hand, pulling him up with her. 'Be sure to put the "do not disturb" notice on the door,' she reminded him, as they went to the bedroom, their arms around each other. Already excited at the idea of making love to her again, he pressed his lips to hers and promised himself they'd always be this happy.

For the next two weeks the idyll continued as the hours flew past all too quickly. In the morning they swam and went snorkelling, and then sunbathed for a while before returning to the shady veranda to enjoy the culinary delights of the island. After a siesta, they explored the nearby beaches and coves and walked through the lush shrubbery that protected the hotel from the main road. Sometimes they picked wild orchids and ginger lilies, which grew in profusion, or they got the hotel to fix them a picnic which they ate by the water's edge. And always they were inseparable, neither wanting nor seeking other people. They were both aware that as soon as they got back to New York, they'd be plunged into work again, Anthony with his own company and Beverley with her column in *Chichi*. They also knew they'd be expected to catch up with their friends, spend occasional weekends at Stockbridge, and generally get back into the swing of things again. It was a prospect that at times filled them with dismay.

'If I had one wish, it would be to live on a desert island, with only you, forever and ever,' Beverley said on their last night.

He held her hand, more in love with her than ever. They'd both had a wonderful two weeks, and he too rather dreaded going back to the hubbub of city life, with its pollution and fumes, its crowds and its crimes.

'We'll come back here,' he promised her.

She looked at him as if she hoped what he said was true. Would they come back? Could they afford to? The trip must have cost Anthony a fortune. Apart from that, there were things one could never recapture; precious moments in time that became the golden days of the past. Something told her, like chilled fingers on her heart, that they'd never come back again. The shadow of Mary still lay over them and was something she couldn't forget, however hard she tried. Would she strike again, with the venom of a woman who believes herself to have been wronged? Or would she submit to the treatment she so obviously needed? Only time would tell.

Chapter Seven

'What's become of Mary?' Beverley asked. She was having a quick lunch with Faye, Nina and Lisette, and knew they'd kept in touch with what was happening. 'Is she coming back to work at Highlight?' It was the first time they'd got together since the wedding and they had a lot of news to catch up on.

'No, she's only just come out of the psychiatric hospital and she's staying with her family in Detroit. In her last letter she said she thought she'd get a job in a local attorney's office,' Faye replied. She'd always been the closest to Mary and had been the one who'd called a paramedic to attend to her at Beverley's wedding.

Lisette shook her head sadly. 'Isn't it awful how some people screw up their lives?'

'She's refusing to date anyone, too,' Nina remarked. 'Even she says she's driving her mom nuts by staying in all the time.'

'How could she have got such a fixation on Anthony?' Lisette asked. 'It's quite scary, isn't it?' She turned to Beverley. 'What did he say about that outburst of hers in church?'

'He was sad, and sorry for her, and embarrassed of course in case anyone thought he had led her on. If

173

Anthony and I weren't so close, it could have ruined everything,' Beverley admitted.

'Do you think she'll ever come back to New York?' Faye asked Nina.

'Who knows? I bet you hope she doesn't, don't you, Beverley?' Lisette interjected.

'I hope she doesn't for her sake. It must be so painful to be obsessed by someone who doesn't return your feelings.'

The others nodded. None of them could imagine behaving in that way. For a moment they ate their corned beef on rye in gloomy silence.

'Let's hope she meets someone nice soon,' Faye remarked.

Lisette's eyes glinted. 'We can't all be as lucky as Beverley. How is His Lordship, by the way?'

Beverley laughed. 'If you mean Anthony, he's fine! You know, I can't get used to this titled bit. It seems such an anachronism in this day and age! Someone called me "Your Ladyship" in a shop the other day, and I looked round, wondering who they were talking to.'

'How come you're "Viscountess" and "Lady Amesbury"?' Faye asked. 'How can you be both?'

Beverley sighed inwardly. She seemed to spend so much time these days explaining the British titles system that it was driving her crazy. As briefly as she could, she repeated what she had told Jenny. 'Honestly,' she added, 'to understand how titles and the peerage works is a study in itself! Since Anthony isn't bothered about using the title, neither am I.' Suddenly Beverley giggled. 'But you should hear Elaine!' she confided. 'She makes everyone in the office refer to me as "Lady Amesbury". It's so embarrassing. I keep saying, "Call me Beverley, for goodness' sake", but the minute they do, she corrects them if she's around.'

'I wonder why people are so riveted by titles?' Lisette asked. 'Everyone I know is impressed by royalty or titles. Even more than they are by money.'

Beverley shrugged. 'I suppose it's to do with history and fantasy and escapism. All that stuff we read as children about the Princess-in-the-Palace and the Knight-in-shining-armour! Fairy tales always had Kings and Queens and Lords and Ladies, didn't they? My favourite was *Sleeping Beauty*. I must have read that story twenty times by the time I was six.'

'Your own life has been rather like a fairy tale, hasn't it?' Lisette observed seriously.

Beverley grinned. 'I have to admit you're right! Not that Anthony and I will ever end up living in a palace, but we do hope to go and stay with his brother in England so we'll be staying in an old castle. We'll never be rich, though. Or live grandly. And I'm sure I'll always have to work. Not that I mind.'

'Talking of work, how *is* Elaine?' Faye asked, curiously. None of them had liked her since *Chichi*'s anniversary party when she'd treated them like dirt, but they were fascinated to know what it was like working for her.

'It's okay,' Beverley replied. 'In fairness, now that the wedding's over, and the pictures were okay, she pretty well leaves me alone to get on with my job.'

'When I saw the issue, with your wedding spread over pages and *pages* . . . I nearly died!' Lisette exclaimed. 'It was some wedding, wasn't it? Were you pleased with the way it was done?'

'Quite,' Beverley replied, but there was some doubt

in her voice. 'I do think it was bad form the way Elaine managed to get into most of the pictures herself. Mom was very peeved. Elaine was acting like my mother, wasn't she?'

'I suppose as Elaine paid for the whole thing, she thought she could do as she liked.'

'*Chichi* paid for it, not Elaine,' Faye corrected her.

'Anyway, Anthony and I had a lovely day,' Beverley said peaceably, 'and an even better honeymoon.'

The others giggled. 'Lucky you,' said Lisette.

'I wish I could meet someone like Anthony,' admitted Nina.

'You can say that again,' Faye said in heartfelt tones.

Beverley grinned, knowing that meeting Anthony had been the most wonderful thing that could have happened to her. Suddenly, she glanced at her wristwatch.

'Hey, I had better be getting back to work,' she exclaimed. 'I've got to call up a whole bunch of socialites and ask them who their favourite designer is.'

'Oh, you poor thing!' Lisette mocked her laughingly.

'*Such* a hard life!' echoed Faye.

'I don't know how you survive,' Nina commiserated.

'Okay, okay.' Beverley was laughing. 'I know I'm not exactly slaving down a salt mine, but the job does have its pressures.'

'Such as?'

'These idle socialites, with nothing to do except look good all the time, can be hell to deal with.'

'I bet! You call them up and say, "Excuse me, this is Lady Amesbury calling from *Chichi*", and dammit, I bet they're like putty in your hands!' Faye said with a joking scorn. 'I bet not one of them has given you a hard time, ever.'

'They're probably falling over themselves to get into your column,' Nina said. 'How can you call that pressure?'

They were all joking and Beverley knew it, but underneath the surface there was that cutting edge, that layer of jealousy that she'd done so well for herself, and she could feel the tiny barbs of envy in their voices.

She laughed to hide the hurt she felt. 'No doubt I'll be fired for getting everyone's name wrong sooner or later,' she quipped, and instantly felt annoyed with herself for being embarrassed by her own success. Why should she feel like apologising to her friends because she'd made a brilliant marriage, been given a fabulous job, and was wonderfully happy? It could have happened to any of them. It was just luck that it had happened to her.

As she walked back to the offices of *Chichi*, she wondered if Anthony's position had distanced him from others? She remembered thinking that if she'd known he was titled before she'd met him, she'd have been shy and in awe. Did people feel like that with her now? Maybe if she went to England, where class seemed to be everything. Surely not at home though, in the States? Deep in thought, she entered the building where *Chichi* occupied the twenty-fifth, twenty-sixth and twenty-seventh floors. Elaine had given her a small office near her own on the top floor, where, if necessary, she could conduct interviews. Mostly she went to the houses and salons of her subjects, though. It was important for her literally to get the 'feel' of the clothes the women she wrote about wore, and study the colours and shapes and textures they most favoured. She could learn more about a woman by looking in her closet, and more about a designer by visiting his workrooms, than she could by just talking to them.

There were two messages waiting for her. One from Anthony saying he'd be home late. The other from Mary, asking her to ring back.

Beverley dialled the Detroit number with feelings of misgiving, and yet how could she ignore Mary's message? Faye had said she'd been discharged from hospital, so that must mean she was better, surely?

When a man's voice answered, Beverley asked to speak to Mary.

'She isn't here. Who are you?' he asked abruptly.

'This is Beverley Amesbury. I just got a message from Mary to call her back. When will she be in please?'

'I tell you, she isn't here.' He sounded impatient, and spoke with a hoarseness that suggested his vocal chords were being relentlessly demolished by cigarettes and liquor.

'You mean she's out?'

'I mean what I say. She isn't here. She's back in New York, and I should know because I'm her father.' There was a click and Beverley found herself staring at the dead receiver in her hand. He'd hung up. So Mary was back in town? So why had she left her Detroit number, for Beverley to call her on? Something cold and crawling shot down Beverley's back. With shaking fingers, she put through a call to Faye and told her what had happened.

'That's strange,' she admitted. 'Look, I'll ring up and ask to speak to her mother. She might be able to tell me what's going on. I've spoken to her before and she sounded sweet. That father of hers is a sonofabitch! He was probably lying because he didn't want you to talk to her.'

'Why?'

'Because we can't be sure what Mary's told him. He may think you really did take Anthony away from her. You know what families are like.'

'*Some* families, perhaps,' Beverley corrected her. 'Will you call me back and tell me what's going on, Faye? The thought of Mary, roaming around New York like a loose cannon, fills me with horror.'

'I know, kiddo. I'll get right back to you,' she promised.

Beverley decided not to say anything to Anthony for the time being, at least not until she'd found out what was going on. No matter how often people assured him he was not to blame for Mary's obsession, she knew he felt badly about it.

Faye was back on the line five minutes later. 'The news is not so hot,' she announced.

'What's happening?' Beverley felt the muscles of her chest contract so that it was hard to breathe while her mind was grappling with the prospect of being harassed by Mary.

'Her father was right. She has left home,' Faye said succinctly.

'And come back to New York?' Beverley asked faintly.

'No one knows. I spoke to her mother who's really worried about her and doesn't know where she is. Neither of us could understand why she left you her home number.'

'When did she leave Detroit, then?'

'Last night.'

'Last night?' Beverley repeated. 'Oh, God, what is she playing at?'

179

'I have a horrible feeling you'll know soon enough,' Faye said drily.

'I suppose I could call the number of her old apartment. Do you know if she's kept it on?'

'No, she gave it up when she came out of hospital. I helped her, in fact, with the packing. She took all her belongings back to Detroit.'

They spoke for a few more minutes, and Beverley decided there was nothing she could do except wait. And hope Mary didn't call her again.

That night, as they cooked supper together, she told Anthony what had happened.

'I can't help feeling threatened,' she confessed as she made some fresh salad dressing. 'Since the wedding, I actually feel she could do anything to get me out of the way.'

Anthony glanced up from trimming the fat off their steaks. He looked stunned. 'You can't be serious!'

'I am, love. I keep getting an awful feeling ... like a premonition ...' Suddenly tears were flowing down her cheeks.

'Sweetheart!' Anthony wiped his hands on a tea towel and took her in his arms. 'This isn't like you!'

Beverley buried her face in his chest. 'I'm so afraid of something happening to us ... to our marriage ... I love you so much and I'm terrified it's all going to end,' she sobbed.

'What's this all about?' he asked horrified. He'd never seen her so upset. Leading her into the living room, he took her to the sofa and they sat down, his arms still around her.

'When did you start feeling like this?' he asked.

'I don't know exactly ... at odd moments, I suppose . . . when something happens to remind me of her . . .'

He handed her his handkerchief and she blew her nose and dabbed her eyes. 'Listen, sweetheart, Mary's sick and everyone knows it. There's nothing she can do to us,' he assured her.

'Sick people can be dangerous.'

'Some are, but Mary's pathetic. She's a drama-queen.' Anthony looked at her tear-stained face and trembling lower lip, and realised just how scared she really was. Mary's outburst at their wedding had unnerved her more than he'd realised.

'I think she's crazy, really crazy,' Beverley admitted brokenly. 'She'll never do you any harm, because she thinks she's in love with you, but I'm afraid she might hurt me if she had the chance.'

'No, of course she wouldn't.' He smiled indulgently. The idea was absurd. It was Beverley who was getting things out of proportion now. 'Listen, sweetheart. Forget all about her, and if she leaves any more messages, ignore them.'

'That's easier said than done. What the hell does she want with me now? It's too late to stop our getting married. Too late to hope to get you away from me . . . too late.' She shook her head. 'Christ, I wish she'd just leave us alone,' she added vehemently.

'So do I,' he agreed. 'Perhaps she will, soon. When she realises it's no good. Then we can forget the whole thing.' He spoke confidently, but privately he wasn't convinced that Mary wouldn't continue to haunt them.

'Should you warn Pamela? Tell her Mary's back in New York?' Beverley suggested.

'I'd already thought of that.' Anthony looked serious

again. 'But I really don't want to get involved. We had Pamela and John to the wedding and I haven't seen them since, and frankly I'd rather not. I think Pamela's done enough harm as it is.'

Beverley nodded. 'You're right.'

'Now, how about that French dressing you were making?' he said, grinning again and pulling her to her feet. 'I don't know about you, but I'm starving.'

'Oh, love, I'm sorry.' She hurried back to the kitchen. Anthony followed, watching her as she measured the wine vinegar and added lemon juice and mustard.

'Did I tell you something, Bevs?' His smile was roguish now.

'What?' She looked back at him, expectantly.

'I love you very much. And I can think of a wonderful way of spending the evening, after we've had dinner!'

'And, pray, My Lord, what way would that be?' she enquired, feigning innocence, although her eyes were dancing.

He grabbed her in a bear hug and held her close. 'If you don't shut up I'll drag you to "My Lady's Chamber" before you even have time to finish that goddam' salad dressing!'

Laughing, they held each other close and he kissed her lips gently.

At that moment the phone rang, loud and shrill, so that they jumped apart, startled.

'I'll take it,' said Anthony grimly, grabbing the receiver from its cradle on the wall. 'Hello?'

Beverley watched, holding her breath. Thirty seconds later he replaced the receiver and looked at her.

'Well?'

'That was Mary all right.' He took a deep breath. 'All

she said was: "I'm back in New York. You know where to find me. I'll be waiting." '

'And you think she realised it was you she was talking to?' Beverley demanded.

He nodded. 'I'm sure she did.'

'How did she sound?'

Anthony averted his gaze and looked uncomfortable. 'Sort of . . . well, sort of seductive,' he said finally. 'It reminded me of the Mae West line: "Come up and see me some time." She was quite suggestive in her tone.'

'It really has started again.' Beverley stirred the salad dressing briskly. 'Let me answer it next time.'

'Perhaps there won't be a next time?' He sounded hopeful.

'Don't bet on it,' she said crisply.

The next morning before she left for work Beverley phoned the New York telephone exchange. 'I'd like our number to be changed,' she told them. 'And I'd like the new one to be unlisted.'

When she arrived at the office, her eyes skimmed her desk to see if there had been any messages for her, but the only one was from a photographer asking how many of his pictures she would need for the next issue.

At eleven o'clock, Elaine sent a message asking her to go along to her office right away. Checking her lipstick and straightening her skirt, Beverley hurried along the elegant hushed corridor.

She found Elaine sitting at her desk with stacks of photographs strewn before her.

'Come and sit down, Beverley,' she said pleasantly. 'I've got an idea for a feature, and I'd like you to write the copy and do some research as well.' Her black hair curved perfectly in line with her taut jaw, and her cream flannel skirt and silk shirt were impeccable. Beverley sat in the white leather chair on the opposite side of the desk and looked at her expectantly.

'The Queen of England is coming to America on a State Visit,' she explained, 'and I want you to do a complete analysis of her wardrobe. Who makes her clothes, her hats, her shoes. What colours she favours, and what styles. We'll be doing a retrospective feature as well, and I want you to get hold of every photograph you can, and select what you think are the best pictures of her wardrobe covering the past forty years.'

'That'll be very interesting,' Beverley commented enthusiastically. 'We can study how her style may have changed over the years, and comment on the development of her taste in clothes.'

'Exactly. She only wears clothes made by British designers so you'll have to get on to them. Let's hope they're co-operative,' Elaine added.

Beverley looked shocked. 'Doesn't she buy from Paris? Or Rome?'

'She doesn't even buy from *us*, my dear,' Elaine said scathingly. 'To say she is conservative is the understatement of the century. Nevertheless, she is the Queen of England and I want us to have some sort of an exclusive over our rivals. Here's a list of her favourite designers in London. There's Hardy Amies and Hartnell . . . and Rayne who make her shoes . . . perhaps they'll let you reproduce some of their original sketches, and then we might be able to put in a photograph of her next to it, in the actual outfit.'

'It's a great idea.' Beverley was thrilled by the assignment. It was something she could really get her teeth into. 'How long do we have?' she enquired.

'The Queen is coming over here in October, so you've got eight weeks in which to assemble everything and write your piece. Then we'll leave space for shots of her while she's here. I want it to be in the Christmas issue.' Elaine started piling up the various photographs of the British Royal Family on her desk, and handing them to Beverley. 'Let me know how you get on. Did I tell you I've had some very nice artwork done to go with your name at the top of your column?'

Beverley looked mystified. She'd expected the heading to be 'Lady Amesbury's Fashion Folder', as they'd first agreed.

'What's it like?' she asked, curiously.

Elaine didn't bat an eyelid as she spoke. 'I looked up Anthony's family in *Debrett's* and we're using his family's coat-of-arms in pale blue as a background to your article each month. We'll be doing a full spread, including pictures, and your copy will run to a thousand words. At the top there'll be a Viscount's coronet, and in big italic lettering which is called "Palace Script" we're putting "Viscountess Amesbury's Viewpoint". Isn't that great?' She gave an ingenuous smile and the scarlet of her lips against the paleness of her skin looked like rubies laid on white satin.

Beverley's eyebrows shot up and she winced inwardly. Trust Elaine to embellish everything with a layer of vulgarity. But as she well knew titles fascinated people. She just hoped Anthony and his family weren't going to mind too much.

'I also want you and Anthony to attend these functions,' Elaine continued, handing her some gilt-edged formal-looking invitations. 'I expect he has his own tuxedo, but you're going to need some new evening dresses. Get them at Bergdorf's, and have the bill sent to *Chichi*.' She smiled again, and Beverley was reminded of Henry referring to Elaine as a White Witch. 'If you're out and about representing *Chichi* as a titled lady, you must look the part,' she added. 'Just don't get anything in white or cream, dear. That's my colour.' Then she rose, bringing their meeting to an end.

Clutching everything, Beverley went back to her own office, wondering how Anthony was going to feel about attending parties with her as a representative of *Chichi*. Flicking through the invitations, she saw they'd been asked to attend a 'Summer Dance' at the Metropolitan Museum of Art, a benefit ball at the Waldorf-Astoria, a gala dinner at the Grant Hyatt Hotel, to honour a former Harvard University President, and the 'Ball of the Year' at the Pierre Hotel. And that was just for the coming week!

Settling at her desk to get on with her work, she was immersed in photographs of the British Royal Family when the phone on her desk purred into life.

'*Chichi*, Editorial Department,' she said automatically.

There was silence on the line but it was a tense silence and she knew instinctively who it was.

'Hello?' She tried to keep her voice steady.

After a moment there was a click. The caller had hung up. Beverley replaced the receiver wondering when Mary would call again.

Beverley awoke with such a splitting headache, she couldn't lift her head off the pillow. Every bone in her body seemed to ache and she felt nauseous.

'You've got a migraine,' Anthony said. 'Lie still, and I'll nip down to the drug store and get you something for it.'

'But I don't get migraine,' she whispered. Even the sound of her own voice seemed to jar, and the light streaming through their bedroom almost blinded her. 'Could you close the curtains, love?' she begged.

'That's definitely a migraine,' he affirmed. 'Acute pain, intolerance to light or sound, and feeling sick.'

She nodded, and then winced at having made the movement. 'I want to die. You'll have to call *Chichi* and say I won't be in today.'

'Poor baby.' He stroked her hair gently. 'I'll be as quick as I can. Keep your eyes shut and don't move.'

'I couldn't if I wanted to.' Damn Mary, she thought miserably. She's to blame for this. For the past six weeks Beverley had been getting anonymous calls at her office, and the strain was getting to her. Mary was also phoning Anthony at his office, but she always asked for him by name, and was quite happy to say who was calling. Anthony, however, never took the calls, instructing his secretary to say he was unavailable.

He'd only been caught once when Mary had called late one evening while he was still at his desk. His secretary had gone home, and without thinking he picked up the phone.

'Anthony, why will you never talk to me?' It was Mary's voice, pleading and tearful. 'Why can't we meet and talk, if nothing else?'

Anthony gathered his wits about him as quickly as he could. The fact he was dealing with someone who was monomaniacal made him feel he had to go easy on her.

'You know that's not possible, Mary,' he replied.

'But why not? I need to see you, Anthony. I love you and I want to be with you. Is that too much to ask?'

'Mary,' he reasoned gently. 'You know there has never been anything between us, and that I'm now a married man. It wouldn't be fair on you or on Beverley if we were to meet.'

She went on pleading and coaxing for several more minutes until Anthony said he had to go. With that he said goodbye and replaced the receiver. Then he took the receiver off the hook.

For a while, Anthony remained at his desk, wondering what the hell to do. This constant pursual was unnerving and troublesome and at times scary. Mary had informed his secretary several times that she was 'going after Beverley', and that Anthony should be made to realise Mary would 'get her' sooner or later. He'd even thought of taking out an injunction to prohibit Mary from contacting either Beverley or himself, but the problem was nobody knew where she was living. She wasn't with her family in Detroit and they'd heard nothing for weeks, and she wasn't living in her New York apartment either. Faye had tried to get hold of her through mutual friends, but without success. Even Pamela and John Hanworth had no idea where she was. It seemed that Mary must be hiding out at some secret address, hell bent on making Beverley's and Anthony's lives a misery.

'She's got some savings,' Faye had told them, 'so she'll be all right for money for the time being.'

Trying to put Mary out of his mind, though it was getting increasingly difficult, Anthony hurried to the drugstore on Lexington. A white-coated pharmacist came forward and he described Beverley's symptoms.

'You say your wife doesn't usually get migraine?'

'I don't think she's ever had one before. She said the pain in her head is dreadful.'

'Umm.' The pharmacist tapped his teeth with the pencil and looked thoughtful. 'I don't want to suggest anything that might harm her if it isn't a migraine she's got,' he said.

Anthony looked alarmed. 'What else could it be? Just a bad headache, you mean?'

'Not necessarily. Lots of things can begin with a severe headache. And a migraine shouldn't be making her ache all over. Has she got backache, d'you know?' He had a kindly face but he made Anthony nervous.

'She's been under a lot of pressure in the last month or so,' he explained anxiously. 'A lot of stress . . . that could cause a migraine, couldn't it?'

'Could be.' The pharmacist sounded non-committal. 'I'll give you something for her. Nothing too strong in case it does more harm than good.' He turned to go into the dispensary, and Anthony stood gazing unseeingly at a large display of toothpaste. What other illnesses started with aches and pain and a splitting head? Flu? Polio? Meningitis? A brain tumour? By the time the pharmacist returned, Anthony was on the brink of panicking.

'Should I get her to a doctor?' he asked, his voice shaking.

'I'd wait and see how she is. If she's worse tomorrow, then it might be wise. In any case, see she has lots of fluids. Has she got a fever?'

Anthony started. He hadn't thought of fevers! 'I don't know. How shall I find out? Should I get a thermometer?'

'No. I wouldn't worry about that at this stage.'

Anthony paid for the medication, wishing he felt more reassured, and then he rushed back to the apartment.

Beverley was in the bathroom being sick when he got back. Cold darts of fear shot through him, leaving him cold.

'Is there anything I can get you, love?' he asked her anxiously. Her face was a delicate shade of green, and she was clutching her head. When she stood up, she seemed to reel dizzily, almost colliding with the bathroom door. Anthony put his arms around her, and half carried her into the bedroom next door.

'I'll be all right in a minute,' she said weakly. 'Could I have some water?'

Propping her up with pillows, because she said her head throbbed more when she was lying flat, he fetched her a glass of iced water, and then sat holding her hand as she swallowed the pills he'd bought for her.

'Shouldn't you be going to work?' she whispered after a while. She felt guilty at keeping him by her side and yet she felt so ill she dreaded being left alone.

'I'm not going in today,' he said softly. 'I'm going to stay with you, and maybe take you to a doctor, to see what's wrong.'

The ghost of her usual smile crossed her face. 'That's nice . . . your staying home, but I'm sure I don't need to see a doctor. I'll be okay once these pills work.'

'I'd still like you to be checked over if you're no better by tomorrow,' Anthony said firmly. As she lay with her eyes closed, and her mouth drooping at the corners, he stroked her cheek. She was warm but he didn't think she had a fever.

'You try and sleep while I make some calls,' he whispered. Then he phoned their local grocery store and gave a large order for provisions to be delivered later in the day, before calling a nearby florist and asking them to send round two dozen long-stemmed pink roses. After a while, he tiptoed back into their bedroom. Beverley still looked ill and wan, but she gave him a little smile as he sat down carefully on the edge of the bed.

'Are you all right, love?' she asked him. 'We need to get in some food and milk . . .' Her voice trailed off as her head pounded with the effort of speaking. Anthony took her hand and squeezed it.

'Everything's under control,' he whispered. 'How are you doing?'

'I suppose I'll live,' she said, her expression wry. Her chestnut hair clung to her temples and there were blue smudges under her eyes. 'Thank God for one thing, anyway.'

'What's that?'

'Our phone number isn't listed,' she replied.

He looked at her thoughtfully, wondering what to do to help relieve the stress she was suffering. 'Why don't we go away for a few days?' he suggested, at last. 'We could do with a break.'

'Do you think we could?' she asked, brightening a little. 'Somewhere really quiet. Just the two of us.'

'I'll fix it,' he promised, taking her gently in his arms. Beverley rested her throbbing head against his shoulder and closed her eyes. Anthony held her close, hating to see her like this, all her sparkle quenched and her usual cheerfulness diminished. He hated the idea, even more, that Mary might be the cause.

The next morning Beverley was no better. She awoke

at six o'clock, the pain in her head making her reach for the pills Anthony had bought yesterday. She felt nauseous again, too, and Anthony became seriously worried.

'I'm taking you to the doctor. You can't go on like this.'

'I'll be all right,' she said bravely. 'I'm sure it will pass. It did yesterday. By the evening I felt fairly okay, didn't I?'

'I still think you should have a check-up. If this were England, of course, you wouldn't have to get dressed and go to some office. Our private doctors pay house calls.' He sounded disgruntled.

Beverley looked up, amazed. 'They come to your home?'

'Of course. You only go to a surgery if you're well enough, or for a routine check-up. Doctors come and visit you any time of the night or day in England, if you're too sick to go out.'

'What a luxury,' Beverley sighed, getting out of bed very slowly, because any sudden movement made her feel as if pounding hammers were attacking her skull.

They took a cab to the doctor's office, having phoned to make an appointment first. The receptionist told them Dr Ronald Draycott would examine Beverley in a few minutes. He'd looked after Anthony when he'd sprained an ankle playing squash the previous year, and Anthony knew him to be a young go-ahead doctor, with a sense of humour.

At last Beverley heard the receptionist say her name.

'Dr Draycott will see you now, Lady Amesbury.'

'Thank you.' Feeling sick again, she walked slowly and carefully into the doctor's consulting room while Anthony waited in reception.

Five minutes passed. Then ten. When fifteen minutes had gone by, Anthony's sense of panic reasserted itself. There must be something seriously wrong for the doctor to take so long. What the hell was he doing? Anthony tried to concentrate on a copy of the *New Yorker* but the print danced before his eyes and his hands started shaking at the thought that there might really be something seriously wrong with Beverley.

When she at last appeared, looking quite calm, Anthony sprang to his feet, anxiety written in every line of his face. He looked at the doctor inquiringly.

'Is my wife all right?' he blurted out.

'Your wife's fine.' Draycott spoke in a matter-of-fact voice. 'I suggest she rests for a few days, but basically she's a very healthy young woman.'

Anthony looked searchingly at him. 'Is it a migraine?'

'Why don't you ask her yourself?' the doctor suggested. He was smiling.

Then Beverly thanked him gravely, and Anthony noticed there was a sudden glow in her cheeks.

'What is it?' he asked.

Beverley hugged his arm and when she looked up at him he saw her eyes were sparkling, the gold flecks glinting in the sunlight that streamed through the surgery window.

'I'm pregnant.'

'You're . . . ?' His eyes widened and then he flung his arms around her. 'Darling, that's wonderful!' he exclaimed. 'That's the most marvellous news I've ever heard! And I've been so worried about you! God, I can't believe it!'

'Neither can I,' she said in a choked voice. She was so happy she didn't know whether to laugh or cry. It had never occurred to her that she'd get pregnant so easily.

Or so quickly. 'Isn't it amazing?' she gasped.

'It's wonderful.' Anthony was looking so pleased it touched her deeply. And he was hugging her still, right there in the middle of the reception area, much to the amusement of the secretary who was pretending not to notice.

'Now I'm going to take you home,' he continued, 'and when you're feeling better, we'll open a bottle of champagne to celebrate. How does that grab you?'

Beverley looked up into his eyes. 'You're a miracle man, aren't you? And do you know something?'

'Lots of things.' He was grinning and deep laughter lines fanned out from around his eyes. 'What in particular did you have in mind?'

'I was thinking that I'm very lucky to be married to you!'

He pretended to preen in a conceited fashion. 'Oh, I know!' he said loftily. Then at the same moment they both remembered Mary and their expressions sobered immediately.

'Yes,' Beverley said seriously. 'I *am* lucky, very lucky,' and for a moment she felt quite sorry for Mary. She had everything Mary had ever wanted. Anthony and the love they shared. A baby on the way. A beautiful home. Enough money between them on which to live comfortably, and for what it was worth, a noble title. But had Mary really wanted all these things or was she the victim of her own obsessive love for a man she could never have? The two things were different; one the reality and the other a fantasy. She was lucky in having the flesh and bone reality, while Mary was still chasing something that had never existed for her in the first place, an illusion, a phantom. But people who believed in a creation of their own mind were dangerous because they couldn't tell the difference between that and the real thing.

Chapter Eight

By the following April, Beverley had turned the spare room into a nursery. The baby was due in the middle of May, and her excitement as the time drew near was reaching fever pitch. If she saw a baby or a small child in the supermarket or in its buggy in the street, her heart squeezed with longing. The tiny star-shaped hands, the small button mouth, the soft folds of a little neck, made her ache to hold her own baby in her arms. For the first time she could understand the longing of a childless woman who was driven to steal babies. Meanwhile, she'd had the nursery painted pale primrose yellow, and had bought some transfers of Bambi, Dumbo and Donald Duck and stuck them on the pretty white chest of drawers and cupboard they'd bought. Anthony had come home with a white rocking chair one day, and she'd made yellow cushions for it. Now all was in readiness. Rachael had been knitting for months, and all the tiny garments were arranged and waiting. A bassinet, with a little white muslin canopy, stood ready in the corner, and already there was a selection of furry animals and toys arranged on a shelf.

They'd decided to postpone their visit to England until the following year, when the baby would be old enough to travel, and now as they awaited its arrival, their evenings were spent leisurely, talking and listening to music, or watching television. It was the last time they would be entirely alone, probably for many years to come, and they were savouring each moment.

Elaine had asked Beverley to continue writing and compiling 'Viscountess Amesbury's Viewpoint' for *Chichi*, but for the next few months the regular staff of *Chichi* would put it together for her.

'I hope you will be able to continue the column,' Elaine stressed one morning, having summoned Beverley into her office. 'It is proving to be as big a success as I thought it would. Our circulation figures have gone up, and I want to build on this social-cum-fashion angle.'

'I'm glad you're pleased,' Beverley responded, smiling. She was feeling rather tired and heavy these days, and her back seemed to ache constantly. However, she didn't want to lose the column. The money she earned was paying for all the little extras that she and Anthony enjoyed so much, like going to concerts and the theatre, good wine for dinner, a visit to the occasional gourmet restaurant, and of course everything for the baby.

'I was wondering,' she said, 'if you'd like me to do one issue on children's clothes, as worn by the trend-setters' children, and maybe President Bush's grandchildren, and I could try and get hold of some aristocratic English children.'

Elaine thought for a moment, her scarlet lips pursed, her long pale hands fingering her pearls. 'We don't really feature children's clothes in *Chichi*, not even in the advertising, but I rather like the idea.' Suddenly she brightened. 'Could you get photographs of the Queen of England's grandchildren? That might be interesting.

"What the Royal Children are Wearing".' She nodded. 'Yes, I like it. Wait until your baby arrives, though. It gives more point to the feature if we feature your child, too. What will it be, by the way?'

Beverley looked taken aback. 'We don't know the sex,' she replied. 'Anthony and I decided we'd rather wait until it was born.'

Elaine shook her head impatiently, pearl drop earrings quivering.

'I mean will it be "Lord" or "Lady"? Surely the baby will have a title.'

'Oh! I see what you mean.' Beverley grinned. Elaine's obsession with titles never abated. 'Either he or she will be "The Honourable".'

Elaine's face was a study. 'Only The Honourable?' she said, not even trying to hide her disappointment. 'I thought a boy might be a Lord or a little girl "Lady Rose" or something?' Her finely pencilled eyebrows arched questioningly.

'Only an Honourable, I'm afraid!' Beverley laughed.

'And never anything more? Your children won't succeed to a higher title later on?' she persisted.

Beverley shook her head. 'When my brother-in-law Henry has a son, he will be the next heir. Anthony is the younger brother, and that's as far as it goes on our side. Honourable is only a courtesy title, anyway.'

Highly amused, and leaving Elaine deflated, Beverley returned to her own office, glad that she only had a few more weeks of pregnancy to go. She'd had an easy eight months, after a bad beginning, but was getting tired very easily these days while sleeping was very difficult as she tried to find a comfortable position.

'At least it's cool,' Anthony pointed out. 'It wouldn't

have been much fun for you if it had been high summer with temperatures in the nineties.'

'Don't even talk about it!' Beverley begged. 'Never let me be pregnant during a hot summer in New York, will you?'

He smiled at her roguishly. 'I'll try to comply with your request!' he said with mock solemnity. 'But I can't always curb my natural impulses, you know!'

'And I should hope not, too!'

As the days dissolved one into another, Beverley became more dreamy and Anthony teased her about her increasing vagueness. She didn't care, though. She'd never been so happy or contented in her life. She only went to the offices of *Chichi* two mornings a week now, to select photographs and decide which socialite to feature in the coming issues, otherwise her time was her own. It seemed that Mary, too, had grown tired of phoning them at their offices during the day, for the number of calls had dwindled and it was several months since either of them had heard from her. Beverley began to hope that her ex-boss had got over her monomania and that they would never hear from her again.

It was cool and fresh on the afternoon when Beverley decided to go to Saks to do some last minute shopping for the baby. In spite of a chest filled with Babygrows, and enough little vests and knitted matinee jackets to clothe a dozen babies, no one had given them a shawl. Beverley yearned for something soft and lacy and warm in which to wrap her child.

Saks was fairly empty when she got there, and walking through the brightly lit elegant ground-floor department, she decided to go up to the eighth floor on the escalator. It always amused her to ride up past the other departments and catch a glimpse of the gorgeous clothes and evening dresses on display. She could hardly wait to get back in the slim-fitting suits she normally wore. The novelty of being pregnant, so exciting at first that she'd wanted to wear voluminous wrap-over dresses from the first month just to show the world her condition, had long since passed. As the gleaming silver escalator glided up past racks of nipped-in-waist dresses and mini-skirts, she longed to lose her bulge.

The delights of the baby department soon made her forget her own uncomfortable bulkiness. One could get carried away, she realised, with all the enchanting infant clothes that were available. If she were to have a dozen children, she could still find something pretty for them to wear.

The shawls were either white or in pastel shades and she was toying with the choice of either buying one in a powder blue soft as thistledown or a gossamer pale pink, when she looked up and caught her reflection in a full-length mirror. She was glad she'd recently had her hair cut shorter. It looked good and fell to her shoulders, gleaming with glossy condition. Her face didn't look so bad either; she'd felt she was getting a bit puffy around the jaw line, but with carefully applied make-up she realised she looked good.

In the second it took to glance at her reflection, her eyes swept down towards her bulky shape and heavily pregnant stomach . . . but she was very slim. Beverley blinked, confused for a second . . . the woman in the mirror wasn't pregnant at all! She started and blinked again . . . and realised the reflection wasn't pregnant *because it wasn't her*. And yet it was. The same colour of hair, shortened as hers was. The same pale skin and the coral-pink lipstick she always wore . . . the same small gold hoop earrings which had become like her signature . . . the trim dark green suit . . .

Beverley stumbled against the counter, gripping it to prevent herself falling because her legs had suddenly become weak and numb. In a moment she was going to be sick or faint.

'A chair . . .' she gasped, but no one heard her. A smart young assistant was speaking brightly, looking past her to the figure beyond.

'There you are, Lady Amesbury.' She was carrying a large Saks shopping bag, which looked as if it contained a dress box. 'Thank you very much. Have a nice day.'

Beverley forced herself forward, willed herself not to lose control. Her mind was spinning and she was gripped by a sense of unreality.

'That's not Lady Amesbury,' she heard herself say, surprising herself by how loud her voice was. 'She's an impostor!'

The assistant looked startled, and Beverley faced the woman who was not her reflection in the mirror at all, but who stood defiantly looking back at her from a few yards away.

'Mary, goddammit! Will you stop this!' she shouted. Beverley felt unnerved and shocked at seeing Mary transformed into her look-alike. The mousey brown hair had been dyed to exactly the same shade as hers and cut short, too. Had Mary been watching her, spying on what she was doing, all these months? She looked closer. The pale skin tone was not natural like hers, but the result of a light foundation. The suit was her style. The earrings an exact copy. Mary continued to watch her, translucent grey eyes staring like a cat.

For a split second Beverly wondered if she was going mad. What the hell was happening? Perhaps she was really Mary? Pregnant, puffy-faced and plain? And the elegant creature who stood before her, being addressed as 'Lady Amesbury', was really Beverley?

'Are you all right, madam?' the assistant asked, in concern. She was looking from one woman to the other with a puzzled expression.

'I'd like to sit down,' Beverley said faintly, feeling hot and sick again. A chair was produced, and the assistant helped her.

'I'll get you a glass of water, madam,' she murmured solicitously and rushed away, calling another assistant to help.

Beverley looked at Mary. 'Why are you doing this?'

'Anthony is mine,' she replied dully. 'The tarot cards have always said so. He belongs to me.'

'You know that's not true,' Beverley defended herself hotly. 'Why won't you accept the fact that there was never anything between you and Anthony in the first place?'

Mary raised her chin, and held the Saks shopping bag tightly in her hand. 'You're lying,' she said calmly. 'I'm expecting Anthony's baby, and I've been buying baby clothes. I'm well known here. Everyone knows I'm really Lady Amesbury. I don't know who you think you are, but you certainly have no right to Anthony.'

Beverley's eyes widened in fear. The woman was insane. Crazy. There was a wildness in her eyes now, such a demented expression of fanatical belief that Beverley experienced a sharp stab of fear.

Struggling heavily to her feet, she tried to attract the attention of one of the other assistants but Mary grabbed her arm. Her fingers were icy and her grip was like a clamp.

'Die!' Mary whispered savagely. 'I hope you're going to die!' She glared threateningly into Beverley's eyes, and the two women, looking as alike as sisters, stood for a moment glaring at each other with the unnatural stillness of shop window dummies. Then Mary turned and hurried away.

'Stop her!' Beverley called out as the first assistant, holding a glass of water, came briskly back. She paused, confused, and glanced at Mary's retreating back view.

'For God's sake, stop her going! Catch her!' she shouted, trying to hurry forward herself, but she was too slow and the shop assistant didn't seem to understand what was going on.

'Here's a nice glass of water, madam, and you'll soon feel better,' she crooned soothingly.

Beverley sank back onto the chair. It was no good. Mary had gone, vanished in the direction of the elevators, and it looked as if the assistant had no intention of going after her.

'Had a quarrel with your sister, have you?' the girl asked sympathetically. 'Never mind. Have a little water and you'll soon feel better.'

'I came in to buy a baby's shawl,' said Beverley numbly. 'And that woman . . . has she been here before? Why did you call her "Lady Amesbury"?'

'She *is* Lady Amesbury. She's bought quite a lot of baby clothes over the last few months. I could see they weren't for her . . . if you see what I mean. Was she buying them for your baby?'

Beverley shook her head. 'She's an impostor. She hasn't got a charge card here in that name, has she?' she added in sudden alarm.

'I don't think she can have because she always pays cash. I thought it was strange, a titled lady and all that, not having a charge card account, or any plastic either, but as long as she paid ... well, it's got nothing to do with me, has it? Now what can I get you? Were you interested in one of those shawls? They're beautifully soft, and we have them in ...'

'No, thank you. I've changed my mind.' Beverley finished the water and rose. 'Thank you,' she added, 'I have to go.'

'You're welcome.' The assistant was obviously puzzled by what had happened, but she saw no need to report it to the buyer of the department. Nobody had shop lifted, and the first lady had paid in cash for her purchase. Apart from some sort of a quarrel between two women who looked like sisters, there was really nothing to report anyway.

Beverley rolled on to her back, gazing up at the darkness of their bedroom, wondering if she ought to awaken Anthony. Shortly after midnight she'd felt a moment's tugging backache, just as she was dropping off to sleep. It had passed after a few moments, but a little while later it had come back again, and now she'd had it several times, and each time it seemed stronger. Could it be the baby arriving? She'd never associated acute backache with the first signs of childbirth, but she'd never had this deep pulling pain before either.

She turned back on to her side, deciding to wait a bit. There was no point in waking up Anthony if it was a false alarm. They'd been late going to bed, as they stayed up talking about Mary, and she knew he had to be up for an early meeting in the morning.

Another pain, even sharper this time, made her catch

her breath, and as if he sensed something, Anthony awoke. Stretching out his hand, he stroked her stomach.

'Are you all right, sweetheart?' he whispered.

'I think so,' she said doubtfully. 'It's just bad backache.'

'Turn around and I'll give you a rub.' He switched on the bedside lamp and, kneeling behind her, started to massage the small of her back with strong but gentle hands.

'Ummm . . .' she mumbled appreciatively. 'That feels good.'

Moving his thumbs in a circular motion, up and down her spine, he was rewarded by little grunts of pleasure from her.

'Oh, that feels so good, love.'

'Do you think you can get back to sleep now?' Anthony asked, after a while.

She rolled towards him, snuggling as close to him as her bulk would allow. 'I haven't been to sleep yet.'

'Are you worrying about Mary?'

'Yeah. It was such a shock . . .' Beverley's voice drifted off as another shaft of pain caught her unawares.

'I bet it was.' They lay in the darkness, holding hands, each immersed in their own thoughts. To Beverley, a woman who impersonated her in every detail, calling herself Anthony's wife and pretending to be pregnant, was an absolute certifiable nut-case. Mary had obviously got to the stage when she actually believed herself to be Anthony's wife too. The creepy thing was the realisation that she must be watching their every move; how else did she know Beverley had recently cut her hair, for example?

Anthony, lying beside her, had more practical

thoughts. Maybe they should take out a court order to stop Mary contacting them? Or get hold of her parents again, and tell them they had to come to New York to find her, so that she could be put into psychiatric care? It wasn't a police matter, he reflected. So far Mary hadn't swindled anyone, and her taunts today to Beverley had been purely verbal so they had no grounds for accusing her of assault. And yet she was beginning to make their lives a misery and Anthony was aware it was affecting Beverley more than it was affecting him. And she was very vulnerable at this time too, he thought.

'Ah-h-h!'

Startled, he turned on the bedside lamp again. Beverley was lying on her side facing him, and she looked scared.

'I've just had a bad pain. I think it is the baby,' she whispered.

'Do you want me to take you to Doctor's Hospital yet?' He was already out of bed, standing anxiously over her.

'I don't know. What do you think?'

'How often are the pains coming?' Anthony had attended natural childbirth classes with her, but now that it had come to the point, he didn't feel like hanging around. The sooner she was in the hands of the experts the better, as far as he was concerned.

'I think about every five minutes,' Beverley replied.

'Then let's get going. I'd rather we arrived too soon than too late,' he added with feeling.

He helped her dress and then slipped into his own clothes. A small case stood ready packed. Seizing it, he took her arm, and together they left the apartment and went to the elevator.

'I wish we had a car,' he fretted as they waited for the lift to arrive.

'Cars are more trouble than they're worth in New York,' Beverley pointed out. 'We'll get a cab quite easily.'

Anthony fervently hoped so. When they arrived in the lobby, he made her sit and wait with the night porter while he went into the street to get a taxi. He was sweating now and his heart was pounding. If the baby started arriving ... or anything happened to Beverley! He breathed deeply to stop himself panicking, but when he saw a vacant yellow cab cruising along the road a minute later, he felt such a rush of relief that he jumped forward, arms outstretched, waving his hands and calling: 'Taxi' in a very loud and very English voice.

When they arrived at Doctor's Hospital, they were directed to the maternity section where the nurse on night duty looked very surprised when they told her who they were and why they'd come.

'You didn't phone us to say you were on your way, did you, Lady Amesbury?' she asked accusingly. 'Have you phoned your own obstetrician?'

'I'm sorry ...' Beverley began, but Anthony interrupted.

'It's my fault, nurse. I'm terribly sorry.' He was turning on all his charm now, and to Beverley's amusement, she could see the starchy nurse melting under the influence of his boyish smile. 'This is our first baby, nurse, and I'm anxious about my wife. I was so afraid the baby might come more quickly than expected.'

The nurse smiled, relenting. Then she took them along a polished corridor smelling of antiseptic and into a small square room with a high hospital bed and some basic furnishing. The only cheerful thing about the room were the floral chintz curtains.

'Get undressed and into bed and the resident doctor will be along to see you in a few minutes,' she said briskly. Then she eyed Beverley up and down. 'I don't think that baby of yours will be arriving for some hours, though.'

'You don't?' Another contraction had just passed and she looked aghast. The pains were bad enough now. If the baby wasn't due for some time yet, how much worse would they get?

'You'll be fine, sweetheart.' Anthony was reassuring.

With a swish of starch and a squeak of sensible black lace-up shoes on the polished floor, the nurse left the room and Beverley started to undress quickly, longing to lie down before the next contraction came.

Almost immediately she went rigid, clutching Anthony's hand as another pain, deeper and stronger this time, took possession of her body.

'I . . . I can't bear it!' she cried. 'Get them to give me something.'

She was scarlet in the face, and her eyes looked blood-shot and panic-stricken.

Anthony looked around wildly. He didn't dare leave her alone in the sterile little room and yet he couldn't bear to see her suffer like this. Then he saw the bell, by the side of the bed, and pressed it hard.

'Hold on, sweetheart,' he begged as she started to cry. 'Remember the breathing exercises? Let's do them together.'

'No, Anthony . . . Oh, my God, here's another one . . .' Her words were cut short as another pain swept through her, sucking the breath out of her body, causing her head to spin and her eyes to prickle with pins and needles. 'Ah-h-h-h!' A wail burst from her open mouth and her nails dug deeply into his hand.

'Pant!' he urged her, trying to keep his own voice steady. 'Pant . . . like this.' He released the air from his lungs in short sharp bursts. 'Like this, sweetheart! Like this!' he urged.

As the wave of pain subsided, she whispered: 'I can't take any more . . . I feel I'm being split in two . . . oh, Jesus! Do something . . . do something!' Then she screamed again, reminding him of a wounded animal.

The contractions seemed to be only moments apart now, coming one on top of the other, in wave after wave, and he was enormously relieved when the door opened and the doctor appeared, accompanied by the nurse.

'Can you give her something?' Anthony asked immediately. 'She's really suffering.' He felt so wretched, standing there unable to do anything to help her, and he prayed the doctor would give her something to knock her out while he delivered the baby.

'Let's see what's going on, shall we?' the doctor asked Beverley. He was totally relaxed and his voice was laid back. Exuding a comfortable air of confidence, his presence was reassuring.

Anthony sat by the head of the bed while he examined Beverley, making happy little humming noises as he did so. He had four children of his own and he'd delivered hundreds of babies. As far as he was concerned, it was a joyful natural occurrence and no big deal.

Another contraction enveloped Beverley, making her cry out again, but when it had passed, the doctor spoke admiringly.

'You're doing very well, little lady. You haven't got

210

far to go before you get to the next stage. Try and hang in there a little longer, and then things will ease up, okay?' He spoke so kindly she opened her eyes for a moment and looked at him gratefully.

'How much longer?' she said in a small voice.

'Only a little while,' he replied easily. Then he turned to Anthony. 'It would help your wife if you supported her shoulders when the time comes. Then she can lean against you when she pushes. All right?'

Anthony nodded, thankful Beverley was now in good hands. The hospital had contacted Beverley's obstetrician, but it looked as if the baby might arrive before he did.

Suddenly things started to happen. He was being helped into a gown and cap, while Beverley was transferred to a trolley to be taken to the delivery room. Two more nurses appeared and as they all hurried down the corridor, Anthony managed to keep hold of Beverley's hand.

'You're doing fine,' the doctor told her cheerfully. When they wheeled her into the large clinical delivery room, Anthony sensed a heightening of tension in the atmosphere.

'Okay, now, Lady Amesbury,' the doctor told her jovially. 'Time for some hard work! You've had a good rest, just lying there doing nothing. Now you've got a job to do! I want you to start pushing in a minute.'

Anthony stared at him, appalled by what seemed to be total lack of sensitivity, but Beverley gave a watery grin and chuckled faintly. The doctor seemed to have the knack of relaxing and reassuring her with his kindly briskness and to Anthony's relief she seemed less fraught now.

The activity in the delivery room stepped up apace as

the nurses fitted Beverley's feet into stirrups and fixed handles on either side of the bed for her to grip. Then they told Anthony to stand by her head, supporting her shoulders. She'd started to cry out in pain again, wrenching screams that were torn from her lungs as she entered the final stages of labour.

'Push! Push!' the doctor commanded. 'Come on, now!'

'I . . . c-can't,' Beverley sobbed.

'Yes, you can. You're doing fine. Next time I tell you to push, give it everything you've got.'

'It's too big . . . I'll never do it,' she wailed, and then as another crashing pain seared through her, she screamed again, and the doctor and nurses commanded: 'Push! Push! That's it! Push harder!' Anthony, feeling sick, wondered how much longer he could bear to watch her suffering like this. It was inhuman. On the farm at Bucklands they wouldn't have let an animal suffer like this.

'Can't you give her something?' he demanded, turning to the doctor, his face pale and sweating. 'A painkiller or something, for God's sake?'

'She's doing fine,' the doctor replied mildly. 'The head has already engaged. It won't be long now.'

'No! No!' Beverley moaned, gripping the handles so tightly the bones of her hands showed through the flesh. 'Stop it coming!' she begged. 'I can't do it . . . it's too big . . . please! Oh, God, please!'

'You're doing great. Come on now. Here we go again. Push! Push!'

On a sobbing gasping breath Beverley pushed until the veins stood out like cords in her neck and her face was scarlet. Holding her shoulders, Anthony supported her as best he knew how. He felt her body tense as she strained down while the nurses made encouraging noises.

'You're nearly there,' the doctor exclaimed. He sounded both excited and pleased. Then he glanced at Anthony with a look of comradeship. They were all in this together; Beverley, Anthony, the doctor and the nurses, all helping to bring into the world a new baby and a new life any minute now. It was a moment of intense emotion.

As another pain overwhelmed Beverley, the doctor spoke commandingly again. 'Push now! Yes . . . come on . . . come on. Push . . . hard . . . harder!'

Anthony felt the prick of tears behind his eyes as he bent over Beverley's shoulder, his cheek almost touching hers. She was in such unbelievable agony and he wished there was something he could do to help her, but she was beyond his help now, beyond his reach. Fighting with the pain which was much worse than either of them had expected, she screamed as she strained and he swore he'd never let her go through this again. One baby would be enough. It would have to be. He couldn't let her endure this agony ever again.

Suddenly she stopped screaming and to his disbelieving ears the sound was taken up by a fainter noise, a thin reedy wail that rose to a little gulping hiccup.

'It's a boy,' Anthony heard the doctor say, holding up the slippery little red creature, and then the tears were streaming down Anthony's cheeks and he was gripping Beverley's shoulders tightly.

'Well done, sweetheart,' he said, his voice choked.

Beverley was crying too, but they were tears of happiness and weakness as she leaned back, gasping and sobbing.

213

'Is he all right?'

'He's perfect!' the doctor assured her. 'We're just going to cut the cord and weigh him, and then he's all yours.'

'Eight pounds, four ounces,' one of the nurses announced triumphantly a few moments later. 'A nice big baby.'

'You surprise me!' Beverley remarked sarcastically, but she was laughing too, her normal resilience flooding back. When the baby was placed in her arms, she looked at him wonderingly. And then she looked at Anthony. Already she could see the likeness. The baby had gold blond hair, and the same features, in miniature, as his father.

'He's beautiful,' she said softly, holding him close to her breast. Anthony, leaning over them both, reached out to touch one of the tiny hands, and was rewarded by little pink fingers wrapping themselves around his finger.

'Look at that!' he gasped.

For several minutes they regarded their offspring with a mixture of amazement and tenderness. When he opened his eyes, blue like Anthony's, Beverley gave a little crow.

'Oh, I love him,' she said impulsively. 'He's absolutely gorgeous.'

'He's wonderful,' Anthony agreed, his voice filled with awe.

'I think you should rest now,' the doctor said firmly. 'We'll wheel you back to your own room, while Junior has a nice bath to clean him up.'

'I do rather feel as if I've been shifting boulders,' Beverley admitted.

'You have,' was his prompt reply as he left the room grinning.

'I'll phone your family while you're sleeping,' Anthony said, kissing her again before he left.

'Give them my love.'

'I will. And I'll be back later.'

'Anthony . . .'

'Yes, sweetheart?'

'I love you. And I love Junior, too.'

He kissed her again. 'And I love both of you,' he whispered.

A pearly pink dawn was breaking over New York as he returned to the apartment and the chill morning air was good and fresh to breathe. Too excited to sleep, he made strong black coffee and then watched from the kitchen window as the skyscrapers turned to pale gold and the mists of the night cleared, revealing a clear blue sky.

A son. They'd got a son. He smiled. Nicholas James Amesbury. Welcome to the world. This is the first day of your life. Silently he toasted his son. If the baby had been a girl they'd been going to call her Charlotte.

Anthony's smile deepened. Maybe next time. Beverley's miraculous recovery once she'd given birth made him realise that of course they'd have more children. But meanwhile they had Nicholas. The most beautiful little boy in the world. He glanced at his wristwatch. No matter what the time was, it was never too early to call up Rachael and Daniel and tell them their first grandchild had been born.

At lunchtime, Anthony returned to the hospital. He'd showered and shaved, put on one of his best suits, and was laden with flowers, a bottle of champagne, a large

215

blue teddy bear he'd bought that morning at F. A. O. Schwartz and a special present for Beverley.

He found her sitting up in bed, looking very perky in one of the white lawn and lace nightdresses she'd bought for her honeymoon, her auburn hair held back with a white satin ribbon.

'Hi, there!' she greeted him in a stage whisper. Then she indicated the hospital bassinet by the side of her bed. 'Guess what?' She was like a little girl with a new toy. 'He's just had his first feed and he's taken to it like a duck to water! He's fallen asleep now. Doesn't he look gorgeous?'

Anthony peered into the cradle and saw Nicholas tucked up on his side, eyes tightly shut, his mouth still going through a sucking motion.

'Is he still hungry?'

Beverley giggled. 'Babies always do that. He's probably dreaming he's feeding.' Then she held out her arms to Anthony and he went to her with loving wonder. Tenderly they kissed.

'I have something for you,' he whispered. There were flowers on her lap, big beautiful pink roses, and champagne by her feet, and the blue teddy bear was propped on the pillow beside her, but Anthony reached into his pocket and withdrew a pale blue box tied with a narrow white satin ribbon.

'Tiffany?' she said, her eyes widening.

'Of course. Only the best for you, sweetheart. See if you like it.' Eagerly, he watched as she opened the box and found a small jewel case inside.

'What is it?' she asked, breathlessly.

He didn't answer but continued to grin as she opened it and saw, lying on a bed of cream velvet, a diamond pendant that very much resembled the design of the Georgian earrings his mother had given her.

'Anthony!' Overcome, she took it out with trembling hands, marvelling at the delicacy of the gold and platinum setting and the fine platinum chain from which the tear-shaped diamond, surrounded by tiny diamond scrolls, hung. Beverley looked at him, unable to speak for a moment. 'Oh!' she gasped. 'It's so beautiful . . . how did you find something that would go with the earrings? Oh, sweetheart!' She was in his arms again, laughing and crying and hugging him as if she could never bear to let him go.

A wail from the cot interrupted Anthony's kisses.

'I'm sure he's hungry again,' Anthony observed, as the baby tried to stuff his tiny fist into his mouth.

Beverley laughed, a joyous sound that filled the room. Then she picked Nicholas out of his crib and held him close. 'I think he wants a cuddle, just like his daddy,' she said. 'I'm going to have my work cut out at this rate.'

Beverley and Anthony decided to spend Christmas and the New Year with her family in Stockbridge, before flying to England in February for their long-promised visit to Henry and Leonora. Nicholas, nearly nine months old, was sitting, crawling, gurgling and grinning, a sunny child who slept soundly at night and played happily during the day in the care of Hayley, Faye's sister, to whom Beverley had given the job of baby-minder. Hayley, who lived with Faye in Beverley's old apartment, was a plump sensible young woman who preferred looking after children to working in an office.

'Can't we get a proper nanny, like Henry has for his daughter?' Anthony had asked at first, but Beverley quickly pointed out that their apartment wasn't big enough to have living-in help. It would be too expensive, too. Nannies demanded high wages and were very inflexible about having time off. In her heart of hearts the thought of a starchy uniformed nanny terrified her, and she eventually confided her fears to Anthony.

He threw back his head, laughing. 'Sweetheart, you wouldn't say that if you'd known my old nanny. She was marvellous: cosy, kind, nursed me through measles, and read aloud to me by the hour. No one could have been less intimidating.'

'But why didn't your mother look after you? She didn't work like I do, did she?'

Anthony shook his head. 'Everyone like us in England has a nanny.'

'By "like us", you mean aristocratic?'

'Not necessarily. Middle-class or monied people have nannies, too.' He smiled. It always amused him trying to explain the class system, because he really didn't understand its complexities himself. He took who he was for granted. He'd been born the second son of an Earl and had always lived in Bucklands Castle, and that, so far as he was concerned, was that. Someone once said, he remembered, that members of the aristocracy don't push for prominence or hustle to be noticed; they simply *are*. Thankfully, Beverley didn't seem as impressed by his title as most people, but there were some aspects of English upper-class life she found intriguing. Like the nanny business.

Working once again on *Chichi*, Beverley was quickly caught up in the world of fashionable women and their wardrobes. She'd also done the feature on the children of celebrities and what they wore, and of course Elaine had insisted Nicholas be photographed in a designer romper suit that Beverley thought was ridiculously expensive.

'We'll pay for it,' Elaine told her grandly. And so the picture had appeared: 'The Honourable Nicholas James Amesbury, son of Viscount and Viscountess Amesbury', and Beverley had sent it to her mother, who had shown it to half the population of Stockbridge.

'You must get photographs taken of all of you when you go to England,' Elaine instructed her one day. 'A family group with the castle in the background. You could have prints done and use it as your Christmas card next year,' she added, brightly.

Beverley shuddered. Elaine's ideas were getting more vulgar by the day. Ever since Princess Diana had attended *Chichi*'s fiftieth anniversary party, Elaine had become even more snobbish and at times it really got on Beverley's nerves.

She was looking forward to going to England in February, though. It would be particularly nice to see Henry again, but she was also longing to meet Leonora, and Anthony's mother, the Dowager Countess of Amesbury.

Rachael and Daniel Franklin wanted it to be a memorable Christmas for their family. How they were all going to squeeze into the little white clapboard house they didn't know, but Josh, home from Washington for the festivities, was going to share a room with Tom, so that Nicholas's cot could go into his room, while an extra bed had been borrowed from a neighbour to be put in Beverley's room for Anthony. It was going to be a cheek-by-jowl family get-together, with Jenny sleeping on the living-room sofa, but everyone was looking forward to it.

'Having a baby in the family makes such a difference,' Rachael kept saying, 'especially since it will be Nicholas's first Christmas.'

Daniel fixed a Christmas tree in a corner of the living room, and underneath it the gaily wrapped presents were stacked high, a large proportion of them labelled, not surprisingly, 'For Nicholas'.

'This is going to be one spoiled baby,' Beverley said, laughing, as they sat down to supper on Christmas Eve. Nicholas was sitting on his grandmother's lap, although he should have been in bed hours ago.

'And why not?' Rachael cooed indulgently. 'He's my precious boy, isn't he!' She kissed the top of his blond head and Daniel groaned theatrically as he gazed down the length of the table at her.

'Ma's off again! Give her a baby and she's happy. No wonder we ended up with four kids.' But his eyes twinkled as he spoke.

'Are you going to be like that, sweetheart?' Anthony teased Beverley.

'Two's going to be quite enough for me,' she replied firmly.

Christmas morning dawned crisp and clear, and after breakfast the presents under the tree were handed out by Daniel and Josh. Soon everyone was ripping off the paper, and exclaiming and laughing and thanking each other, while on the floor, in the middle, Nicholas sat surrounded by gifts, more interested in the bright wrapping paper in most cases than he was by the contents.

Suddenly Beverley was aware Anthony was looking at something he was holding, his brow furrowed, his eyes dagger sharp.

'What is it, love?' she asked.

'This,' he said dully. In his hands he held a slim volume, bound in dark red leather, decorated on the front with gold tooling.

'What is it?'

'The poems of Lord Byron!' Then he picked up the wrapping paper it had been in, and Beverley saw it had come in the mail. With a sinking heart she knew she need ask no more.

'What does she say?' she asked quietly.

Silently, he handed her the book. She opened it and recognised the handwriting: 'Man's love is of man's life a thing apart, 'Tis woman's whole existence'.

It was signed 'Mary'.

Chapter Nine

Storms, with lashing rain and fearsome gales, marked the arrival of the New Year as Beverley and Anthony returned from Stockbridge. Installing Nicholas in his little yellow nursery again, surrounded by all his toys, they unpacked and got settled back in their routine. In five weeks' time, they would be flying to England and there were a lot of arrangements to be made.

Beverley had to get her column for *Chichi* prepared in advance, because she'd be away when the relevant issue went to press, and that meant a lot of forward planning. For Anthony it wasn't so difficult. Being self-employed, he could arrange to be away when he liked, providing his secretary was there.

'What will I need in the way of clothes?' Beverley kept asking. 'If I listen to Elaine, I'll need sixteen ballgowns, a diamond tiara, and a lot of expensive tweed and cashmere worn with pearls!'

Anthony roared with laughter. 'Take something warm,' he advised. 'Trousers, skirts, sweaters, a raincoat and thick shoes. We can lend you anything else you might need. There's always a supply of suitable gear hanging in the gun-room at Bucklands.'

'Such as?' she asked, intrigued.

'Rubber wellies, Barbours, Puffas,' he replied casually.

'Hey!' Beverley exclaimed. 'Are we talking the same language? Puffas? Barbours? What are they?'

'Surely you feature them in *Chichi*? You know, quilted jackets without sleeves, worn over a thick sweater? And waterproof oil-cloth jackets? People wear them for shooting when it's cold and wet.'

She burst out laughing. 'Over here they don't. I can see this trip to England is going to be really educational.'

'I doubt it, sweetheart,' he chuckled. 'Unless you call being buried in a fourteenth-century castle in deepest Oxfordshire educational. Henry and Leonora don't do anything interesting, you know. And neither does Mama, now she's old. There's hunting of course, and shooting, and the odd dinner party ... you'll probably need a long skirt for that ... but otherwise there are just the usual local activities.'

Beverley was longing to meet her in-laws. In her mind she had tried to conjure up pictures of what they would be like, but Anthony's descriptions were characteristically hazy when it came to describing his own family. It wasn't difficult to imagine what the Dowager Countess was like; old, frail, and she sounded as if she were very sweet. His sister Lady Jean Ffitch sounded a real character, but a bit intimidating. Her husband, Colonel Ffitch, was, according to Anthony, plain dull. Then there was Leonora, and Beverley couldn't imagine her at all. Perhaps because Henry had only mentioned her in passing, and had revealed nothing of his feelings towards her, and Anthony seldom spoke of her either.

'She is the daughter of a man from Milton Keynes who owns a chain of garages,' he'd said once when she'd pressed him for details about Leonora.

'That sounds nice,' she replied. 'She must be smart.'

He'd shot her an enigmatic look. 'It's not quite the same in England as it is in the States, love.' Then he paused. 'Smart, yes. But not much else.'

'What do you mean?' She was curious. Was this yet another example of the eccentricities of the British class system?

'Leonora's father happens to be a thoroughly obnoxious, pushy rough diamond,' he explained, his voice dry, 'and although she's considered beautiful, I still fail to understand why Henry married her.'

'Perhaps *she* married him?' Beverley suggested astutely.

'Don't let her intimidate you, sweetheart. She gets awfully grand at times, especially when she feels threatened.'

Beverley snuggled up to Anthony. They were sitting on the big living-room sofa, having a final hot drink before going to bed, and she buried her face in his shoulder.

'She's hardly likely to be intimidated by me,' she murmured.

'I wouldn't be too sure. Anyway, I'll be there to look after you so you've got nothing to worry about.'

She sat upright, looking at him quizzically. 'You're making me nervous, Anthony. Is she really going to hate me?'

'Of course not, sweetheart, but she's going to envy you like hell.'

'Why? What have I got that she hasn't?'

His reply was succinct and brief. 'A son.'

'Nicky?' Her voice rose in astonishment. 'I know he's divine, but even so. She's got a daughter, hasn't she? What's the big deal?'

'Every woman wants a son, I suppose,' he said lightly.

Then he kissed her, full on the lips. 'We can have a daughter next time, can't we?' His eyes were tender.

'Sure, but not just yet, love. Gimme a break! Nicky isn't even one yet.'

Anthony slid his hand up inside her shirt, reaching for the familiar smooth hillocks of her breasts, wanting her always, just as much as he'd done at the beginning.

'There's nothing to stop us keeping in practice, is there?' His smile was roguish.

'Anthony Amesbury, you're insatiable!' she giggled. 'I don't know, you want it morning, noon . . .'

'And night,' he cut in, as he kissed the tip of her nose.

Later, as she lay under him, filled with his love, cradled in their large soft bed, with her arms around his neck, something made her want to remember this moment, to lock in her heart every tender touch, every lingering caress, to savour the feel of him inside her, and recall each trembling ripple that had surged through their bodies as they lay interlocked. She was so lucky to have met him. Luckier still to be so loved by him. 'Come live with me and be my love . . . and we will all the pleasure prove.' Wrapped in each other's arms they fell asleep, their breathing a whisper on the midnight air.

Beverley returned from the offices of *Chichi* later than usual the next evening. Nicholas had already had his bath and Hayley was playing with him in the nursery.

'I'm sorry I'm late,' Beverley said apologetically. 'Have you had a good day, Hayley?'

'Yeah, great, thanks.' She was a strong capable girl, cheerful and good-tempered, but with none of Faye's prettiness. 'He's been really good,' she continued. 'He ate all his lunch, and then we went to Central Park to take some bread to those poor frozen ducks.'

'Hasn't it been a terrible day? I can't remember when it was as cold as this.' She turned to kiss Nicholas's plump cheeks. 'And did Hayley wrap you up all snug and warm, my precious?' she cooed, putting her arms around him.

'Would you like a hot drink before I go? I've just made some coffee,' Hayley offered.

'You're an angel. I'd love some.'

After Beverley had settled Nicholas in his cot for the night, she went into the kitchen where Hayley was peeling some potatoes. A steaming pot of coffee stood ready on the central table.

'What are you doing?' she asked, as she poured the fragrant liquid into a mug. 'You don't have to get our dinner ready, Hayley. You get off home and I'll do it in a minute.'

Hayley shrugged. 'It only takes a couple of seconds, and since you're late I thought you'd be tired,' she said, smiling. 'It's no trouble, really.'

'Thanks. I am a bit frazzled. Elaine was driving us all mad today, changing the whole of the next issue. She's so demanding and exacting. Still, I suppose that's why she is where she is today. She certainly knows how to get things done,' Beverley added with grudging respect.

Twenty minutes later Hayley left, having put on a chicken to roast. Beverley looked at her wrist watch. It was seven o'clock. Anthony should be home any time now. She hurried to the bedroom, deciding to have a quick shower before dinner. It was a relief to get out of her formal work suit and the high-heeled shoes Elaine demanded everyone wear to the office. Once under the soothingly warm flow of water, she could feel herself relaxing. She rubbed the back of her neck, aching from sitting at a desk all day, and then stretched her arms above her head, feeling the water releasing the tension. Thankful that they were not going out, she slipped into her most comfortable slacks and sweater and then opened a bottle of Anthony's favourite wine. They only drank it once or twice a week, and tonight she thought it would warm him up when he got back.

At seven forty-five, there was still no sign of him, and she went to look out of the window. Not that she could see the street below because of a balcony that jutted out on the second floor. It was besides a wild wet night, and the glass of the windows streamed with water while the building shook from time to time with the violent gusts of wind. Anthony was going to be soaked by the time he got home unless he'd been able to pick up a cab, and that was unlikely. There were never any free cabs on a cold wet night in New York.

By eight o'clock, fleeting shadows of doubt were crossing her mind as excuses for his lateness occurred to her. Was it possible she'd got mixed up and they were supposed to meet some place this evening? The theatre or a concert . . . dinner with friends . . . no, that was tomorrow. Tonight, Tuesday, they were definitely spending the evening at home.

Frowning, she decided to wait a few more minutes, having turned the oven down to save the chicken from being burned. If he hadn't shown up by eight-thirty, she'd phone his office. It was something she hated doing, because she felt it made her appear to be such a clinging wife. However, when the gilt carriage clock Henry had given them as a wedding present chimed the half hour in dulcet tones, she grabbed the phone. To hell with what people who shared his office space thought. It was half-past eight, and Anthony was never late.

A minute later, the security guard who manned the main switchboard in the building at night, informed her everyone had gone home.

'A long time ago, Ma'am,' he said cheerfully, though she couldn't imagine what he had to be cheerful about. He came on duty at six-thirty and stayed until seven o'clock the next morning, looking at a bank of close-circuit television screens as he watched for intruders.

'When did the last person leave the building?' Beverley asked. If Anthony had only been able to get away during the past half-hour, she couldn't expect him home quite yet.

'Two hours or more, Ma'am.' Again the cheerfulness. 'It's a bad night, you know. Everyone wanted to get home early, and I don't rightly blame them, Ma'am.'

'Two hours?' she said, stunned.

'That's right, Ma'am. You're going to have to call back in the morning now, Ma'am.'

'Yeah. Thanks.' Thoughtfully, she replaced the receiver. What in God's name could have happened? If it had been anyone but Anthony she could have found a dozen likely explanations. People bumped into friends . . . went to a bar to have a drink . . . grabbed a snack . . . did some shopping . . . the list was endless. But not Anthony. He was reliable, punctual, and she could depend on him. If something unexpected had come up, he'd have called her. And in all the time she'd known him, he'd never once been late.

Beverley curled up on the sofa with her second glass of wine and tried to stay calm. All she wanted was for Anthony to come home. All she needed was the feel of

229

his arms around her and the sound of his voice in her ears. Nervous tension gripped her stomach. It was now nine-fifteen, and inside her a small voice was starting to panic.

'Is that you, Faye? Can I speak to Hayley?'

'Sure, Beverley. Hold on a moment and I'll get her. Is everything all right? Nicky okay?'

'He's fine.' Beverley spoke as if she had a tight band around her chest, inhibiting her breathing.

After a few seconds, Hayley came on the line. 'Hiya!' she said comfortably.

'Listen, Hayley, I'm really sorry to be calling you at this hour, but I wondered if Anthony had left a message for me during the day? Did he call and say he'd be back late?' Her words came out in a rush. It was ten o'clock and she knew she sounded like an overpossessive wife. There was a slight pause on the line and then Hayley spoke.

'No, he didn't call during the day,' she replied. 'Is anything wrong?'

'Probably not. It's just that he hasn't shown up yet and I'm a bit anxious.' It was the understatement of the year, she thought, but she was determined to try and sound calm. 'I guess we got our wires crossed,' she added.

'But Anthony's never late,' Hayley exclaimed. 'You can tell the time by him! Where can he be?'

'He's obviously got caught up with business . . .' she said lamely.

'I'll say he has.' Hayley sounded quite indignant.

'I expect he'll be here soon.'

'Beverley, surely you're worried? Anything could

have happened to him on a night like this. Have you heard the storm? Shouldn't you make some inquiries?'

Hayley was putting her worst fears into words. 'I *am* scared,' she admitted, 'but who can I call? I'm going to be thought crazy if I start making a fuss about a man who's only three and a half hours late getting home! Hell, most husbands get home late! No one's even going to take me seriously.'

'Ummm, I see what you mean. He can hardly be classified as a missing person.' Her dry tones did not hide her usual humorous disposition, and Beverley felt comforted by her matter-of-fact manner.

'Exactly. I'll just have to wait, Hayley. He must come home sooner or later, for God's sake.'

'I bet the chicken in the oven is unhappy!'

Beverley chuckled in spite of herself. 'I think it's going to be a case of doing something quick with an egg, when he shows up.'

'Beverley,' Hayley was serious now, 'if there's anything I can do, you'll let me know, won't you? If you want to go some place, to look for Anthony or anything, I'll nip over and baby-sit, you know.'

'You're sweet, Hayley. I don't see any point in my going to look for him. Where would I start?'

There was nothing she could do but wait. She turned on the CNN channel, poured herself another glass of wine, and made up her mind to stop worrying. She was being stupid. Just because Anthony was normally punctual, it didn't mean anything was wrong because on this one occasion he was late. Very late. She forced herself not to look at the little carriage clock, ticking away so discreetly on the mantelpiece. Instead, she tried to watch television, though it was difficult to concentrate. All the time her mind kept returning to Anthony and what could have happened. If there'd been a breakdown on the subway or a massive traffic jam, she'd have heard it on the local news station. If there'd been a power failure down town and he'd got stuck in some elevator . . . Beverley shuddered. Something was desperately wrong. She could feel it in her bones.

The front door bell rang just before midnight. Bracing herself, she went to answer it.

'Are you . . .' the police lieutenant hesitated, looking down at the notebook he held. 'Are you Viscountess Amesbury?'

'Yes.' It was as if he were talking about someone else. Not Beverley Franklin, from Stockbridge, Massachusetts, working girl, the daughter of teachers, the mother of a small . . .

'What is it?' Her eyes held a thousand desperate questions as she looked up at him, begging him to tell her Anthony was fine, safe, well, on his way home. *Please God, on his way home.*

'May we come in?' He was in uniform, but his companion, who introduced herself quickly as 'Detective O'Conner, Ma'am', was in a dark green raincoat. Her short black hair was plastered to her head with rain, and her face, lightly made-up, was grave. She looked at Beverley watchfully. They both held out their police badges for her to inspect.

'Come in,' Beverley said automatically. Her mind was spinning, wanting to blot out everything that was happening. She didn't want to look at them or hear what they had to say. She wanted it to be the previous night when she'd been in bed with Anthony, so safe in his arms.

'Are you alone, Ma'am?' Detective O'Conner enquired, looking around the living room, taking in the luxurious furnishings, the paintings, the table lamps that gave off a warm light, and the half-finished bottle of wine.

'My son is here . . .' Beverley sank on to the sofa, her legs too weak to support her now. She didn't even ask them what they wanted.

'I'm afraid we have some very bad news for you,' the Lieutenant said slowly. O'Conner shot him a warning look as if to say 'Go steady', and then sat down beside Beverley on the sofa.

'You must have wondered why your husband didn't come home tonight?' she asked softly, encouragingly, as one coaxes something out of a child.

Beverley nodded, her mouth dropping at the corners. Please go away, her mind implored. Please go away and leave me alone to wait for Anthony . . . But she said nothing.

Detective O'Conner took hold of her hands and her grip was strong and steady. 'I'm afraid your husband's been hurt bad. Real bad.' Her accent was pure Bronx, her delivery straightforward.

Beverley dared to raise her eyes and look into the policewoman's. At that moment, she knew she'd lost her youth forever, and nothing would ever be the same again.

'How bad?' she whispered.

'I'm afraid he's dead. He was mugged on Fifty-sixth Street and Lexington earlier this evening, but it seems no one reported finding the body for a coupla hours . . . what with the storm and everything. We'll have more details later . . .'

She went on talking but Beverley's mind had frozen, seeing only a picture of Anthony lying on the sidewalk . . . and no one stopping even to see if he were dead or alive.

Suddenly she jumped to her feet, wrenching her hands away from O'Conner's, knocking over the glass of red wine on the side table. A noise she didn't even recognise burst from her throat in a long keening wail. Then she rushed to the window, and flung it open, as if by doing so she could be nearer to Anthony lying dead on the street. Rain came lashing down, soaking her face and hair, as she gripped the window ledge, and every fibre of her being rejected the news she had just been given.

'NO-o-o-o-o-o . . .' she screamed but the words were dashed from her lips by the storm. 'No! No! Oh, God! God! No-o-o-o!'

Arms gripped her from behind, and half carried her back to the sofa. She fought them off at first but then she weakened, sobbing with hopeless grief.

They stayed with her until Hayley and Faye arrived, summoned by Detective O'Conner who had managed to get the number out of Beverley. Rachael and Daniel Franklin had also been informed, and were driving through the night to be with their daughter. Meanwhile, Beverley had to face another ordeal.

Depending heavily on O'Conner, as she remembered depending on the nurse who had helped deliver Nicholas and who had also been there for her when she needed help, she turned to the policewoman.

'You will come with me, won't you?' she begged. The thought of going to the city morgue to identify

234

Anthony's body was so horrifying she knew she'd never be able to endure it alone.

'Sure thing, Ma'am.' O'Conner's smile was motherly and caring in spite of her manner being strong and robust.

'Do we have to go now?' Beverley's face was swollen and her eyes blurred with tears.

'Better get it over with, Ma'am.'

'We'll stay with Nicholas,' Hayley promised. She, too, was in a state of shock, while Faye wept unashamedly.

They helped Beverley into her thick red winter coat and the ludicrous thought crossed her mind that Elaine would not approve of its colour on such an occasion. 'Black, my dear . . . that's what you should wear . . . black,' Beverley could hear her say.

'We'll bring her back here as soon as we can,' O'Conner told Hayley.

Hayley nodded. 'Sure.'

O'Conner took hold of Beverley's arm. 'Let's go then,' she said as if she too wanted to get the ordeal over.

The morgue smelled of death. The white-tiled walls glittered coldly. The atmosphere was stifling. Even the living seemed to have died somewhere along the way, in spirit if nothing else.

Beverley was taken to a place she would later recall as her idea of hell. It seemed in that room she died too. Swaying, she clung to O'Conner, her knees buckling under her.

'This will only take a moment, Ma'am,' O'Conner assured her, gripping Beverley's arm tightly to prevent her falling. 'You've just got to take a quick look and that's it.'

Breathing heavily through open lips, Beverley went forward, knowing that nothing in her life would ever again be as bad as this moment. If she got through this, she'd get through anything.

The mortuary attendant led her to a trolley on which lay a shape covered by a sheet.

'Our medical examiners will be here in a while to take some samples, Ma'am,' he told her, again in a matter-of-fact voice, and she thought how blasé death had made these people. 'We have to get samples of blood and body fluids and urine . . . and of course scrapings from under his nails to help identify whoever did this to him.'

Involuntarily, Beverley clasped her hand over her mouth to stop the wave of bile rising up in her gullet.

'Are you all right, Ma'am?' she heard O'Conner ask anxiously.

There was a buzzing in her ears now, and the air was full of dancing black spots . . . she staggered but heard the policewoman's voice again.

'Take some deep breaths . . . you're gonna be fine . . . breathe deeply . . . there you go.' The voice from another planet became closer, clearer, and the face of O'Conner swam back into focus.

'I'm okay,' whispered Beverley. Sweat soaked her clothes, and she was trembling.

When they pulled back the sheet, Anthony's face looked perfect. Young and relaxed, he almost seemed to smile as he did when he slept. For a wild tortured moment she wondered if they hadn't made a mistake. He wasn't dead at all. Just sleeping.

'This is your husband?' They wanted verification, and she wanted to scream. 'Yes,' she whispered at last. 'How did he die?'

'Stab wounds. Inflicted from behind. Right into the area around the heart. Death would be instantaneous.' The attendant consulted his notes as he spoke.

'Okay, that's it. Let's go now.' It was the positive voice of O'Conner again. Without another word, Beverley felt herself being led away.

In the car, on the way home, O'Conner explained what would happen next. 'As soon as the medical examiners have finished, your husband's body will be released and then taken to the funeral parlour. I expect you and your family will want to make special arrangements for the funeral,' she added gently. Her part in tonight's tragic ordeal was nearly over. Beverley and her baby son would be in the care of her family and friends. O'Conner looked out of the car window, wanting to hide her embittered expression from the young widow. This was the fourth night in a row she'd had to break the news to someone that a member of their family had been mugged, run down, shot or raped. She'd seen more pain in the past two years than she'd ever dreamed existed, and it was finally getting to her. New York had become a hell-hole. And this was only the first month of the New Year. Four deaths in four nights in her precinct alone. What the hell was it going to be like come August, when the heat brought out the aggression in everyone and the divide between stinking poverty and high living caused dissensions and cost lives?

'Take care of yourself,' she told Beverley, composing her face into lines of cheerful resolve once again as she left her at her apartment door.

'Thank you.' The simple words conveyed more than just mere acknowledgement. O'Conner had been a tower of strength during the last couple of hours, and in spite of everything, for that Beverley would always be grateful.

By dawn, Rachael and Daniel arrived, and Jenny, crying loudly, had come with them. Within minutes, Beverley found herself in the midst of a group of people she loved, who all wanted to do what they could for her except understand the one thing she did want. And that was to be left alone.

'Hayley, will you take Nicholas to the park when he's had his breakfast?' she said gently as she cuddled her baby and thanked God that he was too young to know what had happened.

'I'm going to lie down for a while,' she told her anxious-eyed mother. 'I haven't been to bed yet . . .' Her voice drifted off.

'Of course, you must be exhausted, honey,' Rachael replied. 'I'll go to market as soon as I've made your father's coffee, and then I'll cook us all a big dinner for tonight.'

Incredible, Beverley thought, at a time like this, the mundane things in life are continuing as if nothing has happened. Coffee for her father. Dinner for them all. Dishes to be washed. Rooms to be cleaned. Beds to be made. It would be days before she'd be alone again and yet from now on she was going to be alone for the rest of her life.

Beverley closed her bedroom door quietly and crawled into the neatly made double bed that had not been disturbed, as was usual, by their lovemaking the previous night. Cool and smooth, the sheets encased her like a new envelope. Beverley shut her eyes and tried to let the blessed oblivion of sleep block out the pain, but all that happened was that her mind kept replaying the incidents of the night, over and over again. At one point she dozed off and then, awaking with a start, thought she heard Anthony coming back. The front door clicked shut and she called out: 'Hi, sweetheart . . .'

Then, with a terrible fresh shock that squeezed and twisted her heart, everything came flooding back and all hope of sleep was gone. Lying on her side, her face buried in his pillow, which still bore the faint aroma of his after-shave, she wept in despair. Her loss was so enormous, so incomprehensible, so total, she felt she was clinging to the edge of a deep black hole, a chasm that was going to swallow her up any minute. Hope was just a word now. Happiness a thing she'd once know. As for the future . . . she truly wished as she lay in the bed they had shared only the night before last, that she had died alongside Anthony. Without him there was no life for her. Inconsolable, she lay sobbing until she felt a hand on her shoulder and heard her mother's voice.

'Bevs, darling, do you want us to tell Anthony's family what's happened?' she asked softly. 'Shall Daddy make the call for you?'

Beverley's sobs came to a shuddering halt. Henry. She must get hold of Henry.

'Oh, my God,' she said, reaching for the box of tissues on the bedside table. 'What time is it, Mom?'

'Eleven o'clock. Hayley's taken Nicky into Central Park, and I'm going to make you a cup of tea.'

Beverley tried to think. It would be four o'clock in the afternoon in England. She'd call Henry right away.

'Mom, could you get me some aspirins from the bathroom cabinet?' she begged. 'My head's killing me.' Her face and cheek bones and every tooth in her head ached from crying.

'Yeah, honey. Is there anything I can get you from the doctor's? I think you should have something to help you, right now.'

Beverley heaved herself painfully off the bed. 'Like tranquillisers, you mean? No. It wouldn't help. I'm scared of those things, and sooner or later I've got to come to terms with what's happened.' Having cried her heart out, she felt better now. There were things to be done, and Anthony would expect her to ... she corrected her thoughts, Anthony would have expected her to do, but as she went to the phone a wild voice in her head cried out: But how am I going to do them without him? How am I going to do anything, even survive without him?

She looked up the telephone number of Bucklands Castle in Anthony's address book, and as she dialled, prayed that Henry would be in.

'Hello?' He answered the phone so quickly she thought he must have been standing beside it. He sounded curt, too.

'It's me, Beverley,' she said huskily.

There was a moment's silence, and then he said in a surprised voice: 'My dear Beverley ... I'm sorry, I was expecting someone else. We're all rather at sixes and sevens at the moment, because sadly Leonora has miscarried again and I thought it was her mother on the phone just now.'

Two Amesburys have died on the same day, thought Beverley, and her eyes welled up with sorrow for Henry. 'I'm so sorry ...' she murmured.

'But how are you, my dear? It's good to hear from you.'

'Henry ...' She didn't know how to tell him. Couldn't

find the words. 'Henry . . .' she said again as her voice broke.

'Is anything up, old girl?' He sounded more English than Anthony had ever done and his phraseology was typical of his background.

She remembered the words the police lieutenant had used when he'd first arrived.

'I'm afraid I've got very bad news for you, Henry.' Then she told him everything. In shuddering, gasping breaths at some moments, calm and clear at others, she told him exactly what had happened.

The silence on the line seemed endless before he spoke.

'Dear God.' She could tell he was crying, too. 'Oh, Beverley, I'm so sorry . . . so sorry . . . Oh, Christ, what an awful thing to happen.'

'Can you come over?' she asked. Now that he knew and he was being so supportive and sympathetic, she felt stronger. 'Unless of course . . . you want him buried at Bucklands?' She had to ask that question, although she prayed fervently the answer would be no. England was so far away, thousands of miles. And she still wanted to be near Anthony. Her mother had already said something about having him buried in Stockbridge, in a grave near those of her grandparents. But Anthony belonged to a great English family. Wouldn't they expect to bury one of their sons in the family mausoleum, which Anthony had once told her contained the remains of seven generations of Cumberlands? And if they did, and it was traditional, there was nothing to do but accept the situation.

'My dear Beverley, that is entirely up to you,' Henry was saying, as if he understood how she felt. 'You must decide whatever you think is best, and whatever you think Anthony would have wanted.'

'I'd like it to be at Stockbridge, so I can be near him.' She couldn't continue, but Henry understood.

'That's fine by me,' he said gently. 'Look, I'll fly over tomorrow. Will you be all right until then? You're not on your own, are you?'

Briefly she explained that she had her family with her.

'And you've got one thing to be thankful for,' Henry remarked. 'You've got Nicholas. A beautiful son, and a part of Anthony that will be with you forever.'

'I know.'

When she'd said goodbye, she accepted the cup of tea and aspirins her mother had brought her, and then she went to have a shower. Nicholas would be back from the park soon and she had to remember, no matter how great her loss, that she was going to have to be both mother and father to him now. There would be no one to help her with the day-to-day decisions. No one to look after her and Nicky in the future. They were on their own, and right now she couldn't even begin to think how she was going to manage.

Chapter Ten

'Beverley, are you awake, honey?' Rachael stole into her daughter's bedroom early the next morning. She hated having to disturb Beverley but she had no option.

'Mom? What is it?' She rolled on to her back and opened her eyes. For a split second she thought she was a young girl again, in her room in Stockbridge, with her mother coming to tell her it was time to get up. Then memories came crowding back, crushing her moment of content.

Rachael sat on the edge of the bed and looked down at her with compassion.

'I wouldn't have woken you up if it hadn't been important,' she said apologetically. 'There's someone come to see you.'

Beverley's eyes widened. 'Who?'

'A policewoman. Detective O'Conner. She says she has to ask you a few questions.'

'Oh, God.' Was the misery never going to end? Were there always going to be people making inquiries, stirring up her pain again, when all she wanted was to be left alone? 'Did she say what it was about?' Slowly and stiffly she eased herself out of bed and reached for her terrycloth robe.

243

Rachael shook her head. 'She did say she'd only keep you for a few minutes.'

When Beverley entered the drawing room, she saw Detective O'Conner standing awkwardly in the middle of the room. She looked slimmer today, in a dark blue coat, her short hair brushed becomingly in loose waves. When she saw Beverley, she smiled.

'Good morning, Ma'am. I'm sorry to disturb you but something vital has come up in connection with your husband's death, and I have to ask you a coupla questions.'

'Sit down.' Beverley indicated the sofa. Then she dropped heavily into the nearby armchair. 'What do you want to know?'

Detective O'Conner came straight to the point. 'Does the name Mary Stapelton mean anything to you?'

Beverley looked back at her, shock written in every line of her face. Her hands started to shake.

'Yes,' she replied in a low voice. 'Why?'

'What can you tell me about her, Ma'am?'

'She's got a fixation on Anthony . . .' Beverley began falteringly. 'She wouldn't leave him alone. She used to phone us all the time . . . then she tried to turn herself into my look-alike.' She looked steadily into the calm and friendly face of the policewoman, to whom she felt unaccountably close. 'For months she made our lives a misery . . . she even disrupted our wedding.' Then Beverley stopped, as if struck by a sudden thought. 'She'll be demented now that Anthony's dead . . . has she tried to take her own life? She did that once before, on the day I told her we'd got engaged.'

'She was a friend of yours, then, Ma'am?'

'She was my boss at one time.'

'When did you last see her?' O'Conner reached in her large shoulder bag for her notebook.

'I can't remember. I think it was in Saks, just before Nicky was born. She was calling herself Lady Amesbury.' Beverley leaned forward, frowning. 'What is this all about? What has she done, now?'

'We have reason to believe she was responsible for your husband's death.'

Beverley's jaw dropped and she turned pale. 'Oh, no! Are you sure? Christ, but she was in love with him! She can't have killed him.' She felt sick as she spoke, her heart lurching painfully in her chest. She looked beseechingly into the sympathetic face of O'Conner. 'How do you know that? I thought he was mugged in the street! Stabbed for his wallet! What makes you think it was . . . her?' She couldn't even say the name. It stuck in her gullet, choking her.

O'Conner consulted her notes. 'We found several pictures of your husband in her handbag. They looked as if they'd been cut out of a magazine. Just his head and shoulders. I'd say he was in a group of people but it was only his face she'd kept.'

Beverley buried her face in her hands. 'Our wedding pictures,' she murmured.

'We also found a letter to her mother, telling her what she'd done.'

'What . . . a confession?'

'More or less. She said she was going to kill him, and there was a lot about everything being already ordained. Several times she mentioned tarot cards, and that they had foreseen everything.' She glanced down at her notes. 'At the end of the letter she said she had to carry out the prophecy in order to find fulfilment.' O'Conner

245

looked up again and her tone was blunt and candid.

'Would you know what she's talking about, Ma'am?'

Beverley gave a cry of distress. 'Oh, my God. This is dreadful! She should have been locked away! The woman's crazy! I thought I was the one in danger . . .'

'And you didn't report you were being threatened to the police?'

'No, you don't understand. She never threatened me exactly, it wasn't a police matter. Her family tried to get her to have treatment but she wouldn't . . . and now . . . Oh, I can't bear it!' She broke down, tears streaming down her face. 'I never thought she'd do anything to hurt Anthony of all people. It was me who was standing in her way, or at least that's what she thought.'

'I'm sorry I had to bring you this bad news, Ma'am.' O'Conner shook her head. 'I'm afraid I'm going to have to ask you to make a statement. Just for the record, you know.'

Beverley nodded. 'I'll tell you everything, but none of this is going to bring my husband back, is it?' She took a handkerchief from her dressing gown pocket and wiped her eyes. 'Nothing is going to do that,' she repeated.

'I'm afraid not, Ma'am. But I think you'll find it therapeutic to know who was responsible for your husband's death. There's nothing worse than wondering how something happened and not ever knowing.'

'I suppose you're right. Have you got enough evidence to have her put away for a long time? Will she get the death sentence?'

O'Conner looked at her with an expression Beverley couldn't make out.

'That's not going to be necessary, Ma'am,' she said with finality.

'You mean she'll be committed to a mental institution?'

'No, Ma'am. We found her body on the sidewalk, outside the apartment building where she lived. She'd jumped out of a window on the fourteenth floor. The autopsy revealed she'd died within hours of your husband. At first we were unable to identify her, but last night we gained access to her apartment. That's when we found the photographs of your husband, and her suicide note.'

'Oh, Christ.'

O'Connor spoke again, this time with acerbity. 'Would you happen to know someone called Pamela Hanworth? We're making enquiries about her because Ms Stapelton left her a note too.'

'She was a friend of Mary's. She used to tell her fortune using tarot cards. That was the beginning of all this trouble,' Beverley added bitterly.

'That would explain a lot, Ma'am.' The policewoman made a hurried note. 'Terrible thing, those tarot cards. Especially for anyone who is impressionable. They should be banned.'

'It was Pamela who told Mary that Anthony would marry her eventually.'

'So I gather.' O'Conner's voice was dry. 'Now I understand what she means in her note to Mrs Hanworth.'

For a moment Beverley hesitated, wondering how much more of this she could stand. Somehow she'd been able to accept the thought of Anthony being killed by a common mugger; someone neither of them had known. To realise it was Mary, crazy Mary, added to her grief. At last she felt compelled to ask one more question.

'What did Mary say in her note to Pamela?'

O'Conner frowned, and her eyes looked anxious. 'I don't think you really want to know that, Ma'am.' She gave a quick, slightly false smile. 'No point in giving yourself more pain than you need, is there?'

'I have to know,' Beverley insisted. 'I'll never rest . . . I'll never come to terms with Anthony's death until I understand why it happened.'

'Do you really want to know?' O'Conner still sounded doubtful.

'Yes.'

'Well . . .' she glanced down at the photocopy in her hand. 'The last line says: "So the tarot cards were right all along. Now Anthony and I will be together for the rest of eternity." '

There was silence in the room and Beverley wondered if the policewoman could hear the thumping of her heart. The stupidity of the whole thing made her head reel. The goddamn waste, the utter madness! Anthony had been killed in order to help a neurotic girl fulfil some crazy fantasy which had been fuelled with the aid of a pack of cards. She jumped to her feet, incensed and enraged. For a moment words failed her. How did one put into words what she was feeling? she demanded of herself. She wanted to kill Pamela right now, for being so irresponsible. Feelings of violence flowed through her veins as she paced up and down the room, fists flailing, dry sobs tearing at her throat. If only . . . if only . . . But she knew that down that path lay madness, too. O'Conner was watching her quietly, an expression of deep pity for Beverley's distress on her face. After a few minutes she spoke.

'Would you like me to come back later, Ma'am?'

Beverley stopped in her tracks, threw up her hands in

a gesture of helplessness and then returned to her chair.

'No, let's get it over,' she said resolutely.

Half an hour later O'Conner had written out Beverley's statement, and she'd signed it.

'I hope I won't have to bother you again,' she said as she left. 'Now, you take care of yourself, Ma'am.'

Rachael appeared from the kitchen after the policewoman had gone, offering Beverley coffee and something to eat.

'You must keep your strength up, sweetheart,' she admonished when Beverley refused everything except coffee.

'I know, Mom, but I have no appetite.' Then she told her mother what the policewoman had said.

'I think Daniel ought to go and see that woman, Pam or whatever her name is, and tell her she's responsible for two deaths,' Rachael declared angrily. 'Now go and sit down, and I'll bring you some breakfast.'

At last Beverley succumbed to Rachael's ministrations, the fight draining out of her like sawdust from an old doll. She collapsed on the sofa, exhausted. Everything had become an effort. Thank God her parents, between them, were making all the funeral arrangements. And Hayley had taken charge of Nicholas for the time being. Even Elaine had shown support in her own way by sending round a black suit and hat for her to wear to the funeral. The fact that it came from a top designer was not lost on Beverley, aware that Elaine never did anything for nothing. Cynically she expected Elaine to have arranged for a photographer to take her arriving at Anthony's funeral in three days' time, with a caption saying her outfit was by Oscar de la Renta. What did it matter? Nothing mattered any more. At this moment she had only one thought that consoled her, and that was that the worst thing that could ever happen to her had already happened. From now on, no matter what, nothing would ever be as bad again. This was the bottom line. Whatever life chucked at her in the future was going to be easy to handle by comparison.

Later in the day, Daniel came and sat close beside her and held her hand.

'I know what you're going to say, Daddy, but I don't want to leave New York.'

He looked speculatively at her, seeing her stubborn streak surface. If Beverley set her heart on something, nothing would make her change her mind. He decided not to press the point. A lot depended on the state of Anthony's financial affairs. If he'd carried substantial life insurance, Beverley might be quite well off and that would make things easier for her. Money insulated people from the sordidness of poverty and the violence that so often accompanies it. But if he hadn't? Then it would be impossible to stay in New York, especially with a small child.

'Well, I hope you'll stay with us for a bit,' he said easily. 'Your ma and I like having you home.'

She reached out to touch his hand. 'I know, Daddy.'

Henry arrived in New York that evening, going straight to the Dorset, an elegant English-style hotel where he'd booked himself a suite. He phoned Beverley as soon as he'd unpacked and showered.

'Oh, Henry, I'm so glad you're here,' she said when she heard his voice. He reminded her of Anthony in so many ways and yet he was quite different. More mature, of course, but then he was fourteen years older. And more English in his speech and manner. But they both had the same easy relaxed friendliness, born of being comfortable and confident within themselves.

'How are you bearing up, old thing? It's the most ghastly tragedy. Who would have thought Anthony would be killed on his way home like that? Dear, dear.' He sighed gustily. 'Shall I come over to your place or would you like a quiet dinner in my suite here? We wouldn't be disturbed.'

'I'll come to you,' she replied. It would do her good to get out of the apartment for a few hours and her parents would look after Nicholas.

'Good. Come over as soon as you like, m'dear.' His voice was warm and reassuring.

When she arrived at the Dorset on Fifty-fourth Street, by Fifth Avenue, half an hour later, she found Henry prowling restlessly around his suite, with his jacket discarded over the back of a chair and his shirt unbuttoned at the neck. He was drinking whisky and looked weary and distressed, with dark shadows under his eyes.

'My dear Beverley,' he exclaimed, opening his arms wide. She flew into them, sobbing like a child, and he hugged her close, his warm cheek pressed to hers. He smelled of freshly laundered shirts and expensive cologne.

'What a tragedy. I'm so dreadfully sorry, my dear girl. Poor Anthony. Oh, God, it was a terrible thing to happen. And poor you.' He continued to hug her, murmuring words of sympathy all the time. At last she stopped crying and looked up into his face. His expression was deeply distressed. Then she remembered he'd suffered the loss of a longed for baby as well as his brother.

251

'I'm sorry about your baby, too,' she said, her voice husky with grief. 'It must have been awful for you and Leonora.'

Henry's mouth drooped at the corners.

'It was a boy, too,' he said sadly. 'Poor little fellow.' He gave a quick sigh. 'Ah, well.' He moved away quickly, his eyes over-bright. 'What can I get you to drink, my dear?'

'A club soda, please,' she replied, sinking on to the brocade sofa that faced the faux marble fireplace.

'Nothing stronger? A little brandy, perhaps?'

Beverley shook her head.

When Henry handed her the drink, having topped up his own, he stood before her, a lovable untidy-looking man with his fair hair ruffled and his expression woeful.

'What can I say, Beverley?' His rich deep voice filled the room. 'Nothing I or anyone else says can make any difference, can it? You've suffered a ghastly tragedy . . . the worst . . . but if there's anything I can do to help . . . well . . . you've only got to ask. You know that, don't you, my dear?' He spread his large hands expansively. 'I suppose they've no idea who did it?'

Beverley looked up at him, composed now. Her voice steady.

'Mary Stapelton killed him.'

Henry's jaw dropped, and his eyes widened with incredulity.

'You don't mean it! Jesus Christ, not that nut case who caused the disturbance at your wedding?'

She nodded. 'Then she committed suicide.'

'Dear God!' He clutched his forehead with the palm of his hand. 'What an appalling thing! How absolutely dreadful!'

He stood still for a moment, and then he started

stomping around the room with anger.

'It's such a bloody waste, that's what gets me,' he exclaimed. ''Ant had everything. You, Nicholas, a good future – and then, God Almighty, this terrible thing happens! D'you know something?' he demanded abruptly.

'What?'

He came back to the sofa and dropped heavily on to it beside her. 'It makes one's belief in God a bit shaky, doesn't it?'

There was a boyish candour in the way he spoke, and a certain hint of guilt, as if he expected to be punished for uttering such wicked thoughts. 'He's taken Anthony and the baby all in the space of a few hours! Well, all I can say is, *if* there is a God, and *if* there is a heaven, at least they'll be together now.'

They sat in silence for a few moments, and then Henry rose, blew his nose on a very large white lawn handker- chief and said in a matter-of-fact voice: 'Let's order from Room Service, m'dear. You look as if you could do with a square meal and we've got to keep our strength up. Then you can tell me all the arrangements you've made for the funeral.'

The coffin was taken to the church where they'd been married, only this time there were no summer flowers to decorate the altar, no joyous rendering of Bach, no pretty hats or showers of confetti. There weren't nearly so many people either. Everyone wants to go to a wed- ding, few to a funeral.

Wearing the black couture suit Elaine had sent, and the hat with a veil, Beverley was closely surrounded by Henry, Rachael and Daniel, her brothers Josh and Tom,

253

and of course Jenny. Faye, Hayley, Lisette and Nina had all flown down from New York to be there too, ever faithful friends and loyal companions. Only Elaine was absent, blaming 'pressure of work'.

Holding Nicholas tightly in her arms, Beverley sat in the front pew as if carved from stone. Secondary shock had paralysed her limbs, numbed her feelings, and turned her heart to a block of ice. Calm, and in a state of emotional limbo, she sat dry-eyed, all grief temporarily spent. Around her, those who loved her broke their hearts as much for her as for the loss of Anthony; she looked so brave and yet so vulnerable, a young widow in black with a small child in her arms. With eyes that were devoid of expression, she stared at the oak casket on top of which lay a bouquet of white flowers. The words on the card were simple.

'We will love you and miss you forever. Beverley and Nicholas.'

Afterwards, Henry had arranged for everyone to go back to the Red Lion Inn for refreshments. Detached, composed, feeling remote from everything that was happening, Beverley talked politely to everyone, thanking them for their flowers and words of condolence, accepting their sympathy with quiet graciousness.

'I don't know how she can be so calm,' Faye whispered to Hayley.

'She hasn't been calm at home.' Jenny came up to join them. 'There are times when she's cried herself sick. I don't think she'll ever get over it.'

'You're coming back to New York with me tonight, aren't you?' Faye asked Hayley anxiously. For some reason she hated being on her own in Beverley's old apartment these days.

254

Hayley hitched Nicholas higher on her hip. 'Yeah. She's given me the rest of the week off. I'm worn out with all that's been going on. I'll be glad to take a break.'

'Shall I take Nicky?' Jenny offered, holding out her arms.

'Sure.'

Jenny cuddled him close. 'I'm glad Bevs is staying at home for a little while. I told her she couldn't possibly go back to that empty apartment on her own.'

'She insists on going back to work next week, though,' Hayley pointed out. 'She said work would be therapeutic.'

It was a muted gathering and those who remembered the wedding were particulary affected. At last it was time for Henry to go, because he had to get back to New York to catch an evening flight to England. After he had shaken hands with everyone, he came up to Beverley.

'Goodbye, my dear,' he said, wrapping her in one of his bear hugs. 'Take care of yourself, won't you?' His eyes were sad and tender. 'Ring me if you need anything. Promise?'

She nodded, suddenly finding it hard to speak. It was more difficult to say goodbye to Henry than she'd expected. He was her only link with Anthony now; he'd been a part of Anthony's childhood at Bucklands, and a part of his youth. Henry was linked to Anthony by the bonds of blood and brotherhood. They shared the same parents, the same antecedents, the same roots. To Beverley, it was almost like saying goodbye to a part of Anthony all over again.

Tears streamed down her cheeks now, flooding uncontrollably for having been held back by the dam of delayed shock. Henry pulled her closer.

'Poor little lady,' he said softly. 'Poor little lady.' Then he slipped away, overcome with emotion himself.

It was a week later when Beverley returned with Nicholas to New York. She knew that the longer she remained in the loving shelter of her parents' home, the more difficult it would be to stand on her own feet again. So Hayley was re-installed as baby-minder and on the Monday Beverley returned to the offices of *Chichi*.

'Are you sure you're up to it?' Elaine asked, sweeping into Beverley's office. She was cocooned on this cold February morning in creamy white angora, moulded to her slim figure, and as ever looked elegant and well groomed. Beverley looked up from her desk where she was going through a batch of photographs of society matrons in couture evening gowns, and smiled as brightly as she could. During the past three weeks she'd lost over fifteen pounds, and her cheekbones looked more finely sculpted than ever. Her eyes seemed to have changed too, marked by the deep sadness she couldn't hide.

'I feel better if I keep busy,' she replied, keeping her tone light. 'Anyway, I'll need to earn a living more than ever now I'm on my own.' In the last few days she'd become rather anxious about money, something which she and Anthony had never discussed in any great detail. They'd both earned enough to have a comfortable life-style, but as Anthony had been self-employed, what happened now? His secretary was still working at the shared rented office he'd used, informing clients what had happened and, Beverley presumed, winding down the whole business. But had he taken out a life insurance policy? Was there anything left of the small inheritance he'd received on the death of his father?

These were things she was going to have to find out, and quickly. On her earnings alone she'd barely be able to keep a roof over their heads, far less continue to stay in their large apartment.

'But surely his family will provide for you now?' Elaine asked, breaking into her thoughts.

Beverley raised her chin. 'I wouldn't want that,' she said firmly. 'I'm quite capable of looking after Nicholas and myself.'

'But you shouldn't have to,' Elaine protested with a scandalised expression. 'You're married into one of England's most noble families and even though you're a widow now, you have certain appearances to keep up. How can you do that on your own?'

'All that nonsense about titles and the aristocracy means nothing to me now, Elaine,' Beverley replied candidly. 'I've lost my husband and I have a little boy to look after; frankly, keeping up appearances is way down at the bottom of my list of priorities.'

Elaine gathered her mouth into a tight button. 'Ummm . . .' she said thoughtfully. She seemed to be thinking about something, but then she turned and left the room. 'I've got an important lunch meeting,' she said as she drifted out. 'I'll see you later.'

Beverley settled down to go through a recent batch of coloured photographs taken at a ball in Washington, which had been attended by the President and the First Lady. Barbara Bush was wearing a long silk evening dress in a stunning shade of blue, and it gave Beverley the idea of doing a whole feature on blue gowns. She'd sub-title it 'Blues Ladies', and it would be a bit different from their usual fashion features.

By five o'clock she was exhausted and all she longed to do was to get home, ease herself into a hot bath, and then have an early night. When she got back, Hayley looked tired also.

'How's Nicky been?' Beverley asked.

Hayley groaned good-humouredly. 'He's been a pain! An absolute little horror, all day. I think he missed you.'

At that moment Nicholas came crawling out of the nursery, cooing with delight at seeing his mother.

Beverley scooped him up in her arms and hugged him close.

'How's my precious boy?' she crooned, kissing his smooth rosy cheeks. 'Have you been a bad boy today?'

Gleefully Nicholas grabbed a handful of her hair. 'Da-da!' he gurgled clearly.

It was the first time they'd ever heard him say anything and Hayley winced as she looked anxiously at Beverley to see how she would react.

'Yes, my darling,' Beverley said gently. 'Da-da! I'll tell you all about your lovely Da-da one day. Now, can you say Ma-ma? Ma-ma?'

When Hayley got back to her own apartment that evening she told Faye what had happened.

'D'you know something?' Hayley added. 'Beverley is one remarkable lady. It was so brave, the way she handled Nicky's first word being "Da-da". Can you imagine how awful it must have been for her?'

Anthony's accountant looked at Beverley with concern. 'That's the position, I'm afraid, Lady Amesbury. I wish there was something I could do, but under the circumstances, I'm sorry, I can't help you.'

Beverley nodded, too stunned to take in all the facts

258

and figures he'd been throwing at her for the past half hour, too shocked to make much sense of it all. The bottom line was clear, though, and seemingly irrefutable. Anthony's earnings had stopped at the moment of his death, except for a small amount he was owed by a client. He had no life insurance policy. No accident policy either. Nothing. His current account held a few hundred dollars and no more. There was no portfolio of stocks and shares, no money on deposit; they had been living to the hilt of their joint incomes, and Beverley faced destitution, unless she earned enough to keep herself and Nicholas.

Then she remembered something. 'Didn't he inherit some capital from his father?' she asked.

The accountant nodded, referring to the papers before him. 'That's correct. In fact he came to see me about it some time ago. He wanted to give you a . . . er . . .' He paused in embarrassment, his eyes going to her folded hands on her lap. 'Lord Amesbury wanted you to have a splendid engagement ring, and then he withdrew the rest around the time your son was born. I think he wanted to get you a piece of jewellery.'

The diamond pendant from Tiffany's, she thought, to go with the earrings his mother had sent her.

'That, and the cost of the honeymoon, just about cleared him out,' he concluded. Then he smiled. 'He was thrilled at being able to give you lovely things though, that I do know.'

Beverley looked down at the emerald and diamond ring. She wore it all the time. She even slept in it. It was the most beautiful ring she'd ever seen and she'd loved it from the moment Anthony had given it to her.

'If there's anything I can do at any time, Lady

Amesbury . . .' But the words drifted away, because they both knew it was a polite form of speech and a gracious way to bring their meeting to an end. There was really nothing he could do for her now.

'Thank you,' she replied with equal politeness, but it was with a sinking feeling that she walked out into Park Avenue again, wondering how the hell she was going to manage. Elaine's words kept coming back to her, but there was no way she was going to go begging to Anthony's family. This was her problem, Nicholas was her child, and she'd have to solve her own problems now. The most urgent thing to do was get rid of the apartment. The bank manager had said the rent had been paid monthly by banker's draft and it was due again soon. There was barely enough left in Anthony's account to cover it.

As she walked the few blocks to the offices of *Chichi*, she was thankful that at least she had a job. She'd be able to afford a small apartment, in a less fashionable part of town, but how was she going to pay Hayley to look after Nicholas? Her salary wouldn't stretch to a baby-minder as well as rent and living expenses.

Beverley worked all afternoon, trying to concentrate on 'Blues Ladies', but when she got home that evening she told Hayley what had happened.

'That's tough,' Hayley agreed. 'Jesus, I'm sorry.'

'Yeah. I had hoped to go on living here.' She looked around the rooms she and Anthony had shared, the ornaments they had collected together, and the many wedding presents they'd received. On the mantelpiece, Henry's gilt carriage clock still ticked the hours away, and on the sofa, the two petit point cushions his elder sister, Lady Jean, had given them, depicting the Cumberland coat of arms and crest, glowed in soft shades of blue, gold and deep rosy pink. There were some things she would never part with, no matter what. The clock, the cushions, and of course the Dowager Countess's earrings and the jewellery Anthony had given her. If she had to go hungry, she'd hold on to those things above all else.

'If you didn't have to pay a baby-sitter, you'd be okay on what you earn, wouldn't you?' Hayley asked.

'Yes!'

'I'd love to be able to say I'll work for nothing, but I can't,' Hayley said. 'But why don't you do a deal with your sister Jenny? In return for her board and keep, why not get her to look after Nicholas during the day? As she's so crazy to come to New York, it might be a way out for both of you.'

Beverley looked thoughtful. It certainly was a solution, but was Jenny responsible enough to care for Nicholas? And what about her education?

'Your only alternative is to send Nicky to live in Stockbridge with your parents, and you could visit him at weekends,' Hayley suggested. Beverley turned on her with a horrified expression.

'Oh, I couldn't do that!' she cried. 'I must keep him with me.'

Hayley looked at her sympathetically. 'You might have to, honey,' she said quietly. 'You'd hate to go back to live at home yourself, I suppose?'

Beverley nodded. 'My life's here. I love this city, in spite of everything. And I want only the best for Nicky. I'll work to give him a good home if it's the last thing I do.' There was such determination in her voice Hayley smiled.

261

'You don't think he'd have a better life in the country? Stockbridge is lovely, you know.'

'There's no future in Stockbridge. That's why I left. That's why Jenny's desperate to leave, too, and I don't blame her. New York is throbbing with life . . .'

'And death,' Hayley cut in soberly.

'Yes, but I intend to carve a future for myself and Nicky that will make him proud of me when he grows up,' Beverley said earnestly. 'It's what Anthony would have wanted me to do, I'm sure.'

The next morning Beverley put their apartment in the hands of a rental agency, in order to sub-let it, at the same time asking them to find somewhere small and cheap for her to move to. Then she phoned the colleague of Anthony's who had shared his office and facilities for the past two years. He told her he was sure he could find someone else to take over Anthony's section. He also said he could find another job, within the building, for Anthony's secretary. Much relieved that everything seemed to be falling into place, she called up Rachael when she got home that night.

Briefly, and without a trace of self-pity, Beverley outlined her financial position. 'There's no panic, Mom. I hope I'll be able to move within a couple of weeks, but I thought Jenny might like to come and share with me? Just for a while, anyway. I've worked out that I can give her a little pocket money in return for looking after Nicky while I work.'

Rachael sounded worried. 'How are you going to manage, Beverley? Being a one parent family is no fun, especially when you're short of money, and New York is such a brutal city if you're on your own. Wouldn't you do better to come home, love?'

Beverley had heard it all before. Her mother had never wanted her to work in New York in the first place. All the same arguments were going to be used to stop Jenny coming to the Big Apple, too.

'I know what you're going to say, Mom, but I think Jenny should be given the chance. She's got to leave home sooner or later. If she's with me, I can at least keep an eye on her and maybe, in time, I can persuade her to go back to her studies.'

'I don't know.' Rachael sounded reluctant. 'She's absolutely refusing to go back to school, so I suppose she'd better do something.'

'Talk it over with Daddy and Jenny,' Beverley said, deciding not to push too hard. 'And get her to let me know as soon as possible, Mom.' She tried to sound cool, not wanting her mother to realise how tight her position was.

'Okay, dear. We'll do that.' They talked for a few minutes longer, and then Beverley hung up. She was sailing much nearer the wind than anyone realised, she thought, and it would take only one more thing to go wrong for her whole financial boat to capsize.

Jenny was ecstatic. 'How soon can I come?' she asked Beverley in an excited phone call the next morning. She'd spent most of the night persuading Rachael and Daniel that it was a terrific idea.

'It's not going to be a holiday,' Beverley warned her. 'I want you to come and live with me, but it'll mean staying with Nicky all day, and looking after any child can be exhausting and boring.'

'But I adore Nicky, and I'd much prefer looking after

263

him to working in an office or a restaurant. Oh, it's going to be great! And I promise you I'll be good and not rip off your clothes or be a nuisance,' Jenny added earnestly.

Beverley chuckled. 'That'll be the day! Okay, Jen, then it's settled. I'm looking at a couple of apartments later on today. There'll be so much packing to do when I leave here. I'm thinking of asking Mom and Dad if they'll look after some of my things. I'll never be able to take everything with me to a smaller place.'

'You're on!' Jenny chortled with delight. 'I'll do anything you ask! I can't wait to be in the city.'

She arrived the next day, with a trunkload of clothes, in order 'to get to know my way around before I start work', as she explained to Beverley that evening.

'Hayley can show you how to care for Nicky,' Beverley told her. 'It's going to be unsettling for him when we have to move, but I don't want his routine upset as well.'

'Oh, I'm so excited about coming to live with you! It's going to be marvellous, isn't it, Bevs? And I'll just love looking after Nicky.' And with that she swept her nephew up from the floor, and started covering his blond head with kisses. Beverley had never seen her look so happy. Watching her, playing with Nicky, she hoped the euphoria would last. Her sister was really more suited to disporting herself in a disco than being domestic, but being given real responsibility might just be the making of her.

It was two more days before she found a suitable place for them to live, suitable, that is, because it was rent controlled. Normally, she wouldn't have touched it with a barge pole, but she was being pressured by the management to vacate her apartment as soon as possible because they'd found an elderly couple who wanted to move in right away and were prepared to buy some of the fittings.

'You'll never get as good an offer as this again,' she was told. Whether it was true or not, Beverley wasn't prepared to hang around to find out.

The new apartment was way over on the other side of town, on the lower east side, just by Corlears Moor Park and overlooking Franklin Roosevelt Drive.

One of the reasons she decided to take it, apart from the low rent, was because of its proximity to a park. It would be good for Nicholas to have somewhere out of doors to go to, and the other advantage was there was a crosstown bus that would land her within three blocks of the offices of *Chichi* every morning. The disadvantage of the apartment was that the rooms looked directly onto the expressway that ran alongside the East River, but, as she said to herself, beggars can't be choosers.

At least there was a room for Jenny, another for herself and Nicholas and a small living room. The walls needed painting and there were old worn carpets on the floor, but she concentrated on thinking how she was going to manage in the future, instead of hankering for all she'd lost in the past. Once she'd brought their rugs and sofa and chairs and some of their lamps and pictures, the place would at least be comfortable. They'd manage. They'd have to. Jenny would have to be taught to be tidy and she was going to have to live without the little luxuries of life. Until she had more money, the bulk of their stuff would be stored at Stockbridge.

The day they moved it was snowing, great feathery flakes whirling down, lying wetly on the sidewalk, making everything icy chill and damp.

Beverley had got the day off work, and the removal

men arrived shortly after eight o'clock, ready to empty the apartment. Hayley had come earlier, to give Nicholas his breakfast and to take him back to her place for the day.

'Bring him to the new apartment in the late afternoon, will you, Hayley?' she asked. 'Here's the address. I'll try and get the place as straight as I can before you arrive, so it won't be too much of a shock for him.'

'I'm going to be there to help you,' Jenny pointed out. 'We'll have it all done in no time at all,' she added cheerfully.

When the last piece of furniture and all the packing cases containing her possessions had been stowed into the removal van, some to go to the new apartment and the rest to her parents' home, Beverley sent Jenny ahead while she had a last look round the home that had belonged to her and Anthony. There were so many memories she wanted to make sure were imprinted on her mind, now and forever, before she left for good. Slowly, going from room to room, she lingered in each, recalling how it had been only a few hours ago, digging deeper into her memory to see Anthony lounging on the sofa, watching television, stepping into the shower, his muscular body tanned a golden brown. Or lying in their bed, looking up at her. The images were so strong she almost expected him to walk in through the door at any moment, smiling that roguish smile of his that always melted her heart, telling her he loved her in that warm voice. Her heart ached with the terrible pain of knowing she'd never see him again. He was dead and she was still here, left to bring up their son by herself, left to get through the rest of her life alone.

The empty rooms echoed to the sound of her sobs as

she tried to reconcile herself to what had happened. But she couldn't accept it at this moment; wouldn't accept it. His death had been a needless tragedy, the waste of a life cut off in its prime, and all at once she was consumed by uncontrollable anger.

'How could you let this happen?' she screamed to the empty rooms. 'Goddamn it! How could you have left Nicky and me like this? Why did you ever befriend Mary at all? Why did you even take her out for dinner? Why did you let it happen?'

Her voice rose into a wild crescendo as she reeled from room to room, feeling Anthony's presence, touching the doorknobs he had touched, looking at the things he had looked at, breathing the air he had breathed . . .

'Why did you leave me behind?' she cried at last, her voice dropping pitifully.

They'd told her that rage was all a part of grief; disbelief came first, and then the pain of loss . . . and then the anger and despair. But how long was the journey before she could accept what had happened? How much heartache must she suffer before she could even hope to reach a level of tranquillity?

'Goddammit! I'll never forgive you,' she raged, shouting now. 'It was stupid . . . irresponsible . . . crazy of you to go walking along some back street at night in New York . . . when you knew Mary was crazy!' With clenched fists she thumped the pale peach walls of what had been their bedroom, so that her hands hurt, but the pain went unnoticed. There was too much hurt inside.

Suddenly, frightened by the intensity of feeling that had overwhelmed her, she let the tears flow down her cheeks, angry tears, furious tears, that she wiped away with the back of her hand.

If it hadn't been for her baby . . . for Nicky . . . she didn't finish the sentence, even in her head. Quietly she shut the apartment door behind her and, taking the elevator down to the street, walked out on to the sidewalk without a backward glance.

Chapter Eleven

Nicholas was running around now, getting into everything and full of mischief. By the time Beverley returned home from work each evening, Jenny looked hot and flushed and exhausted.

'You're letting him lead you a dance,' she pointed out when Jenny complained he was too much of a handful. 'For God's sake, don't spoil him! He still needs a rest in the afternoon, so don't let him run around all the time. Be firm with him, Jen. There are things he's allowed to do and things he's not allowed . . . like pulling all the books out of the shelves.'

Some evenings she dreaded going home, wondering what sort of a mess she'd find. Nicholas was very good and sweet-tempered with her, but he seemed to play up when Jenny looked after him.

'He won't do as I say,' her sister whined sulkily. 'Isn't there a toddlers' play group he could go to in the mornings? I think he needs to play with other children.'

'Let him play with other children in the park, for goodness' sake! That's one of the reasons I moved here. Anyway, I can't afford to send him to play school.'

'He'll have to go sooner or later.'

'He's not even two yet!' Beverley protested. The last

few months had gone so quickly she could hardly believe it had been six months since Anthony had been murdered. Six months of a tearing, wrenching pain in her chest, and a constantly throbbing heart. Six months of living in the cramped rooms overlooking the expressway. Six months of eking out her wages from *Chichi*, so she could give Jenny some pocket money, and pay the rent and feed them all. Six months of lonely nights and lonelier dawns, when she awoke to find her teeth so tightly clamped together her jaw ached, and her hands clenched into tight fists. Then she would wonder whether to get up quickly, without disturbing Nicky, so she could distract herself by doing some cleaning, or whether to bury her head beneath the bedclothes and try and block out all that had happened by having a few more minutes' sleep.

Sometimes Nicholas awoke early and as soon as he saw her, from his cot in the corner, he wanted to get up. 'Momma!' he would gurgle in delight. 'Momma . . . S'morning! Get up? Get up?'

She couldn't resist him for long. He looked so enchanting, with his thick straight blond hair and dancing blue eyes, so like Anthony's, and he even had the same grin that spread engagingly across his little face.

'Come on then, you wicked boy,' she would croon, getting out of bed to fetch him. Then she would cuddle him in her arms, and he'd lie snuggled close, his sweet milky breath gently fanning her cheek, his warm little arms around her neck.

He was still too young to be told stories, but she sang softly to him and he loved that. Sometimes he'd hum along tunelessly, but then suddenly he'd get bored.

'Jump!' he'd exclaim, scrambling out from beneath

the bedclothes, and then he'd spring up and down on the bed, as if it was a trampoline, while Beverley held his hands and knew another day had begun.

Soon after that Jenny would emerge from her room, and depending on how late she'd been the night before, would fix some sort of breakfast for them while Beverley showered and put on one of her best suits for work. It wasn't an exciting life, but excitement she could live without. At least she had the security of a regular salary, which enabled her to provide for Nicholas, and she was gradually reaching a calmer phase, a greater acceptance of what had happened, so that on a day to day level she was better able to cope. And as she told herself repeatedly, she had nothing to fear because the worst had already happened, and every day she was learning to survive without Anthony . . . she couldn't call it living yet, living was for the happy, the fulfilled, people who knew hope, but surviving was better than nothing. She was at least existing on a twilight level, and for the moment she was grateful that even that was possible.

On this particular morning she felt more contented than she'd done in a long time. It was hot as she walked the last block to the office, but there was a deliciously cool breeze that played around with her russet hair, grown longer now, and framing her face in a glorious riot of titian red. She was glad, too, that she'd put on her caramel linen button-through dress. She was aware that several people turned to stare admiringly at her, and in a small way that was gratifying. It made her feel like a whole human being again instead of an empty husk. And it did not matter that many of the approving glances came from other women. Her interest in men had gone anyway. Male colleagues at *Chichi* who invited her out for a drink were charmingly but firmly turned down. In fact she hadn't socialised in six months, but part of that was also because Jenny was always desperate to go out every evening and someone had to stay with Nicky. But the major reason was because she wasn't yet ready to join the parade.

When she arrived in her office, she found a memo on her desk. 'Elaine would like to see you immediately.' Nothing unusual in that. They were planning the November issue and no doubt she wanted to put forward some idea for 'Viscountess Amesbury's Viewpoint'.

Running a brush through her hair and touching up her coppery pink lipstick, Beverley picked up her notepad and then walked along the grey and white corridor and tapped on her door.

'Come in,' Elaine called out. She was standing by her desk, dazzling this morning in a white suede skirt, pencil slim and slit at the back, worn with a matching blouson. Bird-like, her dark head cocked to one side, she signalled to Beverley to take a seat while she scribbled something on a pad. Ivory and gold bangles rattled at her wrists as she continued writing, and she seemed in no hurry to tell Beverley why she wanted to see her.

Beverley took the opportunity to look around the incredibly glamorous office and wonder at the woman who had created it. Today there were bowls of white lilies on her desk and on side tables, their heady perfume filling the room. In one of the windows, a life-size crystal horse's head glittered in the sunlight, its facets catching the colours of the rainbow in a myriad of hues, while on the floor white bearskin rugs lay soft as newly fallen snow. Why is she so crazy about white? Beverley wondered for the umpteenth time. White is for virginity and purity, and neither quality she thought, smiling to herself, could possibly have been used to describe Elaine. Then she saw that even past issues of *Chichi* had been bound in batches of six, between white hardboard covers. Only the spine bore the title and then the date in gold lettering. They looked strange on the glass shelves; volumes wrapped in shrouds, blind and dead.

At last Elaine stopped writing and turned to her, smiling, but her eyes remained cold and detached as if they belonged in a different person's face.

'Ah, yes, Beverley,' she said, going round the back of her glass-topped desk and sitting on her white leather chair. She laid down her gold Tiffany pen.

'I expect you've been keeping up with all the happenings in the British Royal Family lately? There's been the divorce of Princess Anne, the Queen's daughter, and then the separation of the Queen's son, the Duke of York, from his wife, Fergie. Not to mention the split between Prince Charles and Princess Diana. Now another royal divorce has just happened, between the Queen's cousin, the Duke of Buckingham, and his wife.'

Beverley nodded. She remembered featuring the Duchess in her column the previous year wearing an exquisite beaded gown by Hardy Amies for a banquet at Buckingham Palace. She was a statuesque young woman, with fair hair and a peaches and cream complexion, who had married into the royal family ten years ago, and had three children.

'Did you know the Duchess's mother was American?' Elaine asked guilelessly. She looked at Beverley squarely and it was impossible to know what she was thinking.

'No, I didn't.' Beverley shook her head.

'Now that her divorce has gone through, she's returning to the States, to get away from the feverish attention
of the media in London. The poor girl has been hounded
by the press for the past few months, and she really
needs to come home and have a break. Her children will
be coming with her.'

'Really?' Beverley smiled politely and wondered
what this was leading up to. Perhaps Elaine wanted her
to set up a photo-feature of the Duchess At Home,
dressed by various American designers, as up to now
she'd have been forced to have her clothes made by
British couturiers.

'It was through her, you know, that I was able to get
Princess Diana to come to our fiftieth anniversary party,'
Elaine continued conversationally. 'I've known her
mother for many years, you see, and so my contacts with
the British Royal Family are very good.'

Bully for you! thought Beverley, but outwardly she
smiled again politely and wished Elaine would get to
the point.

'That being the case . . .' Elaine paused, and Beverley
didn't see it coming, didn't even suspect what was about
to happen.

'That being the case, I have put her under contract to
write "Viewpoint". This is your last issue, I'm afraid,
Beverley.' Elaine's tone was almost gay, her smile spiteful. 'I'm sure you'll understand that the widow of a
Viscount doesn't have the same clout as a royal Duchess,
even if she is divorced from the Duke. I believe the
Queen is very anxious she should remain on friendly
terms with all the members of the royal family, so her
column will be very good for *Chichi*'s image. No doubt,
through her, we shall secure some very good scoops.'

She sat back, and at that moment Beverley realised that the white Bird of Paradise had turned into an evil Bird of Prey.

For a long moment she stared back at Elaine, trying to take in the fact she'd just been fired. The implications were appalling. She was dependent on her salary. Unless she got another job, she'd be wiped out to all intents and purposes.

Tight-lipped, and with a stunned expression, she rose and looked down at Elaine. She couldn't even think of anything to say. Not that it would have made any difference. A royal Duchess, even an ex-one, *did* carry more clout than a penniless Viscountess. Elaine was putting *Chichi* before anything or anyone, as she'd presumably done in the past, and there was no point in fighting her.

'I'd like time off to look for another job,' Beverley said quietly. 'I have a child to support and at this time jobs are scarce. I presume you'll give me a reference?'

Elaine raised finely plucked eyebrows. 'Of course, I'll give you an excellent reference. But surely the Cumberlands should be supporting you? I think it's dreadful that you're forced to work. Henry Cumberland has a duty towards you. Surely he'd feel the family was being let down if you were forced to wait tables, for instance?'

Suddenly she was making it all seem as if it was the fault of Anthony's family. Sounding self righteous, she sat in her all-white parlour like a predatory spider, blaming everyone else. 'Anthony should have had a life insurance policy . . .' she began, but Beverley rounded on her angrily.

'Why should anyone support me? I'm not a charity, for God's sake! Thousands of women bring up their children single-handed and although I'm not doing it by choice, there's no reason why I shouldn't do it. I'll get another job, recession or no recession, but I won't go running to Anthony's family,' she added, raising her chin with a proud gesture.

Elaine shrugged as if she found the whole subject boring. 'That's up to you, of course.' Then she added: 'The Duchess starts working here next Monday. I'd like you to be here all next week, showing her the ropes, helping her to settle in, but after that, you're free to go. You will, of course, be paid up to the end of the month.' Then she rose dismissively, picking up the phone to make a call as she did so.

Without another word, Beverley turned and left the room.

Back in her own office, she put through a call to Charles Floyd. She hadn't seen the head of Highlight Promotions since her wedding, but he'd often sent his good wishes through Faye, and when Anthony died, he'd written her a wonderfully kind letter of condolence.

'Hello, this is Beverley Amesbury,' she explained when she heard his voice.

'Well, how good to hear from you!' he said immediately. His voice was warm, and she could just imagine him sitting in the Madison Avenue offices of the public relations company, impeccable in a summer suit of a soft biscuit shade, the seams straining as he relentlessly put on weight.

'How are things going?' he asked, as if he really cared.

'Can I come and see you?' Beverley's voice shook in spite of her efforts to sound steady.

'Sure,' Charles replied easily. 'How about tomorrow? Sometime in the morning? It would be great to see you again.'

'That would be fine.'

'Shall we say eleven o'clock?'

'Yes. I'll see you then, and thanks.'

When she'd hung up, she put through a second call to Highlight, this time to Faye, whom she knew she could trust implicitly. Briefly she told her what had happened.

'That bitch!' Faye exclaimed hotly. 'How dare she treat you like this? Fancy kicking you out, when she must know you badly need the job!'

'Typical when you think abut it, though,' Beverley pointed out. 'When did Elaine ever make a kind or charitable gesture in her life? Everything's for *Chichi*.'

'Are you really going to put in time next week, showing this royal Duchess what to do?' Faye sounded quite angry at the thought.

'What else can I do? It's not her fault that Elaine has fired me,' Beverley replied reasonably. 'Anyway I've made an appointment to see Charles Floyd tomorrow morning.'

'You have?' Faye sounded startled.

'Yeah. I'm going to ask for my old job back, or anything else he has to offer.'

Beverley was aware of an awkward silence on the phone before Faye spoke again. 'You'll pop in and see us then, won't you?' she said at last.

'Yes, of course I will.' When she hung up she wondered why Faye hadn't sounded more enthusiastic.

Now that she'd become used to sorting out her own problems, she didn't mention the loss of her job to Jenny that night. Her sister would only get in a panic, and anyway there was nothing she could do. Jenny was needed to look after Nicholas. Beverley only hoped she'd be able to continue giving her enough pocket money to keep her happy.

The next morning she left the apartment feeling for some reason more optimistic than she'd done for a long time. To hell with *Chichi*, she thought. The world didn't begin and end with a snobbish fashion magazine, and she might even earn more money by going back to Highlight. With all the experience she'd had on the magazine, surely she'd be worth more to Charles Floyd now? She knew she looked good, too, in a beautiful pale lime green hopsack suit, a reminder that the days of 'charging it to *Chichi* because you must look well dressed' had gone. It made her wonder if she'd ever be able to afford such good clothes again.

After she'd dealt with the mail and sorted out some fashion shots, she slipped out of the office and hailed a cab to take her to her old office. Mounting excitement at the prospect of going back made her heart pound. Now that she thought about it, she'd never been all that happy at *Chichi* anyway. The perks had been terrific and having her own column and byline had given her a great feeling of personal achievement, but she'd missed working with Faye and Lisette and Nina; missed the gossip and the hurried lunch breaks. Missed the quick shopping trips and the way they'd confided in each other.

The receptionist was a stranger to Beverley.

'What name shall I say?' she asked, when Beverley announced she had an appointment with Charles Floyd.

'Beverley Amesbury.'

'Take a seat. Mr Floyd is with someone at the moment but he won't be long.'

'Thanks.'

Beverley sat on the familiar black leather sofa in a corner of the reception area and looked around curiously. There was something different about the atmosphere, but she couldn't quite put her finger on it. Everything looked the same; the walls covered in smartly framed black and white photographs taken by famous photographers, the black table scattered with all the latest glossy magazines, the dramatic touches of scarlet here and there, and yet something was wrong.

The office she'd occupied was at the end of the corridor, and the door was closed. All the internal office doors were closed, she realised, and the babble of voices that usually filtered into the reception area was missing. Then she paused, struck by something. The silence. That was it! The offices of Highlight were uncannily quiet. Usually phones were ringing, people were rushing to and fro with faxes, press releases, products to be photographed, vast mail-shots waiting to be mailed . . .

'It's very quiet this morning?' Beverley observed.

The girl at the reception desk shot her a startled look. 'Quiet? No, it's not particularly quiet,' she replied.

'Have you been here long?'

'Two weeks.'

Beverley nodded in a friendly fashion. 'I expect you enjoy the work. Everyone's very nice.'

The girl tossed back a mass of dark curly hair, which reminded Beverley of a poodle's fur that hadn't been cut for years.

'Yeah.'

The receptionist, she decided, was not of a talkative nature. At that moment the phone on her desk buzzed, and a moment later she was saying:

'Mr Floyd is ready to see you. Do you know the way to his office?'

Beverley jumped to her feet. 'Yes, thanks.'

Charles Floyd was just as she'd remembered him, with one exception. He was much thinner. In fact, as she shook his hand and looked at him more closely, she realised he must have lost over forty pounds. It should have been an improvement, because he'd really been overweight, but somehow it wasn't. He looked gaunt and drawn and for a moment she wondered if he'd been ill.

Charles saw her expression and grinned wryly. 'You're wondering at my new svelte shape?' he teased. 'I've had to have all my suits taken in.'

She eyed him openly now, smiling. 'What did you do? A crash diet?'

He shook his head. 'An imposed loss of weight, over which I had little control,' he replied enigmatically. Then he straightened his shoulders. 'It's great to see you again, Beverley, and you're looking good. You've been through so much. I was shocked to hear about Anthony. What a terrible thing.' He shook his head, gazing at her with sympathy.

'Yes, it was,' she said quietly.

'So?' He raised his bushy eyebrows, and a tired smile creased his now lean face. 'What can I do for you?'

She took a deep breath and told him what had happened. 'I need to get another job as quickly as possible, and I'm free to start working again in two weeks' time, and I wondered if . . .' Now that it had come to the point, she found it difficult to ask him outright if she could have her old job back. There was something forbidding about this thin man sitting opposite her, that had never been there before. Was it true, she wondered, that fat people are always much happier and jollier than thin people?

'I'm afraid that's impossible, Beverley.'

His words cut through her thoughts, startling her by their sheer unexpectedness.

'Oh!' she exclaimed, her hopes dashed. 'You've no vacancies? It doesn't have to be in my old department . . . I mean, I'd be very happy to . . .' Her words trailed off as he looked at her, and for the first time she saw the despair in his eyes.

'We'd love to have you back,' he said gently, 'if there was anything to come back to. This recession has finished us, Beverley. We've lost seventy per cent of our clients . . . seventy per cent! . . . because most of them have gone to the wall. At the moment, we're working with a skeleton staff, but by the end of the month, Highlight will have gone, I'm afraid.'

'No!' Her hand flew to her mouth and she gazed at him, appalled. 'It can't be as bad as that, is it?'

His expression was wry. 'Worse, if anything.'

'My God, I'd no idea . . .' If it meant no job for her, it was a lot worse for Charles Floyd. He'd built up Highlight over the years until it had become one of the top public relations companies in Manhattan. Their list of clients had read like the list of advertisers in *Town & Country*. Top designers, top jewellers, top hotels and restaurants, art galleries, interior decorators, couturiers . . . they'd all gone to Highlight Promotions because it was the best. And Charles Floyd was the man who had made it so.

'I'm so sorry,' she burst out, shocked.

He shrugged again. 'Hence the loss of weight,' he explained, smiling wryly. 'There are two ways to lose weight. Forget all the diets. You either fall in love, or your business goes bust. Either way you can be sure to lose anything up to fifty pounds.'

Beverley nodded, understanding. 'Being widowed does the same,' she vouchsafed.

'I'm sure. God, this is a bad time, isn't it? A bad time for all of us.'

His words reminded her that her visit was pointless. It was a crushing blow, especially as it was so unexpected. Working at *Chichi* on her elitist column, and then going straight home each night to be with Nicholas, she hadn't realised the country's recession had bitten so deep.

'Am I going to have a problem getting another job?' she asked.

Charles Floyd shook his head. 'My advice to you would be to go back home with your little boy. Stockbridge is popular with the tourist trade; you'd have a better chance of finding a job there than you will in New York, and that's a fact.'

'But there's no future for me there.'

'There's more future for you in Stockbridge than there is here, right now.' He shook his head, looking grave. 'You've no idea how bad it is in this town. People are being laid off by the score. Businesses are closing. Bankruptcies are at an all time high. It's hell, Beverley, absolute hell. Get out while you can. Your parents have a nice home, they're both teachers so I expect their jobs are secure. Let them look after you for a bit.'

'I can't do that.' Beverley shook her head. 'I'm a grown woman and I must stand on my own feet and not go running home the first time I get fired.'

He looked at her with renewed respect. 'You're a fighter, aren't you? I wish to God I could give you a job, but at the end of this week I'm shutting down the whole operation. I don't know what the girls who work here

282

are going to do and I feel badly about it. Anyone who has a job in New York right now can consider themselves lucky.'

'That's terrible.'

He nodded. 'No chance of your late husband's family giving you a hand-out, I suppose?'

'Definitely not.' She was beginning to get sick of people thinking she could sponge off the Cumberlands. Now even Charles Floyd was at it. 'Don't worry, I'll manage.' She rose, summoning up a smile. She was glad he thought she was a fighter. It pleased her a lot. And Anthony would have been proud of her, too, trying to manage on her own.

He held out his hand to shake hers. 'I'm really sorry, Beverley. If I ever get back on my feet, you'll be top of the list to be re-employed . . . but don't hold your breath for that to happen!'

She liked his handshake, it was cool and clean and firm.

'Thanks for seeing me anyway,' she said sincerely. 'And all the best.'

'To you, too, my dear,' he replied. 'We're both fighters. We'll both survive. You can bet on it.'

Chapter Twelve

The Duchess of Buckingham arrived at the offices of *Chichi* early on the following Monday. Beverley, determined to conduct herself with dignity during this final week, was already waiting, poised and elegant-looking, when Elaine ushered Serena Buckingham into the room.

'Lady Amesbury will show you everything,' Elaine said, having formally introduced the two women. 'I'm afraid I have to go to a meeting, but if you have any problems, Mr Sternberg will be in his office all morning.'

The Duchess looked with curiosity at Elaine, as if she couldn't quite believe what she saw. Elaine was wearing a matt white ciré trenchcoat, lined with white mink, and white suede boots. Her dark head rose from the soft fur collar like a bird emerging from the snow, and her make-up was so perfect she might have been an enamelled doll.

'I'm sure I'll be fine,' Serena Buckingham assured her. Then she turned and smiled at Beverley. 'I know I'm in very good hands, I just hope you won't find me a complete fool!' Her self-deprecating manner was charming, and in spite of herself Beverley warmed towards this famous beauty who had captured the heart of a royal

Duke but whose marriage had finally foundered because she could no longer tolerate the constraints of life at Buckingham Palace. After all, Beverley reckoned, there was no point in venting her own anger and disappointment on the Duchess. Elaine had proved that she was only interested in people who were useful, and that as soon as you had reached your Sell By Date, you were instantly disposable. It also struck Beverley that maybe the Duchess hadn't as yet realised that Beverley had been kicked off the magazine to make way for her.

'Then I'll leave you to get on with it,' Elaine was saying briskly. She smiled at the Duchess, nodded at Beverley and swept out.

'Well!' Serena Buckingham raised delicate blonde eyebrows as she watched Elaine's figure receding down the corridor. 'What an amazing lady,' she added. 'My mother told me all about her, but this is the first time we've met.'

Beverley smiled diplomatically and gestured to a chair by her desk.

'Shall we start by going through some of the back issues of *Chichi*? It will give you a feel for the type of fashion features we do.'

Serena Buckingham nodded, looking interested. She was a tall woman, in her mid-thirties, possessed of the casual elegance which costs a lot to achieve. Her Armani trouser suit and cream silk shirt were classical, her only jewellery a gold chain bracelet and small gold earrings. A Hermès scarf held her long blonde hair back in a ponytail, and her lightly tanned face was almost devoid of make-up. And yet, Beverley recalled, when she'd seen photographs of the Duchess in her full regalia, with a jewel-encrusted evening dress and a dazzling diamond tiara, she'd been one of the most regal members of the British royal family.

The two women became so engrossed in discussing the editorial pages of *Chichi* that they did not at first notice a figure standing in the doorway, watching them intently. It was Cass Sternberg, big and urbane as ever in a pale grey suit, highly polished shoes on his surprisingly small feet, and a sparkling white shirt with which he wore a deep sky blue silk tie. His grey hair was smoothly combed, and his plump pink face looked even smoother.

'I used to read *Chichi* when I lived over here,' the Duchess was remarking, 'but somehow, once I went to England to get married, I never seemed to have the time.' She shrugged, her lips curling slightly into a disparaging smile.

Listening, head cocked slightly to one side, Cass came forward, his eyes never leaving the Duchess's face. 'Well, we'll give you all the time in the world to read *Chichi* now,' he observed genially. Then he held out his hand. 'Allow me to introduce myself, Your Royal Highness. I'm Cass Sternberg and I'd like to welcome you to *Chichi*. I hope you'll be very happy working for us. We feel very privileged to have you.'

Serena Buckingham looked up, startled. Then she smiled graciously, and Beverley could see how she was able to switch on the charm as she'd no doubt been trained to do when meeting the general public in Britain. Her performance was just too polished to be genuine, but Cass looked dazzled.

'Thank you for giving me the opportunity to work here,' the Duchess replied. 'I'm sure I'm going to love it. Everyone is being so kind.'

Cass bowed and it seemed to Beverley he held on to

the Duchess's hand just a little longer than was necessary.

'As this is your first day, I very much hope you will allow me to take you to lunch, Duchess,' he continued, gazing down at her.

'That's very kind . . .' Serena Buckingham hesitated just long enough not to sound too keen. Then she smiled.

'Thank you. I'd like that.'

Cass beamed and his roly poly chest seemed to expand several inches. 'Then that's settled. My car is outside and I thought you might enjoy going to La Côte Basque.' It was more a statement than a question.

The Duchess rose and she and Cass looked at each other appraisingly. They were about the same height, and for a moment their eyes locked. Then they turned and left the office, Cass solicitously cupping the Duchess's elbow. Her Royal Highness the Duchess of Buckingham had started her first day's work at *Chichi*.

Within three days Cass Sternberg was inviting the Duchess to 'editorial conferences' in his office, which seemed to Beverley, as she cleared her desk in readiness for her departure, to last for anything up to three hours. Serena Buckingham appeared unruffled by this untoward attention. In fact her face lit up whenever Cass walked into their office. She seemed to be busy on several projects too, discussing them with Cass in private but not taking Beverley into her confidence. Once or twice the Duchess excused herself, saying she had to make some phone calls, which she then proceeded to do from the quiet inner sanctum of Cass's office.

When Beverley arrived on the Thursday morning,

her last day but one, the Duchess had already installed herself at what had been Beverley's desk and it was obvious she felt in command of the situation. Today, Beverley noticed, the regal Grace Kelly type beauty was further enhanced by an ice blue bouclé suit and some very fine pearls. She looked up with a bright smile as Beverley came into the room, and there was a definite air of triumph in the way she spoke.

'I've fixed exclusive interviews for the next three issues,' she said. 'I'm going to do individual spreads in future, making my column as much an At Home feature as a fashion report. So much better, don't you think, than covering a mish-mash of well-dressed women at various functions?' Her smile was guileless but her words were a direct criticism of the way Beverley had been compiling the column in the past.

'That sounds like a good idea,' she replied calmly. 'Who have you got?'

The Duchess levelled her gaze at Beverley, but couldn't keep the smugly triumphant note out of her voice.

'Queen Noor of Jordan, Princess Caroline of Monaco and Princess Michael of Kent. We shall also be doing cover shots.'

The first thing that sprang to Beverley's mind was, this dame sure learns fast. Something quite extraordinary was going on. Stunned, she realised Serena Buckingham had mesmerised Cass Sternberg and got him exactly where she wanted him. She'd also over-ruled Elaine, who insisted that only top professional models be used on the cover, and also that the more fashionable women one featured, the bigger the circulation figures. And yet Serena had been so brilliantly clever in getting three scoops in the first week of her employment that Elaine wouldn't be able to object. Especially as the Duchess obviously had Cass's backing in what promised to be a sensational journalistic debut.

'Why, that's great,' she said lamely, wondering what Elaine would say when she found out. There wasn't a damned thing she could do about it, though. It was she who had engaged the Duchess in the first place, and by the looks of it, the Duchess was definitely delivering the goods.

'I'm going out for a while,' Serena Buckingham announced, rising from behind the desk. 'Take any messages for me, will you? There may be a call from Queen Farah Diba's secretary.'

Beverley's mouth tightened. This woman, having taken over her job, her office and her desk, was now treating her like some jumped-up secretary.

At that moment Cass came into the room and as he looked at Serena, eyes darkening with intimacy, smile gentle and tender, Beverley realised with a jolt that the Duchess had even secured possession of Elaine's private territory.

'Hello, Cass,' the Duchess was saying in a low husky voice as he came towards her.

'Hi,' he said softly. 'Are you ready?' A foolish grin spread across his face.

'Yes,' she half whispered, and then without a backward glance left the office with her arm through his.

My God, Beverley reflected, sinking back in her chair. The feathers are really going to fly when the Bird of Prey battles it out with the noble Royal Vulture.

Elaine's hands shook as she tipped two purple capsules

into the palm of her hand. This was more than she could bear. The awareness that Cass was having an affair with the Duchess filled her with fury. And hurt. And deep, deep pain. How could he be doing this to her? Very easily, said a cynical voice in her head. He'd cheated on Maxine for most of their married life, and he'd cheated on her too, for God's sake . . . But never with anyone important before.

Secretaries, shop girls, barmaids and one night stands in general she was prepared to overlook, by pretending to herself they never really happened . . . but this!

Elaine knocked back the two anti-depressants with the vodka and orange she'd already poured out, and then sat at her desk, willing the rising panic and misery to go away. She felt ice-cold, as if her body had been frozen by the chill wind of knowledge. Biting her bottom lip, she fought back tears of despair.

Last night she'd been expecting him to come over to her apartment after a business dinner he had to attend. Maxine was away, staying with her mother in Southampton, and so it was going to be a perfect opportunity for him to stay the night. When he hadn't arrived by midnight she knew in her bones what had happened.

Elaine remembered how he'd summoned the Duchess into his office for a drink, early in the evening when she'd normally have been leaving the office at the same time as Beverley. No doubt, over a glass of wine, he'd arranged to see her later. After his business dinner. So why didn't I do anything to stop them? Elaine asked herself. She knew the answer, of course. She was too frightened. Too scared, for once in her life, to face the truth which was if Cass set his heart on something he had to have it. He was like a spoilt child. And right now, she knew Cass wanted Serena. And the worst part of it was, Elaine knew she couldn't do anything to stop it.

Cocooned in wretchedness, she sat brooding, waiting for the pills to work, demanding of the vodka it do its usual trick of blanketing her raging unhappiness.

Twenty minutes later she still sat at her desk, unable to deal with the pile of work in front of her, unable to do anything except think about Cass and that bitch of a Duchess. In her tortured mind's eye, she could see them together in his office, in a restaurant, back at his apartment, and finally in the kingsized bed he usually shared with Maxine.

Elaine buried her face in her hands. She knew that bed, too. She was also familiar with his wife's dressing table, and her closet, and her adjoining bathroom. Many were the nights she'd stayed with Cass when his wife had been away, and it had given her a kick to assume Maxine's persona. Sometimes she'd spray herself with Maxine's perfume; try on any jewellery that was lying about; slip, literally, into Maxine's high-heeled satin bedroom slippers which matched her pink satin negligée. Then she'd walk around, wishing she was Mrs Cass Sternberg, wishing she was the mother of his three children.

At the memory of them, a son and two daughters, Elaine's face started to crumple. Her jaw sagged and her mouth drooped pitifully. Little wrinkles, which normally never showed under the carefully applied make-up, appeared in a fine tracery while sobs that could no longer be suppressed broke from her throat.

Grief threatened to engulf her. Instead of the vodka giving her a glowing lift, it had pushed her over the edge, into a dark pit, and she was falling fast ... unable to control herself . . . unable to cope any more. Quite simply, something had snapped and she couldn't bear it another minute.

Jumping to her feet, she rushed out of her office and went hurtling down the corridor, a tiny slim figure in a white barathea suit, leaving in her wake a drift of the perfume she always wore, Evyan's White Shoulders.

Passing the open door of Beverley's office, she sped on until she came to Cass's door. It was shut but she flung it open to find Cass sitting at his desk, signing papers. He looked up, startled.

'You son-of-a-bitch!' Elaine screamed. 'How dare you do this to me?'

'What are you talking about?' He rose, red in the face with anger, and what she suspected was also guilt.

'You know very well what I'm talking about. Why didn't you come to me last night?'

'For God's sake, Elaine, keep your voice down!' he admonished, striding around the side of the desk and rushing forward to shut the door. 'Do you want everyone to hear?'

'I don't care who hears,' she sobbed hysterically, collapsing into a chair. 'You've ruined my life . . . you've robbed me of . . .'

'Elaine! Pull yourself together. You're jumping to conclusions, for Christ's sake. What the hell's got into you?'

'I'm not blind. I can see how you've been all week towards that damned Duchess. I wish to God I'd never hired her,' she wept.

'You're being ridiculous,' Cass snapped but his voice carried no conviction. 'I've merely tried to make her feel at home since she joined *Chichi* . . .'

'Yes, your home!' Elaine shot back. 'Don't think I don't know what you were up to last night! Don't think you can fool me! Isn't it enough that I've had to put up with your lies?'

'For Christ's sake, *keep your voice down*, Elaine,' he hissed, furiously. 'You might not mind the entire office knowing your private business, but I do!'

'Why?' she demanded, her voice rising louder. 'Because you don't want people to know how badly you've treated me? Because you would never leave your wife for me? Because you forced me to have an abortion six years ago, and threatened to fire me if I didn't? Is that what you want to keep secret from the rest of the world?' She picked up the heavy bronze figure of a horse he always kept on his desk, and exerting every ounce of strength, threw it at him. '*I don't give a fuck who hears!*' she screamed. 'I won't let you treat me like this.'

Down the corridor, Beverley sat alone in her office, hearing every word through the thin walls that divided them, sickened by the revelations which explained so much. She'd always known about Cass and Elaine's long-term affair, everyone on *Chichi* knew about it, but she'd never guessed that Elaine had aborted a baby. Having a child herself gave her an insight into what Elaine must have suffered as a result; perhaps that was why her moods seemed to swing from time to time, why after a glass of 'orange juice' she seemed much happier, why perhaps she had this fetish with everything white – a sign of mourning in some countries.

'I won't have her working here,' Beverley heard Elaine insisting shrilly.

Cass's voice was low and urgent. 'Stop being so hys-

terical! Having her write a column is a real coup for
Chichi and you know it! Now, for God's sake, pull yourself together and stop this behaviour! It was you who
brought her in!'

'And I'm quite capable of getting rid of her, too.'

'You can't do that . . .' His voice was so low now
Beverley could barely hear what he was saying, but she
heard Elaine screaming back.

'Why can't I? Just watch me! I won't have that woman
take you away from me.' Then her voice broke and she
started sobbing again, and Beverley rose, wanting to
get away, hating being privy to this emotional quarrel,
thankful the Duchess had gone out to 'do some shopping'. As she left to go to the washroom at the far end of
the corridor, she heard Cass speak again. This time his
voice was triumphant.

'You can't get rid of her, because at your insistence,
Elaine, we put her under a two-year contract.
Remember?'

Beverley fled, unable to bear any more. She was glad
now that she was leaving *Chichi*, even if it meant the end
of a glamorous chapter in her life. There was too much
ugliness, too much neurosis, and too much that was
artificial and false to want to make her hang around any
longer. Tomorrow was her last day. And then, as her
mother was fond of saying, the next day would be the
first day of the rest of her life. She had no idea what
the future held, she hadn't even found herself a new job,
but whatever happened, she was determined to face it
with as much courage as she could. Anthony, after all,
would have expected nothing less of her.

Sometimes, in the past few weeks, Beverley had awakened in the middle of the night, overpowered by an

acute sense of anxiety. Like a physical illness it gripped her stomach with cramping tentacles and bound her ribs so tightly she felt she was suffocating.

Added to her grief at losing Anthony she was now desperately worried about money. After two weeks of frantic job searching, she'd been forced to wait tables at a SoHo restaurant called The Blue Cockatoo where the food was fast and cheap, the customers mixed and the hours long. She wouldn't have minded so much if the pay had been good, but as it was she could scarcely manage the rent and the food for the three of them. Was she being crazy to stay in New York when she could have returned with Nicky to Stockbridge? She asked herself that question a thousand times. Her friends thought she was mad, but Jenny of course, wanting to remain in New York herself, was adamant they should stay.

'It's not as if it's affecting Nicky in any way,' she remarked persuasively. She'd got herself a job selling theatre programmes in the evenings, while Beverley stayed in to look after Nicky.

But Rachael and Daniel thought they should all return home, and so did Josh, at least until the recession was over. He called Beverley from Boston one night, sounding deeply concerned.

'Get real, Sis,' he begged her. 'New York is no place without enough money. Go back home. Mom and Dad would love it if you did.'

She got the same advice from Faye and Hayley. 'It was different when you and Anthony had a big apartment in a fashionable area and you were comfortably off,' Hayley pointed out. 'But you live in grottsville now. There are junkies on every street corner, and hookers and down-and-outs and people sitting right on the sidewalk, dying of AIDS. How can you bring up a small child in those surroundings?'

Beverley listened but she didn't want to hear. It had always been her ambition to work and live in New York, ever since she'd been a little girl, and she didn't want to let go of that dream. It spelt independence. Doing her own thing. Being her own person. To go home now would feel like quitting, and there was another reason why she was loath to leave. Manhattan had become synonymous with Anthony and all they had done together from the moment they'd met.

But as the weeks passed, Beverley began to realise the extent to which New York had changed. And so had her perception of it. Maybe it was the lack of money but it no longer seemed the city of opportunity and excitement, of big spenders and a million ways in which they could spend their money. No longer the glittering temple of sybaritic indulgence, it stood now like a poverty-pervaded ruin, bearing the scars of past grandiloquence; a city that smelled of death and decline. And yet she still loved it, loved tracing the routes she and Anthony had taken when they'd first gone out together, walking where they'd walked, passing the restaurants where they'd had dinner and the shops where they'd lingered over their purchases. The only place she couldn't bear to pass was the block where they'd lived. That was too painful, the memories still too sharp.

Every morning, Beverley set out for work, realising this certainly wasn't what she'd planned to do with her life when she'd worked so hard for her scholarship, but realising also that she was lucky at this time to have a job at all. By the end of the day her feet felt like burning coals and she ached all over, but at least she was bringing home a paycheck every week, and Nicky was wanting for nothing. Jenny didn't ask her for anything now that she had her evening job either, and Beverley was impressed at the way her sister had matured in recent months. All of a sudden, Jenny seemed to have grown up and shed her maddening juvenile behaviour.

'I'm very grateful you know, Jen,' Beverley said more than once. 'I feel I'm being selfish keeping you here like this, looking after Nicky all day, and then doing your own job in the evenings; you ought to be finishing your education and leading your own life.'

Jenny smiled. 'I love being here, you know that. And I love looking after Nicky. And let's face it, this wretched recession can't last forever. It'll end one day, and then we'll both do something splendid and be rich again!'

Beverley threw her arms around her, laughing. 'I love you, Jen! Especially now that you've stopped stealing all my best clothes,' she added teasingly.

'You haven't bought anything nice enough to steal, lately,' Jenny giggled. 'And you won't catch me dead in your waitress uniform! Right now, your wardrobe's safe.'

'I'm glad to hear it, not that I plan to go anywhere smart in the foreseeable future.'

'Bevs?' Jenny had been longing to ask her something for a long time now.

'Yeah?'

'Do you wish you could date again? I mean . . . do you want to?'

Beverley drew a deep breath but answered unhesitatingly.

'No, I don't want to, Jen. Not at all. Sometimes I

wonder if I'll ever want to date or have a relationship with anyone ever again.' She paused, thinking. 'You see,' she continued slowly, 'Anthony was the most perfect man in every way as far as I was concerned. He had everything.'

Jenny's brow puckered. 'But what do you do about sex?' she whispered, leaning forward confidentially.

Beverley glanced round their small living room, pretending to look for people. 'Why are you whispering?' she asked again, grinning. 'There's no one here!'

Jenny indicated Nicholas, playing with some bricks in the doorway.

'You know . . . we should be careful what we say.'

'In front of a twenty-two-month-old child?' Beverley asked incredulously. 'It's nice of you to grant him the brilliance of Einstein, but I really don't think it matters what we say at this stage,' she laughed. 'Anyway, to answer your question, I don't even want sex these days. That side of my life seems to have died too. I don't even think about it these days.'

'I think about it all the time,' Jenny admitted. 'I'm scared as hell to do it, because I'm frightened of catching something, but I sure fantasise about it all the time.'

Beverley looked at her with understanding concern. 'I'm glad you're being so mature about it, though, Jen. You should only have sex with someone you know very well, and even then it's wise to take precautions. Do you know what they say these days?'

'What?' Jenny looked wide-eyed and serious. Beverley was the only person she could talk to like this. Rachael would have had a fit and probably been deeply embarrassed.

'They say, when you go to bed with someone, you're

not only going to bed with that particular person, but also with all the people they've slept with during the past five years.'

'Jeez, that's disgusting!' Jenny shuddered. 'It sure puts the dampeners on having a love-life, doesn't it? I think I'll stay a virgin until my wedding night!'

Beverley burst out laughing. 'There's no need to go to extremes, Jen. Just be careful. And discriminating. Get to know someone really well, so you can see what sort of a track record they've got, before you get too involved.'

Beverley loved these times when they could sit and talk. Without Jenny, she wondered if she wouldn't have been tempted to pack her bags and go home. But Jenny managed to cheer her up, and sometimes to make her laugh. If the New York of her dreams was no more, she still wanted to believe that it would all come back one day and she'd be right here to enjoy it.

Jenny was right. The recession couldn't last forever. Nothing ever did.

The following week Beverley got fired from The Blue Cockatoo.

As Beverley made her way home that evening, walking along the dusty sidewalks while the hurly-burly of heavy traffic thundered past, she realised that if she couldn't get another job, she'd have to go on unemployment. There was nothing else for it. She'd have to stay at home with Nicky and try and exist on a state hand-out. But how much would she get? Maybe she'd have to move again, and sub-let the apartment . . . if anyone wanted it. Trying to keep calm, she made up her mind that she *had* to find another job. It was ridiculous, she told herself angrily, that with her degree and work experience, all she'd been able to find was a job waiting tables, and she'd even been fired from that.

'We're having to cut back on staff,' the manager said that morning. 'Business is down for the second month running.'

Quickening her pace she decided to try McDonald's. Surely they'd be able to offer her a job?

But McDonald's had nothing to offer her, and neither did anywhere else she tried. For a week, during which her phone was cut off for non-payment, she applied for dozens of jobs, but to no avail. It seemed that everyone was cutting back. It was the same story wherever she went.

'I'm getting desperate, Jen,' she said one evening as they perched on the high stools in the galley-size kitchen, eating pasta because it was cheap and filling.

Jenny looked around as if for inspiration. 'I wish we had something we could sell.'

'I can't sell my jewellery . . . I couldn't bear to,' Beverley said, biting her lip. The previous week she'd almost been tempted because there were things Nicky badly needed, and there were urgent bills to pay, but when she thought about going to the Diamond District, on Forty-seventh Street, she knew she couldn't go through with it. Her emerald engagement ring, and the diamond pendant Anthony had given her to go with his mother's diamond earrings, were far too precious to part with. To sell them now, no matter how broke she was, would be a betrayal of Anthony's love.

'I'd rather go hungry than sell my jewels,' she said aloud. 'One day I'll give the earrings to Nicky's wife, as Anthony's mother gave them to me.'

Jenny burst out laughing. 'Give the guy a chance! As

you said yourself the other day, he's not even two yet!'

'I know, but I love tradition, and the knowledge that there are things that can be handed down from generation to generation makes me feel good.'

That night, after Jenny had gone to bed, Beverley took her jewellery from its hiding place and spread it on her lap. The emerald and diamond ring glowed with a dazzling depth and she slipped it on her finger, wishing she dare wear it all the time. Then she took the drop earrings and pendant out of their cases and held them in the palm of her hand. The glittering diamonds blazed with a fierce fire as she held them under the light and she remembered how Anthony loved her to wear them. They were a part of her love for him, the jewels he and his mother had given her. She had to find another way to raise money. Through a blur of unshed tears she put them carefully away again, resolving that no matter how bad things got, she would never ever part with them.

Sleep came fitfully to her that night as she tossed about, dozing and dreaming and then waking up with a start as sudden thoughts cut through her slumbers. The situation was becoming desperate, and if she didn't find a job by the end of the week, there'd be nothing for it but to return to Stockbridge, and admit defeat.

The next morning she was up early, determined to make one last concerted effort. She would not be beaten, she told herself sternly. She would not go on unemployment benefit.

Dressing with care in her best dark green suit and brushing her rich chestnut hair until it gleamed, she set off shortly after nine o'clock.

'Wish me luck,' she called to Jenny as she kissed Nicholas goodbye. Jenny emerged from the kitchen where she was making breakfast.

'You look nice,' she said encouragingly. 'A bit up-market for waiting tables, perhaps.'

'Stuff waiting tables,' Beverley replied vigorously. 'I've been underselling myself.' It was true. Depression had been making her feel inadequate. Without Anthony, her self-esteem had been low. Especially since Elaine had fired her. 'Positive thinking, Jen,' she added. 'That's what it's all about. Today I'm going to act like a winner, and see what happens. What have I got to lose, anyway?'

'How did you get on?' Jenny called out, when Beverley returned late that afternoon. She was in the shower, getting ready to go to her job selling theatre programmes. 'Any luck?'

'Do you want the good news . . . or the good news?' Beverley shouted back. There was unmistakable excitement in her voice.

Jenny shot out of the small bathroom, towel draped round her, feet making wet marks on the floor. 'What happened?' she demanded.

Beverley was standing in the middle of the living room, her face radiant. 'I got a job.' At her feet Nicholas was playing with his toys.

'Where? Doing what? How much are you getting?'

'Hey, give me a break!' Beverley laughed. 'The good news is I've got a job as a part-time hotel receptionist, starting Monday. The . . .'

'Which hotel?' Jenny broke in.

'A small hotel on Fifty-first Street and Second Avenue. The Southampton.'

'That's fab, Bevs. And what's the other piece of good news?'

'Next month they'll be hiring me full-time, because their regular receptionist is leaving to go to Europe.'

'Wow!' Jenny flung herself at Beverley. 'That's great! Aren't you thrilled? Oh, it's wonderful, Bevs. We're going to be rich sooner than we thought!'

Laughingly Beverley hugged her back. 'Dream on, sweetheart. The pay's not that great, not as much as I was getting at *Chichi* or anything like, but at least it will keep the wolf from the door, and it will be a helluva lot more interesting than waiting tables.' She swept Nicholas up in her arms and cuddled him. 'I'm going to be able to get some nice things for my precious boy, aren't I?' she cooed, while he grabbed her hair gleefully.

'Toys?' he asked.

'Yes, toys, my darling.' The hardest part of being broke was not being able to get new clothes and toys for Nicky. His babyhood had already passed and now he was a toddler. Soon he would be a small boy, and before long the days of his childhood would be over. It was a thought that saddened her. Anthony was missing the best years of his son's life, and she hadn't the money to make them special either.

'Is that the time?' Jenny exclaimed suddenly, as she pulled on her black skirt and blouse. 'I've got to rush or I'll lose the miserable job I *have* got. By the way, there's a letter from Mom to you. It arrived after you'd gone out this morning. I put it in the kitchen, on top of the fridge.'

'Thanks.' Beverley put Nicholas back on the floor, where he immediately resumed playing with his favourite toy, a little wooden truck he could pull along with a string.

Beverley changed into jeans and a T-shirt before preparing his supper, and it wasn't until he was in his high-chair, spooning mashed banana into his mouth, that she remembered the letter. Since their phone had been cut off, it was the cheapest form of communication and there was something delightfully old fashioned about receiving mail.

Beverley ripped open the envelope with anticipation, longing to hear news from home, wanting to know how Tom was doing at school, and whether her parents liked Josh's new girlfriend.

A moment later, her bitter cry of distress filled the tiny apartment, startling Nicholas and bringing Jenny rushing out of her bedroom, where she had been putting the finishing touches to her make-up.

'What is it?' she asked, alarmed.

Beverley handed her the first page of Rachael's letter as the tears streamed down her cheeks.

Chapter Thirteen

'What is it?' Jenny whispered fearfully, taking the letter with a shaking hand. 'Is it Daddy?'

Beverley shook her head, unable to speak. A few minutes before she'd been happy for the first time in ages. Now this cruel blow had brought back all the pain of the past year, compounding it so that she felt devastated.

Jenny skimmed Rachael's letter, her face turning pale and drawn.

'Oh, God!' she exclaimed, stunned.

Beverley reached for the letter again and re-read it, as if she could hardly believe her eyes. Rachael told of how Anthony's sister, Lady Jean Ffitch, had tried to get hold of Beverley, but as her phone had been cut off, she'd finally put through a call to the Franklins in Stockbridge.

'It seems,' Rachael wrote, 'that while out with the local Hunt, of which he was Master, Henry's horse took a high fence, slipped and fell, and Henry was thrown. He landed badly and broke his neck. Death, Lady Jean told us, would have been instantaneous. As she's been unable to get in touch with you herself, she asked me to let you know . . .'

Henry dead. Beverley sat hunched, her arms wrapped across her stomach, as if to contain the cramping sick pains that were holding her in their grip. First Anthony. Now Henry. Dear, kind, lovable Henry, with his warm bear hugs and reassuring manner. She couldn't believe it, didn't want to believe it, rejected this new heartbreak because she couldn't face it. With Henry gone, her last and final link with Anthony had gone too, and she wept inconsolably as she leant against the kitchen counter.

'Are you all right, Bevs?' Jenny asked anxiously. 'I've got to go to work. Are you sure you'll be all right on your own?'

Beverley nodded, reaching for a tissue. 'It's such a shock,' she said, her voice choked. 'I loved Henry. Even though he lived so far away, it was a comfort to know he was there . . . now I'll never see him again.'

'It's unbelievable, isn't it?' Jenny agreed sorrowfully. 'His poor wife . . . and his daughter. She's just a little girl, isn't she?'

'Yes. I must write to them, and to Anthony and Henry's mother.' Beverley blew her nose and tried to control herself, but the tears kept welling up, as fresh thoughts entered her mind. She turned a woebegone face to Jenny. 'Imagine losing both your sons! Can you think of anything worse? Their poor mother . . . my heart really breaks for her. She's only got Lady Jean now.'

'I know, it's dreadful. Listen, Bevs, I've got to go.' Jenny glanced at her wrist-watch agitatedly. 'Are you sure you'll be okay?'

'Yes, I'll be fine,' Beverley assured her. 'I just wish we had the phone working. I'd like to talk to Mom and Dad myself.'

When Jenny had gone, she picked up Nicky, and, holding him close, turned on the television and settled herself on the sofa with him on her lap. She knew she ought to be giving him his bath and then settling him in bed for the night, but she needed his presence this evening because she couldn't bear to be alone. Nicky was all she had now and as he folded himself into a foetal position against her breast, she held him close, drawing comfort from his presence. Absorbed in a cartoon that filled the screen with colourful images, he lay in her arms until he fell asleep.

Beverley remained on the sofa, not wanting to disturb him, and not having the will to move herself. With eyes that didn't see and a mind that registered nothing, she stayed gazing at the television screen.

Outside the familiar night sounds of Manhattan charged the atmosphere with energy, and down below in the darkened streets life went on as usual, but, drained of emotion, Beverley remained on the sofa, too weary to move, too sick at heart to get herself something to eat.

When Jenny got back at midnight, she found both Beverley and Nicholas asleep on the sofa, with the lights on and the television blaring. Creeping across the room, she switched off the set and then fetched a blanket with which to cover them. She knew she ought to awaken them, so they could go to bed, but she reckoned Beverley needed a few hours' oblivion to help her come to terms with this latest tragedy, and so she left them undisturbed while she tip-toed to her own room.

Beverley wrote to Lady Jean, Leonora and the Dowager Countess. At first, not sure how to word the letters of sympathy, and remembering how formal the English can sometimes be, she composed a couple of drafts, but they were stiff and stilted and so she tore them up and decided to write as she felt, straight from the heart.

'You must be missing him most dreadfully . . .' she put in her letter to old Lady Cumberland to whom she felt the closest although they'd never met. 'I loved Henry, too, and I shall never forget how kind he was to me when Anthony died. Looking at my little Nicholas I cannot bear to think how you must be suffering, having lost both your sons . . .'

When she posted the letters she felt at her lowest ebb. Everything seemed to be going from her; the people she had loved and depended on, the life-style she'd worked so hard to achieve, even her hopes for the future. The moment Anthony had died her world had changed forever, and the inner pain she felt was unrelenting. It was with her when she went to bed, and it was there, even deeper, when she awoke. And all through the long days, she had to carry this black burden around with her, as it sapped her strength, and destroyed her peace of mind. Trying to lose herself in work, she exerted every ounce of energy she could muster to make a success of her job at The Southampton Hotel. It was a bitter experience. Even the general manager referred to the clientele as 'flash and trash' as she learned to handle rudeness, intolerance and humiliation from those who had money but no manners. For the first time she realised how people in the service industry get treated by the general public. If she hadn't needed the money so badly she'd have quit the first week.

Then one evening, a month later, she arrived home to hear voices in the living room, accompanied by the occasional happy squawk from Nicholas.

'Bevs? Is that you?' Jenny called out. 'We've got a visitor.'

Beverley walked slowly into the living room and found herself face to face with a tall angular woman with a large-boned face whose grey hair looked as if it needed expert styling and whose tweeds, though well cut, looked as if they'd been slept in. Round her scrawny neck hung a strand of dull pearls and on her lapel, dingy from lack of cleaning, glinted a brooch with the depth of fire that is only to be found in fine diamonds.

'How do you do. I'm Jean Ffitch,' she announced in a matter-of-fact voice, extending a reddened hand.

Beverley looked at her in astonishment. This woman, who was in her early-fifties, bore no resemblance to either Anthony or Henry. Her eyes were the same sharp blue, but she completely lacked their intrinsic charm and relaxed manner.

'Hi,' said Beverley, trying to pull herself together. 'I'm Beverley.'

'I had rather gathered that,' Lady Jean retorted, though not unkindly. 'Your sister's been telling me what's been happening to you since Anthony's death. Not much fun, I hear.' Her voice was a soft bark, and like Henry she spoke in short sentences.

Beverley picked Nicholas up from where he was playing on the floor and held him close as if for protection.

'We're managing,' she replied stoutly.

Lady Jean sat down again, her slender feet in their sensible low-heeled shoes planted squarely before her. 'I tried to phone you when Henry was killed and I've been trying ever since. Jenny says you haven't been able to pay the bill and it's been cut orf,' she added bluntly, her cut glass accent pronounced.

'I'll be paying it soon,' Beverley replied defensively, hoping Jenny hadn't been saying too much. In spite of everything she still had her pride, and she didn't want Lady Jean to get the impression they were hoping for hand-outs.

'When did you arrive?'

'If you mean New York, yesterday evening. If you mean here, half an hour ago.' Lady Jean glanced at Nicky, who had his head resting on Beverley's shoulder. He was sucking his thumb as he always did when he was tired.

'You'll have to get him out of that habit,' she remarked tartly. 'Anthony was a terrible thumb sucker, too. At least he hasn't got one of those dreadful plastic dummies.'

Beverley tried to catch Jenny's eye, to see if she knew what this unexpected visit was all about, but Jenny shook her head, implying she'd no idea.

'Would you like some coffee?'

'Never touch the stuff. Gives me palpitations,' Lady Jean replied.

'Shall I make some tea?' Jenny suggested. She'd had the stickiest half hour of her life with this bristly woman, and she was looking forward to leaving for work shortly.

'No, thanks.'

Beverley put Nicholas down again, and as he resumed playing with his cart, realised Lady Jean was watching him closely.

'He's big for his age, isn't he?' she remarked after a moment.

'I think he's about average,' Beverley replied mildly. Lady Jean continued to watch him as if she were fascinated.

'Truck's loaded!' Nicholas observed with satisfaction, piling wooden bricks onto his cart.

Then he looked directly at her, a big smile lighting up his face. 'Truck's loaded!' he repeated.

'He's like Anthony, isn't he?' she observed, and her voice was less gruff now.

'Yes,' Beverley agreed. After a moment she continued: 'So what brings you to New York?'

Lady Jean looked up in surprise. 'The need to make contact with you and Nicholas, of course.'

'That's very nice of you,' Beverley replied politely.

'Niceness has got nothing to do with it,' came the swift reply. 'Mother's too old and blind, and I could hardly expect Leonora to come, under the circumstances. So that only left me.'

Beverley looked at her, puzzled. Why did anyone from the Cumberland family have to visit her at all? Were they suddenly concerned about her financial position? Afraid she was going to do something that would bring the family's noble name into disrepute? Or merely curious to see how she was making out on her own?

'So what can I tell you?' Beverley asked. 'You've seen where we live, and as you can tell, Nicky is a normal, healthy, happy little boy.'

Suddenly she realised Lady Jean was looking at her strangely.

'Anthony always told us you were refreshingly naive, but you can't really expect me to believe you don't know why I'm here?' she remonstrated, with a short laugh.

Beverley frowned, not liking her derisive tone. 'I'm afraid I've no idea why you're here. We've been managing okay since Anthony was killed, and we shall go on managing.'

'My dear gel!' Lady Jean's face was incredulous. 'I can

hardly believe this! Don't you realise what's happened? Have you no idea that Henry's death has altered everything?'

'Well . . .' Beverley hedged, feeling disadvantaged. Elaine had made her feel foolish in exactly the same way when she'd got engaged to Anthony. 'I'm not sure I know what you mean.'

'I mean,' said Lady Jean, slowly and deliberately as if she were addressing a stupid child, 'that when poor Henry was killed, Nicholas automatically succeeded to the title.' She looked down at the little blond-haired boy playing at her feet. 'He is now the Earl of Cumberland.'

Beverley couldn't take it in at first, had never made the connection that on Henry's death the title would go to the next male relative in line, who happened to be Nicholas.

'Anthony would have succeeded if he'd been alive,' Lady Jean explained.

'What about Henry's daughter?'

'She remains Lady Juliet Amesbury, as she's always been.'

'My God!' Beverley leaned back in the chair, not knowing what to think. She'd always regarded titles as meaningless, even her own since she married Anthony. What could you *do* with a title? It certainly hadn't helped her in the past few months, but then Elaine would have said Beverley didn't know how to exploit it. She voiced her feelings to Lady Jean now. 'What will it mean . . . now that Nicky's an Earl? It doesn't alter anything, does it? It won't bring his father back? Or his uncle?'

'Good heavens, Beverley!' Lady Jean sounded scandalised. 'What it means is that Nicholas technically owns Bucklands and all that goes with it, though trustees will be looking after it until he comes of age. It also means he will come into a large fortune when he's eighteen. Don't you realise what a heritage this is for the boy? Henry was desperate to have a son to take over when he died. That's why it was so upsetting when Leonora lost a little boy in a miscarriage. They'd been trying for years, but she kept having miscarriages.' She sniffed dispassionately. 'It is a great disappointment to her that she never bore an heir. However, Henry did say to me when he returned from the States after his last visit that Nicholas was a fine little chap, and at least he'd be able to continue the Cumberland line if Leonora never produced a boy.'

Beverley shook her head, bewildered. 'I had no idea, no idea at all.'

'That's why I'm here,' Lady Jean observed.

'What, to tell me all this?'

It was Lady Jean's turn to look astonished. 'To fetch you both. I'm presuming you want to be with Nicholas while he grows up?'

'Wait a minute . . .' Beverley raised her hand. Everything was happening so fast. What on earth was her sister-in-law talking about now? 'Why should you be fetching us? What for?'

'I'm here to take you back with me. Your mother told me of your financial problems, so I've already bought your air tickets, and I suggest we leave for England just as soon as you can manage it.' Lady Jean talked with the assurance of someone who is used to being obeyed.

Beverley looked stunned. 'I don't believe this! We're not going anywhere. This is our home. Our country. My

315

family's here . . . Nicky and I are not going to leave America.'

'You don't seem to understand, Beverley.' Lady Jean spoke slowly and slightly loudly, as English people are inclined to do when addressing foreigners. 'Nicholas must have an English education. He must go to Eton like all his forebears, and on to university. In short he must be brought up in England because he's British and his future lies in Great Britain.'

'He's also half American,' Beverley protested angrily.

'Of course he is, but children adopt their father's nationality, not their mother's.' Seeing how angry and agitated Beverley was becoming, Lady Jean smiled her rusty smile, unused to having to turn on the charm and not finding it an easy task. 'My dear girl, you must see the advantages for Nicholas, and you mustn't deny him what is rightfully his.'

'He can inherit all right, but that surely doesn't mean he has to go to England yet,' Beverley argued. 'If Bucklands isn't his until he's eighteen, why does he have to live in it now?'

'Running a large estate, with a home farm, is a serious business and requires training,' Lady Jean pointed out. 'He might like to go to Cirencester Agricultural College instead of university; that will be up to him. But he can't expect to walk into Bucklands straight from Manhattan when he's eighteen and take over, just like that. It wouldn't be fair on him and it wouldn't be fair on the people who work and live on the estate. He'd be a stranger to them and he wouldn't understand what was expected of him. There's a lot more to a substantial inheritance like this than suddenly finding you've got lots of money in the bank, you know,' she added crisply.

Beverley looked back at her unhappily. She understood what Lady Jean was saying but England was so far away from everything she held dear, and she suddenly felt scared. How would she manage without her parents being a short flight away? How would she survive without all the familiar things that had been her life since she'd been a child? The prospect was daunting, and yet how could she deny Nicky his inheritance? He was being given all the chances Anthony had enjoyed, opportunities she would never be able to give him, and she knew she couldn't stand in his way. And yet . . .

'I'll have to think about it,' she said falteringly. 'It's such a shock . . . it will mean so many changes.'

Lady Jean leaned forward, sensing she was weakening. 'You don't really have anything to think about. Nicholas has to be educated and brought up in England. For goodness' sake, Beverley, think what a wonderful life he has ahead of him. At Bucklands he'll have his own horses, a magnificent estate with forests and the home farm, a castle full of historical treasures, and in time a great deal of money.' She paused and looked round the shabby apartment with the highway running below so that there was always the background noise of the roar of traffic. At that moment, as if on cue, the siren of a police car screamed past at high speed. Lady Jean shrugged her thin tweed-clad shoulders.

'Is this what you want for him, Beverley? Is this how Anthony would have wanted his son to live?'

It was hitting below the belt and Beverley knew it. She raised her chin in a proud gesture. 'New York may not be so hot at the moment, because of the recession, but my home in Stockbridge is beautiful.'

'Then why aren't you and Nicholas living there?'

317

'Because there's no work to be got back home.'

'According to your sister, whom I was talking to while we waited for you to come back, there isn't any work worth having in New York, either,' she remarked sarcastically.

Beverley looked mutinous. 'Things will improve.'

'But why put yourself and Nicholas through all this when you could be living in great comfort in the English countryside?' Lady Jean's tone was incredulous.

'Because . . . because this is *home*,' Beverley stressed, close to tears. She felt confused and bewildered at the suddenness of it all. It was too big a shock to take in all at once. This hard-faced woman, who bore no resemblance to Henry or Anthony, was expecting her to turn her life around all in the space of five minutes, and it simply wasn't possible. She looked down at Nicholas, who was blissfully unaware that the whole of his future was under discussion.

Then she looked up at Lady Jean again, her expression thoughtful.

'Would we have to go right away?' she asked in a small voice.

'If you want a few weeks in which to make your arrangements, that would be all right, but I have to tell you one thing, Beverley.'

'What is it?'

'Don't think you can change your mind the minute my back is turned. The trustees will not subsidise Nicholas's upbringing and education unless he lives in England.'

Beverley sat in silence, knowing now that their going to live in England had been inevitable from the beginning. She'd never had an option or been given a choice. The Cumberland family had banked on the knowledge that no loving mother would deny her son his rightful inheritance, and so Anthony's sister had known what the outcome would be all along. As if she sensed she might have come on too strong, Lady Jean leaned forward again, and her manner was more solicitous.

'This is what Anthony would have wanted for Nicholas, you know. He would have made sure the boy had only the best, just as he and Henry had, wouldn't he?'

Beverley nodded slowly. To keep Nicky in America, just so that she could be near her family, and the country of her birth, would be plain selfish.

Yet, that night, as she lay in bed trying to sleep, her heart ached as she thought of what lay ahead. Nicholas was too young to understand what was happening and he would be happy, no matter what, as long as she was with him. But for her it was different. At the thought of leaving her family behind, she felt overwhelmed with sadness and feelings of dread.

It was their last weekend in America. On Monday Beverley and Nicholas were flying to London, where Lady Jean had arranged for a car to meet them and drive them to Bucklands. Meanwhile Beverley was staying in Stockbridge, relishing the last few days with her parents while they all tried to remain cheerful in spite of the impending separation. Beverley had given up the apartment in Riverside Drive, which at the last moment had seemed so dear to her and Jenny, and now she was all packed, with the bulk of her possessions and wedding presents being shipped to England.

'I can't believe you're going,' Jenny said sorrowfully on the Sunday evening, as they all sat in the garden after

319

supper, watching the sun go down over the distant hills. Jenny had agreed to continue her education as Beverley was no longer going to be living in New York, and she had some far distant ambition to go to England, one day, to seek her own fortune.

'I can't believe it either,' Beverley replied, shaking her head. Her emotions were so mixed she no longer felt sure how she regarded the future. It would be wonderful never to have to worry about money again and wonderful to know Nicky's future was assured. He would be going to Anthony's prep school, Ludgrove, when he was nine, then to Eton, and after that university or agricultural college. At eighteen he would officially inherit Bucklands Castle and a 'considerable fortune', according to Lady Jean. But what of herself? What was she going to do with the rest of her life? Being Nicky's mother would be a full-time job in the immediate future, but as soon as he went away to school, what was she going to do with her time?

'We'll try and visit you next year,' Daniel remarked in his slow comforting way. 'And we'll write to each other, every week. Now that man can travel in outer space, Britain doesn't seem such a long way away, does it?'

Rachael smiled at him in her gentle way, grateful to him for trying to keep their spirits up. 'And we do have a phone!' she added.

'We'll visit you, too, as often as we can,' Beverley said, reaching out to squeeze her mother's hand. 'At least we'll be able to afford to come, which is nice.' Lady Jean had informed her that the trustees had opened a bank account in her name, to provide the day-to-day necessities for herself and Nicholas, and when Beverley heard how much they were giving her, she was amazed.

'What do they consider are "day-to-day" expenses?' she asked Rachael. 'Mink coats and diamond rings?'

'At least you won't have to ask them for money every time you want to buy something,' her mother reminded her wisely. 'You'll have a degree of independence.'

'I know, but aren't the English funny about money? Just before she left, Lady Jean gave me a sealed envelope, with the flight tickets, and said, "This is a little something to tide you over until you arrive in England." ' Beverley smiled at the memory.

'And . . . ?' Jenny asked curiously.

'There was four thousand dollars, in cash. Why couldn't she just have handed it to me and said, "Here's some money in case you're short." '

'The English never discuss money,' Rachael said. 'It's a dirty word with them.'

Surrounded by her family as the dusk closed in around them, Beverley knew she should be thankful for the glittering future that lay before them, but at this moment she wondered how she was going to survive the stiff upper lip English mentality, with its strange customs and its rigid determination to hide all emotion.

As if she knew what her elder daughter was thinking, Rachael leaned over and took her hand.

'Remember, no matter what happens, this will always be your home,' she said softly. 'Daddy and I will always be here for you.'

Beverley gave a watery smile. 'I know. I just wish England was nearer.'

'You married an Englishman, sweetheart, and you'll be living in the country of his birth. Once you're used to it, I'm sure it will be all right.'

'If only I knew what I was letting myself in for it

would be something, but this is like stepping into the unknown, Mom.' Her voice quavered. 'I'm scared. And Anthony's not going to be there to help me cope.' The enormity of going to live in a strange country with a formidable family like the Cumberlands was bad enough in itself, but to have to go alone added to her fears. It wasn't as if she could turn round and come back home if she didn't like it, either. She now had an obligation to Nicky to help prepare him for the great inheritance that lay ahead. For Anthony's sake, as well as Nicky's, she had to be strong enough to cope with whatever awaited her three thousand miles away.

'Remember, honey, Bucklands was part of Anthony and he was part of Bucklands. He loved it and it was his home. Now it's going to be your and Nicholas's home and I'm sure you'll grow to love it too.'

Without Anthony? Beverley thought. This first trip to England would have been a triumphal tour if he had been alive. A celebration of life and love, of memories recaptured and new ones forged. Now she was going to have to face it alone.

When everyone had gone to bed and the old house was silent except for the creaking of its timbers as they shifted back into position through the peaceful hours, Beverley strolled into the deserted garden for the last time, to gaze at the moon-washed countryside. Every tree, every acre of land, each distant mountain, held memories for her which went back to when she'd been a little girl. She remembered telling Anthony the day he asked her to marry him that no matter what happened, a part of her would always be here, in the valley and the forest and up on the mountain slopes. It had been true then, and it was true now. Her soul was cleaved to this soil, her roots buried deep beneath it. To have to leave it now was like severing a vital part of herself, and the pain she felt was the pain of bereavement. Dropping to her knees she spread her palms on the cool crisp grass, and it seemed as if she could feel what the land was feeling. It was as if her heart beat with the rhythm of the season, and the blood flowing through her veins trickled in unison with the streams that coursed down the mountainside from some secret source.

Tonight she was saying goodbye to it all. Her family, her home and the land of her birth. For a moment longer she knelt on the lawn, and then she rose and slowly went back into the house.

PART TWO

England
1992

Chapter Fourteen

'Fasten your seat belts, please, and extinguish your cigarettes,' the disembodied voice announced. 'In a few minutes we shall be coming in to land at Heathrow airport.'

Beverley leaned forward and peered through the small window of the Boeing 747. Rain-laden clouds and a cold blue light shrouded the landscape. It was seven o'clock in the morning and she felt chilled and stiff from the long night flight. Beside her, strapped in his seat, Nicholas slept peacefully, his teddybear clasped to his chest. For a moment she envied the fact he was unaware of the changes that were about to happen in their lives. Oblivious to everything around him, he slumbered on, lulled by the muted roar of the engines, while for Beverley, the journey had been marred by apprehension and anxiety. Now they were about to land. She looked out of the window again and suddenly the clouds melted away to reveal London spread below them like a grey carpet, a haphazard collection of buildings and tiny roads and through it all the Thames winding its way like a silver snake.

Compared to Manhattan with its bold skyline, London looked like a toytown put together by generations of children who, on a whim, had placed buildings side by side, regardless of size or style. Tiny patches of green and brown and grey intermingled with the structures reminded her of a patchwork quilt her grandmother had worked and which was now on her parents' bed. The plane was flying lower and the ground seemed to be coming up to meet them. She could see the buildings more clearly, and then with a rush they were level with the rooftops and swishing along the runway. Nicholas awoke and turned to her with a sleepy grin.

'What are you doing?' he asked as she zipped up her holdall. In the past few months he'd learned to speak very well for a two year old and understood everything she said.

'Time to get going, sweetheart.' The plane was taxiing towards the terminal buildings and when it drew to a halt, a freezing blast of cold damp air told her the cabin crew had opened one of the exit doors. She gave a little shiver, and then unstrapping Nicholas, scooped him up in her arms.

'Going where?' he asked.

'We're going home.'

'To N'York?'

'No, Nicky. Not to New York.'

'To Granny's?'

'We're going to our new home in England.'

''Kay,' he said placidly.

At that moment the passengers started to disembark and hitching him higher on her hip, they moved forward.

Once through passport control, she decided to wait until the stampede to reclaim luggage had subsided. People were scrambling over each other in their efforts to drag their suitcases off the carousel, and with Nicky in her arms, she couldn't compete.

Suddenly a tall black porter appeared at her side with a luggage trolley.

'You wan' help, Ma'am?' he asked cheerfully. He had muscles like Arnold Schwarzenegger and eyes like melting chocolate.

'Yes, please,' Beverley replied gratefully.

'Yo got someone meetin' yo?'

'Yes.'

When they entered the arrivals hall, she scanned the crowds on the other side of the barrier; hundreds of people pressed as if against an invisible window, searching for a familiar face. A child sat on her father's shoulders, looking out eagerly for a relative, an anxious wife craned forward to catch a glimpse of her husband, friends looked out expectantly for each other. With a pang Beverley realised everyone was meeting someone special in their lives, except for her. All she was looking out for was a sign bearing her name.

A moment later she saw it, 'Amesbury' in black lettering on a white card. Hurrying over, with Nicholas in her arms, she found herself looking into the deeply lined but kindly face of a middle-aged man.

'Hi! I'm Beverley Amesbury,' she announced, smiling. Then she indicated the trolley. 'I'm afraid we've got rather a lot of luggage.'

The man inclined his head, almost bowing.

'Good morning, M'Lady. Welcome to England. I'm Percy and I've come to escort you and the young Earl to Bucklands.' His eyes lingered on Nicholas for a moment before he continued: 'If you would be so good as to follow me, there is a car waiting for you.'

'Thank you. Will we be able to get all the cases in the car?'

Percy's smile was reassuring. 'No problem, M'Lady. My son has brought the Range Rover. There will be plenty of room.'

In procession, with Percy leading the way through the crowded terminus, she felt a sudden buzz of excitement. She was actually walking on British soil! She was here, on her way to a new life! And judging by Percy's friendly and reassuring manner, she had the feeling everything was going to be all right after all.

'Okay, my baby?' she whispered in Nicky's ear, hugging him close.

He grinned wickedly at her, reminding her so much of Anthony.

'I'm not a baby!' he said stoutly.

'Of course you're not! This is fun, isn't it? We'll soon be home now.'

'Home,' he echoed, looking around curiously.

The estate car was parked just beyond the exit door. A fair-haired young man jumped out of the driver's seat as soon as he saw them.

Percy hailed him. 'All right, Joe?'

'Yes. They wanted me to move on, but I said I was waiting to pick up a sick child.'

Percy looked askance at Beverley. 'If Joe hadn't spun a bit of a yarn, we'd have had to walk a long way to the car park.'

'Hi, Joe. And thanks,' Beverley greeted him.

Joe inclined his head as his father had done, but he was blushing.

'Good day, M'Lady,' he said shyly.

Within minutes the cases had been loaded into

330

the Range Rover, the porter tipped, and Beverley and Nicholas settled comfortably in the back. Joe got back into the driver's seat with his father beside him.

'Is it far to Bucklands?' Beverley asked as they joined a long line of cars leaving the airport.

'It's only about forty miles from here, M'Lady, but it might take an hour or more to get there because we've hit the rush-hour traffic,' Percy explained. 'Joe and I only took fifty minutes on the way here, but then we did leave at five this morning, to be sure to be in good time.'

'Well, thank you for meeting me,' Beverley replied warmly. 'I don't know how I'd have managed without you both.'

Percy smiled, his wrinkles deepening like the cracks in parched earth. 'Oh, we couldn't have let you and the wee Earl find your own way, could we, Joe?' It was more a statement than a question, and Joe nodded in vehement agreement.

'Anyway, Lady Jean arranged everything,' he added.

'Have you been at Bucklands a long time?'

'All my life, M'Lady. My father worked for the Sixth Earl, and then I took over the job of chief maintenance man when the last Earl inherited . . .' His voice trailed off, catching in his throat.

'You mean Henry?' Beverley said quietly.

'Exactly, and a finer man I've never known. His death was a terrible shock to us all. So sudden. A tragedy. And him without a son, too.'

'I can understand how you feel,' she said softly. 'I didn't know him as well as you, of course, but it broke my heart when he died. With my husband gone, I'd come . . . well, I'd come to depend on Henry.'

'May we express our sympathy and offer you our condolences on your own great loss, M'Lady?' Percy said with old-fashioned formality. 'It's been a very bad time for the Cumberland family. So many tragedies. So much sadness.'

'Thank you, Percy. It has been a bad time for all of us,' she replied reflectively. 'Do you actually live at Bucklands?'

'We have a cottage on the estate, near Home Farm. Joe here will be the fourth generation of Percys to live and work at Bucklands. It started with my grandfather in 1918, when he came back from the First World War, and then my father took over in 1945. Funny that, them both starting after there'd been a war. My father died in 1959 so that's when I left my job in the building trade to carry on in charge of all the estate maintenance. His Lordship used to say: "Percy, you belong here as much as I do!" '

'Percy is your last name?'

'It is indeed, M'Lady. Joe here will be known as Percy when he takes over from me eventually.'

Joe blushed again, easing the car out of the dense traffic and on to the M40.

'So what are you doing now, Joe?' she asked. 'Assisting your father?'

'No, M'Lady. I'm chauffeur to Lady Cumberland these days.'

'She's rather blind, isn't she. I remember my husband telling me she couldn't get around much on her own.'

'I drive the young Lady Cumberland,' he pointed out. 'The Dowager Lady Cumberland never goes anywhere these days. She hasn't left the castle for several years now.'

'I see.'

'Cows!' Nicholas suddenly exclaimed in an excited voice. He'd been sitting very still, little legs stuck straight out in front of him, gazing at the passing landscape.

'More cows!' He pointed to a herd of Jersey cattle that were grazing, their golden coats glistening in the rain that had started to fall.

'Yes, sweetheart.'

'LOTS OF COWS!' he shouted, pink with delight.

Beverley smiled. 'We're not deaf, Nicky,' she said mildly.

He turned to her, blue eyes dancing, smile enraptured.

'Cows,' he breathed in a loud stage whisper.

Percy glanced over his shoulder and he was smiling, too.

'There are lots of animals for you to look at on the farm,' he said. 'We've got cows, sheep, hens, ducks, cats, dogs, and a couple of goats.'

Nicholas was silent for a moment while he digested this fascinating information. Then he spoke gravely.

'I want to see them.'

'Of course, but we have to unpack first, and get settled,' Beverley reminded him.

'Today? Can I see them today?'

'We'll see.'

''Kay.'

Percy spoke again. 'Joe here can take him down to the farm this afternoon if you like, M'Lady.'

'That's very kind. Can I let you know? Nicky and I might have a nap after lunch. We've been flying all night and we're quite tired.'

'I want to see the goats!' Nicholas chanted.

'Maybe later.'

'No, now!' His smile was winning. Beverley was on the point of weakening.

'Joe can take him off your hands while you settle in, M'Lady, if you would like it.'

Beverley gazed out of the window and wondered if everyone at Bucklands was going to be calling her M'Lady all the time. No one in New York had ever addressed her that way, few had even called her 'Lady Amesbury'. It made her feel as if Percy was referring to someone else. Her mother, however, had advised her the night before she left to 'go along with everything at Bucklands' until she found her feet, and then she could make changes if she wanted to.

'The English aristocracy have a different way of doing things,' Rachael had warned her. 'You may not always like what they do or how they act, but wait until you've been there some time and you may find they have a good reason for doing things differently.'

Right now, Beverley longed to tell Percy to call her by her first name, but she guessed it wasn't the done thing, and it might well embarrass him. Give it time, she thought. Take Mom's advice and get the general lie of the land before you say anything.

As they skimmed up the motorway, the skies began to lighten and the mist dissolve. A typical March morning, with strong winds blowing away the aftermath of a rainstorm, reinforced Beverley's belief that it was always grey and invariably wet in England. Although patches of blue sky were emerging through tattered storm clouds, everything seemed to be dripping. Great splodges of water splashed down from the overhanging branches on to the windscreen, while fat blobs of rain shimmered on the car's bonnet. The tyres made a swishing sound as they sent up sprays of water from puddles on the road surface, and a lorry, overtaking them, sprayed them with a million muddy droplets from its backwash.

'Are we there?' Nicholas enquired in his piping voice. 'I want to see the goats.'

'Not long now, M'Lord,' said Percy.

This was too much for Beverley. They could call her what they liked, but this titled bit was absurd for a small child.

'Please call him Nicholas,' she said firmly. 'I want him to be brought up like any other boy, and I think he should be known as Nicholas, at least until he grows up.' It was all very well for her mother to say 'wait and see how they do things', but there was also a lot to be said for starting how she intended to carry on, and that was what she made up her mind to do. She wouldn't be rude or gauche or flout English tradition, but she would point out that this was 1992, she was American and Nicky half-American, and they must be allowed to do certain things in their own way.

Pleased with herself for having come to this decision, she put her arm around Nicholas and hugged him.

'We'll go and see the farm animals this afternoon,' she promised.

'And the goats?' he persisted.

There was a chuckle from the front of the car. 'He's not going to be happy until he's seen those blessed goats, is he?' Percy remarked. 'Meanwhile, in about five minutes, we'll be able to see Bucklands from the road.'

A frisson, half fearful, half excited, prickled down Beverley's spine and her heart gave a nervous lurch. They were almost there. In a matter of minutes she'd see their future home, Nicky's inheritance, the place where Anthony had been born and reared.

Her hands started to tremble and for a moment she

335

felt almost sick. Then she hugged Nicholas closer, almost as if he were a shield behind which she could find protection. If it wasn't for him, she wouldn't be here at all. If it wasn't for Nicky, her future would have lain in America.

They came off the motorway at junction 6, and suddenly they were deep in the heart of lush countryside and quaint winding roads overhung with interlacing branches. Passing through a picture-book village of small stone houses, a pond with ducks nestling under a willow tree, and a manicured village green, Beverley had her first glimpse of rural life in the English countryside. Everything seemed to be in exquisite miniature and she'd never seen grass so green or daffodils growing in front gardens so bright. They came to a bend and Percy pulled off the road and stopped on the grass verge.

'There's Bucklands,' he announced quietly. Beverley followed his gaze and then gasped with amazement.

'It looks as if it came out of a fairy tale!'

Set against the dark foliage of a forest, Bucklands Castle stood just as Anthony had described it, more magnificent than she'd imagined, with its four round towers, one at each corner, and its stonework mellowed to a soft silvery grey, but otherwise familiar, as if in a strange way she already knew it. At that moment, in a natural miracle of perfect timing, the clouds parted as a brisk breeze swept across the valley and like a thousand spotlights the sun shone down brilliantly, illuminating the crenellated ramparts, dazzling on the windows, spilling on to the moat so that the waters shimmered and sparkled.

'It's unreal!' Beverley whispered, stunned.

There was silence in the car as they watched the

powerful sunbeam reveal the historical building in all its glory. It was the most dramatic and splendid sight she had ever seen, and it was obvious Percy and Joe were sensitive to her feelings of awe. Like a magnificent jewel, Bucklands stood in its lush green surroundings as it had stood for hundreds of years and at that moment Beverley had a sudden feeling of closeness to Anthony. The sun coming out seemed to her to be a good omen; a signal perhaps that he was welcoming them and watching over them as they drew near his ancestral home. She pulled Nicky closer, deeply moved, wanting him to remember this moment.

'Look, Nicky. There's your daddy's home, where he lived when he was a little boy. Now it's going to be your home.' She pressed her cheek to his soft rosy little face and wished that Anthony had been there to share this moment.

Nicholas continued to gaze at the distant castle with unwavering eyes. They all watched him, Beverley, Percy and Joe. He was arriving at the seat of his great inheritance and this was his first glimpse of the magnificent home that had belonged to his forebears and would one day be his. Solemnly he turned to his mother and spoke.

'Is that where the goats live?'

The estate car drew to a halt, level with the drawbridge that spanned the moat, and Beverley remembered Anthony telling her this was the only way into Bucklands. The castle stood in the waters of a deep ditch which extended into a lake on the south side, fortified against intruders as it had been in the fourteenth century, and it was an imposing sight.

'Is there no drive up to the door around the other

side?' she asked Percy, eyeing the black waters appre-
hensively. The moat was a death trap for a small child.
She was going to have her work cut out watching
Nicholas all the time in case he fell in.

'No, M'Lady, this is the only way in to the castle,'
Percy explained as he and Joe unloaded her luggage and
carried it across the wooden planked bridge.

Feeling as if she'd stepped into a medieval tale, Beverley clutched Nicholas's hand tightly, and followed.

The heavy oak doors, set behind the raised portcullis,
stood open and led into a stone-flagged lobby, sparsely
furnished with an oak chest and a pair of heavily carved
chairs. Beyond, there was a stone archway which led
into a long wide hall. Here the walls were hung with
hundreds of spears, daggers and swords, displayed in
precise rows of fan-shaped patterns, interspersed with
ancient muskets, used as early as the sixteenth century
by infantry soldiers. Visors and shields, painted with
heraldic arms, glinted over the doorways that led off the
hall. A long narrow Persian rug lay down the centre of
the polished wooden floor.

'Mom, what are they?' Nicholas demanded, pointing
to shining figures guarding one of the doorways.

'Suits of armour. In the olden days soldiers used to
wear them.'

'Can I wear them?'

'They'd be rather big and heavy for you,' Beverley
said, smiling.

'Is there a soldier inside them now?'

Percy, putting down a heavy suitcase, chuckled. 'No
more there isn't, Nicholas. It's a long time since anyone
wore one of those suits. Several hundred years, I'd say.'

'Why?'

Beverley, sensing this could lead to a lengthy interrogation by Nicholas, held his hand tighter. 'Let's get settled before we find out about everything, sweetheart,' she admonished gently. The emptiness and silence of this great hall suddenly unnerved her. It was so unwelcoming and chilly, and once again her heart cried out for Anthony. Or Henry. It would all have been so different if they'd been there. By now Henry would have greeted her with hugs and warm words and the offer of some refreshment. As for Anthony, he'd no doubt have jokingly carried her over the threshold, and then led her by the hand on an exciting magical tour. As it was, she was left standing uncertainly in the oppressive atmosphere of a hall hung with weapons, while Percy and Joe unloaded her luggage from the car.

'Where do I go?' she asked Percy when the last of her cases had been brought in. 'Is everyone out?'

Percy's expression was wry. 'Her Ladyship will still be having breakfast in bed, and the Dowager Lady Cumberland never appears until lunchtime. She'll be in her own wing of the castle. As for Lady Jean . . .' He glanced at his wrist watch. 'Being a magistrate she may already have gone into town to preside in Court, in which case she won't be back for several hours yet.'

Beverley stared at him, unable to believe her ears. She and Nicholas had been flying all night, and this was a strange country in which she was now expected to live, and yet none of the family had the courtesy to be there when she arrived. Their rudeness stunned her. Couldn't Leonora even have got out of bed to greet them on this first morning? And surely Anthony's mother, who had professed such longing to meet her, could have made an exception? And what about Lady Jean or her husband,

Colonel Rupert Ffitch? Was there no one around to bid them welcome and make them feel at home? Feeling utterly deflated, Beverley looked miserably at Percy.

'Do you know which are our rooms? I'd like to freshen up and give Nicholas a bath,' she said.

At that moment a middle-aged woman in a pale blue overall appeared. She was smiling cheerfully, and had a motherly air about her.

'Lady Amesbury?' she said.

Then she looked at Nicholas with undisguised curiosity. 'I'm Alice. Shall I show you to your rooms? Everything is ready for you, and Percy and Joe will bring up your luggage.'

'Thank you,' Beverley replied in relief. 'I was beginning to wonder . . .'

'I'm the housekeeper,' Alice continued, still smiling. Her pointed features were softened by her benign expression and the halo of white curls that framed her face. 'He's a big boy, isn't he?' she remarked, still looking at Nicholas.

'He's two now,' Beverley replied proudly, as they followed Alice up a flight of polished oak stairs.

'That's right,' Alice agreed. 'I remember being told when he was born.'

She led them along the corridor on the first floor and Beverley noticed the walls were hung with portraits of men and women, obviously painted during the eighteenth and nineteenth centuries. The gilt frames were dull from age but the canvasses glowed with the luminosity of Old Masters paintings and she guessed they must be extremely valuable.

'Your room is just along here,' Alice said when they arrived at the end of the corridor. She opened a door

340

and led the way into a large sitting room, furnished with antiques. A bureau stood in one of the windows. A yellow brocade sofa faced the fireplace, laid ready to be lit. Beside it a large basket was filled with logs. The walls were covered with a dull gold and dark turquoise brocaded fabric, and water colour paintings, depicting rural scenes, hung along one wall, their gilt frames catching the light. Heavily shaded table lamps, books, vases and *objets d'art* added to the opulent clutter and, looking around, Beverley realised the room had probably been neither changed nor redecorated since the turn of the century.

'Your bedroom is through here,' Alice was saying, opening heavy oak double doors that led into a room of approximately the same size. Here Chinoiserie abounded, from the large bed with its pagoda-shaped canopy to the yellow silk walls which were handpainted in a Chinese design. There were Chinese vases on the mantelpiece, and the furniture was either red-lacquered or ebony, inlaid with mother-of-pearl cherry blossom. This was the last sort of room Beverley had expected to find in an old English castle and she stood looking around in astonishment.

'The bathroom is through there.' Alice indicated a doorway in the wall opposite the bed. There was pride in her voice. 'The last Earl knocked a hole in the wall so it would adjoin the bedroom,' she added, making it sound as if he'd been responsible for some major act of humanity. 'Only you and Her Ladyship have bathrooms en suite.'

'Thank you,' said Beverley, thinking how different it all was from Anthony's Manhattan apartment. 'Is Nicholas's room next-door?'

Alice looked shocked. 'Oh, no, M'Lady!'

Beverley looked at her sharply. 'Where is he sleeping, then?'

'On the nursery floor, of course. Where the late Earl and Lord Anthony slept when they were small. It's all been got ready. A day nursery and a night nursery, with their own bathroom and a small kitchen. Lady Juliet slept up there until quite recently, but now she's twelve, Her Ladyship thought she'd better have a room on the floor below.' Alice glanced at Nicholas again. 'He'll be ever so happy up in the old nursery.'

Beverley flinched, hating the realisation that all these decisions had been made without her knowledge. She'd wanted Nicholas to sleep in a room next to hers, perhaps even in the same room until he got used to being at Bucklands, and now here was the housekeeper telling her that other arrangements had been made, as if she had no say in the matter.

'Where *is* this nursery?' she asked carefully.

'I'll show you, M'Lady.' Bustling with jollity, which Beverley strongly suspected was a cover-up for deeply profound stupidity, Alice led her up two more flights of carved stairs, each step so highly polished she trod carefully in case she slipped. At last they came to the top floor of the castle, where the ceilings were lower and the grand oil paintings of the lower floors had given way to large framed engravings, many of a religious nature.

With each step, Beverley's disquiet grew. The nursery seemed to be miles away from her room; if he cried out in the night it would be impossible to hear him. She was just about to voice her objections when Alice opened a door and said with a flourish: 'Here we are! And there's Lord Anthony's old rocking horse, all dusted and ready!'

342

Beverley nearly wept when she saw the old wooden horse, standing in the middle of what was the day nursery. His dapple-grey painted coat was battered and chipped, and his leather harness broken. Eyes painted in dark brown and black gazed sadly back at her, as if in mute commiseration, and walking over to it, she stroked the wispy remains of what had once been a mane of real horse hair.

'This used to belong to your daddy,' she said to Nicholas, her voice catching.

'Did he ride it?' Nicholas asked, touching the stirrups.

'He did that!' Alice interjected stoutly. 'I was a chambermaid when His Lordship was a little boy and I remember him sitting on this horse, shouting "Tally-Ho" for all he was worth.'

Beverley turned and looked at the woman with renewed respect. One day, when she felt less emotional, she would ask Alice all about Anthony.

'I want to ride!' Nicholas was already gripping the saddle, trying to lift himself up.

'Up you go then,' Beverley replied, giving him a helping hand.

A minute later he was triumphantly sitting astride the rocking horse, gripping its curved neck, and grinning hugely. 'Look! I'm riding!'

Beverley smiled at him through a sudden glaze of unshed tears, then turned to Alice and spoke quietly.

'I can't possibly have Nicholas sleeping up here, two floors above me,' she said firmly. 'He's had a big enough upheaval already, moving to a new country and a new home, and I want to make sure he's with me until he feels confident and settled. Can you arrange to have a bed put in my room, please?'

Alice looked upset. 'But I've had my orders from Her

Ladyship,' she pointed out. 'Her Ladyship won't allow a young child to sleep on the same floor as her, because it would disturb her in the mornings. Even her daughter Lady Juliet is not allowed a room on that floor. The Dowager Countess sleeps in the west wing, of course. And Lady Jean and Colonel Ffitch have their own house in the grounds. But small children have to be in the nursery,' she added with sudden vehemence.

'I'm not sure I understand you,' said Beverley with deliberate carefulness, as she tried to control her feelings of anger.

'It's like I said, Her Ladyship doesn't want to be disturbed by small children and so I was given strict instructions to get the top floor ready for Nicholas,' she repeated.

Beverley's jaw tightened. She remembered the things Anthony had said about Leonora, and how he'd wondered why Henry had ever married her. Living under the same roof wasn't going to be easy but Beverley knew that if she conceded to Leonora's wishes on this issue, she'd have a problem asserting herself over future issues.

'I'm afraid there's no way I can allow my son to sleep on his own, two floors above me, where I can't hear him if he needs me. He's far too young to be so far away from the adults,' she said firmly.

An expression of heartfelt relief crossed Alice's face, as if she suddenly understood.

'Oh, that's all right, M'Lady. Of course, I forgot to mention that the young Earl won't be alone on the nursery floor.'

'What do you mean?'

'Lady Jean has engaged a nanny to look after him.

She starts on Monday. She'll be keeping an eye on him.'

Tired out by travelling and excitement, Nicholas slept soundly in the middle of Beverley's ornate Chinese bed while she unpacked before having a bath and getting into a change of clothes. It was nearly noon, and so far she had seen none of the Cumberland family. Once Percy and Joe had deposited her cases in the middle of the room, and Alice had brought her some coffee in an antique silver pot, on a tray decorated with a hunting print, she'd been left entirely alone to settle in. No one had come to greet her or ask how she was getting on. There were no flowers or welcoming note in her room, nothing in fact to make her feel that she was joining a family she and Nicholas were to be a part of. If she'd booked an expensive suite in a grand hotel in some foreign country where she knew no one, she would probably have had a warmer welcome, she reflected. For a moment she wondered if it wouldn't be better to turn around and go right back home again. Who needs this? she asked herself stormily. Of one thing she was certain. Both Anthony and Henry would have made sure things were very different if they'd been here. Both men had been renowned for their charm and courtesy. They would never have left her alone on her arrival, without a word of welcome.

After her bath, she lay down beside Nicholas and cradled him in her arms. Tonight he'd sleep in this ridiculous bed with her, if Alice didn't produce a bed for him alongside. And as soon as she saw Leonora or Lady Jean, she'd tell them there was no way she was going to allow a nanny to look after him. On that she was absolutely determined. It might have been all right in the days when Anthony and Henry were babies, but she had no intention of letting anyone else care for her child.

Beverley dozed off, with Nicholas snuggled close to her, and only awoke when he stirred, whimpering.

'What is it, sweetheart?' she asked, instantly alert.

'I want lunch,' he said, clutching his teddybear to his chest. 'When can we have lunch?'

She jumped out of bed, full of resolve. This bunch of rude Brits were not going to spoil things for them. They had as much right to live the way they wanted to as Leonora or anyone else. She would not be pushed around by any of them. This was her home now. And one day the whole pile would belong to Nicholas.

Slipping into her best jeans and wearing one of the silk shirts she'd bought when she'd worked on *Chichi*, she dressed Nicholas in scarlet corded dungarees and a plaid shirt. Then she brushed his golden hair.

'Let's go to lunch, sweetheart,' she said, taking his hand. They went out into the silent corridor, where nothing stirred, and then down the massive carved staircase to the hall below. Beverley sniffed the air hopefully, but there were no delicious cooking smells emanating from the nether regions nor was there a sign of anyone about. This is like the *Marie Celeste*, she thought, determined to keep her sense of humour. She tried to imagine what Anthony would have said if he'd been there. No doubt he'd have made a joke and had her laughing the way he always did.

As they neared the bottom of the stairs Nicholas let go of her hand, and ran through the door that led to the Baronial Hall. His feet pattered on the polished hall.

'I want to see the soldiers!' he shouted, running in the direction of the suits of armour.

Suddenly, Beverley heard a loud gasp, and then a cry that was almost a moan.

'Anthony?' she heard a voice cry out in anguish.

Hurrying forward, she saw an elderly woman in a thick tweed skirt and jacket, with fine snow white hair taken back from her lined face into a bun. She was leaning on a stick and gazing at Nicholas with blue eyes that had a milky glaze and her skin looked as soft and creased as faded silk. She turned sharply when she heard Beverley's footsteps and for a moment they stared at each other, the older woman peering blindly.

'Who's that?' she demanded shrilly. And then she looked back at Nicholas who was staring up at her.

'Oh, my God.' She sighed and put her hand to her mouth. 'It's little Nicholas, isn't it? Just for a moment . . .' Her voice trailed off and ended in a little sob. 'Just for a moment . . . I thought it was Anthony.' Then she drew herself up and smiled sadly. 'But of course it couldn't be. And you, my dear, must be Beverley.' She stretched out her hand. Gravely and gently, Beverley took it.

'Yes, I'm Beverley. And this, as you've gathered, is your grandson.'

The Dowager Countess of Cumberland reached for Nicholas and stroked his gleaming blond hair with tenderness.

'I didn't know you'd arrived, my dear Beverley,' she said in a bewildered voice. 'Leonora told me you weren't expected until tomorrow.'

347

Chapter Fifteen

'I'm most frightfully sorry for the mix-up,' Lady Jean said, striding into the drawing room, hand outstretched, manner brisk and confident as ever. She shook Beverley's hand with a firm grip before turning to Leonora, who was lounging elegantly in the window. 'How could you be such a fool as to get the day wrong! Mother got an awful shock. Thought it was Anthony for a moment,' she said tersely.

'I *know* I told her they were arriving today,' Leonora replied hotly, speaking as if Beverley and Nicholas weren't in the room. 'I remember telling her they'd be here on Wednesday, but you know how forgetful she is.'

The two women glared at each other, much to Beverley's discomfiture. They were such opposite extremes it was difficult to imagine they were sisters-in-law. Jean, with her bristling manner and loping stride encased in tweeds almost as old and baggy as her mother's, was the perfect cliché of a noble English countrywoman, more at home with *Horse & Hound* than *Harper's & Queen*. While Leonora, with her carefully coiffured high-lighted hair, frilly blouse and rash of diamonds, seemed like an actress who was playing a part she had not rehearsed well enough.

'Anyway, I don't see that it matters,' Leonora remarked, fastidiously picking a fleck from her beige suede skirt. 'Alice showed them their rooms.'

Beverley looked at Leonora and realised she was going to be a difficult woman to get along with. Her rather common prettiness was spoilt by a bitter expression of discontent, and her manner was aggressive. At first Beverley had felt moved to speak words of sympathy to her for the loss of Henry, and for her other losses, too; those babies who had not survived, so that she had been unable to provide an heir for Henry. But the words had caught in Beverley's throat, frozen by Leonora's cold expression before they could be given voice. She was a woman who neither gave nor asked for sympathy and Beverley felt chilled. Although they should have had a lot in common, having been married to brothers, it was as if a gigantic gulf divided them and Beverley seriously wondered if she could ever bridge it. Lady Jean was another matter. With her you got what you saw, and that was a forthright no-nonsense woman, genuine from her tightly permed greying hair to the thick soles of her sensible shoes. She was a woman who would not stand for any nonsense, but on the other hand Beverley had the feeling she'd be scrupulously fair, too.

Afternoon tea was about to be served at Bucklands, a repast that Beverley and Nicholas were unaccustomed to but which was obviously an important ritual in the family. Stevens, a very elderly butler who had been with the Cumberlands for nearly thirty years, was bringing in heavy silver trays laden with fine Rockingham cups and saucers, and silver teapots and milk jugs, which he placed on a low table in front of the fireplace, followed by a maid who carried plates of scones, dainty little sandwiches, biscuits and a large homemade walnut cake.

'Cookies!' Nicholas exclaimed gleefully. He laughed with joy, a sound that melted most adult hearts but caused Lady Jean and Leonora to look at him sharply. Then Beverley heard Leonora give a little sigh.

'You'd better put a napkin over his knees so he doesn't drop crumbs on the carpet,' she said in a weary voice.

'Perhaps he could sit up at that table over there,' Lady Jean suggested.

'Once the nanny arrives on Monday there won't be a problem because he'll be having all his meals in the nursery, but in the meantime let's sit him at a table,' she added.

It was now or never. If Beverley didn't assert herself these two women, in their different ways, would have her dancing to their tune like a puppet on a string.

'I wanted to talk to you about that,' Beverley said, settling Nicholas on the sofa beside her, with a tiny cucumber sandwich on a plate in front of him. 'I shall be looking after Nicholas myself, especially now I'm not working, so there was no need for you to engage a nanny for him.'

Lady Jean looked startled and Leonora narrowed her eyes.

'How can you manage without a nanny?' snapped Leonora, waving a slender hand with long red nails. 'A small boy like that – we simply can't have him running wild. Besides, what are you going to do with him at mealtimes?'

It was Beverley's turn to look amazed. 'What do you mean . . . "do with him at mealtimes"? He'll have his meals with me. Who do you suppose he'll have his meals

351

with?' Her voice rose with indignation.

Lady Jean stepped in before Leonora could reply. 'Things are different here, Beverley,' she explained, in her forthright manner. 'Life is fairly formal at Bucklands.' She spread her hands to take in the large and grand drawing room, with its paintings, brocade furnishings and priceless antiques. 'It always has been and it probably always will be, because when you are running a large establishment, with a score of servants, you must have a routine. Life has to be highly organised. Meals have to be properly served: breakfast in the morning room, lunch and dinner in the dining room, and tea in here, in the drawing room. The servants all know what is expected of them, and it isn't fair to upset their duties. That's why, with a small child, there has to be a separate routine, managed by a nanny to suit a child's requirements. That's why there's a kitchen in the nursery quarters. They'll be quite self-contained up there.'

Beverley looked stubborn. 'That may be the way you do things over here, but I'm not having Nicky banished to the top floor in case he upsets anyone's routine. He's my son, and he's going to sleep in my room and have his meals with me.' Protectively, she put her arm around Nicky who was absorbed in tracing the pattern on his plate with his forefinger.

Leonora groaned theatrically. 'Quite out of the question,' she said dismissively.

'You will find it difficult,' Lady Jean warned. 'Nicholas could get very bored and fretful if he has to sit through a two-hour luncheon party, you know. Mother still likes to entertain from time to time, and a lot of Henry's old friends will still expect to come and stay for the shooting.'

'Yes, and I'm not going to have every meal ruined by a small child,' said Leonora. 'Even Juliet is only allowed to join us for luncheon on very special occasions and she's nearly thirteen.'

Beverley stared at her coldly. 'So I've heard,' she replied stiffly. 'If Nicholas's presence upsets you all so much, he and I will be perfectly happy to eat in the kitchen. It's where we usually eat anyway. Anthony always thought it was much more cosy. He loathed formality.'

'With the servants! Eat in the kitchen with the servants!' Leonora was scandalised. She sniffed daintily. 'Out of the question.'

Lady Jean looked at her with ill-disguised irritation. 'Do stop saying "out of the question". This has to be worked out.' She turned back to Beverley. 'Look, let's not be too hasty about all this. The nanny we engaged couldn't start until Monday, and maybe it's just as well. I think you'll see during the next few days that this household is not geared to a small child running about willy-nilly. For one thing, there are a hundred ways in which he could hurt himself, so he will have to be supervised all the time, and the staff just aren't prepared to keep an eye on him. It's not their job. Besides which, you'll find you have to get involved in local matters, and you won't have the time to be with Nicholas, day and night.'

'Yes, who's going to baby-sit if you go out in the evenings?' Leonora demanded, making it clear by her manner that there was no point in counting on her.

Beverley took a deep breath, refusing to be beaten. Carefully she changed her tactics, remembering how clever Elaine Ross had always been at getting her own way, sometimes by devious methods. With a charming smile she turned to Leonora and asked conversationally: 'So how do you manage with Juliet? She's no longer up in the nursery, is she?'

Leonora was unfazed. 'She's at boarding school,' she replied shortly, 'and during the holidays I employ a student-teacher to look after her. Of course, a lot of the time she's staying with her school friends. At the moment she's in the South of France for the Easter holidays with the Duke of Willoughby's daughter, at their villa.'

'How nice for her,' said Beverley calmly. 'I shall engage a local girl perhaps from the village to help me with Nicky, when it is required. Otherwise, I believe a mother should look after her own child as much as possible. Unless, of course, she has a job, which right now doesn't apply to me.' It was as if thoughts of Anthony were giving her the strength to oppose these two formidable women, and she managed to smile as she looked from one to the other. 'We must tell the nanny you engaged that we don't require her now.' She looked down at Nicky, ignoring their baleful stares. 'How about going to look at the animals on the farm before bedtime, sweetheart?' she suggested.

'To see the goats?' he asked excitedly.

'Yes.'

''Kay.' His tone was full of satisfaction. Struggling to his feet from the depths of the brocade sofa he strode over to Leonora and handed her his plate. 'There you are. I'm going to see the goats,' he said with aplomb and then, grabbing his mother's hand, stomped out of the drawing room.

'Goo'bye. See you later,' he called out, as an afterthought.

'The boy's got Anthony's spirit, I'll say that for him,' Lady Jean remarked as she and her husband changed for dinner the next evening. They were in their bedroom in the Dower House, which was situated a quarter of a mile away from the castle on the west side of the estate, and normally reserved for the widows of the Earls of Cumberland. However, when Lady Jean married, her father had given it to her for life and it was an arrangement which suited everyone. Much more comfortable and warm in a chintzy way than Bucklands, it had five bedrooms, a pleasant drawing room and dining room, and a cosy 'den' where they sat in the evenings when they were on their own.

'Nicholas is also the image of Anthony,' she continued. 'Mother got quite a shock when she saw him yesterday.'

'Humph,' responded her husband, but not in a gruff way. Colonel Rupert Ffitch, long since retired from the Brigade of Guards, was a gentleman of leisure if not means, and a man of few words. This was just as well because Lady Jean was a woman of strong opinions who was not afraid to speak her mind, which she continually did.

'Beverley's going to have a problem with Leonora,' she observed, running a tortoiseshell comb with a silver handle through her tight grey curls. 'I was furious when I realised she'd told Mother they weren't arriving until today. She did it on purpose, of course. If I hadn't been in court I'd have known what she was up to. As it was, only Alice was around.' She clicked her tongue with annoyance.

'Humph.'

Lady Jean fastened the clasp of her pearl necklace and regarded herself in the dressing-table mirror. Good looking she was not, and she'd always known it. Her face was too long – 'lantern-jawed' her nanny used to say – her hair was hopelessly fine, and her teeth were long and discoloured, giving her a rather horsey look. However, her fine blue eyes and weather-beaten complexion gave her face an interesting quality and she'd decided at eighteen that if she wasn't going to be a beauty, at least she could make up for it by being lively and intelligent. In fact, with her aristocratic and dignified bearing, she'd never been short of suitors and her marriage to Rupert had been an extremely happy one.

Rising, she smoothed the skirt of her black lace dress, almost green now with age, and flung a black mohair shawl round her shoulders. Having no interest in clothes she'd hardly bought anything new for the past twenty years. Tweed suits, cotton shirts, thick sweaters and a few formal dinner dresses were all she needed. In her opinion, clothes were a waste of time and money and she could never understand Leonora's obsession with them.

'Are you ready, Rupert? We ought to get to Bucklands before everyone else because you can be sure Leonora won't bother to introduce Beverley to anyone.'

'I'm ready, dear.' He gave his black bow-tie a final tweak. In a dinner jacket he was a distinguished-looking man, with his white moustache and military bearing. Together they made a handsome couple.

As it was a blustery and cold evening, they took the car for the short distance to Bucklands, parking it in the drive near the drawbridge.

For a moment Lady Jean stopped to look up at the

ancient castle, captivated by it as she'd been all her life. Because they were giving a dinner party for some of their closest friends and neighbours, to welcome Beverley, all the castle lights were turned on, blazing through the windows, illuminating the surrounding moat. Floodlighting also lit up the exterior, but this was more to prevent accidents than for its theatrical effect. Once, a guest had slipped and fallen into the murky waters, and being unable to swim had been finally hauled out and dragged to dry land by a footman.

'I see we're the first,' she observed with satisfaction. 'That will give me a chance to check that everything has been done properly.'

Colonel Ffitch remained silent. Ever since Henry's death, Jean had acted as if she were mistress of Bucklands and he really couldn't blame her. Mama, as he called the Dowager Countess, was too old to cope, and although Leonora liked to think she was capable of running a stately home, even he could tell she wasn't. Henry had always arranged everything and Bucklands had run like clockwork. Now that Beverley had arrived, the hive would in effect have four queens. Who would be the one who would eventually take command? He hadn't so far met Beverley but he had a gut feeling, reminiscent of his army days, that out of the ranks often came the commanders of the future.

Quietly he followed Jean across the drawbridge, ready to observe with interest the personalities gathered here tonight.

'What the hell have you done to this dress?' Leonora stormed. 'I told you to press it, not pull it out of shape.' She glared angrily at Lizzie, the maid she had annexed

357

to look after her clothes. Lizzie had only been at Bucklands six months, and had been hired as a housemaid by Henry, but the moment he'd died, Leonora proclaimed herself 'too unwell and weak' to look after herself.

Within a week, Lizzie was having to do all her personal laundry by hand, press her clothes each time she wore them, and keep her shoes and handbags polished and in special flannel wrapping. Within a month, Leonora was using her like a ladies' maid and Alice didn't dare say anything. She, like the rest of the staff of Bucklands, loved their positions in the old castle, and had been devoted to Henry and his mother. The young Countess had never won their hearts, and yet here she was, remaining on for probably the rest of her life, with the power to hire or fire. If they wanted to keep their posts, it was important not to cross her.

'I'm sorry, M'Lady,' Lizzie said nervously. 'I used ever such a cool iron.'

'I can't wear it!' Leonora struggled out of the pale blue crêpe dinner dress and flung it across the room. 'You've ruined it!' she screamed. 'That dress cost over a thousand pounds and you've ruined it! How could you have been so clumsy and careless! Lack of education, I suppose,' she added, acidly.

Lizzie flushed angrily and bit her lip.

'Well?' Leonora demanded, standing in her Janet Reger pure silk and lace underclothes. 'What the fuck am I going to wear now?'

Lizzie flew to the large mahogany wardrobe that stood against one of the bedroom walls and opened it.

Enough dresses to stock an exclusive boutique were revealed. There were long ones and short ones, décolleté ones and demure ones, dresses trimmed with feathers,

358

beads, embroidery and sequins.

Leonora, kicking off her Manolo Blahnik pale blue satin shoes, strode over to the wardrobe and regarded the contents with deep discontent.

'That's too dowdy . . . too old . . . a ghastly colour . . . no . . . no . . . no . . . too low-cut, I'll freeze in this damned place . . . that's no good . . . useless . . .' Her commentary continued while Lizzie stood there, shaking.

Suddenly she turned to the maid and spoke sharply. 'What's Lady Amesbury wearing tonight?'

Lizzie looked blank. 'I-I've no idea,' she faltered.

'Well, find out! It's your job to make sure she isn't wearing anything that will . . .' She was going to say 'outshine me', but quickly changed it to '. . . clash with what I'm wearing.'

'How will I do that, M'Lady?' Lizzie looked genuinely puzzled.

Leonora lost her temper again. 'Oh, for God's sake, use a bit of initiative. Ask Alice. Ask the maid that turns down the beds at night. Find an excuse to go to her room and see for yourself!' She slammed the wardrobe doors shut with a crash.

Lizzie fled from the room, glad to get away. For a minute or so she hovered on the landing, trying to collect herself. There was no way she could go back into Lady Cumberland's room and say she hadn't found out what Lady Amesbury was wearing. And yet how was she going to do that? Lizzie bit her lip again and wondered if she should rush down to the kitchens and ask Alice what to do.

'Good evening, Lizzie.' A warm voice, pleasant and friendly, spoke behind her and she spun round to find herself face to face with Beverley, who looked exquisite.

Lizzie could have dropped into a curtsey of gratitude and thankfulness as she saw her coming out of her room, smiling warmly. She was wearing a simple black velvet skirt to the ground, and a black organza top, tucked and ruffled but revealing the creamy gold of her bare shoulders below. With it, Beverley wore the drop earrings and the pendant Anthony had given her.

'Oh, M'Lady!' Lizzie gasped, a smile spreading across her face. 'You look wonderful, if I may say so. Absolutely wonderful.'

Beverley grinned with pleasure. 'Do I really? Thank you, Lizzie. You've just made my evening.' She patted the back of her hair, which she'd wound up into a twist, just as she'd done in the days when she'd worked for Highlight and *Chichi*. She reckoned, as this dinner was supposed to be in her honour, she'd better make a real effort.

'I hope you have a lovely evening, M'Lady,' said Lizzie respectfully. Inside she was glowing. Lady Amesbury had actually remembered her name! And she'd only arrived from America the previous day!

'Thank you, Lizzie.' With another smile Beverley glided away, elegant and beautiful and looking every inch, Lizzie thought, like a real lady.

'Well? Have you found out what she's wearing?' Leonora demanded as soon as she re-entered the bedroom.

'A long black velvet skirt and a black sort of see-through blouse, M'Lady.' She didn't add that they looked like the sort of clothes they pictured in those glossy magazines, that cost a small fortune.

'A skirt and blouse! Ha!' Leonora snorted triumphantly. 'We'll soon show her what being properly dressed is all about!' With her good humour restored, she picked out a bright pink satin evening dress, with a billowing skirt, and a little matching jacket, which fastened diagonally across the front with a frost of diamanté buttons. It was a magnificent outfit to which she added large diamond earrings and for a moment Lizzie thought bitterly that she was certain to outshine Lady Amesbury. Then she took another look at Leonora's face and, seeing the spiteful meanness in her expression, knew she would never be able to compete with the warm and genuine charm of her sister-in-law.

'Get my matching pink shoes,' Leonora commanded. 'And hurry. I want to be downstairs before anyone else.' She did not notice Lizzie's expression of secret exultation as she took the shoes from the cupboard as slowly as she could. With any luck, she reflected, Lady Amesbury would already be greeting the first of the guests in the Baronial Hall.

Beverley skimmed down the polished stairs with a light heart, happy that Nicholas had gone to sleep within minutes of being put to bed. At her insistence, a cot had been brought down from the nursery and put in her room for him the first night, and ever since he had settled down happily. She'd also scored another victory. The nanny had been cancelled that morning, which Lady Jean had told her was very embarrassing but which she'd nevertheless undertaken to do.

'We'll have to compensate her by giving her a month's pay,' Jean grumbled, 'and I don't know how you think you're going to manage without any help.'

'It'll be all right,' Beverley assured her. 'Goodness

knows, I shall have time on my hands now I'm not working. Looking after Nicky is a luxury, compared with waiting tables or being a hotel receptionist.'

Lady Jean thought about this. 'I suppose it must be,' she said at last. She'd never had a job in her life, although she'd always worked on various charity committees and for local activities, and she found it hard to imagine having actually to earn her own living. By the same token she had never contemplated looking after her two children by herself, either.

'I still don't know how you're going to manage,' Lady Jean continued. 'Children are a dreadful tie.'

Beverley smiled. 'I can live with it, and I've made an arrangement with Percy's daughter to babymind when I need help.'

'Clare Percy?' Lady Jean sounded astonished.

'Yes, Clare. I met her when Nicholas and I went to Home Farm, and she says she's got lots of free time in the evenings.'

'But she looks after the animals . . . not children.'

'So?' Beverley's smile deepened. This was her third victory in twenty-four hours, and she was very pleased she was managing to buck the system. 'A baby calf probably needs as much attention as a small child. I found Clare a very sensible and jolly girl and Nicky took to her at once. Especially when she let him hold one of the baby chicks. I think it's all going to work brilliantly.'

'Well . . . we'll see.' Lady Jean still sounded doubtful but she had to admit Beverley was a refreshing change from Leonora, who had packed Juliet off to boarding school at the age of eight, having insisted she be confined to the nursery floor from the moment she was born.

When Beverley arrived in the Baronial Hall, where the light sconces along both walls made the swords and spears glint with a steely sparkle, and the heraldic arms glow with rich colours on the shields, she found Lady Jean and her husband had just arrived.

'Good evening, Beverley,' said Lady Jean, taking command of the situation. 'You haven't met Rupert, have you? Now, has Stevens put the drinks tray in the library? I told him we'd be having champagne unless anyone wanted something different.' She swept ahead, leaving Beverley and Rupert shaking hands.

'How d'you do?' he mumbled from beneath his moustache, and for a moment Beverley got a glimpse of a deeply kind man with sympathetic grey eyes and a patient smile, before he retired once more behind a stiff mask of politeness.

'Hi,' she replied. 'It's very nice to meet you.'

'Humph.'

Then they followed Lady Jean into the library where Stevens was arranging the fluted crystal champagne glasses in rows as neat as soldiers on parade.

'Good evening, Stevens,' she barked.

'Good evening, Lady Jean,' he replied softly. Stevens had known her since she was six, and knew that beneath her abrasiveness lay a heart of gold.

'Everything under control?' she asked, going over to the fireplace where a log fire glowed in the large grate.

'Yes, everything is under control, M'Lady.'

'Make sure all the candles in the dining room are lit before you announce dinner,' she reminded him.

'Yes, M'Lady. Can I perhaps offer you a glass of champagne before the guests arrive?'

363

'You certainly can, Stevens. Although I think the Colonel would prefer whisky. Wouldn't you, Rupert?'

'Please.'

'You'll have champagne, won't you, Beverley?'

'Sure. It's my favourite drink, thanks to Anthony who really introduced me to it,' she replied.

For a moment Stevens turned to look at her, and catching his eye, she saw and recognised a look of sympathy. She smiled at him then, feeling a sudden affinity for someone whom Anthony must have known since he'd been born.

'Oh, both Anthony and Henry liked it,' Lady Jean remarked in her prosaic manner. 'It's all right, but give me a full-bodied Burgundy any day. Stevens, you are serving some of the Burgundy that my brother laid down with the partridges tonight, aren't you?'

Stevens, in spite of his age, glided towards her with the drinks on a small silver tray. 'Yes, M'Lady.'

Beverley, sitting down on one of the sofas by the wide stone mantelpiece, looked round the room with interest. She'd had a quick look at it that morning, as she and Nicholas explored Bucklands, but it had seemed quite different then. Now, with the fire lit and all the lights on, it looked warm and welcoming, furnished with a magnificent collection of books that stretched from floor to ceiling along two walls. Dark blue velvet curtains, trimmed with dull gold brocade edging, hung in richly swagged abundance from the three high arch-shaped windows that filled the third wall, and above the fireplace hung a landscape by Turner dated 1799, glowing with jewel-like colours.

'I love this room,' Beverley said appreciatively as she sipped her champagne. 'I could write in here.'

'Write what? Letters?' Lady Jean asked.

'I wrote a column when I worked on *Chichi*. I'd like to go back to journalism one day, on a free-lance basis, perhaps.'

'You only wrote about fashion, didn't you?' Jean's tone was dismissive.

'Yes, but when I was doing public relations before that, I was required to write press releases about all sort of things.'

'Humph,' said the Colonel. Lady Jean remained silent.

At that moment Leonora swept into the library, pink satin skirt swishing, blonde hair lacquered so that it remained rigid on her skull when she moved.

'Good evening,' she said graciously, her heavily mascaraed eyes sweeping avidly over first Lady Jean's dress and then Beverley's. Then she paused, stunned into silence by Beverley's appearance. A skirt and blouse, my arse! she thought furiously. Wait until she saw that little bitch Lizzie. Beverley looked fantastic, with her chestnut hair coiled up like she'd spent hours at the hairdresser's and an outfit straight from *Vogue*! Leonora was so angry, and suddenly felt so over-dressed, that all coherent thought fled her mind. Absently, she found herself refusing Stevens' offer of a glass of champagne.

'Oh, perhaps I will.' She changed her mind distractedly, grabbing the glass before he took it away. She looked round the library, as if to make sure there were no other nasty surprises. 'You're very early, aren't you, Jean?'

'I'm early because I had to check on all the arrangements,' Lady Jean replied spiritedly. 'With fourteen people coming to dinner, things just can't be left to chance.'

Leonora twirled on her high heels and looked at her sister-in-law balefully.

'The staff are supposed to look after everything,' she said shortly. 'Bring me a cigarette, Stevens.'

'Certainly, M'Lady.' He came forward with a large crested cigarette box on a silver tray, which he offered to her with silent disapproval.

'Filthy habit,' snapped Lady Jean.

'Humph,' agreed the Colonel.

Beverley was mesmerised, observing with appalled fascination the inter-play between the three people who would be part of her life in future. It was like watching the characters in a play, but with the added horrible realisation that there would be no interval and no final bringing down of the curtain.

'Where's Mama?' Lady Jean asked. 'Rupert, go and fetch Mama. She ought to be down by now.'

'I expect she's forgotten,' said Leonora loftily.

'She's blind . . . not batty!'

Leonora shrugged, still furious that Lizzie had misinformed her about Beverley's outfit. She'd never trust the little cow again. If Jean and Rupert hadn't been here, she'd have gone upstairs and changed into something more subtle but now it was too late. For once she hoped some of the other women coming to the dinner party would also have dressed extravagantly, so that between them they could put Beverley in the shade. But she didn't even dare let herself think about the effect Beverley might have on some of the husbands. This American girl could wreak havoc on the social scene, and already Leonora disliked her.

Rupert reappeared with the Dowager a few minutes

later, leaning on his arm but otherwise looking alert and smiling in a grey lace dinner dress worn with a lavender chiffon scarf. Pearls gleamed in her ears and at her throat and her first words as she entered the library were: 'Where's Beverley?'

'I'm here,' she said, coming forward to greet the old lady.

'Ah, Beverley!' Lady Cumberland looked up at her, recognising her now through the mists that had plagued her eyes for the past few years. 'Come and tell me about your day, my dear. How is Nicholas getting on? What has he been doing today?'

'He's been having a ball!' Beverley assured her as she guided her over to the sofa where they sat down, side by side.

A few minutes later the first of the guests arrived, and Beverley was kept busy shaking hands and making small talk as Lady Jean insisted everyone be properly introduced to her. She was grateful, though, knowing that if it had been left to Leonora, she could have sat alone in a corner all evening without talking to a soul. Always, though, she made sure that the Dowager was included in the conversations, for Beverley had quickly realised that although she might not be able to see very well, her mind was as sharp as a razor, and she didn't, Beverley suspect, miss a thing.

When everyone had arrived Stevens announced dinner, and taking her mother-in-law's arm, Beverley walked with her into the grand candle-lit dining room.

'I hope they've put you to sit near me. I do so enjoy your company, my dear.'

'I enjoy your company, too, Lady Cumberland,' Beverley replied warmly. To be with Anthony's mother, with whom she'd always felt an affinity, was the nicest part of being at Bucklands so far.

'Oh, my dear gel,' the old lady exclaimed, stopping in her tracks, 'please call me Mama! And with your own mother so far away in America, I do hope you'll look upon me as your mama.'

Beverley felt close to tears. The old lady's words meant so much to her and she felt so touched, she gripped the blue-veined hand and squeezed it.

'Thank you,' she said simply.

'Of course you must call her "Mama",' said a sharp voice in Beverley's ear, and turning she saw Leonora looking at her with hostile eyes. 'After all, everyone else does,' she added acidly.

The long polished table was a magnificent sight, set out with crystal glasses and silver candlesticks and rose bowls overflowing with blooms from the hot house. The Cumberland dinner service, which had been handed down through successive generations, the white plates and dishes bordered with a band of deep burgundy and gold, was echoed in the burgundy red candles. In front of each guest was a silver pepper pot and salt cellar, and beside it a small card bearing the guest's name.

Smoothly and without fuss, Lady Jean guided people to where they were to sit as if she were the mistress of Bucklands, while Leonora, skittering around in her bright voluminous gown, flirted with the men, making arch *double entendres* to which she managed to give an added crudeness.

The placement arranged by Lady Jean was diplomatic with none of the family positioned at either the head or the foot of the table. Leonora and Rupert were placed down one side and Lady Jean, the Dowager and Beverley down the other. Husbands and wives had been cleverly divided and there were even three single men, two elderly widowers and a bachelor, to make the numbers even.

Beverley found herself seated between a local magistrate, who was a friend of Lady Jean's and whose wife had died the previous year, and Charles Amesbury, a smooth-looking man in his forties, who was introduced to her as a cousin.

'So how are you finding England?' he asked as Stevens filled their glasses with a light dry white wine to go with the first course of smoked salmon.

'I haven't had a chance to look around yet or even get over my jet-lag,' she replied non-committally. Some instinct warned her to be careful what she said until she knew who she could trust. She was still smarting from Leonora's snide remark about calling the Dowager 'Mama'.

'And how are you getting on with the family? You hadn't met any of them before, had you, except for Henry? Jean's a bit formidable, but she's all right really. Rupert doesn't say much, but he's a good chap. Of course, life at Bucklands was a bit different when Henry was alive; he always had a house full of people and loved entertaining. I don't suppose there'll be much in the way of parties in the future.'

Beverley looked at him curiously. Unlike Anthony and Henry he was very swarthy with black hair and the darkest eyes she had ever seen. He also fancied her. She could tell by his body language, his hand occasionally resting on her arm in a gesture of familiarity, and the intimate tone of his voice. It was as if he were saying: Keep close to me and I'll look after you.

'How are you related to the Cumberlands?' she asked.

'Henry and Anthony and I are first cousins. Our grandfather was the Fifth Earl. My mother is Spanish and she and my father live in Madrid. They hate the climate here. I live in the village, you know. Very near,' he added, smiling into her eyes. Then he edged closer and dropped his voice.

'I must say, you're going to liven things up around these parts, and God knows, we could do with a bit of livening up!'

Embarrassed, Beverley looked up and caught his wife Georgina watching her with a sweet and understanding smile. Beverley smiled back, feeling very sorry for this woman who must have a hellish time coping with such a flirtatious husband. Determined to intimate she wasn't in the least interested in Charles, Beverley leaned across the table to include her in their conversation.

'It's so nice, getting to meet all Anthony's family,' she said pointedly. 'I've heard so much about you all and about Bucklands, I can hardly believe I'm really here at last.'

'Well, it's lovely that you're here, Beverley. How is your little boy? And how are you settling down? It must have been a big wrench for you, leaving your family in America.' Georgina was a slim, petite woman with a gentle face and soft fair hair which she wore taken back with two combs. Beverley liked her at once, and warmed to her understanding manner.

'It was tough,' she admitted, 'but of course Nicky is too young to understand, so he's loving every minute of being here. All this open space is so wonderful for a child.'

Georgina nodded. 'He must love the animals on the farm, too.'

Beverley laughed. 'He's crazy about them! I gather you live in the village?'

'On the outskirts of the village. Hunting Lodge. It used to belong to Charles's parents, and when they went abroad they gave it to us. It's nice being within walking distance of Bucklands.'

'Do you have children?' Beverley asked eagerly. 'I want to find some playmates for Nicky.'

'Ours are much older, I'm afraid.' Georgina sounded genuinely regretful. 'We have a daughter of fifteen and a son of twelve. They're both away at school.'

Charles, who had been looking bored at the female level of conversation, remarked: 'Margaret is at the same school as Juliet, although there's a big age gap. You haven't met Juliet yet, I suppose?'

Beverley shook her head.

'She's adorable,' Georgina said. 'Very like Henry, and a delightful little girl. You'll love her.'

'And you've got just the one boy?' Charles remarked, as his eyes swept over her shoulders, gleaming bare through the sheer fabric of her top, and then down to her breasts. It was a gaze of such intensity, especially in front of his wife, that Beverley blushed furiously and, reaching for her glass, took a long sip of wine. At that moment she found herself locking eyes with Leonora, who seemed to be amused by something, from her position on the opposite side of the table.

'Getting to know the locals, Beverley?' she enquired mockingly. Then she flicked her gaze to Charles who looked unconcerned. 'It'll be nice having a new cousin at Bucklands, won't it, Charles?'

In that moment, Beverley instinctively knew Leonora and Charles had been lovers. She dropped her gaze, thinking how hurtful and galling this must all be for Georgina, and wondering if Henry had ever known?

At last, Lady Jean gave the signal for the ladies to leave the men to their cigars and brandy. Beverley followed, as Mama led the way to the drawing room where coffee awaited them. As they walked across the hall, Georgina caught up with her and slipped her arm through Beverley's.

'I'll give you a ring and perhaps you'd like to bring Nicholas to lunch one day? Then we can get to know each other properly.'

'I'd love that,' Beverley replied, looking into the gentle blue eyes and the sweetly smiling face.

'Good. I'll give you a ring. We can have a good old gossip,' Georgina added with a conspiratorial giggle. 'We were all so fond of Anthony and it's really good that you're here now.'

Feeling warmed by Georgina's generosity of spirit, Beverley was careful to avoid being too close to Charles for the rest of the evening. He was probably a harmless flirt, but nevertheless that sort of behaviour could put her in an embarrassing position.

But as all the guests were leaving, Charles slid round to where she stood, saying goodbye, and placed his arm around her waist.

'I'll be seeing a lot more of you,' he whispered in her ear. Stiffening, Beverley turned away and saw Georgina standing close to them. She was looking straight ahead, but Beverley could sense she'd seen them and was pointedly ignoring it.

'For Christ's sake! I'm doing my damnedest to raise

it . . . why can't you leave me alone?' The voice was high-pitched and sharp with fear.

Beverley, coming out of her bedroom with Nicholas on their way down to breakfast, paused and looked across the landing to where Leonora's bedroom door stood ajar. Through the gap she caught a glimpse of Lizzie placing a tray on a table by the side of the bed. In the background her sister-in-law was on the phone.

There was a tug on her hand. 'I forgot my teddy,' Nicholas announced. 'I get him.' Turning, he shot back into their room, leaving her standing there.

'I'll get it as soon as I can!' she heard Leonora exclaim. 'I'm doing my best, for God's sake . . .'

At that moment Lizzie appeared in the doorway, looking flushed. She closed the door carefully behind her and gave Beverley a nervous glance.

'Good morning, Lizzie.'

'G'morning, M'Lady.' Then she scuttled away down the stairs as if she were afraid of something.

'I got teddy!' Nicholas shouted triumphantly as he came hurtling out of their room again, clutching his favourite toy.

'Come along then.' Together they went down the wide polished stairs to the morning room. Beverley, deep in thought, wondered what was going on. Leonora had sounded scared and harassed on the phone just now, but to whom had she been talking? And what was she trying to raise? Money was the only thing Beverley could think of, but why should Leonora be 'doing her damnedest to raise it'?

There was no shortage of money in the Cumberland family, of that Beverley was certain. And she was sure Henry had left Leonora well provided for. One glance at her clothes seemed to confirm the fact that she spent thousands of pounds a year on her wardrobe; they also entertained lavishly, there were at least eight indoor staff from what she'd seen and that was not including Percy, Joe, and all the people who worked on the land. So why should Leonora need money so desperately?

'Are we going to see the goats today?' Nicholas asked through a mouthful of cereal.

'Yes, we are, but don't talk with your mouth full,' Beverley admonished, although she was smiling. 'Clare might let you see the new kittens, too.'

'Do they belong to Clare?'

Beverley paused, longing at moments to say: 'Everything belongs to you, sweetheart, or will one day,' but knowing that was the wrong way to bring Nicholas up, she said instead: 'They belong to the farm.'

'Does the farm belong to Gra?' His eyes, so like Anthony's, were wide and wondering. He'd had trouble saying 'grandma' or 'granny' when he'd first arrived, and the Dowager had been so enchanted at being called 'gra', Beverley had a feeling the abbreviation would stick.

'The farm belongs to our family,' Beverley replied carefully. 'Your daddy lived here when he was a little boy.'

'Where's my daddy now?' He spooned another mouthful of cereal.

It was the question he'd asked so often since he'd learned to talk and every time it made her heart twist with pain. As if he knew he was missing a parent, his curiosity was insatiable.

'Where is he?' he replied.

'Daddy's in Heaven, darling, because he died when you were a baby.'

'Why?'

She sought the simplest explanation. One he would understand without giving him nightmares. 'He had an accident, Nicky.'

He popped another spoonful into his mouth and seemed satisfied.

'Finish your breakfast and we'll go.' Beverley poured herself another cup of coffee, luxuriating in the sybaritic pleasure of having everything done for her. No doubt, in time, she'd get bored with it, but after months of struggling to make ends meet, it was wonderful to find breakfast every morning beautifully cooked and presented, the coffee fragrant and the boiled eggs straight from the farm. It was comforting to have their beds made and the bathroom cleaned, with fresh towels put out every day, and it was reassuring to know that lunch, tea and dinner would be served with elegance and style. Beverley only wished Anthony was here to make it all perfect. As it was, there was only Leonora and Mama for company, and Beverley reflected that such a combination of females, living under one roof, couldn't help but lend itself to a Chekhovian atmosphere at times.

They were crossing the hall, on the way to the gun room where Wellington boots and mackintoshes were kept, when Leonora came rushing down the stairs, her heels tap-tapping on the polished wood. Beverley looked up in greeting, but it was as if Leonora hadn't seen her. She hurried past, a thick wool coat round her shoulders, her hair falling in disarray as if she hadn't even brushed it, and her pale face devoid of make-up.

'Good morning!' said Beverley.

Leonora didn't reply. A moment later, through the gun-room window, Beverley saw her getting into the

Jaguar that was waiting on the far side of the draw-bridge. Joe held the car door open for her and as soon as she was settled in the back, he jumped in, started the engine, and accelerated down the drive, gathering speed all the time.

Chapter Sixteen

Leonora didn't return until mid-afternoon. Beverley was examining the magnificent collection of books in the library when she heard the car coming up the drive and, looking out of the window, saw her sister-in-law hurrying over the drawbridge. She looked calmer though she still had a distracted air. A moment later she burst into the library, and then stopped short when she saw Beverley.

'Oh, I didn't know you were in here,' she said, looking startled.

Beverley looked enquiringly at her. 'Am I in your way?' she asked politely. She'd just come across a fascinating volume of memoirs written by a butler who had worked at Bucklands between 1868 and 1872, while Nicholas played happily on the floor with his toy cars. Fervently, she hoped Leonora wasn't going to join them.

'Er . . .' Leonora looked around the room in a vague manner and then shook her head. 'No, it's all right.' Then she turned and walked out again.

Beverley started reading again, marvelling at the detailed description of life in the old castle a hundred and twenty years ago. There had been twenty-eight indoor servants in those days, the butlers and footmen dressed in scarlet and blue livery, trimmed with silver lace and braid. Silver buckles had adorned their shoes and they wore white stockings and gloves. Reading on, she learned how the Second Countess of Cumberland had given her orders for the day in the morning room, and had managed the running of the castle so brilliantly, the King had described it as 'the finest home in the land'. While the family dined off gold or silver plate 'which was heavy to polish', the servants used pewter plates, goblets and tankards, engraved with the family crest, and before eating in the servants' hall, drank the family's health in ale, from ancient horns. An under-butler would raise his horn and say 'My Lord and Lady' and the servants would respond 'With all my heart'.

Fascinated, Beverley read on while an idea slowly began to form in her brain. She read an account of Christmas 1870 when the revelry both below stairs and above included singing and dancing, amateur theatricals, and much merry making. The village band were also discovered by His Lordship, supine in the snow and scattered around the estate, having collapsed on their way back to the village 'overcome by home brewed ale'. Mummers came to the castle to perform, and on Christmas morning the choir in the local church were as 'pink in the face as peonies', having imbibed ale and hot toast since dawn.

The book gave such a vivid impression of life at Bucklands in the old days that Beverley felt transported to another time and another life, a million miles away from New York and Stockbridge and all that she'd known before. Most interesting of all was the fact that it was all about Anthony's ancestors. She tried to imagine his great-great-grandparents riding through the grounds in the horsedrawn carriage. Entertaining the King at great banquets in the dining room. Holding soireés for the Queen in the drawing room, and hosting weekend house parties for the most noble in the land. For the first time Anthony's background took on real substance. Bucklands might be a fairy tale setting, but the lives that had been lived within its ancient walls were real enough, and the history of the Cumberland family was fascinating. Thoughtfully, she looked over to Nicholas, who was still absorbed in playing with his cars, and felt a sense of renewed shock that he was heir to so much. When she'd first been told by Lady Jean that he was the new Earl, it had seemed as empty and pointless an honour as Anthony's title. What was the use of it? A title had not protected Anthony from the sick horror of Mary and her obsession with him, any more than it had brought Beverley a fortune when she was forced to support Nicholas and herself. But now, as she studied these quaint memoirs, she began to see there was a long heritage to be proud of, and a family history that made extremely interesting reading.

Beverley put the book carefully back on its shelf and decided to talk to Mama about her idea.

At that moment, she heard raised voices in the hall, so loud that even Nicholas looked up, wide-eyed.

'You will let me make the decisions,' Leonora was shouting. 'You should never have let her get rid of that nanny. It was madness. I hate having children around the place, making a noise and cluttering up the place with their mess. He's in the library with her now . . . and he's got all his toys in there. It really isn't on, Jean.'

'Perhaps I can persuade her to have an au pair if she won't have a nanny?' Jean replied.

Beverley had heard enough. Opening the library door she shot into the hall, looking braver than she felt. Lady Jean and Leonora stood facing each other, the former grim-faced and flushed with anger, the latter running her fingers distractedly through her hair.

'I think I should remind you,' Beverley said, glaring at them, 'that neither Nicky nor I are here because we wish to be. Pressure was brought to bear on me to bring him to England. I was told I had no choice but to live at Bucklands and allow Nicky to be brought up here.' She paused for a moment while they both looked at her with astonished expressions. Nicholas wandered out of the library to see what was going on and stood beside his mother, watching the grown-ups intently.

'That being the case,' Beverley continued, 'I think you might show us a little courtesy, not to mention making an effort to make us feel welcome. Nicky has been brought up in the midst of a close and loving family, something which Anthony appreciated, and I don't intend to hand him over to a nanny, or an au pair just because certain people find children a bore. I believe in mothers bringing up their own children. Clare Percy has promised to baby-sit if I need her, and I can leave Nicky at the farm with her for an hour or so each day if I have things to do. If you wish us to remain at Bucklands, he must be allowed the freedom of the place under my supervision.'

It was the longest speech she'd ever remembered making, and she paused to look directly at Leonora before continuing.

'He does *not* clutter up the house with his toys, and he does *not* leave a mess around the place, he's never been allowed to do that, but he is a normal healthy child, and

I can hardly gag him while you have your beauty sleep in the mornings,' she added with a flash of temper.

Leonora looked away for a moment and then back. Her expression was baleful.

'Perhaps you aren't used to living among the aristocracy,' she said spitefully. 'There are standards to be maintained . . .'

'This is getting us nowhere,' Lady Jean cut in hurriedly. 'Providing Nicholas doesn't make too much of a din, I really think we must leave it to Beverley to bring him up as she sees fit.'

Beverley shot her a grateful look. 'His presence is giving Mama a lot of pleasure,' she pointed out. 'Because he's a boy, I think it's helping her to get over the loss of Anthony and Henry. She invited us to watch the children's programme on television in her sitting room yesterday. She said she loved to hear Nicky's remarks, although she can't see much of what's on the screen herself.'

'I'm sure she finds him riveting.' Leonora spoke scornfully. 'Boys are all that count in this family.'

'Don't be silly, Leonora,' Lady Jean said robustly. 'Beverley, if you think you can manage then that's fine, but if you change your mind about having a nanny, I can give you the number of a very good agency.'

'Thank you. I plan to send him to the village play group later in the year. It's only in the mornings and it would be good for him to mix with other children of his age.'

Lady Jean said nothing, but Leonora exploded.

'Oh, well, if you're going to bring him up like that, mixing with the village children, I wash my hands of the whole thing. Don't you realise he'll pick up the most awful working-class accent? The farmers send their children there!' Leonora turned to Lady Jean as if to appeal for her support. 'The next thing is we'll have nits! I heard there was an epidemic of nits among the village children.'

'There's an epidemic of nits in every school in the country at the moment,' Lady Jean retorted, and Beverley could see she was having a problem in keeping a straight face. 'Nits only like very clean hair, you know,' she added conversationally.

'Oh, I give up!' Leonora stormed up the stairs with a dismissive wave of her hand. 'You can all go to hell, for all I care.'

'Thank you,' Lady Jean observed drily. 'I'm sorry about that, Beverley. I hate rudeness. Leonora doesn't seem to be herself these days.'

Beverley remained silent, remembering the fraught conversation she'd overheard that morning.

'Ummm,' she murmured non-committally.

It wasn't until the next day that the extent of Leonora's self-preoccupation became evident.

The twelve-year-old girl sat very upright at the dining-room table, dressed in a grey pleated skirt and dark green sweater, with her long fair hair held back by a black velvet band. Her face was flushed with unshed tears.

'It was awful, Mummy!' she said, her voice rising with distress. 'There I was, stuck at Heathrow, and you'd forgotten to meet me! The Duke was furious. They were all taking another flight on to Scotland, but he said he couldn't leave me on my own. How could you forget, Mummy?' Lady Juliet Amesbury looked badly upset, having only been rescued an hour before by Joe, who had dashed to the airport to collect her on her return from the South of France.

Leonora stabbed furiously at her chicken pilaf with her fork. 'Stop making such a fuss. I hate whining.'

'I'm not whining!' Juliet replied vigorously. She reminded Beverley so much of Henry, with her open expression and candid blue eyes. Her Easter holidays had been spent with a friend from school, near Nice, and she was due back at boarding school in two days' time.

Nicholas wriggled in his high-chair which Beverley had brought down from the nursery as the carved dining-room chairs were far too low for him.

'Ju-let went on a plane!' he announced loudly. He was fascinated by his cousin and had even gone so far as to allow her to hold his teddybear for a few minutes when she'd first arrived. Beverley was delighted with the way Juliet responded. She had spoken to Nicholas gently and sweetly, and put her arms around him.

'I went on a plane!' he informed them cheerfully. 'And Ju-let went on a plane.'

'Shush!' Leonora scowled at him. 'Be quiet while we're having lunch.'

'He's hardly making a noise,' Beverley protested mildly.

The Dowager, who had joined them for lunch today because she said she wanted to see Juliet and hear about her trip, intervened tactfully. Turning to her grand-daughter, she said with a smile: 'I think you've grown since you've been away, haven't you, Juliet darling?'

Juliet turned to her with a quick smile. 'I might have done, Granny. I had a marvellous time. Henrietta and I swam every day, and there was a jacuzzi at the villa, and we went sailing ... the Duke's an awfully good sailor and he allowed us to take it in turns to steer the boat. He taught us all about navigation, too. Henrietta says he's going to give her a little sailing boat when she's eighteen. We had lots of picnics, too, and they had one of those things that detects metal objects in the ground. Henrietta found a five-franc piece on the beach, buried in the sand ...'

'For heaven's sake, Juliet!' her mother exclaimed angrily. 'Will you stop talking! Natter-natter-natter! Your voice goes right through my head.'

Juliet looked crestfallen. 'But Granny asked me about my holiday.'

'I think we can take it Granny has now heard,' Leonora remarked drily.

'I want to hear a great deal more. Why don't you come and see me in my room this afternoon?' the Dowager suggested.

'All right, Granny.'

Leonora was not finished. 'And you can stop going on about not being met this morning, Juliet. It wasn't the end of the world, for goodness' sake.'

'End of the world!' Nicholas repeated with a serious expression, bringing his small fist down on the table. 'End of the world!' he said again sternly.

The Dowager started to laugh, throwing back her head like a young girl. Beverley laughed too. There were times when Nicky was very funny although she had a sneaking feeling he knew when he was playing to the gallery.

'Oh, isn't he adorable?' Juliet exclaimed, reaching out to stroke his cheek. 'I'm so glad you've come to live here, Nicky,' she added impetuously.

'I think he's going to love having a new-found cousin,' Beverley remarked, smiling at the little girl.

'Juliet goes back to school the day after tomorrow,' Leonora remarked as if that were the end of the matter.

'Yes, but there is the summer vacation and that's nice and long, isn't it?' said Beverley.

'Mummy is making me stay with friends for most of the time.'

The Dowager leaned forward and looked into Juliet's face with her misty eyes.

'Perhaps,' she said gently, 'now that Beverley and Nicholas have come to live with us, Mummy will let you stay at Bucklands. That is, if you want to?'

'Oh, I do,' Juliet said earnestly, her blue eyes lighting up. 'Mummy, can't I stay at home next holidays?' she said wheedlingly, her hands clenched anxiously in her lap.

'Out of the question,' said Leonora. Beverley realised this was her favourite phrase. 'You've been invited to Florida, to stay with Cynthia Lloyd and her family, and the Wentworth-Hawkins have invited you up to Scotland . . . I don't want you hanging around here, getting under everyone's feet.'

Beverley looked at Juliet's woebegone face and her heart bled. The girl looked so disappointed and hurt. How could Leonora treat her only child like this? Beverley was on the point of saying something, although she knew it was none of her business, when Juliet spoke.

'Daddy didn't send me away during the holidays when he was alive.'

There was a painful silence in the room and the Dowager shifted uneasily in her chair. Leonora, on the other hand, wasn't in the least put out.

'Well, Daddy isn't alive now, and I say you've got to go and stay with these people. Surely you want to have a good social life? You'll thank me for it when you're older. You'll know everyone by then. You'll get invited to all the best parties, and remember one thing—'

Juliet looked at her unhappily. 'What's that?'

'Most of the girls you know have elder brothers.' Leonora gave a short mirthless laugh. 'Most of them highly eligible, too. At least you'll never be short of dancing partners when you're a debutante.'

'Are there such things as debutantes these days?' Beverley asked artlessly, more to divert the conversation than anything else. She could see Juliet was getting very upset and this was the stickiest lunch she'd ever sat through.

At that moment Nicholas created his own diversion.

'I want to wee!' he said urgently. 'Mummy, I want to wee!'

While Beverley whisked him out of his chair, and Juliet started to giggle, Leonora threw down her table napkin with a gesture of profound impatience.

'This is too much!' she stormed, rising. 'I will not have this chaos! This place is turning into a bear garden. If these children can't behave, they'll have to eat in the nursery, whether they like it or not.'

'Come about twelve-thirty,' Georgina Amesbury suggested. 'Then we can have a drink before luncheon.'

'I'd love that,' Beverley replied. 'See you on Friday.'

When she hung up she felt delighted that Georgina had kept her promise. The one thing she missed about living at Bucklands was having someone near her age to talk to. Leonora was at least ten years older, but seemed more, and Lady Jean was in her early fifties. Talking to

Mama was wonderful, but she was almost more like a grandmother to Beverley than anything else. Georgina, she guessed, was around thirty-five, and on their previous meeting, Beverley had sensed they had a lot in common.

Hunting Lodge, which had originally been part of the Bucklands estate, was a charming grey stone house built on two floors with large receptions rooms, which as Georgina explained had been used for luncheon in the old days when there were large shooting parties.

'Can you imagine,' she told Beverley, as she showed her around, 'that the butlers and footmen from Bucklands carted all the silver and glass down here, and all the food as well, so that the guests could stop and have lunch between drives rather than trek back to the castle? Anyway, Charles' grandfather gave it to his second son as a home, and that's how it came down to us.'

'You must like it much better than living at Bucklands,' Beverley remarked as they sat before a crackling fire in the drawing room, having a drink before luncheon while Nicholas played with a doll's house Georgina had brought down from her daughter's bedroom.

Georgina looked at her and an expression Beverley couldn't quite fathom flickered in her pale eyes. Then it was gone and she was smiling warmly.

'Oh, absolutely. This house is much warmer for one thing!' She laughed merrily. 'When we dine at Bucklands in the winter, I wear *layers* of woollies under my evening dress. How are you liking it?'

'I have to admit it's a great improvement on three rooms overlooking a freeway in the middle of a city!' she laughed.

'But you and Anthony lived in great style, didn't you?

I heard you had your own column on a top magazine, and that you socialised a lot.'

Beverley nodded ruefully. 'We did when Anthony was alive. Things changed when he was killed, and then we had the recession.'

'We've got a terrible recession here, too,' Georgina pointed out.

'It doesn't seem to have affected the family, though. I haven't heard of any cutting back at Bucklands,' Beverley replied.

'Life always was pretty lavish up there. We're the poor branch of the family.' Although Georgina smiled, there was sadness in her expression.

'What does Charles do?'

Georgina picked her words carefully. 'This and that. Nothing very much really. He was left some money by his grandfather, and I suppose when his parents die he'll get a bit, but we'll never be rich.'

This was strange thinking to Beverley. Neither she nor her family had ever waited for 'dead men's boots', as Rachael always described an inheritance. They'd always been taught that one must make one's own way in life.

'So tell me about your children?' Beverley asked.

Georgina's expression melted. 'Oh, Margaret and Tom. They're terrific. I wish they weren't away at school. The holidays go so quickly, and they're growing up so fast.' She gave a quick sigh. 'One wants only the best for one's children, doesn't one? You must be so happy that Nicholas is a boy and will inherit everything.' There was no envy in her voice. She seemed to be happy for Beverley's sake that her son had an assured future.

'To be honest, there are times when I don't know how I feel about it,' Beverley replied candidly. 'I miss

America and my family, and feel quite sad Nicky's not going to be brought up as I was, but on the other hand I couldn't deny him what is rightfully his, could I?'

Georgina nodded sympathetically. 'Perhaps your family will come over and visit you?'

'Oh, they'll certainly do that. And I plan to take Nicky to the States from time to time, so he at least knows what his mom's home is like.'

Talking convivially, the next two hours seemed to fly past as Georgina, without any fuss, served a luncheon of spaghetti bolognaise and salad at the large kitchen table, followed by fruit and cheese and a pot of strawberry yoghurt for Nicholas. She had even unearthed an old high-chair that had belonged to her children, and bought a bottle of fruit juice for him.

'How thoughtful!' Beverley exclaimed, looking round the warm and friendly kitchen. To her relief Charles didn't seem to be at home, and she made a point of not referring to him again.

As she was leaving, Georgina put her hand on Beverley's arm. 'Any time you want to leave Nicholas with me for an hour or so, don't hesitate to ask. I'm here, with very little to do most of the time, and I'd love to look after him.'

Beverley leaned forward and kissed Georgina on the cheek. 'You really are kind, and I do appreciate it. So far, Clare Percy has been helping me but . . .'

'If at anytime she can't, you've got my number. Just give me a ring. I'd be delighted to help.' Her smile was sweet, and as she looked down at Nicholas she patted his head. 'Such a dear little one,' she murmured.

'Thank you very much.' Together she and Nicholas walked down the short drive of Hunting Lodge, while

Georgina stood waving to them from the doorway, her gentle face wreathed in smiles, her fair hair blowing wispily around her head.

'See you soon!' she called out.

A wind was whipping up as Beverley and Nicholas walked back to Bucklands along the Grassy Avenue, and storm clouds were gathering ominously. Then in the distance they heard the rumble of thunder.

'Let's hurry,' Beverley said, grabbing Nicholas' hand. Normally she didn't mind storms but for some reason there was something foreboding in the atmosphere; a presentiment of malevolence in the darkened sky, a premonition of some impending disaster.

Picking up Nicholas and holding him close, she hurried on until the castle was in sight. The wind was stronger now, buffeting her so that her hair blew wildly about. Large drops of rain began to fall. Seized by inexplicable anxiety, she crossed the drawbridge and managed to get inside Bucklands before the rain came lashing down.

'You just escaped the storm in time,' Alice remarked, appearing at that moment.

'Yes,' Beverley replied breathlessly. But she had the feeling it was more than the storm she and Nicky had escaped from. The last time she'd had this strange feeling had been when she'd bumped into Mary, dressed up to resemble her, in the baby clothes department of Saks.

The Dowager Countess sat at the exquisite marquetry writing table in the drawing room of her apartment in the west wing, surrounded by the salvaged mementoes of seven decades. Silver-framed family photographs stood on every surface, together with old lace fans, albums full of snapshots and newspaper clippings from the Court Circular of *The Times*, and ornaments and trinkets collected since her girlhood. Nearly all the furniture had come from her old home too, brought with her to Bucklands when she'd married into the Cumberland family. The paintings she'd inherited from her late father. He'd been a great collector and on the walls hung a small Degas, an impressive landscape by Corot and three sanguine drawings of figures by Watteau.

The room had a tranquil atmosphere, with its slightly shabby rose velvet curtains, the edges long perished from fifty years of sunlight, the chintz furniture covers faded and worn. It was here, since failing sight and an arthritic hip had begun plaguing the Dowager, that she spent most of her time, only venturing downstairs when necessary.

On this bright morning, a week after Juliet had returned to school, Rosemary Cumberland, dressed in her customary tweeds in a dark shade of burgundy, and a creamy lace blouse, peered at the monthly statement that had arrived in the post from Harrods. She'd had an account at the great London store ever since she'd been a young woman and nowadays she did all her shopping from their catalogue. From the magnificent selection of merchandise she selected all her Christmas and birthday presents for family and people who worked on the estate alike. From hampers filled with exotic delicacies to warm bedroom slippers, she made sure that everyone had something according to their needs.

She had only one problem these days. She was getting so blind she could hardly make out the figures on her statement and when it came to writing a cheque, had

difficulty seeing where to write. Henry had been so helpful when he'd been alive, nipping up to her room to fill
in her cheques for her, so that she only had to sign under
his guidance. Now she had no one.

Frustration made her sigh impatiently. Since she'd
started to go blind she'd been told nothing more could
be done.

Sighing again, she scrawled her spidery signature and
hoped that if she'd got it wrong, Harrods' accounts
department would understand.

It was not widely known that Rosemary Cumberland
was a very rich woman in her own right. She'd never
needed financial support from her husband. Born Rosemary Armitage, she'd inherited the Armitage fortune
culled from the prosperous Cornish tin mines that had
originally belonged to her grandfather, and it had
enabled her to have complete financial freedom. Not
that money interested her. She looked upon it as a
commodity to be used for the good of the community.
There were workers on the estate who would be forever
grateful for the helping hand she'd given them, quietly
and discreetly, over the years.

Rising now, she went over to the carved fireplace and
rang the bell beside it. When Stevens came into the
room a few minutes later, she handed him the envelope
addressed to Harrods.

'Will you be so good as to see this gets posted, please?'
she said.

'Certainly, M'Lady.'

The postal van that came up to the castle every morning collected mail as well as delivered it. Stevens walked
sedately down the stairs into the hall, and laid the Dowager's letter on a silver tray left there for the purpose.

There was already some post awaiting collection the next morning; a letter written in Lady Amesbury's handwriting, to an address in America, and another in the young Lady Cumberland's hand, addressed, rather strangely he thought, to someone who lived in Hackney, East London.

Beverley delayed discussing her idea with the Dowager until she'd done more research. The problem was that the thousands of books in the library were not arranged in any particular order so she spent much of her time running up and down the library steps, making some wonderful discoveries but also wasting a lot of time going through books that did not apply to what she wanted to do.

It was a wonderful room to work in, though, with its magnificent ebony floor and pale oak-beamed ceiling. This had become her favourite room in the castle, rivalling the cool elegance of the drawing room and the sombre magnificence of the dining room. While she went through the books, making notes from time to time, Nicholas played happily with his toy cars or climbed on to the windowseats, kneeling on the blue velvet cushions to gaze at the garden and watch the birds.

At last, after a week of systematic research, collecting as much relevant information as she could, Beverley asked her mother-in-law if she could go up and see her one afternoon.

'I've had this idea,' she began as she settled herself in an armchair facing the Dowager with Nicholas playing on the floor between them. 'But I'm going to need your help.'

'Go on, my dear,' said the Dowager encouragingly.

Beverley drew a deep breath. 'I've been looking at the books in the library, and I've found many of them are about the family. Some go right back to AD 1135 when George Amesbury was at the Court of King Stephen. Then there's Thomas Amesbury, whom Anthony told me about; he had an estate near here, during the reign of King Richard II – that was before he bought Bucklands in 1385. It's fascinating stuff. I loved the biography of Harold Amesbury, who was a groom to the bedchamber of King Henry VIII. The family have really been involved in the history of Great Britain, haven't they? And I'd no idea that the first Earl of Cumberland was Lord High Chancellor either!'

'The Amesburys have always been high achievers,' agreed Rosemary. 'They've dedicated themselves to King and Country. So what is your idea, dear girl?'

'I want to write a history of the family. It will probably take me years, but do you think I could have a stab at it?'

'That sounds like an Anthony phrase and I think it's the most brilliant idea,' the Dowager replied immediately. 'You know, it was something I always wanted to do myself, but somehow there was never time and the years passed and then my eyesight started to fail. Oh, Beverley! I think it's a thrilling idea! And who better to do it than you, with all your experience in journalism?'

'I didn't do any serious writing,' Beverley said self-deprecatingly. 'I hope I can do it well enough, because I'd love Nicky to have a complete picture of his family when he's old enough. Something that will give him a sense of pride and a feeling of belonging.'

'I think you're right. The younger generation don't really care too much for family heritage these days.'

She smiled wanly. 'Henry appreciated his antecedents but only wanted to live close to the land, much to Leonora's disappointment. She would so much have loved a life in high society, mixing with the royal family all the time, and all she got was a farm full of animals!'

Beverley grinned, amused at the Dowager's insight into her other daughter-in-law's character.

'And as for Anthony,' she continued, 'he was ambitious to make a lot of money and carve a business career for himself in America, but he had the feeling that having a title would make people think he was a dilettante and a bit of a playboy.'

'He was modest about his lineage, but wasn't ashamed of it,' Beverley pointed out.

'Oh, I know. He was just unassuming and that was one of his great charms. He was a dear boy and I loved him so much.'

'Oh, Mama, I loved him, too. You've no idea how much.'

'I think I know, my dear Beverley. When you got married he wrote to me and said he'd found the most perfect girl in the world. He longed for you and me to meet, and when Nicholas was born he so wanted to bring you both back home to Bucklands so that we could all be together. He loved you more than anything in the world, my dear, and he knew, he realised, how much you loved him too.'

Beverley looked at her mother-in-law through her tears. 'I shall never love anyone again,' she said without a trace of self-pity. 'There will never be another Anthony for me.'

The Dowager reached out and laid her hand on Beverley's arm, her expression full of understanding.

'You will never find another Anthony, that I agree. But I sincerely hope you will find someone to share the rest of your life with, dear girl. You are far too young to remain a widow. I know how dreadfully I missed my husband when he died and I was over sixty! You're a mere child. You have your whole life before you. Don't make the mistake of hanging on to the past, Beverley. Anthony wouldn't have wanted that, he who adored life so much. He told me you had so much love to give; you mustn't let that go to waste.'

Beverley wiped her eyes and gave a watery smile. 'I understand what you're saying, Mama, but I don't know how I could even begin to love anyone again in the way I loved Anthony.'

'Ah, that's not what I said. Of course you won't love anyone in the way you loved him, but I hope you'll find a different sort of love, my dear. A love that will be fulfilling and rewarding in other ways, perhaps.'

'I can't imagine it happening.'

'Of course you can't. Not yet. It's too soon. But give it time . . . at some point it would be good for Nicholas to have a father figure in his life, especially now that Henry's gone too.' Her voice dropped and for the first time since she'd begun talking, emotion showed in the sad lines of her face. 'One must always remember one thing, though.'

'What's that?'

'Something good always comes out of even the most terrible things. You and Nicholas are here with me now, which wouldn't have happened if Henry hadn't been killed. You've no idea, Beverley, how happy your presence has made me. It's like being given the most enormous bonus, just when I thought God had run out of

396

prizes! Dear little Nicholas gives me such joy ... oh, dear girl, you're both making the last few years of my life happy once more, and that is something I certainly didn't think would happen!' She tilted her head with a sprightly movement and clasped her hands together in a girlish gesture.

'I'm so glad.'

'You'll be happy again one day, dear girl, I promise you.'

Beverley shook her head. 'I can't really believe that. I've made up my mind that my life will now be devoted to bringing up Nicky, and helping him to prepare for what lies ahead.'

'I can understand your feeling that way at the moment, but believe me, the heart has a strange way of mending itself. Just when you think nothing nice will ever happen again to you – boom!' The Dowager clapped her hands. 'Something wonderful happens.'

Beverley smiled. 'This is all a long way from my idea of writing the history of the family.'

'It is and it isn't. I'm wiser than I look, you know, and I think, apart from everything else, you'll find writing the book will be cathartic. Much of your deep inner pain will be healed in the process.'

Beverley looked at the old lady with renewed respect. It was obvious that the great sadnesses she had suffered, losing her husband and both her sons, had brought her wisdom and understanding as well as sorrow.

'I'd like to believe you,' Beverley said with sincerity.

'It will happen, dear girl. Meanwhile, I think your idea of writing the history of the Cumberlands is the best thing you could do. You'll have time on your hands when Nicholas starts nursery school, and one thing I do know – there's nothing more depressing than not having enough to do.' The Dowager sighed. 'If only my sight wasn't so bad. There is still so much I could do if I could see. Never mind. If I can help in any way with your book, you know I will.'

'You must have wonderful recollections of coming to Bucklands as a bride?'

'I do, indeed. I know quite a lot about the family, and about Bucklands which you might find useful.'

Beverley leaned forward eagerly. 'Why don't I buy a tape recorder? Then you could talk into it, recounting everything you know, and I could get it transcribed.'

The Dowager looked almost radiant, her pale skin flushing with pleasure.

'Beverley! You really do have the most brilliant ideas! Then I wouldn't have to strain my eyes, would I? And it would give me something really useful to do. Oh, what fun it's going to be!'

Beverley grinned. 'I think it's going to be therapeutic for both of us. I can't wait to get started. I also thought, at the same time, I might catalogue the books in the library. They really need to be got into some order and it's a job I'd enjoy.'

'Dear girl, I think your coming to Bucklands is the best thing that has happened to us for a very long time.'

They continued talking animatedly until, growing bored, Nicholas climbed on to Beverley's knee, demanding to be taken to the farm.

'We'll go in a minute,' she assured him.

'Will you come to the farm, Gra?' he asked the Dowager.

'No, my pet. I don't like going out these days, it makes my hip hurt more, but why don't you go and then you can come back and tell me all about the animals?'

'Yeah!' he crowed.

'So like Anthony!' remarked his grandmother, shaking her head.

'I know.' Beverley picked Nicholas up and gave him a big hug. 'You're just like your daddy, aren't you?'

''Course I'm like my daddy!' he said stoutly. 'Come on, Mummy. Let's go. The goats are waiting to see me!'

Leonora returned from her shopping trip in London later that day, having made Joe drive round in circles, unable to park, while she tried on dresses in Harvey Nichols, suits in Browns, hats at David Shilling and shoes at Manolo Blahnik. Then at one o'clock she asked him to drop her off at San Lorenzo in Beauchamp Place where she said she was meeting a friend for lunch. She'd made it sound like a woman friend, because she didn't trust Joe not to gossip, but of course she'd met Duncan McSwiney, the upwardly mobile young advertising executive with whom she'd been having an affair for the past three months, and they'd gone back to his Pont Street flat afterwards.

She'd enjoyed herself; Duncan was amusing, good in bed and fun to be with. He wasn't serious about her and she suspected he had a string of girlfriends whom she serviced in rotation, but that suited her fine.

Now, as the car cruised down the motorway towards Oxford, on their way back to Bucklands, she brooded on her present situation and felt deeply dissatisfied. It had nothing to do with Duncan.

She'd been fundamentally dissatisfied ever since she'd married Henry thirteen years before. She'd thought then, as a nineteen-year-old bride, that marriage to the

Earl of Cumberland would bring her popularity and power, social acceptance and even a role to play on the fringes of the royal family. At first she'd enjoyed her position as chatelaine of Bucklands Castle, where she reigned supreme, with her mother-in-law in the west wing and Jean in her own house, but gradually she'd come to realise that the aristocracy never quite accepted anyone from the middle classes in the way they accepted one of their own. Anthony had been impossibly snobbish, expressing open amazement that Henry had wanted to marry her, and Jean and the Dowager had been, at best, charmingly patronising. Only Henry, because he'd at first fallen in love with her and realised too late he'd made a dreadful mistake, remained loyal and kind until the end.

Leonora was a lone woman now, kept on at Bucklands because she was Henry's widow, but allowed to live there only under sufferance. She knew they would like her to leave, but she was not going to give them that satisfaction. She intended to hang on to her position, no matter that Beverley and her Yankee brat, as she always thought of Nicholas, were worming their way into the affections of Mama and Jean. For one thing she couldn't afford to leave. Somehow she was going to have to raise an enormous amount of money to meet her debts. Her thin red lips twisted bitterly. Henry had disappointed her in life and he'd done no better in death.

Why hadn't he taken out a life insurance policy? An accident policy? Anything, to avoid her having to live on the small annuity the Cumberlands gave her. And now she was in deep financial waters and even being threatened by the money-lenders she'd gone to. How the hell was she going to get out of this mess?

Chapter Seventeen

'Is there anything I can get you, Mama?' Leonora asked solicitously. The Dowager had been in bed with a heavy cold for the past week and Leonora had been at pains to see she had everything she wanted.

'Nothing, thank you,' Rosemary Cumberland replied. 'Alice gave me some lovely hot soup for luncheon and I'm going to take a little nap now.' The old lady lay propped up against several pillows in her carved Jacobean fourposter bed, looking more frail than ever.

'Ring the bell if you need anything,' Leonora said gushingly. 'I'll make sure you're not disturbed. I thought of going into Oxford to get some new cassettes for you to listen to. You like music, don't you?'

The Dowager closed her eyes and wished Leonora would stop treating her like an imbecile child.

'I think I've got all the music I need,' she replied with a wintry smile. 'I like to listen to my old favourites, you know.'

Leonora looked momentarily deflated and then brightened again.

'How about a few audio books? You can get novels and thrillers and all sorts of books on tape these days.'

For a moment the Dowager thought of explaining

that for the past few evenings Beverley had been reading aloud to her, but she thought better of it. No point in playing one sister-in-law off against the other.

'How kind, my dear,' she murmured instead.

'What shall I get you? A nice romantic novel?'

'How about an autobiography?' the Dowager suggested tactfully. Even Leonora couldn't go wrong with something safe like that written by someone well known.

'Very well. See you later. I shan't be out for long.' Breezily, Leonora swung out of the over-furnished bedroom, a crisp figure in a black wraparound skirt that showed her knees, and a black and white silk blouse.

As the Dowager lay resting, she couldn't help wondering what had brought about the change in Leonora. It was almost as if she'd decided it would be to her advantage to take a leaf out of Beverley's book. Her helpfulness was almost overpowering these days; nothing was too much trouble. She was even complaining less about Nicholas, and her attitude to Beverley seemed much friendlier.

Rosemary Cumberland shrugged her thin shoulders and closed her eyes. All she longed for was peace. She'd suffered too many blows and too much heartbreak to seek anything but tranquillity in the last years of her life. If Leonora had suddenly decided to be pleasanter and more co-operative, then who was she to question why? Be thankful for small mercies, her late husband had always said. And she would. She might have lost her beloved sons in the past two years, but she had two beautiful grandchildren and a daughter-in-law in Beverley who was all one could wish for.

'Thank you, God, for the mercies you have shown

me,' she whispered under her breath. A moment later she was fast asleep.

Leonora dropped her voice in a confidential manner.

'Alice, I don't want the Dowager to be worried about anything; she's not well and I think the time has come, because of her age, when we must all rally round and see that everything runs smoothly for her.'

'I understand, M'Lady,' Alice replied, somewhat surprised. The young Lady Cumberland had never shown anything but irritation with the old lady in the past and now she seemed to be bending over backwards to ingratiate herself. It must be, Alice reflected, because she'd decided to set herself up as a rival to Lady Amesbury, who was popular with everyone on the estate.

'Tell Stevens to bring her mail to me before he takes it up to her, so that she only gets personal post. You know how flustered she always gets when she gets letters from the Inland Revenue, or the bank, or anything official in fact.' She gave a little patronising laugh. 'Old people become rather like children, don't they? We must look after her, though, and protect her from things that make her agitated.'

'Have the doctors said she must be kept quiet?' Alice asked. As far as she was concerned the old lady was as perky as ever, apart from her cold, but maybe there was something wrong with her she didn't know about.

Leonora hesitated and looked down, flicked a speck from the front of her blouse.

'We have to watch her blood pressure,' she said rather vaguely. 'She's been getting rather – er – over-excited, shall we say, when Lady Amesbury's been with her,' she continued as if choosing her words with care. 'This

403

present illness started after they'd spent a day in the library last week – I think it was too much for her, and . . . well, you know. Maybe she was put under some pressure . . .' Leonora let her sentence drift into silence, as if she didn't want to put into words what she was suggesting.

Alice looked back at her with a sullen expression.

'I'll do what I can, M'Lady, but there's only so much I can do. I can't be everywhere at once and if Lady Amesbury won't have a nanny, it's not my job to keep young Nicholas from disturbing the Dowager.'

'Oh, I know that, Alice. Don't worry, I wasn't expecting you to be responsible for Nicholas.' She sighed. 'I'm afraid there's nothing any of us can do to stop him being disruptive around the place and I just hope his presence isn't going to be too much for my mother-in-law. But between us, with Stevens' help, we can protect her from unwelcome post or tiresome telephone calls, can't we?' Leonora smiled graciously. 'The least I can do is to take some of the burden off her shoulders now that my husband is no longer around to help her.'

'Very well, M'Lady.'

'Perhaps you could ask Cook to make her favourite ginger cake for tea? I promised her a nice tea today.'

'It would have to be for tomorrow, Cook could never do it in time for today.'

'Oh, very well.' As if suddenly bored, Leonora made a dismissive gesture with her hand and strode off across the hall and into the drawing room.

Alice stood looking after her thoughtfully. To her way of thinking, the leopard never changed its spots. So what on earth was the young Lady Cumberland up to?

'Will it require a kiss to awaken the Sleeping Beauty?'

The voice was rich with amusement. Startled, Beverley opened her eyes with the unpleasant sensation of realising she'd been watched while she dozed in a garden deckchair.

Standing before her, looking down at her with an expression of insolent intimacy, was Charles Amesbury.

'You scared me!' she exclaimed, feeling rattled. 'How long have you been standing there?'

He shrugged. 'A few minutes. You looked so peaceful it seemed a shame to disturb you.'

'Then why did you?' Beverley sat up, running her hands through her hair, trying to collect her thoughts. It was the most glorious late-April afternoon, hot and cloudless, and she'd decided to spend it in the garden with Nicholas. Percy had recently built a sand pit for him, and she'd bought him a bucket and spade, and at the moment he was solemnly transferring sand from one end to the other, watched by Clare.

'I thought I'd wander by and see how you were getting on.' Charles turned to glance over at Nicky. 'I see the son and heir has adjusted very well to his new position in life.' Without waiting to be asked, he lowered himself on to a nearby seat and then looked at Beverley, his eyes slowly travelling the length of her body.

'And how's his mother getting on?'

'I'm fine,' she replied coolly. The man maddened her. He always seemed to be scoring points and she felt at a disadvantage, sitting there in an old pair of jeans, having just woken up.

He took a packet of Benson & Hedges from his trouser pocket and flicked it open. 'Cigarette?'

She shook her head. 'I don't smoke.'

His eyes were provocative as they stared into hers. 'So what vices do you have?'

Beverley felt herself bristling. She really hated the way he made everything he said sound suggestive. Several answers sprang to mind, but they all sounded either arch or coy. On the other hand, she didn't think she could very well be downright rude.

'How's Georgina?' she asked instead.

He laughed as if he thought her ploy to change the conversation was amusing. 'Why should you want to know how Georgina is?'

'Because I happen to like her and we've become good friends.'

Charles inhaled deeply on his cigarette, watching her closely.

'Is that so?' he asked.

They sat for a few more minutes in silence while a warm breeze ruffled Beverley's hair, playing with the tendrils around her face. Then she spoke.

'Have you come to see Leonora? Or Mama?'

'Neither.' Charles flicked his ash on to the lawn. 'Leonora's a bitch, and I hear Rosemary's in bed with a cold. I hoped you'd entertain me.'

Beverley rose. 'I'm afraid I have to take Nicholas in for tea in a minute. Clare has to get back to the farm in time for milking.'

'Then we'll ask Stevens to bring another cup for me.' He saw she was about to protest, but silenced her with a smile which for an awful flickering moment reminded her of Anthony's. Nicky had that same smile too and she loved it in him, but somehow with Charles she felt repulsed.

Without another word she walked over to the sand pit. Nicholas looked up.

'I've made a castle,' he said, pointing to a misshapen heap of sand.

'So you have, sweetheart. It's beautiful.'

Charles had joined them, his shadow falling across the sand. 'It's almost as nice as your castle, isn't it?' he remarked.

Nicholas looked perplexed. 'It is my castle. I made it.'

'I mean *that* castle.' Charles waved his hand at Bucklands, rising behind them majestically against a clear blue sky.

'That's Gra's castle,' Nicholas said stoutly.

'Whose?' Charles looked questioningly at Beverley.

'Mama's,' she replied shortly. 'Come along, Nicky. It's time we went indoors for tea.'

Obediently, he put down his spade while Clare pulled the cover Percy had made over the sand pit in case it rained in the night. Then, bidding them goodbye, she walked off in the direction of the farm.

'You ought to get him some swings and slides,' Charles observed as he followed Beverley and Nicholas across the lawn, his hands plunged deep into his pockets.

'I'm going to, but so far he's been so busy finding his way around the farm there hasn't been time.'

'And what toys are you going to get for yourself?'

Beverley looked round at him, sharply. 'What do you mean . . . toys?'

'A car? A horse? What do you fancy?' Again there was that wickedly insolent smile.

'I'll probably get myself a car, but I'm going to be fairly busy in the immediate future so I doubt I'll have time for anything else.'

'Busy? Writing your great tome about the family?' His tone was mocking.

'How did you know about that?'

407

'Ah-ha! There are a lot of things I know about you.'

'Including the fact I'm going to catalogue the thousands of books in the library?'

He grinned. 'And the best of British luck to you, too! The book sounds like more fun.'

'It will be. Mama is going to help me by dictating her memoirs into a tape recorder, as she can't see nowadays.'

'Rosemary is a fund of knowledge,' he agreed. 'When I was a boy I used to come and stay here a lot and she used to tell me the most wonderful stories about the old days.'

In spite of herself, Beverley felt a quickening of interest. Nicholas had run ahead of them, his little legs in miniature jeans trotting across the lawn. As she watched him, she felt the familiar pang of wishing Anthony could see him now. He'd have been so proud of his son.

'Get her to tell you all about Great-grandmama,' Charles continued. 'She was a Lady-in-Waiting, you know, to Queen Alexandra. She also had fourteen children, and she taught all her sons Latin! Brilliant woman. Quite a beauty too, I believe. She was the daughter of the Duke of Rochester. Everyone expected her to marry the Prince of Wales, who became Edward VII, but she fell in love with Robert Cumberland and that was that!'

Beverley looked at him in wonder. 'So she might have been Queen of England?'

He nodded. 'Your book should sell well in the States. They're very interested in our royal family and the aristocracy, aren't they?'

'We're all interested in the present royal family, but I don't suppose my book will cut much ice back home.'

'Oh, I don't know! You might make a packet.'

'That isn't actually my intention,' she said crisply. 'I'm really writing it for the benefit of Nicholas, so he has some idea about his father's background. I want him to grow up with a sense of tradition.'

They were crossing the drawbridge now, and she took Nicky's hand protectively.

'His father didn't care much about the history of the family,' Charles remarked, taking another cigarette out of the packet.

Beverley spun on him angrily. 'That's not true! He adored Bucklands. He was also very proud of his family.'

'Then why did he rush off to the States? He could have earned a living in this country. Henry would even have welcomed his living at Bucklands.'

'You may have been Anthony's cousin, but you obviously didn't know him very well. He wanted to support himself. He was aware that Bucklands belonged rightfully to Henry as the elder son. But Anthony had pride. He wanted to make his own way in life.'

Charles threw up his hands in mock surrender. 'Okay! Okay! You needn't be so defensive! But I always felt he didn't care about having a title.'

'He cared,' Beverley replied quietly, 'but he wasn't a show-off, that was the difference.'

'Maybe. I know if I'd had the title I'd have made it work for me!'

'I expect you would.' His words reminded her of what Elaine had always tried to instil in her. 'But Anthony was enough of a man in his own right not to need to lean on his title,' she added with quiet pride.

They were in the Baronial Hall now, and from the drawing room could hear the chink of china as Stevens set out the tea tray.

'Tea!' Nicholas yelled excitedly. 'Tea!'

'Shush!' Beverley said good-humouredly, picking him up to stop him running on the polished floor.

Leonora was already seated behind the silver teapot. When she saw Charles her eyebrows shot up and she looked at them both with cool amusement.

'Hel-lo,' she said, drawing out the word. 'I didn't know you were here, Charles.'

'I was strolling in the grounds and Beverley invited me to tea,' he replied nonchalantly.

'Oh, really?' She looked from one to the other, her eyes gleaming with curiosity. 'Well, now you're here, you'd better sit down.'

While Beverley settled Nicholas at a small table, and put a sandwich on a plate in front of him, she was aware Charles was looking at Leonora with an expression of someone who knew her intimately.

'How's it going?' he asked her chummily.

Leonora froze him with a glare. 'Fine,' she replied abruptly.

His voice dropped. 'Any luck?' he asked, so softly Beverley could hardly hear what he was saying.

Leonora mouthed some angry reply, and then said loudly: 'Beverley, does Nicholas want his milk now?'

Beverley, who had been straining her ears to find out what this interplay between them was about, got up from her seat and reached for the miniature silver tankard Nicholas always drank from. It bore Anthony's initials below the family crest, and had a few dents and scratches from years of nursery use.

'Thanks,' she said lightly.

The next half hour was strained as Charles tried to presume on an old intimacy with Leonora, which she resisted coldly, and at the same time flirt with Beverley.

At last he rose to go and no one tried to stop him.

'Goodbye!' Nicholas piped up, with what would have been rude eagerness had he been an adult.

'Goodbye, young man,' Charles replied, amused. 'Look after your mother.'

Beverley felt herself bristling again. Why did everything he say annoy her so much? It was as if he were the other side of the same coin as Anthony. There was a family similarity there, though not in looks, but whereas everything about Anthony had amused, delighted and thrilled her, everything about Charles had the opposite effect. She found him arrogant to the point of insolence, tiresome in his conceit, repulsive in his playful sexual invitations.

'Goodbye for the moment, Beverley.' His tone suggested he'd be seeing her again shortly.

'Goodbye,' she said firmly. Leading Nicholas out of the drawing room, she was aware of Charles' eyes following her, burning into her back as she went up the stairs. Then she heard him saying something to Leonora, whose reply was loud and angry.

'Mind your own goddamn' business! If it hadn't been for you I wouldn't be in this mess!'

'Isn't it time you took responsibility for your own actions?' she heard him retort. Then, through the banisters, she saw him striding off angrily, leaving Leonora standing alone in the hall.

It was early evening, a week later, and with Nicholas asleep, Beverley decided to go for a walk in the grounds before dinner. There were still parts of the enormous estate she hadn't yet explored, like the small Norman church where in bygone days the Cumberlands had always sat in the front pew, and the Earl had read the lesson every Sunday. She hadn't been to look at the folly either. It stood at the top of a steep grassy incline, an eighteenth-century mock temple built by an earlier Viscountess Amesbury.

It was a mild evening, the air balmy after the heat of the day, the leaves gently rustling in the soft breeze. As she crossed the drawbridge, she saw the punt, moored on the far side of the lake, reminding her that Percy had promised to take her and Nicholas out in it one day. She'd have taken Nicky for a trip round the outside of the castle herself, except that she knew punting required much more skill than rowing. The pole was fifteen feet long and so heavy she could hardly lift it.

Beverley started walking up the knoll, taking it at a leisurely pace, her eyes fixed on the domed roof of the folly and the Corinthian pillars which supported it. It was a charming little temple, whimsical and purposeless, and she thought about the ancestor who had built it and wondered what sort of woman she'd been.

At last she reached the summit and, slightly breathless, stood under the hemispherical roof, looking out at the magnificent view, stretching away into the distance. From this vantage point she was able to see Bucklands as a whole, with its forests and farm, meadows and kitchen gardens, the Grassy Avenue and the exquisite formal rose garden to the south of the castle. It was unbelievable, she reflected, that one day her son would own all this valuable land. Never in her wildest dreams could she have foreseen Nicky's future when he'd been born. Yet she knew that no amount of money or possessions would ever make up for the loss of his father. Nicky had lost the most precious thing of all, one of his parents. All the riches in the world would never be enough to compensate him for that.

'Enjoying the view?' The voice was husky and deep. Beverley spun round, startled and unnerved by the sudden appearance of Charles Amesbury standing a few feet away. He was wearing pale linen trousers and a striped shirt open at the neck. His expression was intimately familiar as he stood there looking at her, feet planted wide, hands in his pockets.

'Do you make a habit of creeping up on people, nearly scaring the life out of them?' Beverley snapped irritably.

Charles smiled lazily. 'How can I help it if you like the same places I like? Anthony and I used this folly as "home" when we played hide-and-seek as boys. I'm glad you like it, too.'

Using the memory of Anthony as a means of getting round her annoyed her deeply. If he and Anthony had been such close chums when they'd been young, how come Anthony had never mentioned it?

'Really?' she replied coolly.

He moved closer. 'So how's everything going? How are you getting along with the in-laws?'

'Fine.'

'Even Leonora?'

'Why not?' She was determined not to be drawn, knowing instinctively that Charles had all the guile of a mischief-maker.

He shrugged, straightening his arms so his hands dug deeper into his pockets. 'She's not everyone's cup of tea. So what do you do with yourself all day?'

Beverley turned her head away, looking at the distant horizon.

'Nicky keeps me busy,' she said briefly.

'But that can't be enough for a young woman like you?'

She could feel him looking at her, from the crown of her titian hair to her slender sandalled feet, and felt uncomfortable and exposed.

'What else do you do?' he coaxed. He'd stepped right beside her, so that his shoulder touched hers. 'A hot-blooded woman like you can't exist on a diet of dusty books and nursery chores. Surely you want something else out of life?'

Beverley looked at him levelly, the gold flecks in her eyes sparking in the evening light. 'Whether or not I eventually want more out of life is a personal matter, Charles.' Her voice was icy now but scrupulously polite.

'But I can offer you a little solace along the way, can't I?' he half whispered, slipping his arm round her waist. 'You're the most desirable woman I've ever met.'

She broke away, cheeks flaming.

'For God's sake, this is ridiculous! I'm not interested, Charles. Can't you understand that?' She started walking down the knoll again, on her way back to the castle. Charles followed, matching his pace to hers, keeping as close to her side as he could.

'But I could make you happy, Beverley. I could make you thrill with renewed life and passion.'

She stopped in her tracks to turn and glare at him.

'I think you're the most insensitive, boorish, tasteless human being I've ever come across!' she told him. 'Will you just leave me alone?' Then she walked on hurriedly, and to her relief he didn't follow.

'Why don't you let me help you, like Henry used to?' Leonora suggested. 'Honestly, Mama, it would be no trouble. Just let me know when you want anything done, like writing a note or filling in a cheque, and I can do it for you as Henry did. Then all you'd have to do is sign your name.'

Rosemary Cumberland felt sorely tempted to accept. Her sight was so bad these days several friends had said they couldn't understand the letters she'd sent them, because she'd written on top of the previous line again and again and they couldn't decipher her words. She sighed deeply, feeling cut off from so many of the activities she'd previously enjoyed, like reading and needlepoint.

'It's very kind of you to offer, Leonora,' she replied, wishing it was Henry who could still see to her affairs. 'I don't want to be a nuisance.'

'Mama! How could it be a bother? It only takes a moment to do a little writing, unless of course you'd rather I hired a part-time secretary for you? Then she could type everything and you could tell her what to put?'

The Dowager shook her head. 'No, I don't think I'd like that.' After all, she reflected, what was the harm in letting Leonora help? She had to admit privately that she'd never really liked her daughter-in-law, and had been dismayed when Henry had married Leonora, but at least the young woman was being kinder to her than she'd been in a long time, and that was a welcome change.

'Very well, my dear,' she conceded, 'if it really wouldn't be too much trouble, I'd be most grateful.'

'It will be no trouble at all,' Leonora replied with warmth. 'Is there anything I can do for you now while I'm here?' She looked over to the marquetry writing

table where Mama always sat to deal with her correspondence.

'I do have to drop a line to Smythson's of Bond Street
to ask them to print some more headed writing paper
and to send me a good supply of envelopes,' Rosemary
Cumberland said.

It only took Leonora a few minutes to write, in her
bold loose round hand, a letter requesting a repeat order
of the enclosed sample of stationery. 'And a hundred
envelopes, Mama? Or two hundred?' she asked.

'You'd better say two hundred, Leonora.'

'Very well.' When she gave it to her mother-in-law to
sign, she watched, head on one side, as the Dowager
scrawled her signature.

'There we are!' Leonora announced brightly. 'No
trouble at all. I'll put it in the hall to be collected tomorrow morning.'

The only thing that grated on the Dowager's nerves,
she thought, as Leonora left the room, was to be spoken
to as if she was a co-operative child.

The Dowager sat up in bed a few days later whilst having
breakfast and looked across the room where she could
see the hazy outline of Alice arranging some flowers in
a vase.

'Surely there was some post for me this morning?'
she asked.

Alice, who had seen several letters addressed to the
Dowager, including one from her bank, smiled
cheerfully.

'Yes, M'Lady. You had some post today. Stevens
brought it up to you. Flower catalogues, weren't they?'
For the past week she'd obeyed young Lady Cumber-

land's instructions, but now she felt uneasy. Supposing those bank letters were important? She'd put them carefully to one side, all the time wondering if she was doing the right thing. Leonora had said she'd handle the Dowager's business affairs in future to prevent the old lady getting fussed, but it struck Alice she was getting into a state because she wasn't receiving much post.

Later that day, Leonora called Alice into the drawing room.

'My mother-in-law tells me there was some post for her this morning, and she wonders why it wasn't brought up to her. What have you been saying, Alice?'

'Nothing, M'Lady. She asked me why she hadn't received any letters and I told her she had – the flower catalogue she always gets from that nursery in Hemel Hempstead.'

Leonora frowned. 'I don't want her worried, Alice. The doctor told me she has to be kept quiet. I'd be grateful, in future, if you'd say nothing to her that might make her agitated.'

'I never did!' Alice flushed hotly.

'That's not the impression I got. You even suggested to her that the post might have gone astray.'

'I never!' Alice repeated, looking aggrieved. 'To soothe her, like, because she said she was used to getting more post, I said something about you know what the post's like these days. It was a general remark, M'Lady. I meant no harm. I never suggested . . .' she faltered.

'Yes, Alice?'

'I never suggested anything had happened to her post, M'Lady.'

'I should think not, because nothing *has* happened to her post. I'm merely trying to spare her the aggravation of having to deal with the Inland Revenue and that sort of thing.'

'Yes, M'Lady.'

Alice withdrew, her heart beating fast, her hands shaking. In future, she decided, she wouldn't go anywhere near the table in the hall where the post was laid out in individual piles each morning; that way she wouldn't know what had arrived and what hadn't. Stevens could sort it out when it was delivered according to the young Lady Cumberland's wishes. Let him be the one who had to answer her awkward questions.

'Do you mean to say you haven't been up to London since you arrived in England?' Georgina asked, her expression stunned.

'I've been so busy settling in, there doesn't seem to have been a moment,' Beverley replied. She'd dropped in to see Georgina while she'd been shopping in the village with Nicholas, and now as they sat in the garden drinking homemade lemon squash, Georgina's amazement made her laugh.

'I don't know how you've been able to resist the temptation!'

'I suppose I feel it would be miserable for Nicky to have to spend a day in town, and so I've avoided going so far.'

'Leave him down here!' Georgina exclaimed. 'Leonora should jolly well have him for the odd day, but as we both know she won't, why don't I look after him?'

'You're very sweet, but I thought of waiting until we were a bit more settled. Perhaps when he starts nursery school.'

'I've got a better idea.' Georgina refilled their glasses

from a tall hand-painted glass jug. 'Let Clare look after him. He likes her, doesn't he? And then we could go together! I could show you all the sights!' Her gentle face lit up with enthusiasm. 'Think what fun it would be.'

For some reason Beverley felt reluctant to leave Nicholas for a whole day, and yet she couldn't think of a real reason to refuse. It was true that he'd be perfectly happy with Clare, who was prepared to look after him at any time, but nevertheless something made her hesitate.

'I'll think about it,' she replied. 'I'm so engrossed in getting together all my notes for this book and getting Mama's reminiscences transcribed . . .' Her words drifted off as if she was over-worked.

'Oh, come on!' Georgina's voice was mildly bantering. 'You go then, and leave Nicholas with me. You should get away from Bucklands and the family sometimes.'

'Can I take a rain check and let you know?'

'Of course, but don't forget, I'll be delighted to look after Nicholas any time.' She reached forward and squeezed Beverley's arm. 'Those of us who have married into this family must stick together and support each other.' Her limpid blue eyes held a look of appeal.

Beverley nodded, guessing her unhappiness at being married to Charles, and wondering why she stuck with him.

'Sure,' she agreed, smiling.

At that moment they heard a car turn into the short drive of Hunting Lodge and pull up outside the front door. Charles clambered out, his arms full of shopping.

'Hello, darling,' Georgina called out with false gaiety. 'Did you get everything?'

He sauntered over, his eyes fixed on Beverley. 'Hello.

I didn't expect to find you here.'

'Hello,' she replied with icy civility.

'Did you remember to get the olive oil?' Georgina asked.

Charles looked bored. 'I got the olive oil. I got the sugar. I got the coffee. I also got some gin, vodka, whisky, martini and sherry, if you must know.'

'My goodness!' Georgina trilled nervously. 'Beverley's going to think this is a house of alcoholics!'

'Oh, surely not?' he replied drily, smiling at Beverley. Then he eyed her glass of lemon squash. 'Can I liven up that fearfully dreary-looking drink for you with a splash of something?'

'No, thank you.' Beverley drained the last of her drink and put the glass down. 'We must be off. It's nearly time for luncheon. Come on, Nicky.'

'Going so soon?' he asked, raising his eyebrows. Then, with a wry smile, he strolled towards the house. 'I'll leave the shopping on the kitchen table, Georgie,' he called out casually over his shoulder.

Beverley said goodbye, the amicable atmosphere gone now, destroyed by the appearance of Charles, so that she and Georgina were rather stiff with each other and there was an awkwardness between them.

Taking Nicholas' hand, Beverley walked back to Bucklands through the coppice that lay between the castle and the village. This was one of her favourite walks, for it was quiet and peaceful in the centre of the forest, and the trees rose high above her, reminding her of the woods back home in Stockbridge. On the outskirts, shrubs grew in profusion, screening the castle from sight. There were rhododendrons and azaleas, hawthorn and laurel bushes, camellias and hydrangeas.

No matter what time of year, there was always something in riotous bloom.

As Beverley emerged at the far edge of the copse, twenty minutes later, a figure emerged from behind one of the bushes. Startled, she stopped in her tracks, staring.

'We meet again.'

'Charles! What on earth are you doing here?' She felt genuinely bewildered. 'How did you get here?' She and Nicholas hadn't exactly hurried, yet here was Charles standing before her, not even breathless.

He shrugged, grinning wickedly. 'I used an amazing invention called a car!'

Beverley flushed, feeling foolish. Nicholas, who was trailing behind, dragging a broken-off piece of branch he'd found, had stopped to prod the earth with it. She turned to call him to hurry up, but before she had time, Charles stepped forward and with a swiftness and sureness of movement, placed one arm around her shoulders, pulling her towards him. Startled, Beverley turned back. His face was only inches away from hers. She opened her mouth to protest hotly but he clamped his lips over hers, holding her pinioned to his side with one arm while he slid his other hand between her legs and stroked her with a skilled touch.

Struggling to pull away from him, her senses reeling with shock, her heart filled with a deep anger, Beverley flailed out with her fists, hitting him in the ribs, in the stomach, trying to aim for his groin, but he held her in a powerful grip and for a moment she thought they were both going to fall. Struggling to keep her balance, stunned by his strength and how helpless she was in his grip, a thousand thoughts flashed through her mind. Uppermost was fury. Raging, seething fury. No one had touched her since Anthony had died. No one but Henry had even held her in a comforting embrace. Yet here was this philanderer, this seducer, this *monster*, violating her, desecrating in her mind the act of love that she and Anthony had shared. Then she remembered Nicholas was only a few yards away.

Summoning up every ounce of strength, she wrenched her head sideways, hurting her neck but freeing her mouth from his.

'Get off me!' she yelled, raising her knee to bring it up into contact with his groin.

Charles let her go immediately, and stepping backwards, stood with arms outstretched, looking at her in surprise. Then he started to chuckle, as if the whole thing had been a joke.

'Can't we even be "kissing cousins"?' he asked sardonically.

Beverley glanced round at Nicholas, who was digging away with concentration, his back to them. 'Don't you ever dare do that again!' she warned in a low voice, so that Nicholas would not hear.

Placing his hands on his hips, he stood looking at her and there was an insolence in his manner she hated.

'What a fuss over nothing,' he remarked coolly. 'You're acting like some bourgeois virgin! Don't you know the upper classes screw around all the time? You'll have to wise up if you're going to be a part of the scene here.'

'If that's what it takes, I'd rather *not* be a part of the scene here,' she said hotly. She was trembling with shock. How could this man be a cousin of Anthony's? And how could he behave like this towards his cousin's widow?

422

'If you ever so much as lay a finger on me again, I'll report you to the police for attempted rape!' she stormed.

'Oh, heavy!' he mocked. 'The Cumberlands would just love that! Can't you see the headlines in the local newspaper? You'd be the laughing stock of the place, my dear Beverley.' Shaking his head and still chuckling, he sauntered off, hands deep in his trouser pockets, jaw raised defiantly.

Feeling suddenly weak, she leaned against a nearby tree, her face buried in her upraised arm. She felt besmirched and humiliated, and more deeply enraged than she'd ever been before. In fury, she pounded her forehead against her arm, as much from a feeling of helplessness as anything else. How was she ever going to be able to look Georgina in the face again? Did she realise her husband was more than just a harmless flirt? And how was she to continue living at Bucklands, to which Charles seemed to have constant access?

'Mom?'

She felt a tugging at her skirt. Looking down she saw Nicholas standing there, still holding his big branch, looking up at her. Pulling herself together, she grabbed his hand.

'Let's go back for lunch,' she said, trying to keep the tears from her voice. Suddenly, she felt so desperately home-sick she wasn't sure how she was going to endure another day in England. She longed for the wise words of her mother, and the comforting advice of her father, and wished with all her heart that she was back in Stockbridge where life was straightforward.

'I'm hungry,' Nicholas announced, trotting beside her.

'Supposing we leave your stick in the garden? Then

we'll get back quicker.' She couldn't bring herself to call Bucklands "home". Worst of all, there was no one she could confide in. No one she could talk to who could tell her how to handle the situation.

''Kay,' said Nicholas, laying it down carefully on the grass. Then he looked at her anxiously. 'Percy won't throw it away, will he?'

Beverley bent down and picked him up, holding him close, trying to block out the memory of that other form pressing himself against her in the copse a few minutes before. Nicholas smelled of baby soap and freshly laundered clothes. She kissed his little round cheeks.

'Why is your face wet, Mom?'

Beverley took a deep breath. She must protect him from the ugliness of life.

'The wind is making my eyes water,' she said, feeling no guilt at lying. Then she hurried across the drawbridge and into the safety of the castle. But was it so safe? Charles seemed to be able to come and go as he liked. The realisation made her aware that she wouldn't be safe from him anywhere.

Clare came to fetch Nicholas after lunch to take him down to the farm. There was nothing he loved more than being with all the animals and it gave Beverley a chance to work on her book. She'd bought a simple tape recorder for the Dowager's use, and now, as they sat in the west wing, they discussed the various aspects of the project.

'You were telling me about the time Anthony's great-grandmother entertained Queen Alexandra?' Beverley prompted. She was glad to have something to do to take her mind off Charles, but her head still ached from the shock and her heart still pounded angrily.

'Ah, yes!' the Dowager replied in delight. 'That was when the Cumberlands had a house in London. When they stayed in town for the season they took twenty servants from here and a wagon loaded with trunks of linen and silver and such foodstuffs as tea, rice, sugar and soap. They even took plants from the garden with which to fill the window boxes of their Eaton Square mansion.'

At that moment there was a knock on her door, and for a moment Beverley froze. Surely Charles wouldn't come in here?

It was Leonora, all smiles until she saw Beverley sitting there.

'Oh!' she exclaimed, startled. Then she saw the tape recorder on the table between them. 'What's that?' she demanded suspiciously.

Beverley explained. 'Mama is recording all she knows about the family for my book.'

'Oh, your book!' She looked disapproving. 'I hope you're not tiring Mama? She hasn't been well, you know.'

'Talking has never tired me, Leonora,' the Dowager replied mildly. 'This book of Beverley's is going to be so exciting, it's really given me something to think about. And, best of all, I don't need to use my eyes, thanks to this marvellous little machine.'

Leonora glared. 'I hope you've got that thing turned off now,' she said. 'Tape recorders are a menace, I think. Anyway, I came to tell you that I'm going to have some people to dinner next Tuesday evening, some friends from London.'

Beverley smiled politely and the Dowager looked hopeful.

'Does that mean you'd rather Beverley and I had

supper up here in my rooms? We wouldn't want to intrude, my dear,' she added with a sweet smile.

'Well . . . er . . .' Leonora looked disconcerted. When Henry had been alive he always insisted his mother join them for dinner, no matter who the guests were, but now Leonora craved a little privacy.

'I'm sure you'd rather have your friends on your own,' Beverley agreed immediately. 'It's no problem.'

Leonora beamed. 'If you're sure?' She made a little show of reluctance. 'As they're all driving down from London, I was going to suggest they stay overnight.'

'That's a very good idea.' The Dowager spoke graciously.

When Leonora had gone, the Dowager immediately started reminiscing again. 'Did I tell you that the family used to go up to London by coach, drawn by four horses, and that a footman in livery stood on the back?'

But Beverley's concentration was shot to pieces, over-powered by the memory of a hot mouth on hers . . . a probing hand . . . and the fear that violation brings. She switched on the 'Record' button discreetly, and let the old lady go on talking.

Chapter Eighteen

On the morning of Leonora's dinner party, Lady Jean stalked up to the castle and arrived in the hall just as Lizzie was collecting Leonora's post to be put on her breakfast tray.

'Good morning.' Her tone was brisk.

'Good morning, M'Lady.'

Lady Jean skimmed the various piles of mail with a practised eye. 'Alice has already sorted them out, has she?'

'I think Mr Stevens did it,' Lizzie replied respectfully.

'Stevens? Anything for my mother? I'm on my way up to see her.'

'Just those, M'Lady.' Lizzie pointed to a catalogue from Harrods and what looked like a charity appeal.

Lady Jean scooped them up, at the same time glancing at Leonora's mail. She could see they mostly looked like bills, addressed to 'Leonora, Countess of Cumberland' as she was now known since Henry's death. Suddenly Lady Jean put out her hand as if to stop Lizzie.

'Wait a minute, that looks like . . .' She picked out a letter half way down the pile. 'Yes, I thought so! This is for Mama. Look, it says "The Dowager Countess of Cumberland". I thought I recognised the envelope. It's from her bank. My sister-in-law goes to another bank altogether.'

'Very well, M'Lady. Stevens must have made a mistake.' Smilingly, Lizzie picked up the tray again.

Lady Jean nodded. 'Poor Stevens. I think it's his eyesight. We'd better make sure he hasn't put any other letters in the wrong pile, don't you think?'

With her usual efficiency, which Lizzie privately thought was bossiness, Lady Jean went through everyone's post.

'The letter to Lady Amesbury has got American stamps on it,' Lizzie observed brightly. 'Shall I take it up to her, as I'm going anyway?'

'I'd leave it here, Lizzie. She can get it herself when she comes down to breakfast.'

'Very well, M'Lady.'

Lizzie trotted off, up to Leonora's bedroom while Lady Jean followed more slowly. When she arrived at the Dowager's rooms in the west wing, she rapped lightly on the bedroom door.

'Come in.'

'Good morning, Mama. How are you today?'

The abrasiveness of Lady Jean was, as always, in marked contrast to the gentleness of her mother.

'Good morning, Jean dear. What brings you over so early?'

The Dowager had already been given her tray by Alice and was sitting up in bed, in a pink woolly shawl, listening to the news on the radio. Her silvery hair, released from the confines of a bun, framed her face in soft waves.

'Turn it off, will you, dear?' she instructed Jean. 'I just wanted to hear what was happening in the world.'

428

Lady Jean did as she was told and then sat on the edge of the bed. 'Here's your post, by the way,' she said.

'Anything interesting?' The Dowager dabbed her mouth with a lace-edged napkin.

'Harrods' catalogue . . .'

'Oh, good! I always like getting that.'

'An appeal from the Royal British Legion, according to the envelope . . .'

'I'll send them a donation.'

'. . . and a letter from your bank.'

'Open it for me, will you, dear? Tell me what they say?'

Lady Jean ripped open the letter from the local branch of the Eastern Bank, and gave a snort. 'I don't know why they waste money sending out all these circulars,' she complained. ' "Our Commitment to Serving You",' she read aloud. ' "We are happy to introduce our new system which will . . ." Oh, do you want to hear any more, Mama?'

The Dowager laughed. 'No, thank you, dear girl. I always throw those sort of things away as soon as they arrive. Have you had breakfast, by the way?'

'Hours ago! Rupert and I were up by six! I've got meetings all afternoon and tonight we've got to be in London for a dinner. Damn' waste of time, but Rupert insists on going as it's a regimental "do".'

'You know, Leonora's got some friends for a dinner party and I believe some of them are staying the night.'

'Who's she asked?'

'She didn't say, but they seem to be her London friends. Five or six of them.'

At that moment there was a sharp tap on the bedroom door, and before she could say anything, the door burst

429

open and Leonora rushed into the room, in an ice blue satin dressing gown, her hair dishevelled, her face unmade-up. When she realised her mother-in-law wasn't alone, she stopped dead in her tracks – 'like a startled filly' as Lady Jean later told her husband.

'Oh! I didn't know you were here!' she exclaimed, looking at her sister-in-law.

'What can we do for you?' Lady Jean asked.

Leonora's eyes flew to the letter lying on the bed.

'Lizzie told me . . .' she faltered as if she was trying to collect her thoughts '. . . told me that the post had got mixed up.'

'Only to the extent that you were about to be given a letter addressed to Mama from her bank,' Lady Jean observed mildly. 'Nothing to get excited about, Leonora. Unless of course you *like* getting letters from banks?'

Leonora gave a high-pitched false laugh, her fingertips to her cheek. 'No, of course I don't! How silly! Why should I like getting letters from banks? I just didn't want Mama to be bothered by any nasty post.'

'It's you who would have been bothered if I hadn't noticed Stevens' mistake.' Lady Jean was looking curiously at Leonora. Her sister-in-law's eyes were still fixed on the Dowager's mail as if she were trying to see what it contained and she seemed highly nervous.

Rosemary Cumberland remained silent, picking up the intonation of their voices, which she did more and more now that her vision was so affected. She could detect a certain hysteria in Leonora's tones and she wondered why. Was she afraid a letter meant for her had been given to her mother-in-law by mistake?

'Let's go into the village, Nicky,' Beverley said as they

finished breakfast. 'I want to do some shopping.'

'For 'weets?' he asked hopefully, his eyes dancing as he tugged off his towelling bib.

'Sweets,' she corrected him. 'Can you say sweets?'

'Yes, 'weets!' he replied firmly. 'We buy weets.'

'Maybe a little box of Smarties, if you're very good,' she promised. 'We can feed the swans on the way, if you like?'

'Yes!' he crowed in delight.

Hand-in-hand, they set off a few minutes later, with Nicholas clutching a bag of stale bread. Crossing the drawbridge, they turned right and walked for a hundred yards along the grassy bank of the moat. Almost immediately half a dozen swans started gliding towards them, followed by several ducks paddling like mad in an effort to get in a good position.

'Break off a small bit of bread and throw it into the water,' Beverley suggested, dropping on to her haunches beside him.

Nicholas gave her a rapturous smile. 'They're coming for their breakfast.'

'That's right.'

Solemnly, he chucked the bread bit by bit into the moat while the birds clustered around, dipping with their bills into the still water to scoop it up. Once or twice the ducks dived deeper, so only their tail feathers stuck straight out of the water, before they bobbed up again.

'Look!' Nicholas giggled with mirth, a rich infectious sound that made Beverley want to laugh too. He pointed a fat little finger at one of the birds. 'Look! He's having a bath! How funny!'

'I expect he's catching a fish.'

He looked up at Beverley with round wondering eyes.

'Are there fish in the moat?'

'Lots of fish. Mostly roach, I believe. Your daddy used to fish in the moat when he was a little boy.'

'Can I fish?'

'Yes. One day. We'll see if we can find his old fishing rod. Let's go now and buy those Smarties.'

Satisfied, he took her hand and trotted beside her as she went the long way round to the village, so that they could walk through the gardens. There was so much to see in the vast grounds of Bucklands, and Beverley enjoyed discovering new avenues and vistas as the days passed. Sometimes they went by the kitchen garden, which was enclosed within the confines of a rosy brick wall. Against this fruit trees espaliered to grow flat hung heavy with purple plums, pears and damsons, while in the centre raspberry canes and strawberry beds lay enclosed in a large netted cage to protect their ruby fruit from the birds. Nicholas loved walking through the greenhouse, too, which was a hundred yards long, and where, in the warm moist atmosphere, peaches and nectarines, grapes and tomatoes, and a wide variety of orchids grew in profusion.

Today, however, Beverley took him down what was known as the Grassy Avenue, a wide turfed path, edged on either side with sycamore, beech, lime and birch. This was the only part of the gardens which was allowed to grow wild, and in the spring the ground was white with snowdrops, growing in great drifts like snow, which made the air heady with their perfume.

'Look!' Nicholas stood stock still and stared. Then he started to quiver with excitement.

'What is it, sweetheart?' Beverley asked, looking where he was pointing.

'A bunny!' he called out. At that moment the wild rabbit hopped rapidly across the grass and disappeared among the undergrowth on the other side of the avenue. Nicholas looked up at Beverley, his face pink with delight.

'I saw a bunny!'

Beverley grinned and picked him up, hugging him close. If only Anthony had been here to share these magic moments, she reflected sadly.

When they arrived in the village of Britwelton, Beverley made for the small general store. She wanted to stock up on shampoo and toothpaste, but also needed to get pads and pencils for her research notes.

The little store, which sold everything from cheese to firelighters, was crowded at this time of the morning and it took her a while to gather all the things she needed.

At last she joined the queue to pay, and as she did so, looked idly at the other shoppers. They were mostly women from the village, some with children, all chatting and gossiping to each other in a warm atmosphere of jovial familiarity. But then suddenly, as if their attention had become focused on something other than themselves, they fell silent. There was a tension in the atmosphere too which she could feel quite strongly. Turning to look about her, as if to discover the source of their preoccupation, she became unpleasantly aware they were staring at Nicholas and herself. All except for two women who were deep in conversation by the bread counter.

'It's them!' murmured the woman who had her back to them.

'Who?' hissed the other, eyes darting around the shop.

'The American and that boy of hers. They say he's not even Lord Amesbury's son!'

As if in a nightmare, Beverley hurried home, dragging Nicholas by the hand.

'Why didn't you get your shopping, Mom?'

She'd flung the shampoo and toothpaste and writing pads down on the counter, and grabbing Nicholas, walked out of the shop, too stunned to do or say anything. Nicholas not Anthony's son! What was this? What the hell was going on?

'I didn't want all that stuff after all,' she replied absently. Her mind was in a turmoil, her thoughts jumbled as she tried to grapple with the enormity of the rumour. It was the type of thing that, if it wasn't squashed at once, could fester and grow and dog Nicholas all the days of his life.

'But we got my 'weets,' he remarked placidly, feeling in his pocket for the little box of Smarties.

'Yes, sweetheart. You got your sweets,' she said, squeezing his hand. What hurt so much was the slur on her and Anthony's love; the very suggestion that she might have had someone else's baby was as wounding as if someone had suggested Anthony had been unfaithful to her. Nicholas was the outcome of their love, and oh God how she'd loved him. How she loved him still although it was eighteen months since Mary had killed him. And how could anyone say Nicky wasn't Anthony's son, when he was the image of his father?

Someone in the village was out to harm them, in the most hurtful way, and she wished now that she'd reacted there and then and told the gossiping women what she thought of them. But she'd been so shocked, so taken aback, that her one idea had been to get away, block it out, pretend that, together with the other awful things that had been going on in the past few days, it hadn't happened.

But it had, and it had to be faced. The question was, how? To get someone prominent in the area like Lady Jean to issue a statement saying of course Nicholas was Anthony's son was only to dignify the slander. But to ignore it might be thought to be condoning it.

Leonora's guests arrived for dinner just before eight o'clock, in a flurry of Golf GTXs, glittering Gianni Versace dresses, hand-made dinner jackets and Louis Vuitton luggage. The women shrieked with laughter, the men talked loudly. With much swaggering and flouncing, the group crossed the drawbridge, admonishing each other in piercing voices not to fall into the moat.

Beverley, watching from her bedroom window, thought how Anthony and Henry would have disliked them. These were Leonora's friends, people she met when she went up to London and had perhaps known from the days before her marriage. No wonder she hadn't wanted Mama or Beverley to be present tonight. This was more Elaine Ross's scene than the Cumberlands'. At a glance, Elaine would have been able to put a price tag on every garment, on each pair of high-heeled shoes and on each jewel worn by these birds of paradise as they swished noisily into the castle.

Turning away from the window, Beverley crept over to the cot that stood near her bed, to make sure Nicholas was asleep before she joined Mama for dinner. He lay curled up on his side, his teddybear clutched in one arm, and as she looked down at him the deep hurt she'd felt earlier in the day came rushing back. There was anger in her heart, too. How could anybody say he wasn't Anthony's son? Who could have started such a vile rumour? Thank God, she reflected, Nicholas was too young to understand. But she feared the rumour would grow and spread like bindweed, choking and strangling everything around its source.

Somehow she was going to have to put a stop to it, for all their sakes. At first she'd thought of telling Mama, but then decided against it. Mama was too old to cope with such unpleasantness, and hadn't she already suffered enough with the loss of both her sons within a year of each other? Why let her know that people in the village were now out to cast doubt on the legitimacy of her only grandson?

Beverley took one last look at Nicholas, and then stole out of the room to make her way to the west wing. She wouldn't stay long. As soon as they'd eaten, she'd find an excuse to slip away, and then she'd go and talk to the only person she knew who might be able to advise her.

Rupert Ffitch opened the front door and stood for a moment staring at Beverley with ill-disguised astonishment.

'Beverley?' His voice rose. 'Goodness me! What can I do for you?'

'May I come in? There's something I want to talk to you both about,' Beverley replied. She looked beautiful on this early summer's evening, in a violet dress that Anthony had always loved, with her hair loose and flowing around her shoulders. Rupert continued to stare at her as if he could hardly believe what he saw. Then he

436

drew himself up, straightened his shoulders and opened the door wider.

'Come in, Beverley.'

'I'm not disturbing your dinner, am I?'

'We've finished. Having a cup of coffee. Can I offer you some?'

Beverley wondered if speaking in short sentences was catching.

'I'd love some coffee, thank you.'

Rupert marched ahead of her, leading the way to the small sitting room where they always sat when they were on their own. Jean sat at a table, working on some papers for the local council.

'Good evening, Beverley,' she said, looking up and removing her glasses. 'Come and sit down. What can we do for you?'

Beverley sat in one of the comfortable armchairs by the fireplace, legs crossed, leaning forward anxiously. 'I'm sorry to bother you, but something has happened and . . . I don't know who else to talk to. I don't want to upset Mama . . .' The words came in a nervous rush.

Lady Jean looked at her curiously then paused before enquiring, 'What is it?'

'I overheard two women in the village shop this morning saying . . .' She faltered, biting her lip, realising she was more hurt and upset than she'd realised.

'Yes?'

'They . . . they said Nicky wasn't Anthony's son!'

'Who said that?' Lady Jean had turned a deep red and her eyes were blazing.

'Two women in the shop. Everyone heard them and they were all looking at us.' Beverley took a quick deep breath, pulling herself together. 'I wish I'd said something at the time . . . but I just froze. I felt numb! How can they say such a thing?'

Lady Jean shot her husband a knowing look. 'I think we all know who's behind this,' she announced grimly.

'Humph!' Rupert retorted. 'Bloody poor show!'

'Who?'

'We all know who wanted a son to inherit everything. We also know she's been jealous of you ever since you and Nicholas arrived.'

'Leonora?'

'Who else?'

'But how can we stop her? The damage has been done. Once a rumour like that gets started, it can get out of hand in no time. And it's so unfair!' Beverley said angrily. 'I feel as mad as hell! Leonora and I haven't exactly become friends, because we're very different sorts of people, but I never thought she'd do a thing like this. It's the sort of slur that could affect Nicky all his life, if we aren't careful!'

'Exactly.' Lady Jean nodded in agreement. 'I'll tell you what we'll do, Beverley. We will give a reception at Bucklands for all the people on the estate, the village people, everyone, and it will be a welcome party for the new Earl of Cumberland, son of the late Viscount Amesbury. Mama must receive the guests, and we'll jolly well make Leonora toe the line. I will not have her upsetting the apple cart just because she's jealous!'

'What I don't understand is what she hoped to gain by saying Anthony wasn't Nicky's father. To discredit me? It doesn't make sense.'

'Whoever said Leonora had any sense?' scoffed Lady Jean. 'Henry made the biggest mistake of his life when he married her.'

'Even supposing Nicky was illegitimate and wasn't the rightful heir, Juliet still couldn't inherit Bucklands, could she?'

'Of course not. It has to go down the male line, as does the title.' Lady Jean gathered up the papers in front of her and, squaring them up, stuffed them into a folder. 'I'll go and see Leonora first thing in the morning and put a stop to her nonsense once and for all.'

Rupert Ffitch, who had remained silent, suddenly spoke.

'She ought to be horse-whipped for spreading lies like that!'

Beverley and his wife looked at him in surprise. He was normally such a mild man, this sudden outburst was all the more surprising. He looked back at them defensively.

'Well, it is disgraceful, isn't it?' he continued. His eyes swept over Beverley as she sat in the big chair, a slim figure with long legs, her hair catching the light so that it glistened with a chestnut glow. 'It's casting aspersions on Beverley's reputation,' he continued, his white moustache bristling.

'We already know that, Rupert. Beverley can look after herself. It's Nicholas we have to protect,' Lady Jean replied with asperity.

'Humph. Even so.' He took a swig of coffee. 'It's a bloody disgrace.'

'It's all so stupid,' Beverley observed. 'Leonora must bear us a very deep grudge to do a thing like this. Supposing Nicholas had been a girl, who would have inherited Bucklands then?'

'Charles,' Lady Jean replied.

Beverley looked stunned. 'Charles Amesbury? I'd no idea!'

'He's Henry and Anthony's first cousin; they had the same grandparents.'

'So . . .' A dawning realisation made Beverley sit up. 'So it could be to his advantage if he could prove Nicholas wasn't Anthony's son? He'd become the new Earl, wouldn't he? And inherit everything?'

'That's true, but Charles' only ambition in life is to get every woman he can into bed. As you've probably noticed,' Lady Jean added drily, 'he's the local Lothario. Georgina has a hell of a time with his constant womanising. Don't know why she puts up with it. He's never been in the slightest bit interested in inheriting Bucklands, though.'

Beverley, who had decided not to mention the squalid episode with Charles in the copse, looked thoughtful. It made more sense to her that someone who had something to gain would spread rumours than someone who was merely being spiteful. She remained silent, though. She hardly knew these people yet. Certainly not well enough to form a judgement on them.

'Don't worry about it any more, Beverley,' Lady Jean was telling her briskly. 'I'll talk to Leonora tomorrow, and then we'll arrange this reception which will make it quite clear that Nicholas is the rightful heir.'

Thanking them, Beverley took her leave, walking slowly back to Bucklands across the moonlit lawns. From the brightly illuminated castle she could hear loud music and the sound of raucous laughter coming through the open windows. Leonora's dinner party sounded as if it was in full swing and all at once a terrible feeling of loneliness and isolation came over her. Home was so far away and she was missing her family more than she had ever thought possible. There was no one in this strange country she felt close to except her precious Nicky, and she had to be strong for him. Oh, Anthony . . . Anthony . . .

A sob rose in her throat, and the tears blinded her. All around her people were whispering lies, making out the great love she had shared with Anthony had not produced Nicky. Making out . . . what? The implications were that she must be a loose woman, a gold digger who had married an eligible man whilst having a baby by someone else . . . it was the most wounding thing that had ever happened to her, and the tears flowed down her cheeks now as she cried uncontrollably.

Homesick, heartsick and utterly desolate, she wept for the love of the man she had lost, and wept for the son they were saying wasn't even his. Little Nicky, her baby, and yet in a way no longer all hers; he'd been claimed by the Cumberland family as the new heir and they were making themselves responsible for the way he was brought up and educated. In a way they had already taken a part of him from her, and at that moment she wished she'd resisted their demands that he should be brought up in England. She wished with all her heart that they were still in Stockbridge, where she'd have had her family, the friends of her childhood, and surroundings that were not so alien to her. But then she resolved that, first and foremost, Nicky was her child, hers and Anthony's. And although he was a Cumberland, he belonged to her and not to them, she told herself, as she wiped her eyes.

But even as these thoughts passed through her mind, she knew she was trapped. There was no going back.

This was where Nicholas belonged, with his father's forebears, and no matter how unhappy she was, she was going to have to stay, too.

As she neared the moat, black and glistening in the dark, she was unaware of a figure, standing among the trees by the Grassy Avenue, watching her. Rock still, hidden by the shadows, it waited until she had crossed the drawbridge and disappeared inside the castle. Then it turned away and silently vanished from sight into the blackness of the night.

Chapter Nineteen

Early the next morning, Lady Jean cornered Leonora in her room as she sat up in bed having breakfast.

'I want to talk to you,' she announced without ceremony, plonking herself on the chintz-covered chaise longue which stood at the foot of the bed. Impatiently she brushed aside a pink cashmere shawl that lay draped over the back.

'What on earth do you want to talk about at this hour?' murmured Leonora. She had a splitting headache and was exhausted, not having got to bed until five o'clock in the morning. 'Can't it wait?'

'No, it can't! There's gossip going around the village emanating from Tilly who runs that little dress shop next to the butcher.'

'Tilly?'

'Yes. I've already established this morning that she is spreading a vile rumour about Nicholas. She says she learned of it from you.'

'Nicholas?'

'Oh, for heaven's sake, Leonora, stop repeating everything! Why have you been saying Nicholas isn't Anthony's son? How could he possibly be anyone else's son? This is malicious and defamatory, you know.

443

Beverley may well sue you for slander and I wouldn't blame her.' Lady Jean snapped shut her thin-lipped mouth and looked at her sister-in-law angrily.

Leonora shot up from her downy nest of pillows, nearly upsetting her breakfast tray.

'I never said anything like that!' she exclaimed. 'How dare Tilly say I said such a thing? She told *me* she'd heard the rumour, but I certainly never started it.'

'And why did you do nothing to stop it?' Lady Jean demanded. 'Why didn't you alert the rest of us? Why didn't you tell Tilly it was a pack of lies?'

Leonora shrugged her bare shoulders. 'You know what villages are like – they're hot-beds for tittle-tattle. I think it's better to ignore it, myself.'

'Well, I don't,' thundered Lady Jean. 'We must put a stop to it at once. I'm going to arrange a reception to welcome Nicholas and his mother to Bucklands, and we're going to invite all the tenants on the estate and people in the village.'

'My, we are rolling out the red carpet, aren't we!'

Lady Jean looked at her levelly. 'Leonora, I'm perfectly well aware that having Beverley and Nicholas here has put your nose out of joint, but I do think you should try to put a good face on it. It's not the boy's fault he's the heir, and I know that Beverley would much have preferred to have remained in the States. If you don't want her to bring a lawsuit against you, I'd button up your mouth and try to be nice to her for a change.'

'I am nice to her, for God's sake,' Leonora wailed. 'If she's got a chip on her shoulder that's her problem, not mine!'

444

'To make sure she's comfortable here is up to all of us, if only for Nicholas' sake,' said Lady Jean severely.

Beverley was also up early, because today her shipment of possessions was arriving from the States. Percy had promised to be on hand with Joe to help unload the heavy stuff and carry it up to the day nursery, which she was planning to turn into a private sitting room-cum-playroom for herself and Nicholas. She wanted to re-create, as much as she could, the style of the living room they'd had in Anthony's Manhattan apartment. It would be a touch of America she could escape to, and a reminder of those first blissful days of her marriage. She also wanted Nicholas to know what his parents' home had been like.

When everything was in place at last, the sofa and chairs, the lamps and pictures, her books and Anthony's small pedestal desk, she looked around in wonder. Everything fitted in perfectly. Henry's little carriage clock ticked away discreetly once again on the mantelpiece, and Anthony's photograph smiled at her from its silver frame on a small side table.

In the corner, the large rush basket she'd bought in Stockbridge was once again filled to the brim with some of Nicholas's toys, and beside it Anthony's old rocking horse, lovingly polished, seemed to survey the room with pride.

'Daddy and I had a room just like this in New York,' she explained, as Nicholas started to pull his toys out of the basket. 'When you were born, we brought you home and laid you on this sofa in your carry-cot.'

'When I was a baby?'

'That's right, sweetheart.'

'I'm not a baby now.' He regarded her with his dancing blue eyes and mischievous grin. 'I'm big now.'

'You certainly are,' Beverley assured him, 'and this room is going to be just for you and me.'

'No one else.'

'That's right. No one else, sweetheart.'

There was a long pause. He seemed deep in thought.

'What is it?' Beverley asked.

'And Gra,' he announced. 'Gra can come in here, can't she? Sometimes?' He nodded his head, coaxing her to agree.

Beverley took him in her arms, hugging him tightly. 'Of course Granny can come in here, too,' she replied warmly.

Leonora was due to have her hair washed that morning at Maison Gerard in Oxford, and as soon as her dinner guests had left for London, she summoned Joe to bring the car up to the castle, half an hour earlier than originally planned.

'I want to stop in the village on the way,' she told him curtly as they drove out of the gates of Bucklands.

'Very well, M'Lady. Any particular part of Britwelton?'

'Yes. The dress shop.'

'Right, M'Lady.'

It was the only one and he'd passed it hundreds of times. The window always displayed just one garment, tastefully draped over an antique chair, and accompanied by an array of earrings and necklaces. It looked a bit pricey, he reflected. Neither his mother nor his sister had ever bought anything there.

When the car drew up outside Tilly's five minutes

later, Leonora hurried inside. Tilly herself, a comfortable middle-aged woman, was going through a rack of new stock, her hair and make-up immaculate, her heels four inch stilettoes.

'Good morning, Lady Cumberland,' she said in a bright but refined voice. 'And how are you today? It's not often we see you so early in the morning. And how can I help you?'

Leonora glared at her, and her eyes were like steel.

'How *dare* you go around saying I told you Nicholas Amesbury might not be the rightful heir? I never said anything like that! I merely said . . .'

'Excuse me, Lady Cumberland, but when I told you what I'd heard, you said you already knew,' Tilly replied hotly. Her face was flaming, and tiny spots of perspiration were gleaming through the heavy make-up on her upper lip.

For a second Leonora looked confused. Then she rose to her own defence. 'I agreed it was *possible* that Anthony Amesbury wasn't his father . . .'

'Exactly.'

'. . . But I didn't start the rumour! Lady Jean has been telling me that you said I'd started it!'

'I never told her you'd started it.' Tilly was angry now. She was not used to being called a liar. 'I said there was talk in the village, and there is! I don't rightly know how it began, but you certainly said you already knew all about it. You did confirm what I'd heard, didn't you?'

Leonora looked mutinous. 'That's beside the point. You should never have quoted me at all. And I can tell you one thing – I'm never going to buy anything from you again.'

'But, M'Lady!'

'I don't like people I can't trust.'

'You can trust me, M'Lady. I'd never in a million years . . .'

But Leonora had swept out of the shop, back into the waiting car.

Tilly watched her go with deep vexation. Lady Cumberland spent a small fortune on clothes and now she'd lost a good customer, just because she'd been foolish enough to ask if what people were saying was true.

'By the way, Beverley, I hope you didn't think it was me who started that stupid rumour about Nicholas,' Leonora remarked casually when she got back from Oxford later that day. She was laden with shopping, and Beverley noticed a lot of it was presents for Mama, like her favourite chocolates and a bottle of the eau-de-cologne she liked so much.

'Whoever did start it has got a very nasty streak in them,' Beverley replied quietly.

'Well, exactly! I quite agree,' Leonora countered swiftly. 'I went in to Tilly's this morning and gave the bitch hell!'

'Who's Tilly?' Beverley looked blank.

Leonora frowned. 'You know, the dress shop in the village. It's Tilly who's been spreading the gossip about Nicholas.'

'There is no gossip about Nicky,' Beverley said curtly.

'Well, you know what I mean. Tilly is the one who has been spreading this horrible rumour . . . and then having the audacity to say she got it from me! I could sue the woman actually,' she added self-righteously.

'But where did this woman Tilly get such an idea from? Who suggested Anthony might not be Nicky's father in the first place, for God's sake?' Beverley wasn't sure whether Leonora was telling the truth or not. She seemed genuinely concerned, but then Beverley remembered what Lady Jean had said.

'I've no idea! She probably made the whole thing up.' Leonora looked evasive. 'Excuse me but I must rush. I'm going to a dinner party tonight in London and I've got to go and get ready.'

Beverley spent the rest of the evening deep in thought. Something wasn't right, but she couldn't put her finger on it. There was something furtive and almost excited in Leonora's manner, and for some reason she didn't think it had anything to do with Leonora's jealousy of herself and Nicholas. She didn't even think it had anything to do with the gossip in the village. Leonora was up to something else, of that she was sure.

Beverley awoke at dawn, the pain in her tooth ripping through her jaw with bolts of agony. She sat up in bed, her hand to her face, and gingerly, with the tip of her tongue, probed her back right-hand molar. The pain seemed deep-rooted, and slipping quietly out of bed, she went to the bathroom next door. For the moment aspirin dissolved on the gum might help, but she'd have to get to a dentist as soon as possible.

Nicholas was awake when she got back to the bedroom, and she read to him for a while, although the pain was still bad. She'd always had good teeth, and this was something new in her experience, a violent jabbing pain that at moments took her breath away.

As soon as she had dressed Nicholas and herself, she crossed the landing and tapped on Leonora's bedroom door.

'Come in,' snapped a waspish voice. Leonora was lying in bed, drinking tea and looking dreadful. When she saw them she groaned.

'What on earth is it, Beverley? Don't you know it's only eight o'clock?' She hadn't got back from the party in London until four o'clock in the morning, and she was suffering from a terrible hangover.

'I'm sorry, Leonora, but I've got terrible toothache and I wondered if you could recommend a dentist? I've got to get it dealt with right away because the pain is killing me.' Beverley held her hand to her jaw, letting the warmth of her palm seep into her face.

Leonora groaned theatrically.

'Oh, God. There's no one locally. They're a bunch of butchers around here. If a tooth hurts they just pull it out.'

'So do you know a dentist in London I could go to?' Beverley asked in desperation.

Leonora lay silently for a moment, gazing at the ceiling as if she was having difficulty in concentrating.

'I go to Mr Hunt. He's in Portman Place and he's very good,' she said at last.

'Thanks,' said Beverley in relief. 'I suppose I can find him in the phone book?'

'If you bring me my address book I can give it to you,' Leonora offered wearily.

Trying to hide her surprise at this helpfulness, Beverley was about to thank her when Nicholas, who had been standing looking at Leonora with interest, asked loudly: 'What's wrong with your face?'

Startled, Leonora glared at him, and her hands flew to her face. 'Nothing's wrong with my face. Is there?' she looked at Beverley for reassurance.

'Your face is fine,' Beverley replied. 'I think Nicky is just used to seeing you wearing make-up.' In spite of her suffering, she was having a problem keeping a straight face. Leonora did look staggeringly different without her customary cosmetics.

Leonora flopped back on to her pillows, closing her eyes as if she too was suffering deeply.

'Where is your address book?' Beverley asked.

'On the dressing table . . . over there.' Her sister-in-law waved a hand in the direction of the window.

The dressing table was kidney-shaped, flounced in pink organza, frilled and gathered, be-ribboned and ruched.

'Why has it got a dress on?' Nicholas demanded.

'Shush!' Beverley whispered, scanning the mess of bottles, brushes, make-up, hair lacquer, jewellery, perfume, and papers. Leonora must deal with her correspondence while she puts on her face in the morning, Beverley concluded, eyeing the clutter.

'It's a dark red address book,' Leonora said in a weak voice as she struggled up on to one elbow to have another sip of her tea.

Beverley saw it, tucked among a higgledy-piggledy assortment of bills and letters. She reached to pull it out, and by mistake dislodged a letter typed on business headed paper. She didn't mean to read it but her training in public relations and journalism had given her the ability to absorb the contents of a page in seconds. She could absorb the words as if by osmosis, and what she took in, in those few moments, left her stunned.

'Here it is,' she said aloud, carrying the address book across the room and handing it to Leonora. Her mind was spinning. She wondered how her sister-in-law was able to remain so relatively calm in the face of such worry?

'Mr Hunt,' said Leonora, reading aloud. 'Here is the address and the phone number.' She handed the book, open at the right page, to Beverley. 'Copy it down for yourself and be sure to tell him I sent you, otherwise he might keep you waiting weeks for an appointment.'

'Thanks.'

'I shan't be needing the car today; Joe can drive you to London. You're bound to get lost on your own,' she added ungraciously.

'Thanks,' said Beverley again.

Mr Hunt's secretary informed her he could 'fit her in' at twelve noon. Clare agreed to look after Nicholas and Joe said he would drive her up to London and bring her back again with pleasure. With everything arranged, Beverley dressed in one of the expensive New York suits, that Elaine had said were 'musts' for a summer wardrobe, and with it wore high-heeled shoes, a matching handbag, and large gold earrings. It was the first time she'd worn smart clothes during the day, and when Leonora saw her, as she was departing, she looked her up and down in amazement.

'You're only going to the dentist, aren't you?' she remarked rudely, her eyes flicking over every detail of Beverley's outfit.

'Yes, but it is in London,' she replied. 'I always used to dress like this when I worked in Manhattan.'

'What a pity Mr Hunt's too old to appreciate the effort you've made.'

'I haven't made an effort for the dentist but for myself,' Beverley replied evenly. 'I'm in so much pain, at least it's good to know I look okay, even if I feel dreadful.'

Once in the enveloping leather comfort of the Jaguar, with Joe at the wheel, Beverley thought about the letter she'd seen on Leonora's dressing table. Several things struck her with force. First, it was from a firm of money-lenders in Hackney, East London. They were threatening her in no uncertain terms about a large amount of money they'd lent her, and demanding payment in full, with interest, within the next ten days. The figures had jumped off the page as Beverley had scanned the letter. She owed them three hundred and eighty thousand pounds.

So that, Beverley realised, explained the telephone conversation she'd overheard in which Leonora had said she was doing her best to raise funds. It still didn't explain, though, how she'd got into such debt.

'We're just coming to the outskirts of London, M'Lady,' Joe announced, breaking into her thoughts.

Beverley looked at the row upon row of ugly two-storey houses, and realised that the suburbs of any city are its worst feature. Entering New York was enough to make you wish you'd never made the trip, until the magical moment when you saw the towering sky-scrapers etched starkly against the sky.

'How long before we get to the centre?' she asked. Several aspirins had eased the pain and she was feeling more cheerful.

'In about twenty minutes, M'Lady. When you've been to the dentist, would you like me to drive you to some of the famous places, just for a quick look? Like the Houses of Parliament and Buckingham Palace, perhaps?'

'If there's time, I'd love that. I told your sister we'd be back to collect Nicky from her at teatime and I promised the Dowager I'd get something for her in Harrods.'

Mr Hunt turned out to be charming, soothing and able. He assured Beverley he could relieve the pain, but she should make several more appointments in the near future.

'I've never had any trouble with my teeth,' she protested. 'And I've had regular check-ups all my life.'

'Have you been ill? Suffered some shock that could have traumatised your system?' he asked in a fatherly way.

She told him about Anthony's death and having to uproot herself to come and live in England.

'And this was not long after you'd had a baby?' he asked sympathetically.

Beverley nodded. She didn't go into the months of financial worry and work to make ends meet so that often she went hungry in order that Nicholas and Jenny could eat. She didn't mention the pain of leaving the lovely apartment she'd shared with Anthony and moving to a grotty little flat overlooking a freeway.

'You should take a course of vitamins,' he advised, 'but in the meanwhile I'll patch you up so you'll be out of pain.'

On her way out, Beverley made three more appointments with his secretary. She made one for Nicholas, too, so she could have his baby teeth checked.

Joe was waiting by the car, a shy smile on his face.

'I've worked out a route between here and Harrods that passes several interesting landmarks, M'Lady,' he said with quiet pride when she was settled in the back of the car.

'Have you really?' For a moment she felt like a young girl again, excited and full of anticipation.

In his soft voice, Joe pointed out places of interest to

her, slowing down if the traffic allowed it so that she could get a good view.

They were places she'd heard of, too, because Anthony had mentioned them; Regent Street and Piccadilly Circus, the Houses of Parliament and the Thames, The Mall and Buckingham Palace, Hyde Park Corner and Knightsbridge. And the one element that made the ancient city so unmistakably London to her was the big red buses. On every film she'd ever seen set in London, it was always the red buses that distinguished it from any other city.

'It's enchanting!' Beverley exclaimed several times. 'I can't believe I'm not looking at picture postcards!'

At last they came to Harrods, majestically dominating the Brompton Road. Joe dropped her off at one of the main entrances.

Beverley looked up at the grand Edwardian architecture, in rosy pink brick and stonework, and realised it was bigger than Saks, Bloomingdales and Bergdorf Goodman's put together.

'I'll be waiting at the Basil Street entrance, M'Lady.'

'What happens if I get lost?' she joked.

'Ask a green man,' Joe informed her gravely.

'A green man?' She looked bewildered.

He nodded, indicating the top-hatted doormen in their dark green livery. 'They'll direct you, M'Lady.'

Laughing, Beverley waved to him before entering the glassy portals of the most magnificent store in the world.

Mama had asked her to buy a special type of French cheese she was afraid would go off if it was sent. Beverley was quickly directed to the right department, and a few minutes later had secured her purchase. The temptation to look around some of the other departments was irresistible, and an hour later she found herself laden with cosmetics, perfume, tights, a gorgeous scarf, some clothes and toys for Nicholas, and some bath oil for Mama.

This was the first shopping spree she'd had since Anthony had died, and she'd enjoyed it immensely. She finally had to ask an assistant how to get to the Basil Street exit.

'Right through the men's department, over there, Madam,' she was told by a polite young woman. 'You can't miss it.'

'Thanks.' She set off, clutching all her parcels and feeling guilty at keeping Joe waiting so long. Racks of suits, jackets, overcoats and trousers filled the rear street-level department, interspersed by displays of all the accessories any well-to-do man could ever want. When she'd been married she'd so loved to help Anthony choose his clothes, and now as she gazed at a display of cashmere sweaters in a range of soft colours, she longed to have someone for whom she could buy one.

A tall dark-haired man was holding one up, at arm's length, judging its size. For a second she stopped to look at his backview. There was something familiar about him and the way he inclined his head. Was it a colleague from her days at Highlight? Or someone she'd worked with on *Chichi*?

At that moment he saw her too, and a look of incredulity, followed by delight, spread across his face.

'Beverley! What in the world are you doing here?'

Then it came back to her in a bitter sweet rush of memory. Stockbridge airport on a summer's afternoon . . . a dinner party in a garden that night when

Henry arrived late . . . the laughter and the camaraderie . . . the joy of the occasion . . .

'Bertie!' she croaked.

'My dear Beverley!' He put his hands on her shoulders and kissed her warmly on both cheeks. 'I've thought about you so often.' He shook his head and his eyes searched her face almost tenderly. 'You've been through so much. It was so devastating about Anthony. I could hardly believe it at the time.'

Beverley smiled up into his face, remembering how close he and Anthony had always been. 'You wrote such a beautiful letter,' she said gratefully. 'I did appreciate it.'

'You're looking terrific. What are you doing in London?'

'I live over here now. You know Henry was . . .'

'Oh, God, yes! Unbelievable.' He shook his head again in distress. 'But why have you left America? What about your family?'

'Nicky . . . he's the new Earl.'

'Christ! I hadn't thought of that! Don't tell me you're living at Bucklands?'

'Yes, we are. The family insist he's educated over here, and so here we are! But what about you, Bertie? What are you doing with yourself?' It was so good to see him again she felt elated. He was better looking than she remembered, or did he just seem more handsome when no longer compared to Anthony?

'I'm still trying to earn an honest crust in this damnable recession. I work for Semple, Lawrence and Carpenter – you know, the merchant bankers?'

'And you obviously live in London?'

'I've got a house in Launceston Place, thanks to my

old dad who made the property over to me when I left university. In case you don't know, that's in Kensington, not far from here.'

'Listen, Bertie, I've got to rush. I've kept the driver waiting for God knows how long while I shopped . . .'

'Beverley.' He caught her hand and squeezed it in both of his. 'Let's get together some time. If I'd known you were in England I'd have contacted you before now. I'll call you at Bucklands, okay?'

'Great.'

'Bucklands, eh?' Bertie grinned and shook his head. 'I haven't stayed at Bucklands since Ant went to live in America. Fancy your living there now. How's Rosemary?'

'Fine, apart from her sight.'

He turned and walked with her to the exit. Joe had managed to park nearby and was standing by the car. As soon as he saw her, he came forward to relieve her of her parcels.

'I'm sorry I've been so long,' Beverley apologised.

'Good Lord, it's Joe!' exclaimed Bertie.

Joe smiled, blushing slightly as he always did. 'Good afternoon, M'Lord.'

'Anthony and I taught Joe to play cricket when we were lads,' Bertie explained.

'You did that, M'Lord,' Joe replied sheepishly. 'Never could bat either, could I?'

With much laughter, Bertie kissed Beverley goodbye, and with Joe at the wheel, they drove off in a cloud of good humour. Beverley hadn't felt so happy for a very long time. Georgina was right. She should get away from Bucklands occasionally.

Beverley knew something was wrong the moment she

saw the two fire engines. She leaned forward in the car and spoke urgently to Joe.

'Look! There must be a fire at Home Farm!'

Joe, who was just about to go straight up the drive to the castle, instead took a sharp left turn and, gathering speed, drove down the lane that would take them straight into the farm yard.

'It looks like one of the barns,' he observed as they drew nearer. Acrid smoke plumed up into the sky before being whipped away by the breeze.

'I wonder what's happened.' She was straining forward anxiously, trying to see what was happening, unable to voice her terror. Nicky was spending the day at the farm with Clare.

'Quickly, Joe,' she begged. 'I'm scared about Nicky.'

'I'm going as fast as I dare, M'Lady. We don't want to go ending up in the ditch. Don't worry about young Nicholas. My sister will have taken good care of him.'

'Oh, I know, Joe. It's just that fires spread so quickly! Especially when there's straw and hay about!' Beverley wrung her hands with feverish impatience, seeing they still had several hundred yards to go before they reached the barns and the farm house itself.

'There's me dad!' Joe exclaimed as he swung the car into the yard and braked hard. The quadrangle was filled with firemen, but most of them were coiling up their hosepipes and only one remained, training his hose into the interior of one of the barns. Percy was standing with Walter Masters, the farm manager for the estate, and they were looking at the charred remains of some bales of hay that had been pitchforked out on to the cobbles. Pools of water and burnt hay, mingled with mud, covered the ground and the air smelled pungently of burning wood and straw.

Beverley was out of the car and running over to where Percy was standing, oblivious of splashing her legs and pale cream shoes in her anxiety to find out what had happened.

'Where's Nicky?' she asked in panic. 'What's happened?'

Percy was the first to reply. 'There's no need to worry, M'Lady. Clare got him out in the nick of time.'

Beverley clamped her hand over her mouth and realised she was shaking all over. 'Is he all right?' she gasped, feeling sick.

'He's fine. Not a scratch on him, thanks be.' But Percy looked grey and his face was smoke-streaked. Then she realised they all looked grey and shaken; Walter Masters, the lads who helped him, even the fireman.

'Where is he?' She looked round frantically. Oh, why had she stayed so long in London today? She cursed herself for all the dawdling she'd done, and felt guilty that while she'd been away, something dreadful might have happened to Nicky.

'You'll find him in the kitchen. He's having his tea.' Percy nodded in the direction of the comfortable-looking grey stone building which led off the courtyard.

Without another word, she fled across the yard, dodging the puddles as best as she could, but so desperate to get to Nicky that she didn't care what happened. Pushing the front door open, she heard voices coming from the big old kitchen at the back.

'Nicky?' she called out as she ran along the passage. Then she burst into the warm room, where the glorious smell of baking bread still lingered in the air, and there, sitting at the scrubbed table, tucking into a large piece of fruit cake, was Nicholas. His cotton shirt sleeves had

460

been rolled above his elbows like a workman and he waved happily as she rushed over to him.

'Hi, Mom!'

'Nicky. Are you all right, darling?' She knelt by his chair, looking into his face. He was rosy polished and scrubbed, and smiled at her with glee.

'I'm having tea!'

'I can see that, sweetheart.' Feeling weak with relief, Beverley rose, trembling, and looked at Clare and Mrs Masters, who were watching her with anxious eyes. Clare had been crying, her eyes red and swollen, and was clutching a handkerchief. The farmer's wife looked concerned.

Beverley sat down suddenly on the chair next to Nicholas and felt quite faint. 'What happened?' she asked in a voice that seemed to come from far away.

'What you need is a strong cup of tea with a lot of sugar,' Mrs Masters remarked, reaching for a large brown china teapot.

'What happened, Clare?' Beverley said again.

'I was only gone for two minutes, M'Lady.' Clare started weeping again. 'The lads were working in the yard. He wasn't alone or anything. Oh, I'm so terribly sorry . . . terribly sorry. If anything had happened to the little lad . . .' She became overcome with sobs, and couldn't continue.

Nicholas, Beverley noticed, had also gone rather quiet as he watched his mother.

She reached out and laid a hand on Clare's shoulder.

'I'm not blaming you, Clare. I just want to know what happened?' she asked gently.

'When I gets back to Nicholas, the hay's caught a-fire, and he's standing there watching the flames!' She buried

461

her face in her hands, shaking her head as she did so.

'And you picked him up and took him out of the barn?' Beverley coaxed.

Clare nodded. 'That's right. He weren't hurt. But he might have been.'

'Yes. He might have been,' Beverley repeated slowly. 'But how did the fire start? Had someone been smoking in the barn?'

'No, M'Lady.'

'Then what happened?'

'When I got back, Nicholas was still fiddling with some matches . . .'

'Matches!' The very word was like a spear striking her heart. 'How in God's name did he come to be playing with matches?'

'I-I d-don't know, M'Lady, and that's the honest to God's truth. I'd never let him have matches.'

Beverley spun on Nicholas, relief that he was all right in spite of what had happened, making her suddenly angry.

'What were you doing with matches, Nicky? That's very naughty! Matches are dangerous.'

His mouth drooped at the corners, and he looked down into his lap.

'Nicky?'

'I found them,' he whispered, his breath catching in a sob.

'Where did you find them, sweetheart?' Surely people didn't leave boxes of matches lying around on a farm? She frowned. 'Come on, Nicky.'

His bottom lip quivering, he whispered, 'I found them.'

'You. . . . where, Nicky? I won't be angry if you tell

me the truth. Where did you find them?'

He gulped, raised his head and looked at her with his candid blue eyes.

'I was playing with the kittens . . . and one ran off . . . and I ran after him.'

'Yes?'

'I caught him . . . and I took him into the barn . . . I wanted to let him ride in my wheelbarrow.'

Nicholas had been given a toy wheelbarrow by Clare some weeks before, and it was his pride and joy.

'What happened then, Nicky?'

'I found the matches in my wheelbarrow.'

'In your . . .?' She turned to Clare. 'Is that possible?' she asked.

'I don't rightly know how, M'Lady. He had his wheelbarrow with him all the time . . . it was only when I went into the house for a minute that he must have gone after the kitten . . . and someone must have dropped the matches into his barrow then.'

'But who could have done such a thing?' Beverley looked unconvinced. 'Who could have been so careless?'

'I'm sure it weren't any of the lads, M'Lady. None of 'em smokes,' observed Mrs Masters who had been listening to the conversation with a grave expression on her face.

Beverley frowned, shaking her head. 'I'm not suggesting it was, Mrs Masters, but how did Nicky get hold of them in the first place?'

'I found them! In my wheelbarrow!' Nicholas piped up. He was enjoying himself now, and being the centre of attention made him feel important.

'I wouldn't have had this happen for the world,

M'Lady,' Clare said sorrowfully.

'It's obviously not your fault, Clare, I know how careful you are. I'd just like to get hold of the person who behaved in such an irresponsible way, though. I'd better get Nicky home now. It'll soon be time for his bath,' Beverley said, rising. 'And thank you for getting to him in time. That's what counts, Clare. You saved him today.'

'You won't be letting me care for him again though, will you, M'Lady?' Her expression was woebegone.

'Of course I will, Clare. It could have happened if I'd been looking after him. One can't keep one's eye on a child every moment of the day,' Beverley reasoned.

'Oh, next time I will! I'll get me mum to watch him if I have to leave him for even a second.'

Joe was still waiting by the car when she and Nicholas went into the farm yard again. The lads had swept the place clean, but there was still the acrid smell of burning in the air.

As Beverley climbed into the back of the Jaguar, she took a last look at the barn. Due to prompt action no one had been hurt and the damage had been superficial, but when she thought what might have happened, she shuddered. Nicholas was the most precious thing in her life. If anything had happened to him ... But she couldn't bear even to think about it. Nicky was her reason for carrying on, for living. Without him she would feel tempted to give up.

Chapter Twenty

'Of course it would never have happened if you'd had a proper nanny,' Leonora observed with a note of triumph in her voice.

'Don't you think you should reconsider, Beverley?' Lady Jean asked.

It was a week later, and the Dowager was giving a family lunch party to welcome Juliet home for the summer holidays. She'd invited Charles and Georgina Amesbury as well; the first time Beverley had seen him since he'd pounced on her in the copse. To her surprise his manner towards her was as furtively flirtatious and suggestive as ever, as if their encounter had never happened, and if she was embarrassed to see him again, he most certainly was not.

'I think Clare is perfectly able to look after Nicky when I need help,' Beverley protested.

'But look what happened!' Lady Jean expostulated. 'He might have been killed!'

'Oh, it's too awful to think about,' said Georgina, shaking her head. 'It's almost as if there were a curse on the Cumberlands. First Anthony. Then Henry. And now . . .'

'Stuff and nonsense!' Lady Jean snapped angrily.

'What a silly thing to say.' She looked worriedly at her mother, who had been deeply shaken by the incident. 'Just because some damn' fool must have been smoking in the farm yard, and dropped his matches by mistake, doesn't mean we're jinxed.'

'Damned carelessness, if you ask me,' Rupert Ffitch admonished. 'Filthy habit, smoking.'

'That puts me in my place,' Charles remarked ruefully, stuffing his packet of Benson & Hedges into his pocket again.

'I don't think an occasional cigarette does anyone any harm,' Leonora said, who smoked no more than four or five cigarettes a day.

'That is beside the point.' Lady Jean spoke severely. 'As I said to you when you first arrived, Beverley, there are a dozen ways in which Nicholas could hurt himself around here; he really needs to be supervised all the time.'

Beverley flushed, stung by such a barrage of criticism. 'He is watched all the time. I don't blame Clare for what happened. It was just one of those things and she felt terrible about it.' She knew Clare would never have left Nicky, even for a couple of minutes, if she'd thought he could come to any harm. As it had turned out, the girl had suffered a terrible fright which would no doubt make her doubly careful in the future.

Little Lady Juliet, sitting next to Nicholas at the long formal dining-room table, had been listening to every word. She reached out and stroked his hand.

'And I'll help look after you now I'm back, won't I, Nicky?'

Nicholas regarded his cousin with a roguish grin.

'And I'll look after you!' he piped up.

Georgina smiled. 'Oh, aren't they sweet together? Such dear little things!' She looked at Juliet earnestly. 'Do you love your little cousin very much?'

'Yes,' Juliet replied with an embarrassed giggle.

'You haven't forgotten you're going to Scotland, have you, Juliet?' Leonora pointed out. 'And the Lloyds have invited you to Florida for ten days.' She'd also appointed a student-teacher for the next few weeks to look after Juliet and make her keep up her studies. She was a girl of twenty-three called Wendy Johnson who had been highly recommended by Juliet's head mistress. She was due to arrive the following day.

Juliet looked crestfallen and Beverley remembered the conversation between mother and daughter in the Easter holidays.

'Do I have to go to the Lloyds', Mummy? I want to stay at Bucklands. You know I hate going away,' Juliet pleaded, twisting her thin hands in her lap, a nervous gesture Beverley had observed before when the child was unhappy.

Leonora glanced across at her with distaste. In her opinion Juliet was a whining edition of Henry and it irked her even to look at her daughter at times.

'We'll discuss this later,' she said coldly, aware that the others were watching them.

An uncomfortable silence fell on the assembled group, broken a couple of times by a throaty 'Humph!' from Rupert Ffitch. Then the Dowager spoke.

'I would like to say,' she paused to smile at everyone around the table, 'that as I am an old lady . . .' to which there was a chorus of 'Not at all' and 'Nonsense' . . . 'I would like to see as much of my grandchildren as possible. That being the case, can't you indulge me a little,

Leonora dear? Can't you let Juliet stay at home for most of the holidays so we can spend some time together? She and Nicholas and I?' Her tone was quietly persuasive and yet spoken with the confidence of someone who knows they will get their own way in the end.

Leonora looked appalled for a moment, but then in an amazing volte-face, which took everyone by surprise, she looked at the Dowager with a tender expression. 'Oh, of course, Mama! I know you love to have her around. I'm always afraid it's too much for you, though?'

Astonished, Beverley watched the change in Leonora's manner and instinctively wondered what she was playing at. Even Mama seemed a little taken aback by how quickly she had succumbed.

'It's not too much for me providing I don't have to run around the grounds with them,' Rosemary Cumberland said drily.

'Juliet is welcome to spend a lot of time with Nicky and me if she wouldn't find it too boring,' Beverley suggested. 'We'd love to have you do things with us, wouldn't we, Nicky?'

'Yeah!' he yelled.

While Beverley told him to be quieter, Georgina leaned forward eagerly, her face alight with enthusiasm.

'We've got Tom and Margaret coming home from school at the end of the week, Juliet and Nicholas can come and play at our place. We can have picnics and organise games . . . what do you say, Beverley?'

'Sounds like hell to me,' Charles interjected.

'That's very kind, thank you,' Beverley said to Georgina, ignoring him.

When lunch came to an end, Beverley noticed that

Charles tried to engage Leonora in private conversation, whispering to her in the hall outside the dining room, but it was obvious she wasn't going to respond and Beverley heard her say: 'Mind your own damn' business, Charles.' Then she stalked off without a backward glance.

Shrugging, he turned to Beverley. 'What the hell's got into Leonora these days?'

'I really wouldn't know,' she replied coldly.

'But you live under the same roof! Why is she blowing hot and cold with Mama?' He looked genuinely bewildered and rather concerned.

'I have no idea.' She hated even having to answer the man. There was something about him she was allergic to, and she had to be honest and admit to herself she'd felt like that from the first moment she'd met him. It was the arrogance and conceit that got to her, as if he were sure every woman was longing for his touch. Beverley wished with all her heart he was not a part of the family and that she was not forced to be in his company from time to time.

'You know she's up to her eyes in debt,' Charles was saying in a low voice. 'And I mean heavy debt.'

Beverley turned away, not wanting to get involved. She already knew her sister-in-law owed a great deal of money, but it was none of her business. More especially, she did not wish to discuss the matter with Charles. Georgina stepped towards her at that moment.

'Wasn't that a lovely lunch? There's nowhere in the world for entertaining like Bucklands, is there?' She looked around the Baronial Hall with a starry-eyed expression, her eyes lingering lovingly on the heraldic shields. 'I just adore this place, don't you?'

Beverly hesitated before answering. She admired the beauty of Bucklands, certainly, and was aware of the great history that lay within its thick walls, but to say she loved it . . .

'Perhaps I haven't been here long enough for the place to get under my skin,' she replied slowly. 'I certainly like it here but I'm not sure I actually love it yet.'

'I don't know how you can resist it,' Georgina laughed. 'But then, I always was a sucker for stately homes and all that.'

'We know.' Charles' voice was brittle dry. For a moment his eyes skimmed over his pretty wife, and Beverley noticed there wasn't a flicker of affection in his expression.

'I don't think I've been in England long enough to get bitten by the stately home bug!' Beverley joked in an effort to lighten the atmosphere. 'But if I'm true to my countrymen, I'll be addicted in no time.'

The party broke up as everyone began saying goodbye. Lady Jean and her husband were going up to London to attend a banquet in the Mansion House – 'Christ, how dreary!' Charles observed – and Mama wanted to have a rest before tea.

'Let's go in the garden,' Beverley suggested to Juliet. She agreed with alacrity, and they each took Nicholas by the hand and went off to the area set aside for his sandpit. Beside it, Percy had assembled a climbing frame Beverley had bought plus a double swing. As soon as Juliet saw this she let out a whoop of joy.

'Oh, what fun!' she exclaimed. 'Mummy would never let me have anything like this when I was small!'

While she and Nicholas played happily together, in spite of the age difference, Beverley relaxed in a deck

470

chair, watching them and thinking about Leonora. She wished she could believe that her sister-in-law genuinely wanted to please Mama and be kind to her, and yet at the back of her mind hovered the thought that her attempts at being nice didn't ring true.

'There'll be a hundred guests,' Lady Jean told Beverley on the morning of the reception they were holding to welcome Nicholas to Bucklands. She'd taken it upon herself to make all the arrangements and as the weather was fine and warm, had decided it should take the form of a garden party.

Long trestle tables were being set up in the shade of a magnificent chestnut tree at one end of the west lawn, and small tables and chairs were dotted around for those who wanted to sit.

'I've ordered masses of sandwiches and scones,' Jean continued, consulting her clip-board, 'and there will be cakes and biscuits, and strawberries and cream. There will also be a choice of tea or iced coffee, and orange juice for all the children.'

Beverley smiled, remembering all the functions she'd helped organise when she'd been at Highlight. It seemed a party was a party, no matter in what part of the world it was held.

'That sounds great,' she replied. 'Is there anything I can do?'

'No, thank you, Beverley. Everything's under control. Just make sure Nicholas is looking clean and tidy at four o'clock when everyone arrives.' With that she strode off on her long legs, enjoying the opportunity of being in charge once again.

'You'd really think this was still her home, the way she

takes over,' Leonora observed crossly as she came out of the castle to watch the preparations in progress.

'In a way I suppose it still is,' Beverley pointed out. 'She was born here, and she's never really left, has she?'

'Her bossiness used to drive Henry mad! And now she seems determined to run all our lives. I can't think why we have to go through all this nonsense of welcoming Nicholas today! He's not even going to remember, when he's older.'

'It's being held to try and quash those horrible rumours,' Beverley replied hotly. 'I hope that, once and for all, this will do the trick.'

'It's hard on Juliet, though,' Leonora replied bitterly.

Beverley looked concerned. 'Oh, I wouldn't want her to feel she wasn't just as important as Nicky.'

'It's inevitable, isn't it? She's only a girl. It's boys that count in this establishment.'

'But this party isn't to do with the fact that Nicky's a boy . . . it's to do with his being Anthony's son.'

'Do you believe that?' Leonora's face had hardened into ugly lines of discontent. 'This family never stop making me feel inadequate because I didn't produce an heir!'

'I'm sure you're wrong, Leonora. They all adore Juliet. It's no one's fault you didn't have a son,' she added sincerely, suddenly sorry for Leonora. The woman's unhappiness was no doubt genuine and Beverley had a sneaking feeling that it was true that the Cumberlands would have liked her more if she'd produced a son and heir.

'Try telling them that,' Leonora snapped. 'I suppose I'd better put Juliet into a party frock this afternoon. God knows what I'm going to wear.'

472

At a quarter-to-four, Beverley took Nicholas down to the garden, dressed in the royal blue linen shorts she'd bought him at Harrods, and a white shirt. With his hair brushed smooth he looked adorable. Then Juliet appeared, accompanied by her holiday minder, Wendy Johnson. She was a quaint old-fashioned-looking girl who reminded Beverley of a Victorian doll. Her saucer eyes were fringed by long black eyelashes, and her rosy cheeks were round and solid. Blonde hair, parted in the middle and held back by a black ribbon at the nape of her neck enhanced the porcelain doll-like look, as did her ankle-length cotton dress in a pattern of tiny rose-buds on a cream background. She seemed to be rather dazed at finding herself at Bucklands, and it had been Juliet who had spent the previous week showing her around.

'Are you excited, Nicky?' Juliet asked as they all stood on the lawn, waiting for the first of the guests to arrive.

Nicholas was eyeing the buffet with deep interest. Tiny sandwiches, jam-filled scones, cakes and biscuits, and great bowls of fresh strawberries were placed in readiness, whilst behind a large old silver samovar, Stevens stood poised to serve cups of tea.

'I think it all looks wonderful,' Beverley said, survey-ing the typically English scene. She'd decided to wear the caramel-coloured linen dress she'd had in New York, which set off her auburn hair so perfectly and she felt confident, knowing she looked good. Jean, on the other hand, had plumped for a plain dark blue dress, cut on severe lines, while Leonora was in a riot of multi-coloured frilled chiffon and spiky heels which kept sink-ing into the lawn.

Charles and Georgina were among the first arrivals

473

bringing Tom and Margaret with them. Juliet and Margaret immediately went into a giggling huddle, talking and whispering conspiratorially, but Tom hung around his mother, watching her all the time, while Georgina, Beverley noticed, constantly placed her hand on his shoulder or his back, and every now and again stroked his hair. It was as if she couldn't bear not to be touching him all the time, and having him near her.

'What a lovely occasion this is,' she remarked, smiling down at Nicholas. She made an attempt to introduce Tom to his 'new little cousin' but Tom looked singularly unimpressed and sullen.

'I think this is going to be a bit boring for the younger ones,' Beverley remarked, looking sympathetically at Tom. He reminded her of her own brother Tom, except that he'd never been the clinging type. But then Rachael had never been one of those mothers who had let any of them languish at her apron strings.

'Perhaps we can organise some games after tea,' Beverley continued hopefully. With Charles and Rupert Ffitch being the only men in the family now, she wondered if she ought to arrange something.

'My dear, you needn't worry about the girls,' Georgina observed indulgently. 'What Margaret and Juliet find to talk about I'll never know, but Margaret has always got on terrifically well with Juliet, although she's nearly three years older.'

'That's nice,' Beverley agreed.

Soon the lawn was crowded with the local people, the women in their best flower-patterned frocks, many of them wearing little straw hats, and the majority of the men in suits, with neat ties and shirts. It seemed the village had turned out to take full advantage of the hospitality being offered at Bucklands.

And seated in the middle of the throng the Dowager held court as everyone came forward to shake her hand. Regal in grey, with long ropes of pearls, she exuded an old world graciousness and charm.

'This is my grandson Nicholas, Anthony's boy,' she said repeatedly as he played at her feet with his toy cars and Beverley did her best to stop him running around. It meant so much to her that he was being publicly acknowledged as Anthony's son and she'd promised him a surprise if he was 'a good boy'.

'This should put an end to the tittle-tattle,' she heard a voice say in her ear and, turning, realised with dread it was Charles.

'I sincerely hope so,' she replied stiffly. Georgina was watching them, with Tom still by her side, and Beverley immediately moved away to speak to Mrs Masters and her husband from Home Farm.

'He don't seem no worse for his adventure,' Mrs Masters remarked cheerfully, indicating Nicholas. She was got up in a deep pink dress, bought specially for the occasion, a shade that blended with her own high colouring.

'He's fine, thank God,' Beverley agreed.

'Yes, I heard we had a pyromaniac in the family!' Charles had followed Beverley and was smiling with sardonic amusement. 'What's he going to do next, Beverley? Set fire to the forest? Burn down Bucklands?' He chuckled at his own wit.

Beverley ignored him, but Mrs Masters giggled.

'Eh, I hope not, Mr Amesbury,' she said. 'What a thing to say!' She rocked on her heels and looked coy. 'We don't want no more frights, now do we?'

Charles, who had lit a cigarette, inhaled deeply and then looked over to the buffet where Stevens was dispensing the tea into exquisite Rockingham china cups and saucers.

'What does one have to do around here to get a decent drink, Beverley?' he enquired insolently.

For the first time she turned to face him, looking at him levelly as she spoke.

'If tea isn't good enough, then I suggest you go home if you want something stronger.'

He stroked the crown of his head with a gesture of annoyed frustration, moving out of earshot of the Masters as he did so.

'For heavens' sake, Beverley! How long are you going to keep up this vendetta? You're a grown woman, for God's sake. Why can't you take a more sophisticated attitude to life?' His voice was low so that no one else could hear what he was saying, but she was nevertheless aware that several people were looking at them curiously.

'Okay, so I shouldn't have kissed you the other day, but Christ, you're a very desirable woman,' he continued huskily. 'Do you blame me for wanting you? I've never wanted any woman so much in my life.'

'Charles, you've got to stop this nonsense,' she said briskly. 'I'm not interested and that's that. Now please leave me alone. I've already warned you and I meant what I said.' As she spoke, she started walking towards the buffet to get herself something to eat, but Charles followed her, seemingly not caring that he might be making a spectacle of himself.

'Think about your wife, if you won't consider my feelings,' Beverley retorted in an angry whisper. 'I can promise you one thing – you're wasting your time with me.'

They'd reached the buffet and she helped herself to a sandwich.

He put his head close to hers and spoke softly. 'Oh, I wouldn't be too sure. I'm a very patient man.'

She could smell the tobacco on his breath, mingled with a waft of his aftershave. A wave of revulsion swept over her and she'd never longed for Anthony's presence more, to protect her from this loathsome man who was his cousin. For a moment she closed her eyes and when she opened them again, Charles appeared to be staring at a car coming slowly up the drive.

Beverley followed his gaze, and saw an open-topped red sports car. Its sole occupant, a man in his forties, parked near the drawbridge and then got out.

Charles let out a long low whistle. 'Here comes trouble,' he said softly, his eyes narrowing. The man was strolling slowly towards them now, weaving his way through the groups of guests, his eyes intent on one person only. Dressed in a loud pin-striped suit, pale yellow silk tie and highly polished shoes, he cut a raffish figure amongst the country locals. As he came nearer, Beverley saw the winking of a diamond set in the heavy gold ring he was wearing, and the quick gleam of a Rolex wristwatch.

Her first thought was, Trust Charles to have such a disreputable friend. The man looked like a gangster. But why had he come looking for Charles at Bucklands? she wondered. Why hadn't he gone to Hunting Lodge?

Lady Jean had spotted him too, and was watching him with an expression of concerned alertness, as if bracing herself for some unpleasantness. Beverley glanced quickly at Charles, but he registered nothing but curiosity. At that moment Beverley realised the man wasn't heading for Charles at all. It was someone beyond them he had his sights on and, turning, Beverley saw Leonora, her face turned ashen, her eyes dark pools of horror. For a moment she swayed and it looked as if she were going to faint, but the man had reached her by then and was gripping one of her arms to prevent her falling.

People stared and strained to hear what was being said between the young Countess of Cumberland and the flash-looking stranger, but he was bustling Leonora unceremoniously towards the castle, while she stumbled on the lawn in her high heels, looking shocked and distressed.

At that moment Georgina came hurrying up to where Charles and Beverley stood.

'Who was that, Charles?' she asked breathlessly.

'How should I know?' he replied vaguely. 'Probably one of Leonora's London friends.' Then he strolled off, puffing away at his cigarette in a casual manner.

Georgina turned troubled eyes to Beverley. 'I hope she's not in any sort of trouble. Do you think I should go and find out if there's anything I can do?'

Beverley hesitated. 'I don't know. It's up to you. Personally, I don't think she'd thank me if I stuck my nose into her affairs.'

Georgina looked slightly offended. 'I don't want to interfere. I merely thought I might be of some help. Everyone has always been so against Leonora, and I feel quite sorry for her at times.'

'So do I,' Beverley agreed, 'but I still don't think she'd like me to get too close. But you are a different matter. You've known her much longer than I have, and I'm sure she's very fond of you.'

Georgina's smile was self-depreciating. 'My dear, I only do what I can.' She looked over to Bucklands. 'They seem to have gone inside. I'll leave it for a few minutes then I'll go and see if there is anything I can do.'

For the next twenty minutes Beverley found herself making conversation with some of the village people, noticing a distinct change in their attitude. Some seemed rather embarrassed at facing her but others talked to her warmly about Nicholas and she realised that Jean's idea of holding this party had been worthwhile.

At last the guests began to drift away in twos and threes, and noticing the Dowager looked tired, Beverley went over to her.

'Mama, what a lovely party it's been. Shall Nicky and I escort you back inside?' she asked gently.

The Dowager looked up at her with milky eyes and smiled. 'Dear Beverley, I think that would be lovely. Hasn't Nicholas been an angel all afternoon? I've been so proud of him . . . and of you too, my dear.'

'It's been a wonderful afternoon, Mama, and thank you for everything.' Beverley slipped her arm through her mother-in-law's and together they walked slowly across the lawn while Nicholas, in a burst of energy brought on by remembering he was due for a surprise, circled around them with arms outstretched, pretending to be an aeroplane.

'Steady on, Nicky!' Beverley called out, in case he bumped into one of the departing guests.

'Buz-z-z-z-z-z-z!' he droned excitedly. 'When can I have my surprise, Mom?'

'As soon as Granny is settled in her room.'

The Dowager laughed. 'So like Anthony! You should have seen him on Christmas morning when he was a little boy . . .' and as she started to reminisce, Beverley had a vivid picture of Anthony when he'd been small, running and playing around Bucklands as Nicholas did now.

Once the Dowager was in her own quarters, with Alice to make her some fresh tea, Beverley took Nicholas back to the garden.

'Can I have my surprise now, Mom?' he kept asking.

'Yes, you can,' Beverley promised.

'Where is it?' He stood in his smart new clothes and looked around curiously at the sweeping lawns where the servants were clearing away the tables and chairs.

'Supposing we try by the swings and slides?' she suggested in a teasing voice.

''Kay.' He trotted off round the side of the moat to where, in a secluded clearing, his play corner had been set up. Then he saw it.

'A pool!' he yelled, heading for the pale blue inflatable paddling pool which Percy had filled from a hose pipe earlier in the day.

Nicholas started to tug off his shoes. 'I'm going in! I'm going to get wet!'

Beverley laughed. 'Okay, Buster. Let's get your clothes off first.'

A minute later, he was splashing naked in the pool, a look of rapturous pleasure on his face.

Then Beverley heard it: raised and angry voices, a woman's and a man's, coming from the direction of the drawbridge. She couldn't see what was happening from where they were, but she recognised Leonora's voice screaming: 'Get the hell out of here!'

Then there was the roar of a car engine, and a minute later the sports car came into sight, careering away along the drive, screaming at full throttle. When it vanished into the distance there was silence. Beverley waited and watched while Nicholas played in his pool, unconcerned.

Then she saw Leonora and Charles walking slowly across the lawn, deep in conversation.

Chapter Twenty-One

Beverley arrived at Langan's Brasserie to find Bertie Goring already seated on a high stool at the bar. He was watching the revolving doors with eager eyes and when he saw her, his face lit up.

'Beverley! How good to see you again. I'm so glad you could make lunch today,' he exclaimed, kissing her on both cheeks.

'Hi, Bertie.' She eased herself up on to the stool next to his and smiled warmly. He looked every inch the City businessman in an impeccable dark blue suit and discreet silk tie with his pale blue shirt, but his expression was delightfully boyish and his dark eyes twinkled as he looked back at her.

'Champagne?' he asked.

'Ummm. I'd love some,' she replied, nodding.

'How did you get on at the dentist?'

'Fine. I've got to go again, but at least I'm not in any pain.'

'You're looking great.'

'Thanks,' she said, grinning. She felt great, too. Getting away from Bucklands now and again was like taking a breath of fresh air – invigorating, refreshing and inspiring. She'd driven up to London with Leonora, who said she had 'things to do' but was in no mood to reveal her plans, and then Joe had dropped her off in Knightsbridge before taking Beverley on to the dentist. Both Nicholas and Juliet, in the care of Wendy, were spending the day at Georgina's, so they could be with Tom and Margaret, and for once, Beverley felt carefree and with more zest for living than she'd felt in a long time. Sipping her champagne, she looked around the fashionable brasserie, which was just off Piccadilly and which she'd heard was part-owned by Michael Caine, and experienced the frisson of pleasure she remembered feeling when Anthony had taken her to smart restaurants in New York.

'How's everything going?' Bertie asked.

'Nicky loves being at Bucklands. It's a heaven on earth for a child, isn't it?'

Bertie nodded. 'I was about thirteen when Anthony first invited me to stay and it made me wish we had a country place like that. Alas,' he grinned ruefully, 'the Gorings don't have the Cumberlands' wealth. When my parents were alive we had a nice place in Wiltshire, and the house I now have in Launceston Place. When they died, though, the death duties were so heavy I had to sell Hanby Court. As I work in London, I felt a home up here would be more sensible than a house in the country.'

'I didn't know your parents were dead,' Beverley said. When she came to think of it, she knew practically nothing about Bertie, except that he was the Marquess of Goring, and a friend of Anthony's since their days together at Eton.

'Do you have brothers or sisters?'

He shook his head. 'I think just one of me was enough

for Ma and Pa!' he joked. 'They were quite middle-aged when I was born, and as I was a boy, I think they felt they'd done their bit.'

Beverley smiled knowingly. 'Ah, yes. The familiar story of how vital it is to produce a son.' She shook her head. 'It seems to be a theme that haunts me these days. Don't girls ever inherit in this country?'

'Sometimes, but not often,' Bertie admitted, laughing.

At that moment, an elegant-looking young woman in a black suit who was the maître d' came up to them holding two large menus.

'Your table is ready, Lord Goring,' she said pleasantly.

A few minutes later they were seated at a table in one of the windows, their refilled champagne glasses before them, and a waiter hovering to take their order.

'This is fun,' Beverley exclaimed impulsively. 'I'm getting to like England more and more by the minute!'

Bertie laughed. 'It's not a bad place. Now, what are we going to eat?'

The next two hours flew past so quickly Beverley couldn't believe it when she saw the hands of her watch say it was after three. They'd talked non-stop as he'd told her so much about the youth he'd shared with Anthony, and how they'd only gone their own ways when Anthony decided to live in New York, that she'd lost all sense of time.

'I must get to the Ritz!' she gasped. 'I'd no idea it was so late.'

'I'll walk you there, it's only at the end of the road,' said Bertie, asking for the bill.

'Thank goodness! I was afraid it might be miles away. I haven't got the hang of London yet. This is only my second time here.'

'What are you doing at the Ritz?'

'Meeting Leonora. We're going back together in the car.'

'Driven by Joe?'

Beverley nodded. 'I must get a British driving licence. Then I'll buy a car and be independent . . . that is, when I've mastered driving on the wrong side of the road!'

'If you want any help or advice about cars, let me know.'

'Thanks. I'll probably take you up on that.'

As they walked up Stratton Street towards Piccadilly in the mellow afternoon sunshine, Beverley looked up at Bertie, realising he was even taller than Anthony had been. They were still talking about the Cumberland family.

'Did you get to know Leonora well in the days when you stayed at Bucklands?' she asked curiously.

'Hardly at all, really. Henry, being older than Ant and myself, had his own set of friends. Ant and I never liked Leonora, though.' He paused before adding, 'How are you getting on with her?'

Beverley gave a little grimace. 'It's a tricky situation.' She longed to tell him more, but until she knew him better felt the need to be discreet and loyal to the Cumberlands.

'Why are you meeting her at the Ritz? Was she lunching there?'

'I don't know, Bertie. I have no idea what she does when she comes to London. Shops, I suppose. Meets friends.'

'And lovers?'

Beverley looked surprised for a moment, but then nodded slowly. 'I suppose she could be. Do you remember Charles Amesbury, the cousin who lives nearby?'

'God, yes!' Bertie chuckled. 'A woman-chaser if ever I met one! Why?'

'I've got a feeling Leonora's had an affair with him at some point.'

Bertie shrugged. 'More than likely. She was always cheating on Henry.'

'Poor Henry.' Beverley gave a little sigh. Then she added vehemently, 'I can't stand Charles.'

'Been pursuing you, has he? I bet he has, the bastard!' Bertie suddenly sounded cross.

'It's Georgina I feel sorry for.'

'She's a sweet person from what I can remember. It must be hell being married to someone like Charles. How does she cope?'

'Sometimes I wonder. She's so patient and calm and always smiling.' Beverley gave a little grunt of impatience. 'I'd kill him if he were my husband.'

They turned into Piccadilly, and Bertie pointed out the magnificent turn-of-the-century building which dominated the opposite side of the street.

'There's the Ritz,' he told her.

'And there's Leonora,' said Beverley in a flat voice. Her sister-in-law was standing by the car talking to Joe, who was holding open the door for her.

'Let's cross the road here.' Bertie grabbed Beverley's hand, and they ran across the busy street, dodging the traffic, Bertie swift and assured, Beverley giving little gasps of fright as buses and taxis swooped past too close for her liking.

Breathless and laughing, they reached the pavement just as Leonora looked up and saw them. Her eyes narrowed.

487

'Why, Bertie!' she exclaimed shrilly. 'What are you doing here?' She offered a cool painted cheek and her eyes looked deeply into his from under the brim of the large black straw hat she was wearing.

'How are you, Leonora?' he asked politely.

'You're late, you know, Beverley,' she said, turning to her sister-in-law. 'I want to get out of London before the rush hour starts.'

'I'm sorry. I lost track of the time.'

'Let's get going then.' Without another word she climbed into the back of the car and crossed her elegant legs.

Bertie grabbed Beverley's arm. 'When am I going to see you again?' he asked.

Aware that Leonora was watching them and listening to every word they said, she replied lightly: 'Why don't I give you a ring?'

He nodded, as if understanding she didn't want to make plans in front of Leonora. 'Better still,' he said, 'I'll give *you* a ring.'

'Okay, and thank you for a lovely lunch.' Her words were conventional but her eyes were warm, the gold flecks in them glinting in the sunlight.

'Great. Be in touch.' With a grin, he saw her into the car and as Joe pulled away from the kerb, he waved.

There was silence for about a minute before Leonora said cattily: 'You're a dark horse I must say. Fancy your having lunch with old Bertie Goring. Ha! He was Anthony's best friend, you know.'

'That was why I was having lunch with him,' Beverley responded coolly. 'Anthony was very fond of Bertie and he was the best man at our wedding.'

'So he was.' Leonora gazed with tired eyes at the

surrounding traffic, and then, reaching up, removed her hat. To Beverley's relief she lapsed into silence for the rest of the journey back to Bucklands.

Leonora felt a chill of panic as she read the letter from the bank, addressed to her mother-in-law.

> I felt I should let you know that items due for payment today will create an overdraft of fourteen thousand, five hundred and twenty pounds, unless credit is received later today. You may wish to arrange a transfer of funds from your deposit account, and I enclose a transfer form for your use . . . Alternatively you might like to arrange an appointment to see me, in order to discuss disposing of some of your gilt-edged securities . . .

The letter continued for several more lines, but they became lost to Leonora as her mind seemed to drift from its moorings and spin into free-fall, leaving her sweating with fear. How was she going to get out of this one? She'd managed to get the Dowager to sign several cheques, which she thought were made out to Harrods or Smythson's or the like, but which were in fact made out to Leonora herself. And for very large amounts, too. The last one had been for ten thousand pounds, but when she'd given it to the Dowager to sign, it had been made out for ten pounds only. Not that it mattered because Mama could barely see where to sign, Leonora reflected, far less make out the amounts written in. Then she added in the noughts and the word 'thousand', and finally made out the cheque in her maiden name,

Leonora Dudley. As soon as she'd paid it into the bank in London where she had an account in the name of Dudley, she was able to pay something towards settling her debts. In the plural now. Not only did she owe the firm of money lenders in Hackney another twenty-eight thousand pounds, but the Caspian Casino were hounding her too, demanding she settle her losses and refusing to let her play again until she did. It would be a long time before she'd get over the shock of seeing one of their directors turning up at the garden party. Charles guessed, of course, but then it was he who had introduced her to the world of gambling and the Caspian Casino in the first place. From then on she'd joined all the other London casinos, including the Ritz which was her favourite.

'But you didn't have to get hooked!' he'd protested when she told him how much she owed the Caspian. And the money lenders.

Leonora sat hunched on her bed, her arms wrapped around her stomach as if she had a pain and her eyes starting from her head as she contemplated the future. She *must* stop this compulsion to try her luck at the gaming wheel, but it was so exciting . . . so irresistible. The opportunity to make a fortune at the turn of a card or the dropping of a tiny white ivory ball was so compulsive she couldn't resist it. To Leonora, gambling was more potent than alcohol, more arousing than sex. The buzz she got from it was the most compelling pleasure she had ever known. And yet in the last year she'd lost four hundred and fifty thousand pounds. Which she didn't have. And now she'd cleaned out Mama's current account over the past few weeks, and the bank were asking for money to be transferred from the deposit account.

Dressing, swiftly with hands that shook, she ran a brush through her hair and wondered on what pretext she could get Mama to sign the form? And how much did she have on deposit? It would be necessary to go through Mama's papers and find the relevant bank statements, and she'd have to find an excuse to do that.

Leonora's greatest fear, though, was that the bank manager in Oxford would want to talk to the Dowager on the phone. Stevens, who answered all the calls, saying: 'Bucklands. Can I help you?' had been instructed by her to refer all calls from the bank, the Inland Revenue, and anyone else of a business nature to Leonora, and only to put through personal calls to the Dowager.

As hardly anyone phoned Rosemary Cumberland these days, this had not so far presented any problems. But in case anything should go wrong, if for instance she was in London on the day and Stevens disobeyed her orders, Leonora had planned what to do. She would say her mother-in-law was suffering from the beginnings of senile dementia, sometimes being rational, other times not knowing what she was doing. Leonora would say when that happened, she insisted on giving her money in the belief she was still Miss Leonora Dudley, and that she hadn't wanted to upset the Dowager by refusing. It wasn't a convincing yarn, and yet on the other hand, the truth was unlikely ever to come out. With Henry dead, no one else knew about the Dowager's financial affairs or how much money she had, and as long as she herself wasn't made aware of the situation, Leonora felt relatively safe.

'Good morning, Mama!' she greeted the Dowager with gaiety when she entered her room a few minutes later.

'Good morning, Leonora.' Rosemary Cumberland

wished that Leonora wouldn't come bursting into her room first thing every morning, disturbing her when she was listening to the radio as she had her breakfast, but the change in her attitude was so welcome, she didn't want anything to upset her.

'Such a bore, Mama, but could you sign this tax return? I'll deal with it for you, so don't worry about it.' She placed the transfer form on the blotter Mama always used, but just to be sure the Dowager couldn't see what it really was, held a genuine tax payslip over the top of it.

'Oh, dear, it's never ending!' Rosemary Cumberland grumbled. 'Is it my imagination or are they sending more forms to be dealt with these days? I'm sure I don't remember Henry bringing me so many things to sign!'

Leonora was adept at thinking on her feet. 'You're right, Mama. There has been more paperwork recently. The reason is that everything got neglected immediately after Henry was killed . . . and I was too upset to help you with your affairs . . . and so we're having to deal with a back-log of tax demands. I think we're almost straight again, though,' she added brightly.

'Thank goodness for that. Do they want any money? Do we owe them anything?' She scrawled her signature, and then handed the pen back to her daughter-in-law.

Leonora paused, pretending to read the form. 'They don't say how much, I think this is a sort of assessment. Why don't you sign a couple of cheques, and then I only have to fill them in when they tell you how much you owe.'

'Very well, dear.' Rosemary Cumberland detested

any form of paperwork or accounts. Someone had done it for her all her life and she felt quite grateful to Leonora for taking the burden off her now. 'Pass me the cheque book and let's get on with it.'

With guidance, she signed three blank cheques, and then leaned back against her pillows with a sigh of relief. 'Thank God that's done!' she said thankfully.

Leonora's laugh was tinkling. 'Well done, Mama!' She spoke as if to a young child. Returning the blotter to Mama's writing table, she pretended to search for the reply-paid envelope the Inland Revenue had 'enclosed for your use', as she put it, whilst in reality taking out the folder of bank statements which gave details of the amount in the deposit account. The last one was dated months before and she realised that since Henry's death, there had been no one to keep them in order. Rosemary Cumberland had just been stuffing them into a drawer, still in their envelopes, and it took her several minutes to find the most recent. Stunned, she saw that her mother-in-law had nearly a million pounds on deposit. More than enough to see Leonora out of trouble.

'There we are!' she said gaily, shutting the drawer and rising. 'I'm sure I won't have to bother you again, Mama. And I'll make sure this goes into the post in the morning.'

'You're very kind, Leonora,' the Dowager replied, wishing she could feel more fond of this daughter-in-law. After all, she was being very helpful these days. Perhaps, Rosemary reflected, she could have liked Leonora more if only she didn't keep comparing her to Beverley, to whom she felt increasingly close.

Leonora, hurrying triumphantly downstairs, knew that if she could resist gambling, she'd be able to settle her debts once and for all. But could she resist? Could she bear to deprive herself of the buzz that was as addictive as a drug?

Bertie phoned Beverley a few days later. 'How about lunch again?' he asked in his breezy fashion. He was finding himself thinking about her more and more these days, marvelling at how lucky Anthony had been to have found such a wonderful young woman.

'I'd like that,' he heard Beverley reply. 'I do have one more appointment with my dentist, next Tuesday. Is that any good?'

'Perfect.' They arranged to meet at a little Italian restaurant off Jermyn Street, and when Bertie hung up, he was torn between elation and depression. He was thrilled that she'd agreed to meet him again, and yet the very fact that she'd agreed so easily made him aware she regarded him as a friend only, a friend of her late husband and no more. She obviously did not regard meeting him as having a date, and he wondered if she ever would? Would she ever get over the death of Anthony? Would she ever fall in love again so that she could live life to the full? It made his heart sink when he realised that might never happen . . . and what a waste it would be, too. A beautiful healthy young woman like Beverley, with the whole of her life before her, should be in a loving relationship, he told himself. Not stuck in the country with a clutch of women, all older than herself.

Dashing from his office in Threadneedle Street, where the merchant bank he worked for had been established since the turn of the century, Bertie managed to get to the restaurant a few minutes before Beverley. When she arrived, the waiter was just about to serve the champagne Bertie had ordered.

'What's this?' Beverley asked, grinning at him. 'Are you celebrating something or do you always drink champagne for lunch?'

'Only on special occasions,' he replied, smiling at her. 'And because I happen to know you like it,' he added.

'That's really sweet of you.' She was touched by the gesture. 'How are you?' Her gold flecked eyes scanned his face, and he thought how well she was looking, with her skin lightly tanned and her hair like burnished copper.

'In terrific form,' he replied.

'I came up by train so thank goodness I don't have to rush off to meet Leonora today,' Beverley announced when they'd ordered. 'And Nicky and Juliet are spending the day with Georgina Amesbury again, so I don't have to hurry back to him, either.'

'That's good.' He loved her naturally disarming way of expressing herself, without affectation or guile. 'How's Nicholas? I'm longing to see him.'

Beverley's face lit up. 'Why don't you come down for a weekend? I know Mama would love to see you and you'd like to visit Bucklands after such a long time, wouldn't you?'

'I'd love to,' Bertie replied, needing no persuasion. 'It would be great to see the old place again.'

'Then how about this weekend?' Her eagerness was apparent; she was with someone who had known Anthony nearly all his life and warmed towards him with a naturalness that he found wonderful, but it once again put him firmly in the category of old family friend and nothing more.

'I could be with you in time for dinner Friday night?' he suggested.

'Great! Let's hope Leonora's out then we can have a cosy supper on our own, and you can have a peep at Nicky.'

Her enthusiasm was infectious. Bertie toasted her, clinking his glass with hers. 'Here's to you, Beverley! And to little Nicholas, too!'

She laughed, a joyous sound that made Bertie's heart miss a beat.

'It really is good to have met up with you again,' she said. 'I didn't know a soul when I arrived in this country, apart from Jean whom I'd only met a few times in New York, and now, between you and Georgina Amesbury, I don't feel nearly so lonely.' Her expression was sincere, her eyes candid. 'Wouldn't it have been wonderful if Anthony could have been here with us now?'

Bertie nodded. He missed Anthony too. It would be strange going back to Bucklands without him. Strange and sad. They'd shared so much of their youth, and like brothers their dreams and aspirations too. Anthony had always thought the grass was greener on the other side of the Atlantic, but Bertie had never expected him to settle there for good. He'd imagined, in the fullness of time, that he and Anthony would end up like a couple of real old codgers, meeting at Boodle's or White's for lunch and talking about the latest number of innings at Lord's. They'd have discussed their children, and maybe grandchildren, and have reminisced about the Good Old Days. Now it was not to be. The days of their youth, so golden and full of promise, were a thing of the past, never to be recaptured, and without Anthony the world was a poorer place.

'You miss him, too, don't you?' Beverley said gently, watching him. Her own eyes held a glimmer of unshed tears. 'We all miss him. Nicky, Mama, all the people who work at Bucklands – he was a very special person.'

'Yes, he was. A fine man, Beverley, and a very kind one. Anthony wouldn't have knowingly hurt a living thing.'

'That's what makes his death doubly bad,' she observed. 'He was kind to Mary, nothing more, but eventually that kindness cost him his life.'

Bertie nodded. 'I couldn't believe what had happened. It must have been the most terrible shock for you.'

'It was,' she said quietly.

'And what does the future hold for you now, Beverley?'

She replied without hesitation, 'Looking after Nicky, bringing him up to be as fine a person as his father. Maybe I'll become a free-lance journalist in time. That is, when I've finished writing the history of the Cumberlands, which is going to take ages.'

'You'll never go back to live in the States?'

Beverley shook her head. 'Not while Nicky needs me. Not until he's grown-up.'

'Do you miss your family?'

'Very much, sometimes. I hope they'll be coming over in the fall, but I have to remember that Nicky's future must come first. I don't want even to think about going home again, because I know it would unsettle me.' She smiled wistfully, thinking of Rachael and Daniel, and Jenny, Josh and Tom. So many thousands of miles away. A part of her past that was gone forever.

'I'm sure, in time, you'll love England,' Bertie

497

remarked hopefully. 'It's not a bad place to be, and Bucklands is especially lovely.'

'You're right. I've only been here a few months so it's not surprising I'm still finding it all a little strange. Unlike Nicky,' she added with a grin. 'He's so happy and is having such a wonderful time, I couldn't ask more out of life, for his sake.'

Once again, as they talked, the time flew past, and Bertie abandoned all thoughts of going back to the office. He could always say he was entertaining an important client. Beverley was in no hurry, either. She'd already checked the train timetable, and as long as she got back in time to put Nicky to bed, she knew Georgina would take good care of him at Hunting Lodge.

'How about a walk in the park?' Bertie suggested, as they finished their second cup of coffee. 'Green Park is quite near.' He looked out of the restaurant window. 'It looks like a fabulous afternoon; far too sunny to stay indoors.'

'Yes, I'd like that.'

They left Signor Sassi's a few minutes later, and companionably Beverley linked her arm through Bertie's. They walked the length of Jermyn Street, looking into the windows of some of the most exclusive and expensive shops in London and then crossing St James's Street, passed the Ritz before coming to the pastoral country atmosphere of Green Park. Walking under the trees, Beverley looked around appreciatively.

'It's almost like being in the depth of the country,' she remarked. 'And you say Piccadilly is only a quarter of a mile away?'

'Follow me, and I'll have another surprise for you,' he replied mysteriously. They set off, walking south across the shady park.

'I must get to know London better,' Beverley observed. 'It's so vast and sprawling, isn't it? Unlike Manhattan, with its grid system, where it's impossible to get lost.'

'I'll buy you an A to Z map!' Bertie promised. 'Then the next time you come up, you'll know where everything is.'

Ahead, Beverley could see they were approaching a road that ran through the park. 'Where are you taking me?' she asked, intrigued.

'In a minute, you'll see.'

They walked another three hundred yards, and then as the trees thinned out, she saw the great grey stone building, set in a vast courtyard behind gilt railings.

'Oh! It's Buckingham Palace!' she exclaimed. 'Joe drove me past it, the first time I came to London, but I hadn't noticed it was set in such an amazing position.'

'The Queen also has a garden, at the back, which is almost the same size as Green Park,' Bertie told her. 'What you Americans would call a back yard,' he added, chuckling.

'Some yard!' Beverley giggled.

They crossed The Mall and entered St James's Park, which she thought was even prettier than Green Park, with its fountains and lake, and flower beds brimming with colourful blooms on this hot summer's afternoon.

'I had no idea London was so beautiful,' she remarked, as they sat on a bench, overlooking the lake, where geese and swans and ducks glided up and down.

'You are seeing the best part,' Bertie reminded her. 'Go three or four miles in any direction, and it's a different story.'

'What about where you live?'

'Launceston Place is pretty stunning, actually,' he

admitted. Then he sat upright, struck by an idea. 'Why don't you come back and see it? We could have tea and I could show you around?'

Beverley glanced at her watch. It was four o'clock. 'As long as I catch the five-thirty train,' she pointed out.

'Great!' Bertie's lean face lit up, and his dark velvety eyes twinkled with pleasure. 'We'll get a cab and be home in ten minutes.'

As soon as Beverley saw Launceston Place she was enchanted.

It was a quiet Kensington road, lined on both sides with white stucco houses, set back from the pavement behind small front gardens. Elegant black railings and gates, behind which shrubs and small trees grew in profusion, gave the buildings a gracious air. Short flights of steps, some tiled in black and white, some marbled, led up to the front doors, most of which were painted black, and in some cases formal porticoes and pillars gave the houses an air of restrained grandeur.

'It's beautiful,' Beverley said as they got out of the taxi and she stood looking up and down the length of the street. 'What pretty houses. Are they very old?'

'Turn of the century, I suppose. My parents bought this one at the end of the war for a few hundred pounds. Not a bad investment when you come to think of it.' Taking his keys out of his pocket, Bertie led the way up the stone-flagged path to the front door.

'What's it worth now?' Beverley asked, looking up at the charming bow-shaped window of the ground-floor drawing room. The house had four storeys, including the semi-basement, and she wondered at a single man living in such a big house.

'It's been valued at over half a million pounds,' Bertie

replied, leading the way into the front hall which was decorated in a sunny shade of yellow, with a black and white tiled marble floor. 'Come in. Mrs Brooks should still be here. I'll get her to make us a cup of tea.'

Beverley waited in the drawing room, while Bertie went in search of his housekeeper, and looked around. It was slightly shabby, in the very English way she'd come to recognise as typifying the upper classes. Everything was of superb quality, but age and wear and tear had laid a mellowing patina over paintwork and furniture, from the tapestry rugs to the swagged brocade curtains, softening the colours and giving the place a very lived-in look.

It was also very obviously a bachelor's pad. Piles of old newspapers, catalogues and magazines were stacked up on side tables. Boxes of ammunition stood on a desk, and she remembered how he'd told her he loved shooting. Then she spotted what looked like a rifle, in its canvas case, propped in a corner near the window. There was not a plant or flower in sight, nor even any photographs of a personal nature.

'Tea will be here in a minute,' Bertie announced, striding back into the room. 'Meanwhile, would you like to see the rest of the house?'

Beverley rose, grinning. 'There's nothing I'd like more. I got a taste for looking around other people's homes when I worked on *Chichi*. You can tell so much about someone by seeing how they live,' she added candidly.

Bertie laughed. 'Well, don't blame me for the decor! My mother chose all the curtains and wallpapers and everything, and I haven't done anything to the place since my parents died.' He looked ruefully at the stair carpet, which was a dark shade of moss green and showing signs of being threadbare. 'I'll have to get down to it one day, but frankly I don't know where to start.'

There were six bedrooms, Beverley discovered, and three pleasant but old-fashioned bathrooms. A large formal dining room, a cosy study and the drawing room took up the ground floor, and in the basement a kitchen, maid's sitting room and a utility room were adequate for a man living on his own, but like the rest of the house, painfully old fashioned to Beverley's eye.

The proportions of the rooms, however, were perfect, and they were all light and airy. In the hands of someone who knew what they were doing, it could be turned into an exquisite home; stylish, comfortable and chic.

Mrs Brooks brought them tea, eyeing Beverley with typical female curiosity.

'Is there anything else you'll be wanting?' she asked in a soft Irish brogue.

'That's all, thanks,' Bertie told her breezily. Then he turned to Beverley. 'Go on. You be mother!'

Laughing and feeling more comfortably relaxed than she'd done for a long time, Beverley poured the tea and Bertie pushed a plate of chocolate biscuits towards her.

'Help yourself,' he said, munching happily.

Beverley smiled at him. 'Did Anthony come here often?'

Bertie nodded. 'Quite a lot. He'd often stay the night if we'd been to a party rather than driving back to Bucklands. Then he got himself a tiny flat in Cliveden Place. That was before he left for America.'

She looked around the room again, picturing Anthony in this setting, sitting in these chairs, looking out of that window.

'Oh, God, I miss him,' she said suddenly.

Bertie looked startled for a moment by the vehemence of her tone, then gazed at her sympathetically. 'I don't blame you, Beverley. It's going to take time.'

'A very long time,' she echoed with conviction.

He leaned forward, looking at her intently. 'It'll happen, though. One day you'll suddenly realise the worst is over. The pain will have subsided, and only the happy memories will be left.'

'How can you be so sure?' she asked doubtfully. 'There are times when I feel I'll never get over it.'

There was a pause, as if he was wondering whether to go ahead and tell her something or not. She watched him curiously, knowing he was holding back. Then he decided to speak.

'When I was twenty-three I got engaged to a girl I was crazy about. I loved her more than anything in the world and we planned to get married. Everything in the garden was rosy until she became ill, quite suddenly. Cancer was diagnosed. She died eight months later.'

Beverley gasped. 'Oh, Bertie! I'd no idea. How awful. I'm so sorry.'

He smiled gently at her. 'Don't be, Beverley. I'm completely over it now, though I must admit it took a couple of years. I only told you to give you hope for the future. One day you will realise it's over. Then you'll be free to fall in love again.' He didn't add 'like I've done'. It was too soon to tell her that already, after only three meetings, he'd come to realise that he was crazy about her. To tell her now might ruin everything. He was going to have to be patient and very gentle, so that the first move eventually came from her. Otherwise she might think he was trying to take over everything that had belonged to Anthony and that would be fatal.

'I'll take your word for it, but I honestly can't see it happening,' Beverley replied. She remembered having almost exactly the same conversation with Mama not long ago, when she, too, had assured her she would fall in love again one day.

'Well, don't worry about it now,' Bertie said lightly, offering her another chocolate biscuit. 'When it happens, it happens.'

After that they chattered about general topics until Beverley suddenly looked at her watch.

'My train!' she gasped. 'It's nearly five-thirty now! I'll have to catch the next one.'

'I had no idea it was so late,' he admitted. 'When is the next one?'

'Six-thirty. Can I use your phone? If I tell Clare to go and pick up Nicky from Hunting Lodge, then she can take him back to Bucklands and put him to bed for me.'

'Of course. The phone's in the study. Let me show you.'

Clare was willing and happy to pick Nicholas up from Georgina Amesbury.

'I'll see he has a good supper and I'll pop him into a bath before he goes to bed,' she assured Beverley. 'Don't worry about a thing, M'Lady.'

'Thank you, I'm very grateful,' Beverley assured her. Then she turned to Bertie who had come back into the room. 'It's all fixed. Clare is going to look after Nicky for me.'

He looked relieved. 'Great. Why don't I drive you to the station? Then that would give us time to have a glass of wine or something before you leave. What d'you say?'

Beverley laughed. 'I'd say we're turning into a couple of alcoholics at this rate! But why not? I don't know when I'm coming up to London again, so I might as well enjoy myself.'

Chapter Twenty-Two

It was nearly eight o'clock when Beverley was dropped off at Bucklands by the taxi she'd taken from the station. Leonara was just about to enter the drawing room when she stopped and regarded Beverley's smart silk dress and high-heeled shoes with a sideways glance.

'Been shopping?' she asked.

'Not today. I've been to the dentist.'

Leonora's eyes widened in mock amazement. 'And what's he been filling today?' She laughed crudely. 'My dear Beverley, it's nearly time for dinner! Don't expect anyone to believe that tall story!' As she spoke she went over to the drinks tray which Stevens always put in the drawing room in the evening, and poured herself a gin and tonic.

Beverley flushed with annoyance, wishing now she'd said nothing. 'I was looking at the sights,' she explained lamely.

'I'll say. Want a drink?' Leonora lit herself a cigarette with a silver lighter and settled herself on the sofa. 'Mama was getting quite worried about you, but I told her you knew how to look after yourself . . . and you do, don't you, Beverley?'

There was something sinister in her tone, but

Beverley chose to ignore it. Instead she remarked: 'I'd better pop up and see her right away.'

'Don't bother. She's decided to come down for dinner tonight, though God knows why. Juliet has already had her supper and there's only us.'

'Yes, I know, but . . .' Beverley broke off as footsteps came thundering along the hall, urgent running footsteps, skidding and pounding on the polished wood floor. A man's voice shouted something in alarm, and then a woman's voice, gasping as if in horror, cried out.

Beverley reached the hall first and nearly bumped into Percy, who was being followed by Joe. His face was white and his eyes dark shadowy pools of fear. Alice was standing looking at them, her jaw slack and her mouth agape with horror. 'M'Lady!' Joe exclaimed when he saw her. 'Young Nicholas is leaning out of the bedroom window! I've just seen him from the garden!' He'd obviously been running for his breathing was laboured. 'He's hanging right out!'

'Oh, my God!' Beverley felt herself freeze for a second and then she started running towards the staircase. Alice was already ahead of her, but she couldn't go as fast and so Beverley tore ahead, charging up the steps two at a time, her heart pounding, her mind edging towards panic. Percy and Joe were racing behind her and at the bottom of the stairs, Stevens was making a valiant effort to hurry.

'Don't let's startle him,' Percy warned, close on Beverley's heels. Her only thought was to get to Nicky, though, before it was too late. There was a forty-foot drop from their bedroom window to the black waters of the moat below, but more dangerous were the jutting-out stone buttresses that supported the ancient walls. If he were to strike one of them as he fell . . .

'Oh, God. Oh, please God!' Beverley mouthed the words, her mind spinning with petrifying dread at what she might find. Not Nicholas. Not her beloved baby . . . Her legs had become so weak they could hardly carry her as she struggled to the top of the polished oak stairs and then ran along the corridor to her bedroom. The door was shut. She seized the handle with hands that shook violently, and then from somewhere at the back of her mind came Percy's words: 'Don't startle him.'

Hardly able to breathe so great was her fear now, she forced herself to open the door slowly and softly, turning the handle with care. Then she entered on tip-toe. The room was in semi-darkness, dusk having descended with summer's swiftness after a sunny day. She looked across the over-furnished bedroom with its Chinese bed and artifacts, to the windows. The curtains had been pulled back from one of them, and standing, wobbling precariously on the arm of a chair, leaning far out with his elbows resting on the ledge, was Nicholas. He was straining to see something far below and did not turn as Beverley crept stealthily towards him. Silhouetted against the purple landscape, he wriggled further forward, so that only his toes reached the chair.

With a diving running plunge, Beverley flung herself forward, eyes fixed on the little golden-haired figure in the striped pyjamas, her arms outstretched to grab him before he tumbled out of sight.

She was within a few feet of him when he suddenly turned, almost losing his balance as he saw her.

'Nicky!' she cried out, almost within reach of him. The chair wobbled and a fleeting look of fear crossed his face as he clung to the window ledge, his feet no longer even touching the chair, his weight too far forward.

'Nicky!' She grabbed him around the middle and pulled him bodily away from the window. Then she crushed him to her as if she could never bear to let him go.

'What were you doing?' she scolded, through tears of relief. 'You must never go near an open window! It's dangerous! Do you hear me? You might have fallen out!'

Percy and Joe stood braced to perform an act of rescue, their pent-up adrenaline-charged energy making them hover anxiously, while Alice joined by a panting Stevens stood in the doorway weeping.

Beverley collapsed into the chair, Nicholas on her lap.

'I wanted to see if the swans had gone to bed,' he whispered. He looked subdued and shaken by his mother's scolding.

Beverley hugged him tightly, stroking his blond hair with a feverish hand. 'Promise me you'll never, never lean out of a window again.'

He looked up into her face. ''Kay.'

A sudden thought struck Beverley. 'Who opened the window in the first place?' she demanded, looking at the others. 'They are never to be opened while Nicky is around.'

Percy spoke. 'That's just what I was wondering, M'Lady. It's a lucky thing that I was walking past on my way home when I happened to look up at Bucklands and see the young master, leaning right out. I shouted at him to go back but I don't think he heard me.'

Nicholas looked up at Percy. 'Have the swans gone to bed?'

Percy smiled, a forced grin that twisted his drawn face.

'I don't rightly know, Nicholas. But you listen to your mother. You don't want to go leaning out of windows again. It's real dangerous.'

'I wanted to see,' he declared, perking up. He looked over at Joe, Alice and Stevens with curiosity. 'What are you doing?'

'They've come to see if you're all right,' Beverley told him. Then she turned to Percy again. 'Where's Clare?'

Alice stepped forward. 'She went home more than an hour ago, M'Lady. After she put Nicholas to bed.'

'Did anyone else come in here after that? Clare wouldn't have left the window open, with the curtains drawn back, of that I'm certain.'

'No, it can't have been Clare,' Percy agreed. 'We've got a rule in our house about windows being locked if there are children around. My Clare knows that as well as anyone.'

'Then who else could it be?' Beverley asked distractedly. Fear at what might have happened made her angry. 'Did anyone else come into your room, after Clare had gone?' she asked Nicky. 'Did Juliet come and see you?'

Nicholas shook his head and started playing with the string of pearls round her neck.

'And I never comes upstairs in the evening,' Alice announced defensively.

'Well, he couldn't have opened it by himself, it's far too heavy.'

Percy and Joe went over to the heavy sashcord window and closed it. 'No child could open that,' said Joe.

'A lady opened it,' Nicholas announced suddenly. 'And she woke me up.'

Beverley looked at him, stunned. So someone *had*

entered their bedroom after he'd been settled for the night, and had then opened their window. Against all the rules. She had always said no one was to disturb him when he'd been put to bed. And certainly, no one was allowed to open their bedroom window.

'Who was it, sweetheart?' she asked, trying to keep her voice steady.

'I don't know.' He was getting tired now, grinding one of his fists into his eye. 'I wanted to see if the swans had gone to bed,' he repeated sleepily.

'Yes, I know, Nicky.' Beverley spoke soothingly. 'But did you see who it was? Which lady opened your window and woke you up?'

The atmosphere in the room was tense now, with Percy, Joe, Alice and Stevens straining to hear Nicky's reply. Alice, in particular, looked nervous because if it was Lizzie or one of the other maids she might be held responsible.

Nicholas started whimpering. 'I . . . I didn't . . . see.'

'You must have seen, darling. It isn't dark yet. Who was it, Nicky? Why are you saying you couldn't see?' She hated pressurising him like this, but she had an urgent need to know who had been responsible for putting her son's life in danger.

Nicholas gave a dry shuddering sob. 'She was going out the door.'

It was a reasonable explanation. Whoever had come into their room had pulled back the curtains, opened the window, leaving a wide gap of about three feet, and had then awakened Nicky before slipping out of the room.

'And you didn't see who it was?' Beverley persisted.

Nicky shook his head, stuffed his thumb into his mouth and refused to say any more.

'Could you fix proper locks, with keys, on to these windows tomorrow, Percy?'

'That's exactly what I was thinking, M'Lady. I'll go round the whole castle, checking every window and making sure they can't be opened without a key.'

'Of course, all the windows on the nursery floor have bars so no child could fall out of them,' Alice remarked in a voice that suggested if Beverley had allowed Nicholas to sleep upstairs in the first place, none of this would have happened.

'I know, but we're talking about this floor,' she replied firmly. Then she looked back at Percy again. 'Thank you for raising the alarm so quickly. You may well have saved Nicky's life.'

'M'Lady, I just thank providence that I happened to be passing at that moment. A real bit of luck that was.'

'Well, thank you anyway.' Beverley rose and, carrying Nicholas over to his cot, lowered him gently into it. He was almost asleep again, and as she pulled the coverlet up over him, the knowledge of what might have happened hit her in a fresh rush of overwhelming horror.

Some dreadful certainty, a deep gut feeling, told Beverley that whoever had opened the window had meant to harm Nicholas. And in a way that would look like an accident, too. She thought back to the fire in the barn. Had that been a deliberate attempt on his life? If it had succeeded, it too could have been made to look like a tragic accident.

As Beverley got ready for dinner she couldn't help wondering why Leonora hadn't rushed upstairs with everyone else to see what was happening. Was it because she knew what they would find? Was it in fact Leonora, whose bedroom was across the landing from Beverley's, who had gone into the room and deliberately opened the window? But why? What had she, or Juliet for that matter, to gain if anything happened to Nicholas?

Convinced that Clare had nothing to do with it, Beverley thought about the other women in the house. There was Wendy who had been in bed with a migraine which was why Juliet and Nicholas had spent the day at Georgina's, and there was Mama, Alice and the maids. None of them would do anything so foolish. There were only two possible explanations. Either it was a woman from the village – but a stranger would have been spotted wandering around the castle – or Nicky was mistaken and it hadn't been a woman at all, but a man. A man with a lot to gain if Nicholas was out of the way.

In the drawing room, Leonora and the Dowager waited to go in to dinner.

'Ah, there you are, dear girl! I was wondering what had happened to you,' the Dowager said smilingly as Beverley entered the room, and at that moment she realised her mother-in-law didn't know what had happened.

'I'm sorry . . .' Beverley apologised, glancing at Leonora. Her sister-in-law shot her a warning look, but was it to spare the Dowager the shock of hearing her beloved grandson had been in danger, or to protect herself?

'I was settling Nicky,' Beverley said lamely.

But throughout dinner she was aware of an atmosphere of constraint as Stevens, still looking pale, plodded round the dining room serving them. And all the time her suspicions grew. So did the belief that Nicholas could be in danger.

'You don't mean it!' Bertie's expression was stunned.

'Why should anyone want to hurt Nicholas, for God's sake?'

He'd arrived the previous evening, and as he and Beverley strolled in the rose garden after dinner, she told him about the incident of the open window.

'I don't think the fire in the barn was an accident either,' she continued. 'Why should a box of matches end up in Nicky's wheelbarrow, for God's sake? I think someone deliberately threw them there while Nicky was chasing the kitten, and you know what small children are like. He found them and thought, Wow! A new toy!'

Bertie looked concerned. 'Have you told anyone else about your suspicions? This sounds really serious, Beverley.' His dark eyes were grave as they looked into hers.

'I mentioned it to my mother on the phone, but she's so far away. It's hard for her to imagine what it's like here. She said perhaps I was getting things out of proportion. A couple of accidents, or near accidents, don't add up to an attempt on Nicky's life – and I agree with her. It's other things, though, that make me suspicious. There was a rumour going round the village not long after we arrived, that Anthony wasn't really Nicky's father . . .'

'What?' He looked aghast.

Beverley nodded her head. 'Jean thought Leonora had started it, but she strenuously denied doing so.'

'What's she to gain, though?'

'Maybe she just wants to make my life hell. She's very bitter she hasn't got a son.'

'Charles Amesbury would have succeeded if Nicholas hadn't been born, wouldn't he?'

'Yes.'

'Do you think he could be behind these so-called accidents?'

Beverley sighed deeply. 'He certainly has a motive.'

They'd reached the far end of the garden, and sitting on a wooden seat set under an arbour of white roses, they watched the sun slowly setting in the west.

Bertie looked at her profile, marvelling at her almost perfect bone structure and the creaminess of her skin.

'But you don't think it's him?' he asked intuitively.

She turned to look at Bertie and her expression was perplexed.

'Much as I dislike him, I somehow can't see him plotting to get rid of a child in order to inherit. I honestly can't.' She spread her hands expressively. 'I may be wrong, but I truly believe he has no ambition to be the next Earl or live at Bucklands . . . he's too *lazy*! Except when it comes to one thing and that's chasing women.' Her mouth tightened at the memory of Charles' attempt to make love to her in the copse. 'He has enough money to live on, and a very nice house. He's unpretentious as far as belonging to a titled family is concerned . . .' She paused uncertainly, thinking of the contradictions in Charles' personality. Hadn't he criticised Anthony for not caring enough about his title? Hadn't he said that if it had been him, he'd have made a title work for him?

'He has the motive and the opportunity,' Bertie pointed out, breaking into her thoughts. 'He seems to be able to pop into Bucklands at any time. Couldn't he have crept into Nicky's room and opened the window?'

'But Nicky did say he saw a woman leaving the room.'

'Maybe he did. That doesn't mean Charles hadn't gone into your room earlier. Maybe he was looking for you, hoping to find you there. Maybe he acted on impulse . . . saw opening the window as an opportunity

516

of endangering Nicky's life. Perhaps, after he'd gone, one of the maids went into the room to check on it, and it was her backview Nicky saw as she was leaving.'

'That's true,' Beverley admitted, 'although the maids turn down the beds and draw the curtains much earlier in the evening, before Nicky even has his bath. I've questioned them but they all deny going into my room at that hour.'

Bertie looked thoughtful. 'Charles is also one of the few people who still smoke, isn't he?'

'Yes, but so does Leonora.'

'Supposing Charles was at the farm for some reason, the day of the fire? He's more likely to have been there than Leonora, isn't he? Maybe he acted on impulse once again? He saw Nicky's wheelbarrow and just chucked his matches into it to see what would happen. With children of his own, he'd guess that Nicky would start playing with them.'

'Oh, God, this is awful,' Beverley exclaimed. 'What am I going to do, Bertie? I feel I daren't leave Nicky alone for a moment. I trust Clare, but even she hasn't been able to prevent these near disasters happening.'

'Maybe nothing more will happen,' Bertie said comfortingly. 'You haven't got enough to go on to inform the police, I'm afraid. Everything that's happened, apart from the rumour about his legitimacy, could have been purely accidental. You need proof before you report the circumstances as suspicious.'

When the shadows lengthened, and the rosy landscape turned to violet, they strolled slowly back to Bucklands, Bertie with his arm linked through hers. For a moment he thought of saying something; he had this great urge to comfort and protect her, but somehow, he knew she would reject any feelings of love on his part. It was too soon. Beverley had come this far alone, and he was sure she wouldn't want to relinquish her independence yet. Somehow he was going to have to be patient and be there for her as a friend, if nothing else.

Suddenly she gripped his arm tighter and stopped dead.

'Did you see that?' She was looking in the direction of the flowering shrubs that edged the copse.

'See what?' He peered with narrowed eyes but darkness was closing in quickly and it was difficult to see clearly.

'Someone's over there . . . I saw them move,' she said tensely.

'Among those shrubs?'

Beverley nodded. Without another word, Bertie sprinted silently forward across the lawn, his long legs stretching athletically, his eyes fixed on the shrubbery ahead. Beverley ran after him but she couldn't keep up with his pace and he disappeared among the bushes and the trees beyond. It was dark in the copse and she paused, hearing the thud of his footfalls on the soft mulchy ground until they receded and the place became an eerie shady area of malevolence which she felt too scared to enter. Memories of Charles forcing himself on her came rushing back and so every shrub and tree became a threat that lurked ominously, foreboding evil. An owl hooting in the distance made her start; a rustle in the undergrowth caused her heart to skip a beat. Then she heard the swish of leaves being disturbed and, holding her breath while she stood stock still, waited as the rustling came nearer. Then she heard her name being whispered.

'Beverley?'

It was Bertie. He stumbled as he drew nearer and she could feel his breath, hot and sweet, on her face.

'Did you see who it was?' she asked in a low voice.

'No. I only caught a glimpse of someone running away,' he panted.

'Could it have been Charles?'

Taking her arm protectively, he led her across the lawn. 'I've no idea. It was too dark and whoever it was was going at a hell of a pace. Why do you think it might be Charles. More likely a poacher, I'd say.'

'Because Charles practically tried to rape me, just near this spot.'

'He did what? Oh, Christ!' Bertie sounded disgusted.

They'd reached the drawbridge and as they entered the castle, Stevens came towards them.

'Ah, M'Lady,' he said as soon as he saw Beverley. 'There's a phone call for the young Lady Cumberland. I can't find her anywhere. Has she by any chance been walking in the garden with you?'

Beverley and Bertie looked at each other and when Beverley replied she chose her words with care.

'She hasn't been with us, Stevens.'

He seemed tired and distracted. 'The gentleman on the phone is being very offensive, but I can't help it if I can't find her, can I?' Disgruntled, he turned away and shuffled off to deal with the caller, muttering under his breath.

'Oh dear!' Beverley remarked. 'I can guess who that is.'

'Who? One of her boyfriends?' Bertie spoke in a low voice so they would not be overheard.

Beverley shook her head. 'More likely a moneylender,

or the owner of a casino where Charles tells me she owes a lot of money.'

'Does she gamble?' Bertie sounded astonished. 'I'm sure she never did when Henry was alive.'

'I don't know how long it's been going on, but I know for a fact that she owes over three hundred thousand to a firm of moneylenders.'

'Three hundred...! Whew!' He looked shaken. 'That's going it a bit, I must say.'

Drinking coffee in the library a few minutes later, Bertie turned to Beverley with troubled eyes.

'Charles didn't really try to rape you, did he?' he asked.

'He didn't get the chance, but he grabbed me in the coppice and got me in a clinch before I knew what was happening,' Beverley admitted. 'He's left me alone since then so perhaps he's got the message, but he really is the most repulsive creature I've ever met.'

'His wife must have a hell of a life,' Bertie agreed. 'I wonder why she puts up with it?'

'God knows. Perhaps she loves him. I'm sure she's unhappy, though. Imagine being married to someone who plays around all the time.'

'Poor Georgina.' He sounded sympathetic. 'It must be awkward for you, with Charles in hot pursuit isn't it?'

She shrugged. 'I've managed to avoid him recently. He'll soon find someone else to interest him, I'm sure.'

Bertie looked at her, sitting curled up on the leather sofa, her shoes off and her feet tucked under her, her hair a fiery gold in the soft library lights.

'You need someone to look after you,' he said, deciding to take a chance after all. 'Someone who can take care of you and Nicky,' he added huskily.

Beverley rested her head on one of the blue velvet cushions and gazed up at the beamed ceiling. 'No, I don't,' she replied gently, her intuition telling her what he was hinting at. 'I've looked after myself since I left college, and I've managed to look after Nicky too, since Anthony died. I manage very well, you know,' she added, smiling.

'But you can't want to be on your own forever,' he ventured.

She turned to him then, her gaze level, her expression resolute.

'Falling in love and getting married again is definitely not on my agenda.'

Bertie looked abashed and she noticed his hands were shaking as he put down his coffee cup.

'Really?' he asked in a hollow voice. 'Don't you ever want to marry again?'

'I don't think I do,' she replied truthfully. 'I loved Anthony so much I can't imagine myself loving anyone else again in that way. We had something so special, Bertie.' Her eyes suddenly filled with tears and she looked away so he would not see her pain, but instead he rose from the chair he'd been sitting in and sat down on the sofa beside her.

'I know you did, love,' he murmured, putting his arm around her shoulders. He longed to hold her close and kiss away her tears and tell her he loved her, but he knew he had to hold his peace. It was going to take time, maybe a long time, before she was ready for love again, and unless he wanted to risk losing her altogether, he must remain silent.

'How long will it take, Bertie?' she wept, resting her head on his shoulder for a moment. 'How long will it be before I feel a whole woman again? You've been through this. Will the hurting ever stop?'

He laid his cheek carefully against her hair and her perfume made him dizzy with longing. He closed his eyes, cherishing this moment of closeness, but when he spoke he forced his voice to be strong and positive.

'I promise you it doesn't last forever. One day, you'll suddenly feel a lightening of the spirit, a lifting of all the greyness and misery, and you'll realise you've joined the human race again.'

She raised her head and wiped away the tears with the tips of her fingers. 'Will I really?' She gave him a shaky smile. 'You promise?'

'I'll bet you a pound to a penny!' he teased. Then he paused, hesitating before he spoke again. 'You do know I'll always be around, don't you?' he said boldly. 'However long it takes.'

Beverley averted her gaze, suddenly embarrassed. 'You mustn't do that, Bertie. You'll always be my best friend, as you were Anthony's, but don't wait for miracles. The part of me that has to do with loving a man . . . in that way . . . is dead. I have no feelings like that at all now. So please don't wait. You must get on with your own life as I must get on with mine, and my main concern at the moment is Nicky.'

'I understand, I really do,' he assured her. 'But remember what I've said. As to Nicky, are you forced to live at Bucklands? Why don't you take a flat in London so you're both away from here and Charles and Leonora and all the unpleasantness?'

Beverley looked startled. 'I think it would cause an

awful rift if I moved to London. It wouldn't be much fun for Nicky either. We've just left a big town. Even I don't want to live in a city again, right now.'

Bertie hid the disappointment he felt. Just for a moment he'd found the perfect excuse to have her living near him, so he could see her more often.

'So what do you plan to do?' he asked.

'Keep an even closer watch on Nicky,' she asserted firmly.

They were in the hall saying goodnight a few minutes later when Leonora appeared through the main entrance, windblown and ruffled-looking. She seemed startled to find them there, and barely paused as she crossed the hall and started climbing the stairs.

'What's it like out?' Bertie asked conversationally. 'It was a bit blustery earlier on.'

Leonora glanced at him briefly. 'It is rather windy,' she replied. When she reached the first-floor landing, she hurried off in the direction of her room.

Beverley and Bertie looked at each other.

'Where's she been?' he whispered. 'Is she still having a thing with Charles?'

Beverley thought back to the day of the garden party, and how she'd seen Leonora and Charles coming out of Bucklands, deep in conversation after the departure of the casino owner.

'I don't know,' she replied thoughtfully.

'Did you notice her stockings or tights or whatever she was wearing?' he asked.

Beverley blinked, puzzled. 'Why should I? They were black, weren't they?'

Bertie nodded. 'I noticed, before dinner this evening, she had a ladder up the back of her right leg. It surprised me, because she's someone who is always so particular about her appearance.'

'I expect she caught it on something. What are you saying?'

'As she was going up the stairs just now, I saw the ladder was on the back of her left leg,' he replied quietly.

Lady Jean and her husband always attended Morning Service on Sundays at the small parish church that formed part of the estate. She considered it her duty as a committed Christian, and Rupert went along with her for the sake of peace. This Sunday morning, however, she arrived at Bucklands while everyone was still having breakfast, accompanied by her husband.

'I presume you're all coming with me this morning?' she asked, looking up and down the breakfast table. Beverley, buttering a piece of toast for Nicholas, looked up, amused. Sometimes she went to church taking Nicholas with her, but if he was in a slightly fractious mood, they stayed behind. Today, however, Jean managed to make the suggestion sound like a royal command.

'You'll be coming, won't you, Bertie?' she barked encouragingly. 'And, Wendy, you will accompany Juliet. As it's such a nice day, I'm going to see if Mama will come, too.'

'Is Mummy going?' Juliet piped up.

A frosty smile crossed Jean's face. 'When did your mother last go to church?' she said drily. 'From memory, I'd say the last time Leonora went to church was for her own wedding.'

'She was at Daddy's funeral,' Juliet pointed out, loyally.

'Yes, of course she was,' Jean cut in swiftly. 'Maybe

you'd like to tell her we're all going this morning, and I hope she'll join us in the family pew.'

'Humph!' said Rupert Ffitch, from the doorway, where he stood watching Beverley as she tended to Nicholas' needs. He thought he'd never seen her looking so beautiful, with her hair flowing loose around her shoulders, and the skin of her bare arms, in a sleeveless summer dress, creamy and smooth. Mesmerised, he gazed at her from afar, and wished he was twenty years younger.

'Shall we all meet in the porch of St Luke's at ten-fifty?' Jean suggested.

There were murmurs and nods of assent.

'Right!' said Jean, turning on her heel. 'Let's go up and see Mama, Rupert.'

Bertie chuckled when they'd left the room. 'Jean hasn't changed since I was at Eton with Ant! I remember her then, coming in here while we were having our eggs and B., telling us it was time to get ready for church. God, how the years have flown!'

'Have you known Aunt Jean all your life?' Juliet asked, round-eyed.

'Almost. It seems like a lifetime anyway,' he replied. Then he turned to Beverley. 'If you don't want to take Nicky to church, I'd be very happy to look after him for a bit?'

'Really?' Beverley looked at him in surprise. 'Is that because you're longing for an excuse not to have to go to church yourself? I bet it is!' she laughed banteringly.

Bertie grinned. 'Well . . . I'd like to get to know him better. He's such a grand little chap, and actually I'm very fond of children.' He looked slightly sheepish. 'I'm probably a frustrated dad myself.'

Beverley grinned. 'Okay! You've got yourself a deal! I feel I have to go, duty and all that, but it is rather tedious for Nicky at his age. What will you do? Take him to play in his paddling pool? It's warm enough.'

Bertie addressed Nicholas solemnly. 'What shall we do this morning? Discuss affairs of state? Decide how the country should be run?'

Nicholas giggled. 'Go on the swings!' he exclaimed loudly. 'And feed the goats!'

Bertie rumpled Nicholas' hair. 'You're a farmer's lad, aren't you!' he teased. 'I bet you like to ride on the tractor.'

'Yeah!' He looked excited. 'Mom, can I ride on the tractor?'

'You've started something now,' Beverley informed Bertie, smiling. 'There's nothing he loves more than going over to the farm.'

'Then that's what we'll do.' Bertie sounded genuinely enthusiastic, and Beverley thought with a pang how much Anthony would have enjoyed the company of his son. They could have done so much together, and Anthony could have shown Nicky all the places where he'd played when he'd been a boy, and they could have had a great time together. Anthony would have been so proud of Nicky, too. The little boy was bright for his age, and already the possessor of a sense of humour.

'You're a lucky boy,' Beverley said warmly as she took off his towelling bib. 'You're going to have much more fun this morning than I am.'

'Can I go to the farm with you, too?' Juliet begged.

Wendy looked questioningly at Beverley, seeing it as a way of getting out of going to church herself.

Beverley looked doubtful. 'You'll have to ask your

mother,' she said, thinking back to the previous evening when Leonora had returned from being out somewhere with the run in her ladder on a different leg to when she'd gone out. How observant of Bertie to notice such a thing.

When she saw Charles, accompanied by Georgina and their children in church, a couple of hours later, she returned his greeting coolly while showing Georgina great warmth. Beverley thought she looked tired today, and weary and dispirited. Her summer dress hung limply on her scrawny body, and the dark blue straw hat she wore had a battered look about it, suggesting it had been around for several years. Even her fair hair looked wispier than usual, as it hung in tendrils around her ears.

After the service, Georgina came over to her as they all stood outside the church and kissed her on the cheek.

'I heard about your awful fright the other evening . . . with Nicholas,' she said sympathetically. 'My dear, I'm always terrified of open windows with children.'

Beverley nodded, looking into the pale blue eyes that were so bright and tender. 'It was an awful experience,' she agreed. 'Thank God Percy saw him and we got to him in time.'

'And you've no idea who opened the window?' Georgina sounded scandalised that such a thing could happen. As she spoke, she was stroking Tom's shoulder absent-mindedly.

'No idea at all. He says he thinks he saw a woman leaving the room, but I can't think who it could have been.'

'Oh, he's just a baby, how can he be sure?' Georgina said indulgently. 'I think it was the most awful thing to happen.'

527

'I know. Like the fire in the barn.'

'Well, children do get into awful scrapes, you know. Sometimes I wonder how they survive at all! Tom fused all the lights when he was about two, and nearly blew himself up as well, by stuffing the foil top from a bottle of milk into the electric toaster. Didn't you, Tom?'

He grinned, but remained silent.

'Yes,' Beverley agreed, 'but there are accidents and accidents. These things happened to Nicky; he didn't engineer them out of naughtiness or playfulness.'

'I wouldn't worry,' Georgina said soothingly, patting her arm.

It seemed everyone in the village had heard about Nicholas and the open window – the story spread, no doubt, by the Percy family – and many people came up to Beverley to offer her their sympathy. Only Charles for once ignored her, although he talked to Mama and Jean, and gave Wendy lingering looks with his lustful eyes.

'He's very attractive, isn't he?' she observed in a quiet voice to Beverley as they all walked slowly back to Bucklands for lunch.

Beverley looked at her, startled. 'Charles? Do you think so?'

Wendy sighed, her full-lipped mouth tilting up at the corners, making her look more like a doll with a fixed expression than ever. 'Oh, yes,' she breathed. 'He's so sophisticated, too. A real man-of-the-world.'

Beverley didn't know whether to pity this nineteen-year-old girl or feel angry with her. It was clear that she'd never had experience of men like Charles before, and the potential situation rang warning bells in Beverley's head.

'Well, he's married so that puts paid to that, doesn't it?' she said in a brisk but friendly way. 'He's bad news as far as women are concerned, and his wife's the one I feel sorry for.'

Wendy pondered this last remark, and then whispered softly: 'She is a bit drab though, isn't she? You can understand a man wanting someone a bit more exciting . . .' Her voice trailed off, and Beverley knew instinctively she was finishing the sentence in her head with the words: '. . . like me.'

'Wendy, any woman who gets involved with Charles is asking for trouble,' Beverley said severely. They were ahead of all the others now, but they still spoke in low voices for fear of being overheard.

Blushing, almost simpering, Wendy looked at Beverley with starry saucer eyes.

'But I already have,' she whispered. 'We were at the folly last night. You won't tell anyone, will you?'

Beverley's heart sank, appalled by Charles' relentless pursuit of women, and the pang of resulting hurt she felt for Georgina. Staggered also by the apparent juvenile naivety of Wendy. In a minute she'd be telling her Charles really cared.

'He's told me how much he loves me,' Wendy continued, right on cue. 'He's so wonderful!'

'Oh, my God, Wendy,' Beverley groaned, hating to have to disillusion the girl, but fearful for her at the same time. 'You have to stop this right away. How much longer are you supposed to look after Juliet? The summer holidays must be nearly over, aren't they? And she's going to stay with friends in Scotland.'

'Leonora has booked me to stay for another two and a half weeks. She wants me here for the last few days, after Juliet returns from Scotland, before she goes back to school.'

'Take my advice and get the hell out of it now, Wendy.' Beverley spoke fiercely. 'You'll be doing yourself no favours by staying. You'll get hurt, badly hurt, if you really care about him. Go, before it's too late.'

Wendy smiled at her with sweet condescension. 'It's not like that,' she said softly. 'Last night, Charles told me how much I mean to him. This is the real thing . . . for both of us.'

Later, as Beverley confided in Bertie as they sat in the garden after lunch, she said: 'This rules out the affair we thought Charles was still having with Leonora, doesn't it. If Wendy was with him last night . . .'

Bertie nodded. 'You're right. Then who do you suppose Leonora was with?'

Chapter Twenty-Three

'Come back at noon,' Leonora curtly told Joe as he dropped her off outside a dark red brick Victorian house in Pont Street.

Duncan McSwiney was waiting for her in his second-floor flat, still in a dressing gown, his bed unmade because he knew it would soon be rumpled again. As soon as he opened the door for her, he reached out with greedy hands to grasp her breasts, but she pushed him away.

'Not now, Duncan,' she said crisply. 'I want your help.'

He looked faintly astonished and not a little put out. He ran a hand over his slickly combed blond hair and his expression was disconcerted.

'What sort of help?' he asked doubtfully.

'You have a typewriter, don't you?'

'What do you want with a typewriter, for God's sake?'

'It may surprise you to know that my father insisted I took a typing course before I married Henry.' Leonora knew he sometimes had his secretary come to the flat at weekends if there was urgent work to attend to. 'I want to do a letter, a confidential letter,' she stressed, 'and you're the only person I know who won't talk.'

'Okay, but what is it about?'

'Oh, just a family matter,' she said vaguely. 'It'll only take a few minutes and then, as they say, I'm all yours,' she added with a seductive smile.

When Duncan had set up his rather old-fashioned portable machine on a corner of the dining-room table, Leonora took the handwritten draft she'd worked on the previous night out of her handbag.

'Make me some coffee while I do this, darling,' she begged, giving him her most alluring glance. 'I'm just dying for something hot and wet.'

He came up behind her and, sliding his hands from her shoulders down to her breasts, nuzzled her neck.

'You smell wonderful,' he murmured. 'I want you now.'

'Work before pleasure,' she chided softly, feeling his hardness pressing into her back. 'I want you too, but be a love and let me get this out of the way first.'

'All right. I can't think what letter could be more important than getting into bed with me but I'll leave you in peace. Five minutes only, though. Okay?'

'You're an angel,' she cooed. Although she hadn't typed for years she quickly got to work and ten minutes later the letter was finished. Addressed to Mr Brimpton, the Manager of the Eastern Bank in Oxford, it stated, in answer to his query about her future requirements, that she'd been forced in the past few months to draw large amounts of money from her current and deposit accounts in order to pay off the debts incurred by her daughter-in-law, Beverley, the Viscountess Amesbury. This was a highly confidential matter, the letter continued, and she did not wish the rest of her family to know anything about it. In conclusion the letter stressed that there was still eighteen thousand pounds owing to various shops in the United States which had been run up by Lady Amesbury before she left for England, but she very much hoped when she'd paid them that would be the end of the matter. The letter ended 'yours sincerely' and then there was a gap before she typed 'Rosemary, Countess of Cumberland'.

As soon as she got back to Bucklands, she'd get Mama to put her signature to it. That should keep the bank quiet for a while, and satisfy the Manager's queries about the state of Mama's financial affairs.

Beverley was reading aloud to the Dowager when Leonora came swanning into her sitting room later that day.

'Oh, are you very busy?' she demanded, although it was obvious they weren't. Beverley rested *Jane Eyre* on her lap and wondered why Leonora looked so flushed.

'What can we do for you, dear?' the Dowager enquired, although she did not invite Leonora to sit down.

'Oh, nothing,' she said airily. She brought her powers of quick invention into play. 'I was going to suggest we give a dinner party at the end of the month, there are a lot of people we should ask, but there's no hurry. We can talk about it another time.'

'That sounds like a nice idea,' Mama replied blandly. 'Let's talk about it tomorrow, shall we?'

Beverley couldn't fail to notice how disgruntled Leonora looked. She tucked the folder she was carrying under her arm with a cross little toss of her head and made for the door again. When she'd gone, Rosemary Cumberland turned her almost blind eyes to Beverley.

'For once she didn't seem to have any papers for me

to sign!' she said conspiratorially. 'Leonora makes such heavy weather of everything. When Henry looked after my affairs there didn't seem anything like so much to be done. I shouldn't criticise, because it's kind of her to go to all the trouble in the first place, but it does seem endless.'

'What business papers to be signed?' Beverley asked curiously. It surprised her that Mama had any 'business' to see to in the first place. Unaware of her mother-in-law's private fortune, she presumed she received an allowance from the estate, as she herself did.

Mama sighed. 'Oh, it's endless, dear girl. She explained to me there was a backlog of tax returns or whatever . . . I never understand these things and not being able to *see* properly . . .' She broke off in frustration. 'She said we're nearly up to date. You see, nothing was attended to after Henry was killed.'

Beverley looked perplexed. 'Shouldn't you have a proper accountant if it involves tax? I thought Leonora merely wrote out cheques to pay bills which you then signed. I didn't know there was more to it than that.'

'Well . . .' Mama looked confused and slightly flustered. 'That's what she said. I do have rather a lot of money, left me by my father, that has nothing to do with the Cumberland money, so I suppose . . . Well, there probably is a lot to see to.' She sighed again, and her hands picked restlessly at the tweed of her skirt.

'If there's as much work as you say, shouldn't you have the help of someone professional?' Beverley asked carefully. An icy frisson had swept down her back as a dreadful suspicion occurred to her. Leonora was in debt, heavily so. What if she was somehow stealing from her mother-in-law?

'It's always been so straightforward, dear girl, Henry was able to manage beautifully. Leonora said the other day that everything was under control, so I don't suppose there will be any more forms to sign for a while.' Although she tried to sound calm, there was agitation in her voice and her cheeks were flushed.

'Anything to do with accounts or tax is a real bore, isn't it?' Beverley agreed understandingly. 'I used to leave everything like that to Anthony, but I haven't got to grips with the situation over here yet.'

'You needn't worry, my dear. Your and Nicholas' finances are looked after by the Cumberland estate which employs accountants to take care of everything. My situation is different, and should be much simpler in fact.' She gave a soft and rather strained laugh. 'It's only poor Leonora who makes such heavy weather of paying a few bills.'

Nothing more was said. Beverley continued to read *Jane Eyre* aloud, and wondered how she was going to find out exactly what was going on.

All too quickly the summer holidays came to an end, and it was time for Juliet to return to school. Margaret and Tom Amesbury were due back at their respective schools the following day, too, so Beverley and Georgina decided to organise a picnic in the folly.

'We've never done anything like this before,' Juliet said excitedly. 'Do you think Mummy will come?'

The day was fine and sunny, although it was now September. In high spirits they all set off up the steep grassy incline to the folly, carrying rugs and picnic hampers. The cook at Bucklands had gone to a lot of trouble preparing things she thought the children would like, and there were miniature hamburgers in little baps, hot sausages, crisps and popcorn, and blackberry fool in individual ramekin dishes.

'Wow!' Nicholas yelled, as Georgina and Wendy set out the food. They laughed at his wide-eyed earnest enthusiasm. 'Can we start?' he demanded, reaching for a sausage.

'Hang on a minute, Nicky,' Beverley said. She was in charge of drinks, opening cans of Coca-Cola and orange juice and pouring them into plastic beakers. 'You must wait until we're ready.'

'Wendy,' Georgina called out, 'why don't you organise a game of hide-and-seek down in the copse while Beverley and I get lunch organised? By the time you come back, it will be ready.'

'All right.' Wendy grabbed Nicholas' hand. 'Let's go! Who's going to be "It"?'

Shrieking with laughter, Tom, Margaret, and Juliet went hurtling down the slope from the folly, followed by Wendy and Nicholas who was scampering as fast as his legs would carry him. Beverley stood watching them with an indulgent smile.

'It's good they all get on so well together, isn't it?' Georgina observed, as she put out cardboard plates patterned with a design of clowns and balloons, and matching paper napkins.

'That's because they're all the same blood,' Beverley pointed out. Then she paused and stared down to the bottom of the hillock.

'Look who's coming!' she said in a low voice.

'Not Char—?' Georgina broke off, flushing. 'Oh, it's Leonora!' she said quickly. 'What's that she's carrying?'

'It looks like a bag of something . . . I do believe it's

bottles of wine!' Beverley stood up and hailed Leonora. 'Hi there! What have you got?'

Leonora reached the folly, puffing and panting. 'I thought that if this bloody picnic was going to be made bearable, we'd have to get smashed, so I've brought some wine and some decent glasses.' She sank, as if exhausted, on to one of the rugs. 'I even remembered the corkscrew, too.'

Georgina laughed merrily. 'You're brilliant, Leonora,' she said. 'I was just thinking how nice a glass of wine would be. Weren't you, Beverley?'

'I never refuse a glass of wine!' Beverley responded with equally forced bonhomie. 'This is going to be some picnic, isn't it!' They'd both privately hoped Leonora would stay away, but as she'd decided to join them, there was nothing for it but to act graciously.

Methodically, Georgina unpacked the food, putting the sandwiches and other delicacies on to plates spread out on a red and white checked tablecloth, and the fresh fruit into a basket.

'Let's open the wine and then call the children,' Georgina said at last. 'Everything's ready.'

Beverley rose to her feet. 'Come on, boys and girls!' she called loudly. 'Time for lunch.'

'Coming,' Wendy called back from the copse below.

A minute later, pink in the face from exertion, the children came clambering up the slope, with Wendy, flushed and laughing, bringing up the rear.

Nicholas seated himself on the rug beside Beverley.

'Can I start now?'

'Yes,' she assured him, smiling. A sudden silence fell over the children as they started to eat while the grown-ups sipped their wine.

'Amazing how food keeps them quiet,' Leonora remarked, with a note of thankfulness in her voice. She leaned back against one of the grey stone pillars of the folly. 'God, I needed this,' she murmured as she finished her glass of wine. 'Roll on term time!'

'That's an awful thing to say.' Georgina turned on her angrily. 'I can't bear it when Tom and Margaret have to go back. I wish Charles hadn't insisted they go away to school at all. I really miss them.'

'I'm not exactly looking forward to this public school business myself,' Beverley remarked drily. 'We don't have that sort of thing in the States. Nicky certainly isn't going away until he has to.'

'You mean when he's seven?'

'*Seven?* Certainly not. Jean said he'd have to go to prep school when he was nine, but I still think that's barbaric,' Beverley responded hotly.

'Oh, it's heartbreaking,' Georgina agreed, her hand going up involuntarily to stroke Tom's back. 'I always cry.'

'Oh, for God's sake!' Leonora spoke scornfully. 'You'll turn Tom into a mother's boy! Juliet went to boarding school at eight and it hasn't hurt her, has it?' She looked across at her daughter with an expression Beverley couldn't quite fathom. It was part pride, but tinged with displeasure.

'I don't mind it now, Mummy, but I wasn't at all happy at first,' Juliet said candidly.

After they'd had the picnic, the children having eaten almost everything, Beverley suggested a game of Consequences.

'I've brought paper and pencils so we can all have a go,' she said.

538

'How do you play it?' Juliet asked.

'We're each given a sheet of paper, and we start off writing a man's name. Then we fold it over and pass it to the next person and they write a woman's name.'

'Then what?'

'Then we put where the man and the woman met. After that it's "he said to her" . . . and then "she said to him" . . . and "the consequences were", and when we've each written that, we pass the paper once more and then we read the whole thing aloud,' Beverley explained.

Nicky grabbed paper and pencil and enthusiastically started to scrawl.

'I think I'd better help you, sweetheart,' she said, taking hold of his hand. With concentration they all started to play, carefully folding over the paper before they passed it on to the person on their left, so they could not see what had been previously written.

'All done?' Beverley asked at last. 'Pass them on once more.'

'Can I be the first to read mine?' Margaret asked, unfolding her sheet of paper.

'Go ahead.'

'Right.' Margaret cleared her throat and began. 'Father Christmas met Cinderella at the Bowling Alley, and he said to her "Will you marry me?" and she said to him "Get stuffed" and the consequences were the world population exploded!' Margaret looked up, blushing and laughing, while Tom and Juliet shrieked with laughter.

'You next, Juliet,' Beverley prompted.

'Madonna met Donald Duck . . .' Juliet dissolved into giggles, and for the next few minutes, as everyone read aloud what had been written with their joint efforts, there was great amusement. Margaret and Juliet were rolling on the ground, chortling with merriment. Then it was Beverley's turn, and for the first time she unfolded her paper. It was coincidence, of course, she told herself. No one could have planned the finished page to read the way it did, but it gave her a shock. For a moment, she froze, unable to speak.

'Go on,' Georgina urged her. 'Is it very rude?'

Beverley shook her head, playing for time. 'It's just silly.'

'Well, let's hear it,' Leonora said impatiently.

Beverley took a deep breath. 'Jack met Jill at the cinema, and he said to her "What's for dinner?" and she said to him "You're good-looking" and the consequences were they got married.'

'Is that all?' Juliet looked disappointed.

'I said it was silly,' Beverley remarked lightly, screwing up the piece of paper into a tight ball, and then throwing it away with such force that it landed in the branches of the trees in the copse below. There was an awkward silence, and if Leonora, Georgina or Wendy thought her action strange, she knew they would presume it was because it was not suitable for the children to hear. But imprinted on her mind was what had really been written, and it sent a chill down her spine. Yet none of them knew what the previous person had put, so it could only have been chance that the result filled her with fear.

'Nicholas met Wendy', it had read, 'at the folly. He said to her "Give me a sweet", she said to him "I'm a witch" and the consequences were they both dropped down dead.'

Nicholas started to feel ill later that afternoon. At first, when he complained he couldn't see the pictures in a book they were looking at, Beverley thought perhaps he had something in his eye. He was rubbing them with his knuckles and whimpering.

'Let's have a look, sweetheart,' she said, lifting him on to her knee. They were upstairs in 'their' room, playing games before he had his supper. He kept rubbing his eyes and she had to prise his hands away from his face.

'What's the matter, Nicky? Let Mummy see what's wrong?'

Looking into his forget-me-not eyes a moment later, she was startled to see that they looked almost black. Then she realised his pupils were so dilated hardly any of the blue showed. He was also very hot and flushed.

'Thirsty!' he whined pitifully. 'I'm thirsty.'

'Sit there, Nicky, and I'll get you a drink.' Beverley felt uneasy. Nicky was never ill. Perhaps he was coming down with one of the childish ailments she'd read about in her baby books; measles, mumps, scarlet fever. As soon as she'd got him some water, she'd look up sore eyes and a fever in her *Children's Medical Dictionary*.

'Mom, what's wrong with your face?' Nicky said fretfully, as she held him on her lap again, giving him sips of water.

'My face?' Startled, Beverley put her hand up to her cheek. 'Nothing's wrong with my face . . . why?'

'It's funny . . .' he said, but he didn't seem to be looking at her. He was gazing straight ahead, and with a stabbing bolt of fear, Beverley knew where she'd seen that disoriented look before. Mama sometimes looked like that, when she'd lost her bearings and couldn't see where she was. *Nicky was going blind*.

'My God, Nicky!' She lifted him up so that he was

541

standing on her lap. 'What is it? What's the matter? Can't you *see*?'

He was crying loudly now and his skin seemed more red and dry than ever. She had no experience of childish ailments but it was obvious he was very unwell. Holding him close, she hurried down from the nursery floor to her bedroom, calling out for Leonora as she did so. She must have had experience with Juliet, and she would certainly know the name of the local doctor.

Running a cool bath, she decided to bathe Nicky, to help bring down his fever.

'What's the matter?' Leonora asked, coming into the room.

'Can you ring for the doctor, Leonora? There's something terribly wrong with Nicky. He's burning up. He can't seem to see properly, either!' Beverley's voice caught. She was stripping off his cotton shirt and shorts. Then she gasped aloud.

'Look!' Her eyes were transfixed, looking at his small chest in horror. His heart was beating so rapidly it looked as if his chest was fibrillating, and she could actually hear the rapid thud-thud of his heartbeat. 'Quick! Phone for an ambulance! Oh, God! What *is* it?' Even in her limited experience, she knew this was no ordinary ailment. Nicky seemed completely confused and disorientated now, his eyes like shining black buttons, his face scarlet.

'Children run high fevers very easily,' Leonora remarked calmly. 'I wouldn't worry. He'll probably be all right in the morning.'

'He's sick, Leonora! Can't you see that?' Beverley was beside herself with worry. As she lowered Nicky into the water, he was wriggling and screaming, his whole body crimson now, glowing with heat.

'Is there anything I can do?' Wendy appeared in the bathroom doorway, too, her round eyes staring, her small mouth open. 'Oh! What's wrong with him?' she gasped when she saw Nicky.

'*Please!* Will someone get an ambulance! I've got to get him to hospital.'

'Okay. Don't worry. I'll phone right away.' It was Wendy speaking. Leonora still stood there, watching Nicky.

'Oh, please God,' Beverley kept muttering under her breath, as she sponged him down. 'Can you see now, Nicky?' she asked. 'Can you see Mommy?'

'Drink . . . I want a drink!' His arms flailed around blindly, as if he didn't know where he was.

'All right, sweetheart. I'll get you a drink.' She lifted him out of the bath, flung a towel around him, and then, pushing past Leonora, hurried back into her bedroom where she'd left the water.

'Will they take long to get here?' she asked distractedly.

'What? The ambulance?' Leonora was edging her way out of the room.

'Yes. Where's the nearest hospital? Oxford?'

'Yes. Oxford. It should be here in fifteen or twenty minutes. I'm . . . I'm just going to see if Mama is all right,' she added as she left the room.

'There, my baby,' Beverley whispered softly, rocking Nicky gently in an effort to soothe him. 'You're going to be all right, sweetheart.' She stroked his brow and it was fiery hot beneath her fingers. And was it her imagination . . . or was he breathing more rapidly now? His little heart was still pounding, and she felt he was reaching a crisis point. Maybe the fever was about to break, she thought hopefully. Maybe in a few minutes she would see the welcome rash of measles, or the ugly spots of chicken pox.

Then it happened. Nicky seemed to arch his back and grow rigid, his arms and legs stuck out straight and immobile, so that he looked like a stiff doll. A moment later he was jerking violently, so that she could hardly hold him on her lap, and when she cried out his name repeatedly he neither seemed to hear nor see her.

'Nicky!' All the pain in the world was in her distraught cry. 'Nicky . . . Nicky!' In some crazy way she was sure that if she could only make him hear her, if she could only make contact with her child who seemed to be lost in a world of blind misery, if she could just reach into him, he would get better. He was a part of her, so surely she could link her mind and her soul to his, to bring him out of the convulsions that had now taken possession of his small body, as an earthquake takes possession of the terrain?

Holding him as tightly as she could, Beverley sat on her bed, praying the ambulance would arrive soon.

Years seemed to pass; at first Wendy came back to say the ambulance was on its way, then Alice appeared with Mama who had heard the commotion.

'Dear girl.' Her milky eyes looked towards the Chinese bed where Beverley sat holding Nicky. 'What's wrong with him?' She looked stricken, and Beverley knew she mustn't frighten her.

'He's got a bug of some sort, Mama,' she replied, forcing herself to sound calm. 'He's running a high temperature so I'm not taking any chances. I'm getting him to a hospital as quickly as I can . . . even if it does only

544

turn out to be chicken-pox.' Her voice quavered and she had to bite her lip to stop herself breaking into sobs.

'Poor child.' Mama walked slowly over to the bed, feeling the way with one hand, supported by a walking stick in the other. 'Children do run frightening fevers, you know. Anthony used to scare me to death when he got ill.'

'Really?' Beverley looked up at her mother-in-law, aching for her to say it was nothing; that Anthony had the same sort of attack when he was small and it was nothing. Instead the Dowager reached out her hand, finding Nicholas' head more by instinct than sight. She placed her delicate palm gently on his forehead, and then withdrew it with a little gasp.

'Goodness! He is hot,' she murmured. Then she placed her hand on Beverley's shoulder. 'I know it's easy to say "don't worry", dear girl, but it won't do you or Nicholas any good. The doctors will know what to do. We must just have faith in God. It's all we can do.'

Beverley nodded mutely, unable to speak. Nicky looked small and vulnerable, but at the same time as if he had been possessed by some terrible evil force. Black eye-balls glared unseeingly at Beverley, and the writhing of his limbs, jerking spasmodically, shook his small frame.

Alice watched him from the foot of the bed where she was standing. 'That's a fit he's having,' she said. 'I wouldn't be surprised if he's not epileptic.'

Beverley heard Mama give a low moan. At that moment, they heard the wailing siren of an ambulance.

'Thank God,' Beverley exclaimed, rising to her feet with Nicholas in her arms. He was still wrapped in a towel but she grabbed a soft lacy woollen shawl from his cot and draped it over him.

'Take care, dear girl. I'll be praying for you,' Mama promised.

'Oh, Mama!' Beverley kissed her cheek and found it cold and damp. Then she hurried out of her room and down the stairs to meet the ambulance.

'He's got a high fever . . . and convulsions . . . and the pupils of his eyes are dilated,' she said breathlessly, as kind and willing hands reached out to take Nicholas from her, and help her into the ambulance. The paramedics carried out a swift examination of Nicholas as he lay on a stretcher, and the ambulance screamed through the country lanes on its way back to Oxford. Through a haze of fear and wretchedness, Beverley was aware of a barrage of questions being hurled at her. Had he been sick? Had diarrhoea? Complained of pain anywhere? She answered as best as she could, praying they would tell her at any moment that it was nothing serious. As they talked to each other in medical terms and she strained to hear if she could understand what they were saying, she caught the words 'high toxicity'.

Fear made her cold.

'What's wrong with him?' she whispered.

'Has he been out today? In the countryside?' one of the paramedics asked.

Beverley nodded. 'We had a picnic. Why?'

The paramedics exchanged looks.

'Atropa Belladonna . . . to give it its correct name,' one of them said.

The other made a note on his clipboard before turning to Beverley. 'More commonly known as Deadly Nightshade. I'm afraid your son's been poisoned.'

How? How could it have happened? Beverley asked

herself the question over and over again, as she sat in the waiting area of the casualty department of St Marriot's Hospital. Nicholas had been rushed to intensive care and although she'd desperately wanted to go with him they told her, tactfully and firmly, that she'd be much better waiting until they had some news for her.

'But he's going to be all right, isn't he?' she begged one of the doctors, as he asked her Nicky's age and medical history.

'We're going to pump out his stomach, and try and induce vomiting, too, and then we'll administer a tannic acid solution. It's good you got him here so quickly . . .' He broke off, leaving Beverley in no doubt that if Nicholas hadn't been attended to at once it would have been too late.

'You say he was on a picnic? Is it possible he ate some Deadly Nightshade berries, thinking they were ordinary berries?' His dark gentle eyes looked searchingly into hers and she noticed that his face, dark-skinned suggesting he was Indian, was grave.

'As far as I know he didn't eat any berries at all. We all had the same things to eat . . . sandwiches, crisps, you know. Unless, of course . . .' She broke off, and her hand flew to her mouth.

'Yes?'

'He was playing hide and seek with his cousins before the picnic, they were in the coppice where there are lots of shrubs . . .' She paused, thinking. 'They were being looked after by a grown-up, though. A student teacher, in fact. I'm sure she'd have seen if Nicky had eaten anything.'

'Well, we're doing all we can for him. We'll give him some pilocarpine . . .'

547

'What will that do?'

'It'll help restore the visual disturbance. You know what happens when someone gets poisoned by Atropa Belladonna, I suppose?'

'I have no idea.'

'It paralyses the parasympathetic nervous system, blocking the action of nerve endings. That's why your son's pupils dilated.' He gave a little grunt. 'Belladonna is Italian for "Beautiful Woman". In the Renaissance, women applied the plant to their eyes to dilate their pupils and make themselves look more beautiful.' His smile was wry and tired. 'You're not supposed to eat it, though.'

'He will be all right, won't he, doctor?'

'We're doing our best. The great thing is you got him here before he fell into a coma. I'll be getting back now.'

'When can I see him?'

He hesitated before answering. 'We'll let you know,' he said at last, then he strode off, his white surgical coat almost crackling with starch.

While she waited for news, Beverley played a game in her head but it wasn't really a game at all. She was trying to remember the positions of everyone at the picnic. They'd all sat in a circle after lunch playing Consequences, and the last line of the game she'd read aloud, 'They both dropped down dead', had been handed to her by Wendy. So that meant she had written it. What worried Beverley was who had filled in the sheet of paper before it got to Wendy? In what order had everyone sat in the circle, taking part, with the exception of Nicky, who had sat on her knee? Beverley closed her eyes, concentrating, because whether it was a coincidence or not, the contents of that sheet of paper now seemed like a warning of what was about to happen.

She visualised the scene: the tartan rugs spread on the ground and, in the centre, the red and white checked tablecloth with all the food and drink set out. If Wendy had been sitting on her right . . . who had been sitting next to Wendy? Margaret. Beyond Margaret, Beverley remembered seeing Leonora, reclining with her glass of wine and a cigarette. Then came Tom and Georgina, and beside Georgina, on Beverley's left, Juliet. She had it now! The circle of adults and children. All taking part in the pencil and paper game of Consequences. It didn't take her long to work out who had written what, if Wendy had been the last one to fill the bottom line, before passing it to her to read aloud.

Juliet must have written 'Nicky met . . . ' and Georgina had filled in 'Wendy'. Then Tom must have written 'They met at the folly'. After him Leonora had put 'Give me a sweet'. In reply, Margaret had scribbled 'I'm a witch', while Wendy had added the last line . . . and the consequence was 'They both dropped down dead'.

As the paper was folded over after each person had written, there was no way, if the play was fair, that the next person in line would know what the previous person had put. And yet . . . was there complicity between some of the players? Those who realised a warning should be issued? And had the others unwittingly added to making sense of the final finished page?

Beverley's head was reeling, trying to piece together what might have happened, and all around her the hustle and bustle and sense of emergency generated by a hospital casualty department deepened her feelings of panic. She had no doubt now that someone was trying to harm Nicky, kill him even. But why? Sitting with her head in her hands, her mind tried to grapple with the situation. Which one of them was it?

Or had Nicky picked the poisonous berries himself and eaten them?

Bertie Goring dialled the Bucklands number on impulse. He'd had a long day in the City and now that he was home suddenly felt a great desire to talk to Beverley. Stevens answered, his stentorian tones formal and grave.

'May I speak to Lady Amesbury?' Bertie asked. As he spoke he looked around his drawing room, remembering how she had sat in the chair by the fire the last time she'd been here, sipping tea, her glorious chestnut hair framing her face, her gold-flecked eyes looking at him candidly as they talked.

'I'm afraid Her Ladyship is not available,' he heard Stevens say.

'What? . . . Oh!' Disappointment swept through him like a tidal wave. 'When will she be back?'

'Who is that, please?'

'Lord Goring.'

'Oh, M'Lord. I beg your pardon. I didn't recognise your voice. I'm afraid Lady Amesbury is at the hospital . . .'

'My God, what's happened? Is she all right?' Bertie's heart lurched in his rib cage and he lowered himself slowly and carefully on to his chintz sofa as if he had suddenly become very delicate.

Stevens sounded strained. 'It's young Nicholas, I'm afraid, M'Lord. He was taken to St Marriot's Hospital, over in Oxford, and Lady Amesbury went with him.'

A different sort of alarm filled Bertie now. Children sometimes had terrible accidents, but at least, if Beverley was all right, he might be able to do something to comfort her.

'What happened?'

'The little boy suddenly became most unwell . . . I'm not sure of the details yet. No doubt Her Ladyship will be informing us in due course.'

'St Marriot's Hospital, Oxford, did you say? Thank you, Stevens.' Bertie hung up, hurried into the hall and picked his car keys off the console table. A minute later he was striding along Launceston Place to his car. He could be in Oxford in just over an hour as long as he didn't get caught up in heavy traffic. His only thought as he eased the clutch out, was to get to Beverley. If anything had happened to Nicholas, and Stevens had sounded worried although he hadn't said much, then he must get to her as quickly as possible. She'd borne too much alone. Too many painful days. Too many lonely nights. The desire to take her in his arms and hold her enveloped him in a cloak of longing. Oh, God, he reflected, would she ever get over Anthony? Would she ever allow him to love her and look after her for the rest of her life? He wanted to be with her so much his body ached and he felt, at times, as if the top of his head was going to blow off.

When he arrived in Oxford, he pulled in to a garage and asked the way to St Marriot's. He did not have far to go. Leaving his car in the hospital car park where it said 'Doctors Only', he hurried through the main entrance.

'I believe you have a little boy . . . I think he's had an accident . . . the name is Amesbury . . . or it might be Cumberland,' he said breathlessly to the nurse on duty at the reception desk.

She looked at him strangely. 'When was he admitted?'

'Er . . . by ambulance. Some time this afternoon. His mother was with him.'

She spent several moments stabbing away at a computer, her beady eyes watching the screen like a hungry bird trying to spot a worm.

'He hasn't been admitted to a ward,' she announced finally. 'I should try the casualty department, if I were you. Along the corridor, turn left, go to the end, and it's on your right. Are you a relative?'

'Thanks. I'm an uncle,' Bertie lied, hurrying away before she could stop him.

When he saw Beverley, sitting alone on a bench, he thought his heart would break. Her eyes were red from crying, and she looked desolate, a handkerchief clutched in one hand, a forlorn stoop to her shoulders.

She didn't see him at first, but as he came and stood quietly before her, she looked up and gave a little cry. Then she jumped to her feet and he put his arms around her. Sobbing, she let herself be held without resistance as she buried her face in his shoulder.

'Bertie . . . Oh, Bertie . . . what are you doing here?' she asked. 'How did you know I was here?'

Bertie looked tenderly into her face. 'Stevens told me. How's Nicholas? What's happened? Has he had a fall?'

Holding his hand, Beverley pulled him down beside her on the bench, and told him what had happened. 'I'm waiting to hear how he is.'

'Dear God!' He looked stunned and his face had grown pale. Then he shook his head. 'It couldn't have been deliberate, surely?'

'How else did he get to eat Deadly Nightshade?' she asked. Now that Bertie, dear kind reliable Bertie was here, she felt calmer. 'Nicky knows he mustn't eat any-

552

thing that grows wild; he was taught that when we stayed in Stockbridge, before coming to England. If he's been poisoned, somebody gave him something. The only time I wasn't with him today was when they were all playing Hide-and-Seek; otherwise we all had the same things to eat on the picnic.'

'Are you sure he didn't eat a few berries? Deadly Nightshade has always grown in profusion in the copse. I remember being warned about it when I stayed at Bucklands as a boy,' Bertie pointed out.

'I phoned Bucklands a few minutes before you arrived and I spoke to Wendy. She swears Nicky didn't put anything in his mouth, and says she was holding his hand most of the time. She said he'd have had purple stains around his lips if he'd eaten a berry.'

Bertie nodded slowly and thoughtfully. 'Something's going on though, Beverley. This is one "accident" too many. I really think you should tell the police.'

Beverley didn't answer. There was still a part of her that couldn't seriously believe anyone would want to hurt Nicholas, and yet ... Bertie was right. This did seem like one accident too many.

Lady Jean, arriving back from a day in London, hurried over to the castle as soon as Rupert told her what had happened. Since Beverley had talked to Wendy on the phone, everyone now knew what was wrong with Nicky.

'Whatever next?' she stormed, looking from Leonora to Mama. 'Beverley simply *must* get a nanny. Nicholas is the future of Bucklands; the future of the family. If anything happened to him it would be catastrophic.'

The Dowager fiddled fretfully with the silk scarf on her knee.

'But Beverley was with him all the time,' she protested.

'Except when he went off with Wendy and the other children,' Leonora intervened. 'I tell you, that child is accident prone! Juliet never had anything happen to her, but then we always had a proper nanny, as you say. If you ask me, whether she means to or not, I think Beverley almost wills disasters to happen. She likes being the centre of attention and . . .'

'Now you're being silly, Leonora,' Jean snapped crossly. 'Where's Wendy?'

'She's upstairs with Juliet. She's very upset. She seemed to think Beverley was blaming her at first,' the Dowager said. 'But I assured her Beverley was not like that.'

'Where are the others?'

Leonora looked up lazily. 'Georgina? And Tom and Margaret? They went home after the picnic. I doubt if they even know what's happened. Nicholas didn't become ill until later.'

'I might give Georgina a ring, just to make sure her children are all right.' Jean shook her head, worried. 'I'd better speak to Cook, in case something has got mixed up in the kitchen and we *all* go down with poisoning!'

'They did have blackberry fool for lunch,' the Dowager remarked.

Jean looked at her, stunned. 'Blackberry! Then that's it! Some goddamn bloody fool has mixed up blackberries and Deadly Nightshade berries . . . but why aren't the others ill in that case?'

Leonora shrugged. 'I didn't have any myself because of my diet.'

'Dear God!' Lady Jean stomped around the room in her sensible shoes. 'I'd better get to the kitchens at once, before the stupid woman puts toadstools instead of mushrooms in the chicken casserole or something, and we all end up in hospital!'

'I hope the others are all right,' the Dowager said, alarmed. 'Leonora, could you ring Georgina? Find out how they are?'

'We'd have heard if they'd been taken ill.'

'Not necessarily. I know all about Atropa Belladonna. Sometimes there's no reaction for several days. It's one of the most deadly poisons there are. I always did hate having it growing in the grounds.'

'Very well.' With exaggerated patience, Leonora strolled into the hall, and dialled the Amesburys' number.

'We're all fine,' Georgina exclaimed. 'Surely little Nicky can't really have been poisoned, can he?' she added anxiously. 'He seemed fine on the picnic.'

'Well, that's what Beverley said when she rang from the hospital a little while ago, but you know what a drama-queen she is.'

'Oh, that's not fair,' Georgina protested. 'She must be out of her mind with worry! Is there anything I can do?'

'Not a thing. They're both at the hospital and I've no idea when they'll be back. Mama just wanted to make sure you were all okay.'

'Please thank her, Leonora, and tell her we're fine. How serious is Nicholas' condition? He is going to be all right, isn't he?'

'I don't think anyone knows yet. He seemed to be having some sort of fit when he left here in the ambulance.'

Georgina gasped. 'Oh, my God! As bad as that? The next stage after convulsions is a coma, followed by death. Oh, poor Beverley! I can't bear to think how she must be feeling.'

'If there's any news we'll let you know,' Leonora replied. 'I'd better go back to Mama now.'

'Of course, my dear. And you will let me know if there's anything I can do? This is the most tragic thing that could have happened.'

It was late evening and the frenetic activity in the casualty department had quietened down. Only two people, besides Beverley and Bertie, waited for news, sitting on the hard benches under the glare of unshaded lights.

'Christ, I wonder when we'll hear something?' Beverley groaned, straightening her aching back.

'Shall I find someone who can tell us what's happening?' Bertie had been fetching her endless cups of coffee from a vending machine and he was worried about her. She looked ready to crack at any moment and he couldn't even bring himself to think how she'd react if the news about Nicky was bad.

'Could you, Bertie? I'm getting desperate. It must be two hours since they told us there was no change in his condition.' She shook her head in despair. 'What are they *doing* to my baby?'

At that moment the doctor who had questioned her when she'd first brought Nicholas in appeared at the end of the corridor which led to the intensive care unit. He was walking towards them slowly and wearily, his face drawn by tiredness, his expression implacable.

Watching him approach, trying to gauge his emotions, Beverley half rose from the bench but then sank back, her legs too weak to support her. Dread robbed her of reason, and her heart played a drum-roll of terror in her chest.

Chapter Twenty-Four

'I threw the rest of them out, Lady Jean,' the cook admitted in a quivering voice. 'When I heard Nicholas had got food poisoning, I was afraid someone else would take one of my little ramekin dishes of blackberry fool out of the fridge and get ill too.' A plump woman of uncertain age, she stood by the kitchen table, her expression a mixture of alarm and self-righteousness.

'What else did you throw out, Gladys?' Jean sounded exasperated.

'There weren't nothing else. They'd finished the hamburgers, and all the sandwiches. Anyway, Wendy said he's been poisoned by berries . . .'

'Deadly Nightshade berries, Gladys. Not blackberries.'

Gladys looked indignant. 'Well, I didn't go putting no Deadly Nightshade berries in the fool! If they got there, it wasn't me!'

Lady Jean looked at her thoughtfully. 'Where did the blackberries come from? Were they our own, or did they come from a shop?'

'They were our own, of course. We don't go buying someone else's produce when we've got things in plenty at Bucklands.'

'So one of the gardeners picked them and brought them to you, here in the kitchen? How many individual puddings did you make?'

'A dozen, Lady Jean. And all from the same mixture.'

'And how many were consumed?'

'Five. Then, when I hear what's happened, I chucks out the rest.'

'And no one else has been struck down so far . . .' Jean paused, her brow puckered. 'I wish to God you'd asked someone before throwing away the remaining ones.'

Gladys drew herself up, folding her hands over her extended stomach. 'In all the years I've worked here, there's never been a case of food poisoning, Lady Jean. I was very upset to hear about young Nicholas, although I can't think how it happened . . . I'd have noticed if there were any other sort of berry mixed in with the blackberries . . . but I had to be sure no one else got ill. I was just doing my job, M'Lady,' she added with dignity.

'Of course, Gladys. No one's blaming you,' Lady Jean said hurriedly. It was true that the cook had been with the family for nearly eighteen years, and the food had always been perfect. 'Let's just hope the others who ate the fool are all right.' Then she sighed worriedly. 'The trouble is, we may not know for several days.'

'He's going to be all right, but I'd like to keep him here under observation for a couple of days,' the doctor told Beverley. 'He's very young to have suffered such a serious form of poisoning.'

Beverley suddenly realised she had a splitting headache. She still couldn't believe, after all the hours of waiting, that Nicky was really going to be all right.

'Thank God,' she kept saying. 'Thank you for all you've done.' But inside she was thinking: Is it true? Can I really allow myself to believe he's going to be all right? Relief made her suddenly feel nauseous, and her head was throbbing agonisingly.

Bertie had his arm round her shoulders and was beaming at the doctor with delight. 'That's great news,' he said repeatedly.

'Your son's sleeping now, so why don't you have a quick look at him and then go home and have a good night's sleep yourself?' the doctor suggested, smiling now. 'You look exhausted.'

Beverley nodded. 'Where is he?'

They were led down the corridor to a large room filled with every type of resuscitation equipment. A nurse sat by a narrow bed in the corner, watching over Nicholas. He was sleeping peacefully, with his thumb in his mouth, and it was hard to believe that he'd had a close brush with death only hours before.

Beverley looked down at him, longing to hold him close but knowing it would be wrong to disturb him. Instead she watched him as he slept, and as a feeling of great love overwhelmed her, she said a silent prayer of thanks.

The nurse looked up and smiled. 'You and your husband can probably take him home tomorrow,' she whispered. 'He's doing much better than we expected.'

Beverley felt Bertie's grip on her arm tighten, but she only smiled. It was hardly surprising the nurse would presume she was married to Bertie. After all he'd been with her all evening, as concerned about Nicky as she was.

'I'll drive you back to Bucklands,' Bertie offered, as

they left St Marriot's a few minutes later.

'Thanks. Why don't you stay the night? It's a long haul back to London at this hour,' she suggested.

Juliet had gone back to school by the time Nicholas was released from hospital, and Wendy had left, too, returning to the kindergarten in London where she was a student teacher. No one else had become ill as a result of eating Gladys' blackberry fool, and so the matter came to an uneasy rest, as far as Beverley was concerned.

'What can I do?' she asked Bertie, during one of their now frequent phone conversations. 'The evidence has been destroyed. God knows how Nicky came to have Deadly Nightshade poisoning; perhaps it didn't have anything to do with the fool. Perhaps he got hold of a leaf or a twig and put it in his mouth. Mama says every part of the plant including the roots is highly poisonous. Maybe, as Leonora keeps saying, he's just accident prone.' There was doubt in her voice as she spoke. 'Somehow I don't believe that. Everything was fine until we came here, and now this is the third time his life has been in danger.'

'I wish you'd come to live in London.' There was longing in Bertie's voice. He no longer cared that she knew how deeply in love he was with her.

'I can't leave here, Bertie. Maybe when Nicky goes off to school I'll get myself an apartment in London, but not right now.'

'But I want to see more of you. I can't expect you and the Cumberlands to invite me down all the time, you know. When am I going to see you again?'

Beverley laughed gently. She was very fond of Bertie, but she didn't love him in the way he wanted, and she felt it was unfair to encourage him. 'I don't know. Maybe I'll come up to London to do some shopping. I'm going to need warm clothes if I'm to survive the winter in England, so perhaps we could meet for lunch.'

'Why not stay the night in town? I can book you into an hotel if you'd rather, and we might take in a show and go somewhere nice for dinner? What d'you say?' He sounded so desperate she hadn't the heart to refuse outright.

'Maybe, later on,' she stalled. 'I'll let you know when I decide to come.'

'Make it soon, Beverley.'

'Yes. Okay.'

'And try and arrange to stay overnight.'

'That will be difficult because I don't want to leave Nicky. He's been quite insecure since he was ill.'

'Then we'll meet for lunch?'

'Yeah. Great. Talk to you soon.'

'I'll ring you tomorrow.'

As Beverley hung up she thought fleetingly how nice it would have been if she could have fallen in love with Bertie. He was one of the kindest, nicest men she'd ever met apart from Anthony, and he clearly adored Nicky, too. Then she sighed, knowing she couldn't force feelings that weren't there. But somehow, without hurting him, she was going to have to make him understand she was unable to return his love.

Rosemary Cumberland sat on the edge of her bed looking deeply agitated.

'Alice,' she commanded, leaving her breakfast tray untouched, 'get Joe to come round with the car in half-an-hour.'

Alice looked scared. The usually mild-mannered

Dowager seemed to be in a terrible state and this was the first time she'd ordered the car in years.

'Yes, M'Lady. Where shall I tell Joe to take you?'

'Don't tell him anything!' snapped the Dowager. 'Do that, and then come back and help me dress, please.'

'Very well, M'Lady.' Alice hurried from the room and as she scuttled down the stairs bumped into Lizzie who was bringing up Leonora's breakfast tray.

'Mind out, girl!' Alice said shrilly. 'The Dowager's in a right old state this morning and I've got to get hold of Joe.'

Lizzie paused, round-eyed, resting the heavy tray on the banister for a moment. 'Why?'

'Gawd knows! She rings the bell for me, and when I gets to her room, she'd climbing out of bed, and won't eat her breakfast. Proper state she's in!' Alice paused, struck by a sudden thought. ''Ere . . . did you or Stevens take up her tray this morning?'

'I did, 'cause Mr Stevens, he said he didn't feel too good.'

'Was there anything in the post for her?'

Lizzie nodded knowingly. 'Mr Stevens, he don't see too well neither, does he? I found a letter for the Dowager on young Lady Cumberland's pile, so I takes it up with her breakfast.'

Alice suddenly felt faint, the blood draining from her face, making her skin look waxy. 'Oh, my Gawd!' she moaned. 'Now there'll be trouble!'

'What d'you mean?' Lizzie sounded indignant. 'I was only doing my job! What's wrong with the Dowager having her post?'

'You don't understand. . . .'

'The poor old thing doesn't have much of a life!

Why shouldn't she get her letters?'

'Hush, girl, for Gawd's sake! The damage has been done, and I wouldn't like to be in your shoes when young Lady Cumberland finds out, that's all.' Then Alice hurried away to phone Joe.

By the time she got back, the Dowager was already half-dressed. Almost immediately she sent Alice on another errand.

'Be so good as to go and tell Lady Amesbury I wish to see her right away, will you, Alice? It's very urgent, but don't tell anyone else.'

Alice's eyes widened. So Beverley Amesbury was involved too, was she? She'd suspected Leonora Cumberland was up to something, but it was a shock to find Lady Amesbury might be a part of it.

'Yes, M'Lady. And will you be wanting to see the young Lady Cumberland, too?' Alice enquired boldly.

'Oh, my goodness, no!' The Dowager looked appalled. 'Don't tell her anything . . . don't say I'm going to . . . well, I'm going out. I only wish to have a private word with Lady Amesbury.'

'Very well.' Alice hurried from the room a second time, and scurried with no little excitement back to the main part of the castle. When she tapped on Beverley's door, there was no answer and Alice realised it was later than she thought. Beverley and Nicholas would already be having breakfast downstairs.

'Is she unwell, Alice?' Beverley asked immediately when she received the Dowager's message.

'No, I don't rightly think she's ill, M'Lady. More like, well, sort of worked up about something.'

Beverley looked at her sharply. 'I'll go to her right away. Could you keep an eye on Nicky for a moment, please? He's had his cereal, but could you butter some toast for him to have with his boiled egg?'

'Yes, certainly, M'Lady.' Secretly Alice loved being with Nicky and helping out at odd moments, but she would never have admitted it. Her job was housekeeper. She had no intention of being turned into an unofficial nanny. But as soon as Beverley had left the room, she sat down facing Nicholas and smiled at him. 'And how is my lambkin this morning?' she asked softly.

On arriving in the Dowager's apartments, Beverley found her mother-in-law putting on a dark red felt hat that had seen better days. Over her tweed suit, although it was summer, she also wore a dark red mohair wrap.

'Ah, there you are, dear girl,' Rosemary Cumberland greeted her.

Beverley looked at her in astonishment. 'Where are you going?' The Dowager hadn't ventured out of the castle since she'd arrived, except for the one occasion she'd gone to church.

'My dear, something awful has happened. I've got to go into Oxford right away. Can you possibly come with me?' she begged. 'I don't think I can get through this alone.'

Lady Jean stood stock still, her eyes narrowed, her expression stunned. She was standing by the village green, having done some shopping in the local general store, and she was just about to cross the road when out of the Hare and Hound she saw two familiar figures emerge, look furtively up and down the street, and then scurry off towards the bus stop. Her first thought was that it was very early in the morning for anyone to be drinking in a pub, and then she gasped at her own naivety. People stayed at the Hare and Hounds. Bed and breakfast was in the region of fifteen pounds a night, she believed. The girl had been carrying a small suitcase, and the man had put his arm around her waist, just for a second, before they hurried up the street. It took no imagination to know they were lovers. Charles and Wendy. Lady Jean felt as if a heavy weight had been heaped on her shoulders by this unwelcome knowledge. Charles and Wendy! Enjoying what must have been a night of love ... or sex ... or whatever they called it, right here in the village, not a quarter of a mile away from Hunting Lodge.

Suppose they'd been seen, Jean thought with alarm, but then realised they *had* been seen, by her. It left her feeling soiled, that quick glimpse of their intimacy. It was as if she'd read someone's private diary or opened a letter addressed to someone else. Knowledge gained by such means besmirches the finder and makes them part of the guilt. And how was she going to look Georgina in the face again?

Grimly, Jean crossed the street to go to the baker's on the other side, and at precisely that moment she recognised the familiar outline of the Jaguar from Bucklands, driven by Joe. Thinking he would have Leonora in the back, she raised her hand to wave politely, only to get her second shock of the morning. Sitting very upright on the back seat she saw Mama with Beverley beside her. They were looking straight ahead and did not see her. A moment later the car had swept on, going in the direction of Oxford.

Leonora awoke feeling more relaxed than she'd done for months. Not only had she cleared all her debts, but her sex life had improved beyond her wildest dreams. Rex Harper, who owned the Caspian Casino, had become her lover in recent weeks and she'd dumped Duncan McSwiney as a result. Rex was a stud to end all studs as far as she was concerned, and he thought nothing of driving to Oxford for a few hours in the evening to meet her in an hotel, before returning to London in time to close the casino. More than that, he'd given her unlimited credit to gamble in the future, telling his general manager she was 'financially sound'. Which was no more than she deserved, Leonora reflected, thinking of all the thousands of pounds she'd lost at roulette. Rex Harper had done very well out of her. She'd decided, though, not to gamble any more. She'd managed to get away with systematically helping herself to Mama's fortune to pay back her losses, but even Mama's money wasn't going to last forever. Quit while you're even, she told herself. She'd paid off all her debts and got away with it. She'd also had a lot of excitement and fun . . . Oh, God! the wonderful heart-stopping buzz of waiting for that little ivory ball to drop into the right number! But now she'd get her kicks out of being with Rex, although she hadn't as yet told him she wouldn't be gambling any more.

She sat up in bed, stretched her arms above her head, and decided she would go up to London today and maybe stay overnight. Rex had a large flat in Finchley and he'd told her she could stay there with him at any time. Glancing at her wrist watch, she saw it was nearly ten o'clock. If she sent a message to Joe to come to Bucklands in an hour, he could drive her up to London and she could be with Rex by lunchtime. He never got up until noon, preferring to lounge in bed with the newspapers and endless cups of coffee. Supposing she surprised him? Elated at the prospect, she sprang out of bed and rang for Lizzie. The thought of an afternoon in bed with Rex was even more exciting than the thought of an afternoon gambling, she realised. Rex with his massive cock and almost permanent erection. Rex who was happy to do anything she wanted, which was a lot more than Henry had been prepared to do when it came to sex.

Lizzie appeared at the bedroom door, having knocked first. 'You rang for me, M'Lady?' she enquired nervously. Alice's warning of the young Lady Cumberland's wrath when she discovered how the Dowager's post had been given to her direct made Lizzie quake at the knees.

'Tell Joe to bring the car round in an hour, will you? I want him to take me to London.'

'Yes, M'Lady, but Joe . . . he ain't here,' Lizzie replied.

Leonora frowned with irritation. 'I wish to goodness Lady Amesbury would get herself a car,' she snapped. 'It's most inconvenient her getting Joe to drive her when she wants to go out. I suppose he's taken her shopping, has he?'

'I think it's really the Dowager he had to take out, but Lady Amesbury went, too. I heard them telling him to take them to Oxford,' Lizzie said chattily and then instantly regretted it. Leonora had turned to glare at her with fury.

'The Dowager?' she said shrilly. 'What do you mean, the Dowager? She never goes anywhere. You must be mistaken.' Lizzie detected the underlying fear in her voice.

'Well, I thinks it was the Dowager . . .' Lizzie faltered, trying to edge out of the room.

'Jesus Christ!' Leonora's face showed real alarm now.

'Did they say what they were doing in Oxford?'

Lizzie shook her head. 'I don't rightly know, M'Lady. Will that be all?'

Leonora didn't answer but went over to the bedroom window to gaze up the length of the drive, as if she hoped to see the car returning. She was shaking all over, filled with a sense of impending doom. Had they found out what she'd been doing? And what could they do about it? Every signature on every cheque had been genuinely signed by Rosemary Cumberland herself. She'd signed all the letters of instruction to the bank, too.

'Get out! Get out and leave me alone!' Leonora suddenly screamed at Lizzie. 'What are you standing there for?'

As Lizzie scuttled away, Léonora picked up a hair-brush from her dressing table and threw it at Lizzie's retreating figure. Then she collapsed on to a chair and rocked back and forth in a turmoil of misery. To have got this far. To have paid off all her debts, so that she needn't embezzle any more of Mama's money . . . and to have it discovered now! Moaning, she held her head in her hands, too upset even to plan what she was going to do next. Say Mama was senile? No, too many people knew she wasn't. Oh, God, dear God! Tears sprang to her eyes. She was ruined. Finished. Even Rex wouldn't want to have anything more to do with her now. And then it came to her with fearful clarity that perhaps Rex was only interested in her because he thought she had unlimited funds with which to gamble . . .

Rosemary Cumberland and Beverley gazed at the manager of the Eastern Bank as if they could hardly believe their ears. Nothing he said seemed to make sense . . . except for the fact that over half a million pounds had been withdrawn from the Dowager's current and deposit accounts in the last few months.

'But I haven't withdrawn that sort of money,' Rosemary Cumberland said, her voice low. 'You know I haven't! How could you let this happen without informing me before?'

Mr Brimpton, the new young manager brought in to give the bank the sort of easy-going image it was hoped would appeal to the undergraduates of Oxford, turned and glanced nervously at Beverley. It was bad enough having to face a half-blind old lady who didn't seem to know what she was doing, but he felt most uncomfortable in the presence of this bright young daughter-in-law of hers who, according to the Dowager's last letter, had left massive debts in the United States which she seemed to feel honour bound to settle.

'Lady Cumberland,' he began in embarrassment, 'it *is* your signature on each and every cheque. We have no reason to suppose your signature has been forged, and it is not uncommon, especially if someone suffers from poor sight, for someone else to fill in the details. It is only because the amounts have been rather large that I thought I'd better write to you clarifying the situation.'

Rosemary Cumberland nodded.

Beverley looked at her sharply. 'How did you manage to read the letter, Mama?'

'I asked Lizzie to tell me what it said, when she brought it up on my breakfast tray this morning. You see, I've had a feeling recently, that something was wrong. I'm afraid I made her promise she wouldn't tell anyone. The fewer people who know about this the better.'

Mr Brimpton leaned forward, smooth young face apprehensive. The last thing he wanted was a case brought against the Eastern Bank for negligence.

'You don't intend to pursue this matter further?' he asked hopefully.

'Mama, you *must*!' Beverley cut in, scandalised. Then she turned to him angrily. 'What did you suppose my mother-in-law was doing with that sort of money? It's obvious someone has been stealing from her.'

His blush deepened as he drew a letter out of a folder on his desk. 'Lady Cumberland did in fact give us a perfectly reasonable explanation in her letter of the second of September,' he said carefully.

'What am I supposed to have said?' Rosemary Cumberland asked drily. 'Along with signing dozens of cheques, which I admit to, I seem to have been rather busy.'

'Shall I read it to you?' Mr Brimpton asked diffidently.

'If you would be so kind.'

Mr Brimpton, scarlet and sweating by now, cleared his throat and began. It wasn't until he got to the line '. . . in order to pay off the debts incurred by my daughter-in-law, Beverley, the Viscountess Amesbury . . .' that both women gasped.

'*What!*' said Beverley, appalled. She turned to the Dowager in bewilderment. 'What does it mean?'

Rosemary Cumberland looked crushed. 'If I signed that letter, I certainly didn't write it.'

'Then who . . . ?'

The Dowager remained silent, her lips pressed together, the distress in her milky eyes pitiful to see. Beverley instantly knew the answer but of course Mr Brimpton didn't.

'If you did not write this letter then I think the Fraud

Squad should be called in,' he said at once, relieved that this did not seem to be a massive error on the part of the bank.

'Wait!' Rosemary Cumberland's tone was imperious for once. 'I have to have time to think about this.'

'But, Lady Cumberland, if someone has been embezzling your funds, by taking advantage of your blindness, then this is definitely a case for the police. Have you any idea who is behind this?'

'Oh, yes, I know all right,' she replied. There was a pause before she added brokenly, 'And it hurts a lot. It's someone I foolishly trusted . . .' Her voice broke and she stretched out her hand to lay it on Beverley's arm. 'I would, however, like to make one thing very clear. Lady Amesbury doesn't have and has never had any debts. She has not received a single penny from me at any time, so you must forget the contents of that letter. And now I wish to go back to Bucklands to think about this matter. Will you please give Lady Amesbury copies of all my bank statements, everything pertaining to this business, please? Then, when I've made up my mind what to do, I will let you know.'

'Certainly, Lady Cumberland.'

Going back to Bucklands in the car, Beverley and Mama remained silent, stunned by what they'd learned, each lost in their own thoughts. It was only as they were going up the drive that the Dowager turned to Beverley and said softly: 'Don't mention this matter to anyone for the time being. We will carry on as if nothing has happened, dear girl. I need time to think before I decide whether to inform the police or not.'

During the next few days an uneasy atmosphere hung over Bucklands like gathering storm clouds. Beverley could feel an undercurrent brewing beneath the smooth surface of everyday life, and she had a growing feeling that something momentous was going to break. Leonora was jumpy and every time Beverley saw her she appeared anxious, as if she were expecting bad news. Mama, in contrast, stayed in her rooms in the west wing, refusing to discuss anything and being very withdrawn. Lady Jean, on the other hand, strode around the estate, glowering and preoccupied, and when Charles strolled over for tea one day, she nearly bit his head off when she heard him asking Leonora if Wendy was returning to Bucklands for the Christmas holidays to look after Juliet.

Beverley found the pervasive feeling of distrust and animosity so unpleasant she walked over to Hunting Lodge on several occasions, to get away from it. Only Georgina seemed serene, smiling and welcoming as usual, and Beverley found her house a warm haven of glowing log fires and fragrant cups of coffee. There were toys for Nicholas to play with, light-hearted conversation to indulge in, and as long as Charles was out, the two women could relax and while away a few hours.

'It's so cosy here,' Beverley remarked one afternoon. 'I wish Bucklands was as warm and comfortable as this.'

Georgina smiled. 'You're not wild about the old place, are you?'

'It's so enormous,' Beverley admitted. 'The rooms are so big. Rooms should be designed in proportion to people, not like aircraft hangars!'

'But they're so beautiful,' Georgina enthused. Her eyes flickered to Nicholas. 'And to think it will all belong to him one day. Did you get a shock when you realised he was the heir?'

'I was staggered, to put it mildly.'

'He's a lucky boy.'

When the time came for Beverley to go, Georgina invited her for lunch the following day. 'We'll be on our own. Charles is terribly tied up with some new business venture he's involved in, in London, so what do you say?'

'I have a better idea. Bertie Goring is coming for the weekend. He's arriving later this evening. Why don't you come to us, if you're going to be on your own? Percy has promised, at long last, to take us punting on the moat.'

Georgina's small features lit up. 'What a splendid idea. Oh, I'd love that, Beverley.'

'Great. That's fixed, then.'

'Tell me.' She leaned forward confidentially. 'Are you and Bertie Goring getting together? I mean, is romance in the air?'

Beverley chortled. 'Bertie is the best friend I've got, apart from yourself of course. But there's no romance. As all the best people say, "We're just good friends".'

'Oh, dear! I'd hoped there'd be wedding bells in due course.' Georgina's eyes seemed to blaze with merriment.

'Not a chance! You're just an incurable romantic!'

'Oh, I *know*!' Georgina laughed. 'But it seems to me you protesteth too much!'

Bertie arrived in time for dinner, having driven down from London. He brought with him a battery-operated toy dog that sat up and begged and made barking noises for Nicholas, and a silk scarf for Beverley, in the shades of green she loved so much.

'You're spoiling us,' she chided gently. Bertie was one of the most generous people she'd ever known, but it worried her that he spent so much money on them. 'You've got to stop giving us all these wonderful presents.'

'But I enjoy doing it,' he protested, grinning. His face was tanned from having been out of doors every weekend during the long hot summer, and he looked leaner and more attractive than ever. 'Let me loose in a toy department and I'm as happy as Larry! I love seeing what I can find for Nicky. Do you think he'd like a train set for his birthday?'

Beverley couldn't resist laughing. 'You mean, you'd like a train set to play with, don't you?'

He nodded sheepishly. 'Now tell me, how have things been here?' He hadn't seen Beverley for a couple of weeks, and he worried about both her and Nicky.

She shrugged. 'Very strained. Leonora is avoiding us all – that is when she's here. She's been spending a lot of time in London and so has Charles; whether they're seeing each other or not, I've no idea. Mama remains in the west wing and doesn't encourage any of us to spend time with her. Nothing's been the same since she found Leonora had been helping herself to a large fortune. Even Jean is being bad-tempered.' She shook her head. 'There are times when I really hate it here!' she said vehemently. 'If it wasn't for Georgina, I'd go crazy.'

Bertie looked sympathetic. 'Nicky's been all right, though? No more "accidents" or anything like that?'

'Thank God, no. My mother's certain I've imagined he's been deliberately put in danger by someone. She said all the incidents could have been genuine mishaps and I suppose she's right.'

'Even the poisoning?'

'When you think of it, they were all playing Hide-and-Seek in the copse, and you know how children put things in their mouth. Leonora never touched the picnic food. Now if a glass of wine had been tampered with, that would have been different.'

Bertie sighed deeply. 'Let's hope that's the end of the matter, then.'

Leonora had gone out again, and so they dined alone. Afterwards they took a stroll in the garden, which was bathed in the mellow light of a harvest moon. Beverley took Bertie's arm, grateful for his friendship, and he responded with a tenderness that was protective as well as loving. Neither spoke much. Beverley was thinking about her family so far away and wondering when she could persuade them to come and visit, and Bertie was wishing she could return his love. He wanted her now more than he had ever wanted anyone. There wasn't a single particle of Beverley that he didn't adore, but with a growing feeling of inner despair, he was beginning to realise she might never return that love.

Suddenly Beverley shivered.

'Are you cold?' he asked at once.

'No.' She shook her head and looked troubled. 'But I always get the feeling we're being watched in this part of the garden.'

'Like the night we disturbed a poacher in the copse?'

'If it was a poacher,' she said quietly.

At twelve-thirty the next day, Beverley and Bertie waited in the library for Leonora and Georgina to join them for a drink before lunch. Nicholas was jumping restlessly around the room, longing to go in the punt.

'Can't we go now?' he kept asking Beverley.

'After lunch,' she promised. 'We have to wait for Percy.'

Bertie spoke. 'We don't actually need Percy. I'm an expert punter. Anthony and I were out in that old punt in all weathers. It's as easy as pie.'

'Really?' Beverley looked doubtful. 'Isn't it very heavy, though? It looks such an awkward type of boat, with its flat bottom and blunt ends.'

Bertie laughed. 'Don't forget the moat's not that deep. It's only meant to glide about in, you know.'

'Okay! You can be chief punter,' Beverley replied.

'Yeah!' Nicholas crowed, delighted. 'Can't we go now?'

Leonora appeared at that moment, looking wan and tired. She greeted Bertie coolly before helping herself to a gin and tonic from the drinks tray.

'We're going punting,' Nicholas told her excitedly. 'You're coming, too!'

'I think not,' she replied. 'I hate going in boats.'

'Why?' he asked. 'Why do you hate going in boats?'

Leonora sighed theatrically. 'For God's sake, do stop your child asking "why?" all the time, Beverley. It's so wearing,' she said, before slumping as if exhausted into one of the leather chairs.

The arrival of Georgina at that moment prevented Beverley from answering. She was accompanied by Charles.

'I thought you had business in London today?' Beverley said to him after she'd kissed Georgina in greeting.

'Don't tell me you'd rather I wasn't here?' he replied mockingly. 'Beverley, you've wounded me deeply.' He lit a cigarette and accepted a proffered drink from

Leonora. 'When I heard we were all going punting, I couldn't resist!'

Georgina's expression seemed fixed in a tight smile and her eyes were evasive. 'Yes, he's given up a day's work just to be with us,' she said lightly.

'So what sort of business do you do that takes you to London on a Saturday?' Bertie asked, in an obvious effort to be sociable. Beverley knew how much he'd always disliked Charles, and if she'd known he was coming today she'd never have invited Georgina.

Charles drew deeply on his cigarette before puffing out a series of perfect smoke rings that had Nicholas enchanted.

'This and that,' he replied casually.

Lunch was a strained affair as Stevens hobbled around the long table serving everyone and Beverley and Bertie tried to keep some sort of conversation going. She'd also sent a message to Percy that they wouldn't need to disturb his afternoon off, and Stevens had come back to her to say Percy had quite understood but he'd be around in any case if he were needed.

At last they all trooped into the garden, led by an excited Nicholas.

'We're going in the punt!' he kept saying gleefully.

'You can count me out,' Leonora retorted, hugging her cashmere jacket around her shoulders. 'The wind's really chilly.'

'But it's going to be such fun!' Georgina exclaimed, catching hold of Nicky's hand.

The moat stretched out into a large lake on the southern side of the castle. Edged with bulrushes and reeds, it curved its way to the woods on the far side, a perfect haven for wild birds. Ducks, geese and swans nested by the sides, and on this late September afternoon, a stiff breeze ruffled the normally glassy surface.

While Charles and Leonora sat on a wooden seat by the landing stage, Beverley and Georgina, with Nicholas, clambered on board. Bertie untied the boat and, taking the long wooden pole, pushed them off gently from the side. Without making so much as a ripple, the punt glided forward and Nicky gave a whoop of delight.

'We're going!' he called out, clapping his hands.

Bertie, standing at one end, feet apart, propelled the punt towards the centre of the lake, his strong muscular arms bare to the elbow, his expression delighted.

'Isn't this great?' he said, smiling down at Beverley. She was sitting in the middle with Nicholas beside her, her long legs encased in white jeans with which she wore a navy blue sweater. She looked about sixteen as she grinned back at him.

'The castle looks different from here, doesn't it?' she observed. 'I suppose I've never seen it from this angle.'

They all looked up at the towering grey stone walls, supported by massive buttresses.

'Isn't it magnificent?' Georgina said, in a quiet voice. 'I think it's the most beautiful castle on earth.'

Bertie laughed. 'Ever the romantic, eh, Georgina? What about Windsor Castle? Or some of those Scottish castles?'

'Or even those multi-turreted castles in Liechtenstein and Bavaria?' Beverley pointed out. 'I've only seen them in pictures, but they look pretty terrific.'

Bertie guided the punt over to the far side, and then, to avoid disturbing the wild fowl, edged it round the outer walls of the castle. When they finally got back to

the landing stage half an hour later, Leonora and
Charles were still deep in conversation.

Helped by Bertie, Nicholas was the first to scramble
on to land.

'You've got to come too, 'Nora,' he said excitedly to
Leonora. He stretched his arm in a wide arc. 'We've
been right over there!'

'Good,' she replied tersely.

Georgina and Beverley climbed out of the punt, too,
while Bertie slipped the mooring rope loosely over a
nearby bollard.

'You must be exhausted,' said Beverley, seeing the
film of sweat on his forehead.

'Not at all. It's all a knack, really, not brute strength.'

'I want to go again! Let's go again!' Nicholas crowed.

'Give us a break, buster,' Beverley said. 'We've only
just been.'

'I want to go again, Mummy.'

Suddenly Beverley looked across to the castle
entrance, a couple of hundred yards away. 'Look!
There's Mama! I do believe she's coming out to join us.'

The Dowager was standing in the doorway of the
castle, leaning heavily on her stick. Then she shuffled
slowly forward.

'Bertie, let's go and help her,' Beverley said eagerly.
This was the first time Rosemary Cumberland had come
downstairs since the visit to the bank, and Beverley
sprinted along the grass verge, followed by Bertie. As
soon as she heard them approach, she stood stock still,
her head cocked to one side.

'Beverley?' she called out uncertainly, peering as
through a mist.

'Yes, Mama, and here's Bertie,' said Beverley, kissing

her mother-in-law affectionately.

Bertie stepped forward and kissed her, too. 'Rosemary, how good to see you,' he said warmly.

'My dear Bertie.' Her smile was radiant, and Beverley realised that whatever personal hell the Dowager had passed through in recent days was now over. It was as if a terrible storm had given way to a calm sunny day, and a wave of relief swept through Beverley. Rosemary Cumberland's face was once again serene and smiling, and she seemed quite light-hearted as she took Bertie's arm and allowed him to guide her across the drawbridge.

'Alice told me you were all punting and I decided I must come and join in the fun,' she remarked gaily, waving her stick.

'We haven't seen nearly enough of you lately,' Beverley replied. 'How are you feeling? You look well.'

The Dowager paused to gaze at Beverley. 'It's been torture, dear girl. Absolute torture, wondering what I should do.'

'I'm sure.' Beverley smiled sympathetically.

'But at last, I've come to a decision. I've finally made up my mind what to do.' Her tone was resolute. 'You can tell Bertie all about it later, but in the meantime I've decided to . . .' She broke off as a piercing scream came echoing across the waters of the moat.

Beverley froze, spun round to see what was happening, and then gasped in horror.

Chapter Twenty-Five

'Nicky! Nicky!' Beverley ran screaming towards the landing stage.

Leonora, Charles and Georgina were standing watching, staring as if mesmerised at the sight of the punt drifting away from the bank. Nicholas was standing up in it at one end, a look of terror on his face, as an angry swan came thudding with a drumbeat of mighty wings across the surface of the lake towards him.

'Mummy!' he wailed piteously.

'Nicky, sit down!' Beverley yelled. 'Sit down!'

Bertie, racing beside her, cupped his hands around his mouth and shouted to Nicky, too, but the little boy was too paralysed with fear to do anything except stand, trembling violently. Then the swan, in a splashing skirmish of water, came to a halt beside the punt, its wings still thundering with a fearful beating sound that reverberated in the air.

'*Mummy!*' Panicking, Nicholas stepped back in an effort to get away from the jabbing, hissing yellow beak, and the long white neck that coiled and recoiled like a frenzied snake. The swan was a powerful creature, protective of its family and territory. With a wing span of six feet, it had the power to break a man's leg with a single stroke.

'Sit down, Nicky. Mummy's coming!' Beverley's voice was a hoarse roar, shot through with panic.

At that moment, Nicholas lost his balance, wobbling precariously on the edge of the punt, and then with a scream toppled backwards. Horrified, Beverley saw the murky waters of the moat close over his head as he disappeared from sight. There was a little rippling disturbance on the surface, and the silence was only broken by the beating of the swan's wings as it peered into the depths.

'He can't swim!' Beverley cried out. She and Bertie were still fifty yards away from the edge. She thought of the icy cold water and the choking clinging weeds that could ensnare even a strong swimmer.

Suddenly, Georgina seemed to wake up as if from a deep reverie. She glanced at Leonora and Charles as if she'd only just become aware of their presence. Then she kicked off her shoes and plunged into the moat, striking out through reeds and rushes to get to Nicholas.

'She'll never do it,' Beverley heard Bertie exclaim. A moment later he too plunged into the moat, but he took a running dive and emerged out of the water ahead of Georgina.

Nicholas was flailing frantically now, gasping for air and fighting a desperate battle with the waters that kept closing over his head. The swan, mounted on the punt, was punching the air with weaving head and sledgehammer wings, hissing fearsomely at the small boy.

Bertie swam forward strongly, with wide clean breast strokes, but Georgina seemed stuck in the rushes as she trod water frantically, the slimy weeds draping themselves around her neck and shoulders like strange jewellery.

'I can't get to him!' she gasped.

'Bertie's nearly there,' Beverley shouted back, her eyes never leaving the spot where Nicky thrashed around. He was spluttering as he struggled, coughing and choking and crying all at the same time.

'I've got him!' Bertie yelled a few seconds later, as he lifted Nicholas out of the water and away from the swan.

Beverley sank to her knees on the grass as a rush of relief and weakness sapped the strength from her limbs.

Then she watched as Bertie started swimming back to the bank with Nicholas riding on his back, holding on with his arms around Bertie's neck. Slowly, almost agonisingly, Georgina was following, her face a ghastly white.

'Are you okay?' Beverley shouted.

Georgina didn't reply but Bertie gave a cheerful: 'Yeah, great!' Something in the way Nicky was hanging on to him, his cheek pressed against Bertie's, touched her deeply. It was the look of total trust in Nicky's expression as he clung, dripping, to the man who had rescued him, and it was the resolute strength in Bertie's face as he sliced smoothly through the water that caused an almost painful sensation in her heart. For a moment she didn't know whether to laugh or cry. Overwhelmed by conflicting emotions, she held her breath as if in pain.

A dark corner of her soul had been illuminated in that moment and a veil stripped away, revealing something she hadn't realised before. With fatherly care, Bertie was bringing Nicky back to her, and suddenly she realised the impossible had happened. The part of her that had lain dormant, numb and devoid of feeling since Anthony had died, had been awakened with a kind of thawing ache so that she felt raw and tender inside.

Bertie looked up at her as he drew near the bank and

their eyes locked as if he too was aware something had happened.

Leaning forward, she lifted Nicky off his shoulders and he climbed on to the landing stage.

'Are you all right?' she whispered. When she expected her maternal feelings to be uppermost, she was shocked to find herself consumed with desire for Bertie. His lean tanned face and dark velvety eyes, bronzed muscular arms and long lean frame, dominated her emotional horizon. Fiercely she wanted him, in a way she'd almost forgotten existed. Every nerve ending in her body cried out for his touch and as she held Nicky against her with one arm, she reached out for Bertie with the other as if it were the most natural thing to do.

There was a look of surprised tenderness on Bertie's face as he put his arms around both of them.

'We'd better get Nicky into a hot bath, darling,' he whispered.

Beverley nodded, unable to speak. For a long moment they stood close, their heads together, lost in a world of their own, until they heard Charles shouting at Georgina.

'What the bloody hell do you think you're doing?' he stormed. 'You're not even a good swimmer.'

Beverley turned and watched as Georgina emerged from the water looking like a bedraggled kitten, hair matted to her head, clothes moulded to her thin body. More than that, her spirit seemed crushed, and there was a look of desperate unhappiness in her eyes.

Beverley's heart went out to her. Even though she'd been brave, Charles was still treating her with contempt. In a fury she turned on him.

'Don't talk to Georgina like that!' she said angrily. 'It

was wonderful of her to rush to Nicky's rescue. I notice *you* didn't do a thing to help.'

Charles stared at her but she couldn't make out the expression in his eyes. 'One hero in the family is enough,' he commented drily.

Beverley ignored the gibe. 'But how did it happen in the first place?' She noticed the long pole was still lying on the grass where Bertie had left it. 'Nicky couldn't have pushed off on his own. The punt's far too heavy.'

'I'd also slipped the mooring rope over the bollard,' Bertie pointed out. They both looked at Nicholas, but he was shivering and starting to cry.

'Let's settle this later. We must get him into dry clothes,' said Beverley, but as she turned to go she fancied she saw a look of fear in Leonora's eyes. Could she and Charles have done it between them? Because he wanted Bucklands, and she needed the money?

'I had decided to do nothing about the money,' Mama confided to Beverley and Bertie as they sat talking quietly in the library a little later. Nicholas, after a hot bath, seemed to have come to no harm, and Bertie, holding Beverley's hand as if he could never bear to let it go, sat in dry clothes beside her, listening intently.

'You'd decided to let Leonora get away with it?' Beverley said.

The Dowager nodded. 'That was my intention. Mainly for the sake of poor little Juliet, really. It's bad enough that she's lost her father, but to have her mother accused of embezzlement!' Then she gazed in the direction of Beverley. 'But if what you say is true, that changes everything.'

'I don't believe today was a mishap, Rosemary,' Bertie

vouchsafed. 'I think this was one of several attempts to create the conditions for an "accident".'

'But to try and hurt a child!' She sounded appalled. 'I can hardly believe it. Could Leonora really have done such a dreadful thing?'

'She may have had help from Charles. They still seem to be close friends,' Beverley interjected.

'But why? What could she have against little Nicholas? He's the sweetest child.'

'Leonora has always resented him, Mama. I think she hates the fact it isn't her child who's the heir. Maybe losing so many babies in miscarriages has affected her mind.'

Bertie looked gravely at the Dowager. 'There is no way Nicky could have lifted the rope off the bollard and pushed the punt away from the bank all by himself. I think whoever did it, waited until Nicky had climbed on board again and then seized the opportunity while the rest of us were distracted by your appearance on the drawbridge.'

Rosemary Cumberland was silent for a moment, deep in thought. When she spoke her voice was urgent.

'Will you phone Jean, dear girl?' she asked Beverley. 'Will you ask her to come over here, right away? She knows all about the law and I think we should talk to her before we accuse Leonora of anything.'

Beverley hurried into the hall, knowing that Charles and Leonora were still in the garden. She kept her voice low, though, as she asked Jean to come over at once as Mama wanted to see her.

Meanwhile Mama had turned to Bertie and laid her hand on his arm.

'It's so wonderful to have you staying here again, my

dear Bertie. Just like the old days when you used to visit
Anthony. But now you're here to see Beverley and I
think that's the best thing that has happened for a long
time.' Her expression softened and her smile was gentle.
'Beverley really needs you, Bertie, and so does Nicholas.
I hope we shall be seeing a great deal of you in the
future.'

Bertie laid his hand over hers, clasping it in his strong
fingers. He wanted her to feel the warmth of his grip
even if she couldn't see the expression in his eyes.

'Beverley and Nicky mean the world to me,
Rosemary.'

Suddenly her voice quavered with joy. 'My dear boy,
I'm so glad. It's what Anthony would have wanted,
you know.'

'I hope so. I'll do everything I can to make them
happy.'

At that moment Beverley came back into the room.
One glance told her what they'd been talking about. A
flush spread to her cheeks as she looked at Bertie and
gave him a secret knowing smile that sent his heart
racing.

'Jean and Rupert are coming over right away. I didn't
tell her what it was about but she seemed to guess
something was wrong,' she told Mama.

'Good. Shut the door, dear girl, so we won't be disturbed. Where are the others?'

'Georgina's upstairs having a bath and I've lent her
some dry clothes. The others are in the garden.'

There was a pause and Mama shook her head. 'Poor
Georgina. She has to put up with so much suffering.'

'I can guess what this is about,' Lady Jean said briskly as

she plonked herself down on a chair by the library fire, having thrown a couple of logs on it first. 'Charles is up to his old tricks, of course.'

'Disgraceful!' Rupert Ffitch mumbled.

'I'm not sure I know what you mean, dear girl?'

'If you don't, you're the only person around here who doesn't, Mama,' Jean barked. 'He's screwing around with that gel Wendy.'

'Oh!' said the Dowager. 'I thought it was Leonora.'

'It used to be but that's been over for ages. They're just friends now,' Jean declared knowledgeably.

'You're very well informed,' her mother said mildly. 'But there is something rather more serious we want to discuss with you. Beverley dear, will you tell Jean all that's been happening?'

As briefly as she could, Beverley outlined the four incidents that had put Nicholas's life in danger.

'And you suspect Leonora?'

'Yes. We also think she may have had help from Charles, especially today,' said Bertie.

'Are you sure? These are very serious accusations.'

'I've come to the conclusion it must be her,' Beverley said earnestly. 'She could have opened my bedroom window after Nicky had gone to sleep . . . he did say he saw a woman's backview leaving the room when he awoke. She could have put Deadly Nightshade in his blackberry fool when no one was looking on the picnic. She was by the punt just now. She smokes, too. She could have been the one who dropped the box of matches into Nicky's wheelbarrow. She's the only person who has always been around when these "accidents" have happened!'

'And there's the question of the money, too,' the

Dowager said almost to herself.

Jean spun round to look at her mother. 'What money?'

Rosemary Cumberland told Jean about the visit to the Eastern Bank the previous week. 'I had decided,' she concluded, 'not to bring charges because of Juliet. My idea was to tell Leonora that if she left Bucklands for good, I'd ignore the stolen money. But now . . .' Her lips trembled. 'If she's really tried to harm Nicholas, we will have to do something.'

Rupert Ffitch, who had remained sitting ramrod stiff in aghast silence, suddenly exploded, his face red as he spluttered with rage.

'It's bloody disgraceful! The woman ought to be horse-whipped! We can't have this sort of behaviour at Bucklands! For God's sake . . . we must call the police. At once.'

'Yes, Rupert,' Jean said patiently but not without firmness, 'but what we have to decide is the best way to handle this situation. We do have to think about the family, you know. The Cumberlands have never been involved in anything like this and the last thing we want is the whole county gossiping about us.'

At that moment the drawing-room door opened and they all stopped talking. Stevens was bringing in afternoon tea, followed by one of the maids with plates of sandwiches and cakes. It struck Beverley that this daily ritual would probably have been carried out even if Nicky had drowned.

'Ah, tea!' Rupert was given to stating the obvious. 'Everything stops for tea,' he added pointedly, giving the others a series of obvious winks.

After a few minutes, they were joined by Leonora and

Charles, and a moment later Georgina, swamped by the skirt and sweater Beverley had loaned her which was several sizes too big for her slight frame.

The conversation immediately became general as Stevens set out the tea things with laborious care and precision. When he finally left the room, the tension mounted so that it became an almost palpable force. Beverley could feel her nerves straining unbearably as Jean seemed to be summoning her strength for the attack. Leonora seemed aware of it too, because she suddenly became stiff and wary like an animal scenting danger. Without moving her head, her eyes darted anxiously around the room, yet they avoided contact with the others. Only Charles seemed totally at ease as he lounged in a chair and lit a cigarette.

'Come and sit down,' Beverley said warmly to Georgina who was hovering uncertainly. 'Are you warm again? The moat must have been freezing.'

'I'm fine,' she replied in her gentle voice. Her smile was wan and she still looked deathly pale. 'I had a lovely hot bath. The most important thing is, how is Nicky?' She looked over to where he was sitting on the sofa beside Mama, tucking into a sandwich.

Jean had automatically taken charge of pouring the tea, as if she were mistress of Bucklands. No one spoke. The silence became a black hole into which they were all sucked and rendered mute. For a moment Beverley felt as if she couldn't stand the agonising uneasiness that filled the library like a smothering blanket of apprehension, for another second. When Jean finally broke the silence they all jumped.

'Leonora,' she began. 'There is something we want to say to . . .'

Her words were interrupted by a gentle tap-tap on the library door. Butlers never knock, and so knowing it couldn't be Stevens, Jean frowned. 'Come in,' she commanded.

The door opened and Percy stood there in his dark green apron over his beige corduroy trousers, as if he had come straight from work although it was Saturday afternoon.

'What is it, Percy?' Jean asked.

He looked acutely uncomfortable, shuffling from foot to foot as if the floor was hot. He cleared his throat but did not speak.

'Out with it, man,' Jean barked, though her tone was friendly.

'Can I have a word with you, please, Lady Jean?' He spoke so quietly, his words became almost lost in the lofty book-lined room.

'What . . . now?'

He nodded, and Beverley suddenly became aware he was trembling and looked deeply upset.

'Can't it wait, Percy? We're just about to have a family discussion and this really isn't the best time.'

He took a step forward. 'No, it can't wait, Lady Jean.' Then he looked at Nicholas, who was watching him with wide-eyed interest. 'It concerns young Nicholas and how he nearly got drowned this afternoon. I saw what happened, as I was fixing some loose tiles on the roof.'

The effect of his words was electrifying, and Beverley felt her heart leap with a strange and terrible excitement. There was a witness who had seen what had happened! Now there would be no more guessing, no more speculation. And, at last, Nicky would be safe. She glanced at Bertie who was looking at Percy in astonishment, and then looked across at Leonora. Did she look frightened? While she was trying to gauge Leonora's expression, Georgina startled them all by jumping to her feet with a long thin scream of anguish. There was a wild shining in her eyes and she was clasping her head with both hands as if she were afraid it would break away from her neck.

'All right!' she rasped, her voice high-pitched and pierced with agony. '*All right!* But can you blame me? Married to him!' She pointed at Charles with white trembling fingers. 'I've had seventeen years of hell and humiliation with not enough money and no future! I've had to put up with all his affairs and I knew nothing would change unless I made it change. It's not fair! Why shouldn't I have the things I want for myself . . . and for Tom? Why shouldn't *Tom* have only the best of everything?'

Beverley felt an icy chill crawl down her spine. When had she last heard the rantings of a woman who could not have what she wanted? Aghast, she looked at Georgina who had been her friend and did not recognise the contorted white face and bloodshot eyes that glared back into hers.

'I have a son, too, you know.' Georgina spoke in a small, sharp, mad voice that sounded as if it belonged to someone else. 'A son who could inherit all this!' Her arms swept in a wide arc as she looked up at the beamed ceiling. 'All this . . . if it wasn't for Nicholas! He's the only thing that stands between Tom and everything I've ever wanted for him!' Then sobs overwhelmed her, racking sobs that convulsed her thin body. The others sat mesmerised as Georgina seemed to disintegrate before their eyes. All the years of a carefully contrived appear-

594

ance of serene normality had split wide, revealing the inner turmoil of an obsessed woman.

'Only Nicholas stands in the way . . .' She was rocking backwards and forwards, her keening a thin trail of sound. Then she turned on Percy, her clenched fists beating the air. 'So you saw me today . . . *so what*? I only pushed out the punt with my foot while his mother was sucking up to the old woman! While the others talked. No one realises how unhappy I am . . . Jesus Christ, I hate you all!' Her voice rose in a wail and at that moment Beverley was again reminded of Mary, screaming at her wedding, tortured by some inner demon because she couldn't have the one thing she wanted. With Mary it had been Anthony. With Georgina it was Bucklands and everything that went with it.

'Wait a minute!' It was Leonora talking. They all turned to look at her, and she was staring at Georgina with a stunned expression. 'Was it you who arranged the other so-called accidents that have happened to Nicky?'

Tears started to course silently now down Georgina's cheeks. 'I wanted him dead. I couldn't let a small child stand in the way, could I? Tom should have all this one day and I should be here to enjoy it with him.'

Lady Jean was looking grim-faced. 'Charles would inherit if anything happened to Nicholas,' she said harshly. 'Have you thought of that?'

Georgina sank into a chair, arms clasped around her ribs as if she was in pain. 'Of course I've thought of that, but Charles can't live forever, can he? And then everything will belong to Tom . . . my boy . . . my baby . . .'

'Dear God . . . dear God,' Mama was whispering aloud. She looked old and frail as she listened to what was going on, and Beverley reached out to take her hand.

'It's all right, Mama,' she said quietly. 'Nicholas is quite safe now.'

Georgina jumped to her feet like a Jack-in-the-Box and started pacing the room, up and down, up and down, up and down. When she spoke again her voice was quite normal.

'I had hoped to get people to believe Nicky wasn't Anthony's son, so I told Tilly in the village he was illegitimate, but that didn't work out.' She paused, staring out of the window to where the long shadows darkened and deepened as the sun sank below the horizon.

'After that it was easy,' she continued. 'So easy. You've no idea how vulnerable a small child is. A little push . . . a tiny shove . . . the day I brought Juliet back here, when Wendy was in bed with a migraine and Clare had already fetched Nicky and put him to bed, I just nipped into your room, Beverley, opened the window and then woke him up before I crept out again. It nearly worked too, didn't it?'

A heavy silence pervaded the room as they sat, chilled by her words and the way in which she had uttered them. There was no more remorse or feeling in the way she spoke, than if she'd been describing a shopping trip. Coolly and without emotion she stood there boasting about how she'd tried to kill a child of two.

'Did you try and poison him, too? At the picnic?' Beverley asked in a small voice.

Georgina spun on her. 'Easy!' she spat. 'Easy-peasy! I'd already picked some Deadly Nightshade berries and I put them in his pudding! He ate it all up like a lamb, didn't he?' Then she started to laugh, an awful bubbling sound that seemed to fill her throat, gurgling to the surface before erupting. 'Everyone thought Wendy was responsible . . . Wendy who is fucking my husband . . . Wendy the scheming little bitch . . . Wendy with the big cunt . . .'

Springing to his feet, Charles seized her arm and started to drag her to the door where Percy still stood, an unhappy embarrassed look on his face.

'We're going home,' Charles said, without looking at the others.

'What about the fire in the barn?' Jean asked. 'Did you start that too, Georgina?'

Georgina tore away from Charles' grasp. 'You're all a bunch of fools,' she screamed. '*Of course* I put the matches in his wheelbarrow! I hoped you'd think it was Charles because he smokes! Ha! What a joke that would have been!' She threw back her head then, her mouth open wide in a silent howl. Her madness was terrible to see, a twisted unbalanced insanity that caused manic laughter one minute and then swung to tragic sadness the next.

'But why did you try and save Nicky in the moat just now?' Beverley asked in desperation. It was such a shock to find it was Georgina and not Leonora who had tried to harm Nicky, she still couldn't take it in.

'So that no one would suspect me of pushing out the punt in the first place,' Georgina whispered, overcome with tears again. 'There were so many of you around . . . and I wanted you all to admire me . . . and have some use for me, and I realised one of you would rescue him anyway.'

'Come along,' Charles was saying, briskly but not unkindly. He took her arm again, but she clung to the back of a sofa, sobbing broken-heartedly, resisting him with all her strength, hanging on to the furniture with hysterical fervour as if it could save her.

'I'll phone for an ambulance,' Beverley heard Jean say in a low voice as she hurried from the room.

'You can't put me away!' Georgina cried out intuitively. 'I belong here. This should be my home . . . and Tom's.' She turned to look at Beverley with hate-filled eyes. 'Why should you live here? Oh, God! The hundreds of evenings I've spent in the copse, watching the lights go on in the castle, thinking of you all living in this beautiful place while I . . . while I . . .'

She was unable to continue. Sliding out of Charles' grip, she slumped to the floor, overcome with silent choking sobs. She was still there, huddled in Beverley's clothes which were much too big for her, when the ambulance crew arrived twenty minutes later.

Bertie's hands caressed her as gently as if this was the first time she'd ever made love, as if she were a virgin who had entrusted herself to him. He stroked her breasts with tender fingertips, kissing her nipples so that she tingled with desire, and then he held her close, so close she could feel every part of his body pressed against hers.

It had been so long since she'd felt like this, it almost did feel like the first time. Returning his kisses, she delighted in the scent of his skin and hair and the warm firmness of his lips

'I love you,' she whispered, surprising herself. She'd been so sure she'd never feel like this again, but here she was, tightly clasped in Bertie's arms, wanting him with a deep longing that filled every particle of her being.

'Oh, Beverley . . . Beverley.' He whispered her name again and again as he kissed her face, her eyes, the lobes of her ears. 'I've been in love with you from the beginning, from the first moment I saw you in Harrods that day . . . God, I was so afraid you'd never feel the same way.'

She cupped his face in her hands, looking deeply into his dark eyes. 'But I do, Bertie, I do. The past is the past, and now all I want is you.' By the dim glow of the bedside lamp in his bedroom at Bucklands, she could not mistake the love in his eyes.

'I want you more than anything else on earth,' he whispered. 'I want to feel you, to taste you, to become a part of you.'

For answer she kissed him deeply, probing the softness of his mouth with her tongue, stroking his hair and the back of his neck with soft caresses, cradling his manhood in her hands until he groaned with desire.

Then, taking his hand, she guided it to where she wanted him to touch her most, and as he stroked her tenderly, she found herself beginning to peak. Ripples of exquisite pleasure surged through her now, making her arch her back and gasp.

'Oh, Bertie, yes . . . yes . . . oh, darling!' she cried out, desperate in her need to have him and hold him inside her.

'Beverley . . .' He was all hers now, rocking her with a gentle force, filling her with his love and strength until he too cried out.

'Oh, God, I love you so much,' he gasped, and then he kissed her again, a tender binding kiss that told her more than words could have done just how much she meant to him.

For a long time they lay locked together, revelling in their new-found passion, arms clasped around each other.

'I can hardly believe how happy I am,' Beverley whispered, still feeling dazed by what had happened. The whole day had been unreal, but the most wonderful part of it was that she'd broken out from the icy capsule of frozen feelings that had locked in her emotions since Anthony had died, and she was freed from the past. For the first time she felt whole again, a woman with desires and hopes and a zest for living that she'd feared would never return. As if he sensed what she was thinking, Bertie gazed into her eyes.

'You can believe in this, can't you?' he whispered.

'Oh, yes, Bertie. Yes. I've never believed in anything more,' she replied, the gold flecks in her eyes glittering with joy now.

They lay together for a long time, each lost in their own thoughts and yet closer than either could have imagined ever being. After a while, Beverley spoke.

'In spite of everything, I can't help feeling sorry for Georgina, you know. We were such good friends. I'd no idea she was obsessed with getting Bucklands. But then I didn't know, at first, that Mary was obsessed with Anthony. It's strange how life works out, isn't it?' She was thinking about Leonora too, who after a long and confidential talk with Mama had emerged red-eyed from the library and had gone upstairs to pack. As far as the servants and the workers on the estate were concerned, she was moving back to London to be near her friends and family and would only come back to Bucklands during the school holidays when Juliet was at home. That was the way Mama wanted things arranged, and so Jean, Rupert and Beverley agreed to go along with it. Leonora would always be able to look after herself, of that Beverley was sure, but what of Georgina?

'Do you think she'll be kept in a mental home?' she asked sadly. 'Will they be able to cure her?'

'I don't know, sweetheart,' Bertie replied. 'It's a tragedy, really, and Charles isn't going to hang around either.'

Beverley stirred, propping herself up on her elbow, to look into Bertie's face. 'What do you mean?'

'He's going off with Wendy.'

'You're not serious? She's only a young girl, and Charles must be forty-five at least.'

Bertie nodded knowledgeably. 'He told me he plans to marry Wendy. Says she'd be a marvellous mother for Margaret and Tom. He's got it all worked out.'

She flopped back on the pillows, stunned. 'It's unbelievable! What a day this has been! When I woke up this morning . . .'

'. . . you never guessed you'd end up in the spare room with me tonight,' Bertie interjected, grinning at her.

She laughed, a joyous sound that made him long to kiss her again. 'I certainly didn't,' she admitted.

Bertie pulled her close again. 'But you've no regrets?' He nuzzled her neck, closing his eyes as her perfume made him dizzy, arousing him again. 'And you'll marry me, sweetheart? And we'll divide our time between London and Bucklands . . .' His voice became languorous with renewed longing.

'. . . and we'll live happily ever after.' Henry's words came back to her, the words he spoken when he'd made a speech at her wedding to Anthony.

601

She was sure she'd live happily ever after now, not with Anthony, her first great love and Nicky's father, but with Bertie; wonderful, loving Bertie, who had always been there when she needed him. His lips were brushing hers now, lightly and gently, and as his arms closed tight around her, she was filled by the most glorious feeling of being set free and floating away into limitless space. Returning his kiss with a passion she had not felt for so long, she knew that this was the right thing to do. The legacy of love Anthony had left them was in the very fabric of Bucklands and in the love they shared for Nicholas and for each other.